Mr.Shahi, is a fantastic writer, who writes for the people. His writing enraptures readers with his beautiful culturally loaded heartrending stories. Also, he is a poet who writes poems in which he shows grief, loss and coping from different angles, which touch the hearts of every one.

Kazem Bimar Psy.D.

Professor

International Language Institute of Monterey, CA

Shahi Sadat restores to us our humanity by focusing on our loves and hates and on the bittersweet awakening from the illusions often generated by our passions. He achieves this without ever losing hope that humanity can prevail.

Vida Pavesich

Professor of Philosophy

Diablo Valley College

Shahi Sadat writes about love and betrayal, war and death and the survival of hope. Out of mix of cultures and experiences, out of a confrontation between eastern and western values a strong and authentic voice emerges, which consistently on those things that unites us rather than those things that divide. The themes may be sorrow or beauty, suffering or love, but the effect is always uplifting, always a reaffirmation of how much wonder exists in the world.

MARK G. EDELSTEIN, Ph.D.

Former President of Diablo Valley College

I much admire the beautiful thoughts and powerful message that is so wonderfully expressed through Shahi's delicate writing.
Fedric Johnson, Ph.D.

Music Instructor at Diablo Valley College.

Shahi writes for others. It is this nature of Shahi's that I am confident will ring through out the reader's mind, whether that reader gains insights of the world through Shahi's eye via German, Pashto, Hindi, Farsi, or English. His voice rings out in mine.

David Vela

Professor of Literature at Diablo Valley College

DANCING IN TERROR

SHASHI SADAT

DANCING IN TERROR

Dancing In Terror

Published by Tate Publishing & Enterprises, LLC
127 E. Trade Center Terrace | Mustang, Oklahoma 73064 USA
1.888.361.9473 | www.tatepublishing.com

Tate Publishing is committed to excellence in the publishing industry. The company reflects the philosophy established by the founders, based on Psalm 68:11,
"The Lord gave the word and great was the company of those who published it."

Cover design by Nikolai Purpura
Interior design by Mary Jean Archival

Published in the United States of America

ISBN: 978-1-63185-253-4
Fiction / General
14.04.28

To Laila and Rustam Khan for the past,
Khwaga for the present,
and
Heela and Leema for the future

I am grateful to Diablo Valley College,
San Francisco State University,
their faculty, and Puente for their contribution
to my knowledge.

ACKNOWLEDGMENTS

I want to thank Allen Horne,
who has accompanied me on this journey.

INTRODUCTION

I AM STANDING BESIDE the Auzingianai River in Srakala, the village where I was born, and the wind is soft and the trees are green and birds are roosting on the branches of the trees, the green trees. I can hear the birds chattering; their eyes peer at me, the eyes of the river, the eyes of Afghanistan reflecting a landscape of shifting patterns and hues, of generations in a land that arose thousands of years ago. When I hear the songs of the birds, I am hearing the voice of my country; when I look into the eyes of the Auzingianai River, I am seeing my own eyes. I am suffused with the wonder of it all for I am part of it.

The scene shifts. I am being attacked by wolves. I try to fight them off, but I cannot move. Centuries of struggle, of invasions, of conquerors, of kings and treaties and allegiances. This also is Afghanistan. And these too are part of me. For I am Pashtoon!

PART I

BACKGROUND

In 1973, King Zahir Shah had been in power in Afghanistan for almost forty years. It was at this time that things began to change, and what set them in motion was the ongoing dispute about Pakhtunistan, which had formerly been in Afghanistan and which was now under Punjabi authority. This came about in the following way: In the late nineteenth century, the Colonial British Empire created the Durand Line, a 2,700-mile boundary separating British India from Afghanistan. Pakhtunistan, originally part of Afghanistan and about one-third the size of California, became a semiautonomous region behind the Durand Line and remained under the aegis of the British. When Pakistan was created in 1947, the British included Pakhtunistan as part of their territory. Afghanistan never agreed to this parceling of their land, nor was it accepted by the Pakhtunistan people, and there had been—and continues to be—clashes along the border between the two countries.

Throughout his reign, King Zahir had tried to find a peaceful solution to this struggle, regularly appealing to the United Nations to help him work out an arrangement with Pakistan so that Pakhtunistan could be reunited with his country. But it was all to no avail. When the king asked President Nixon to intervene, he refused because of America's alliance with Pakistan in their struggle against the Soviets. Zahir's cousin, Mohammad Dawud, who was prime minister, thought there could be no peaceful agreements with Pakistan and wanted to wage war to reclaim the territory. Dawud suggested that they turn to Russia, but the king vetoed that idea. During this time, he was having problems with his eyes and went to Rome to consult a specialist. While he was in Italy in the summer of 1973, Dawud staged a successful and bloodless coup and named himself as president.

Once established, Dawud asked the Russians for military assistance so that he could reclaim Pakhtunistan. Russia agreed, and thousands of Afghans were sent to be trained in the Soviet Union. This was a decision Dawud would later come to regret as the relations between his government and the Soviets deteriorated. In 1978, Noor Mohammad Taraki, an Afghan Communist party leader supported by the Soviet Union, overthrew the government and assassinated Dawud and his entire family. Within a short time, however, conflict erupted between non-Communists and Communists as well as between the various Communist factions, rifts that Taraki was ill-equipped to deal with. He was only in power for a few months when Hafizullah Amin, a deputy prime minister who had been educated in America, overthrew Taraki and had him executed, becoming the new leader. Amin was under the backing of the KGB, who never trusted him and who monitored his every move. The turmoil continued with frequent uprisings and demonstrations that were met with lethal force. Afghan against Afghan.

CHAPTER ONE

IT WAS OLD LADY Gulapa who told us about the wraiths. She said that they hid in the cornfields and that her husband Atal had to fight them whenever he went outside the walls of our village. We'd gather around her while she smoked *tamako* from a hookah and told us stories of death and mutilation, of banishment and torture, of ghouls who pulled out the still-beating hearts of small children and drank the blood. I was best friends with her son Khialo, and we couldn't get enough of her tales, nor could the other village children, including my sister Meena and my brother Sial, even though they were older and maintained that they didn't believe in such nonsense. We would all sit in a semicircle, hardly daring to breathe while Gulapa unveiled yet another episode of what was a never-ending battle against the monsters of the abyss.

"One day my poor Atal was out planting tomatoes. It was hot for spring, but the freshly turned earth was cool and the work went easy. He had almost finished when he heard a baby crying. He stopped what he was doing and looked around. Now at the far edge of the field, there was an ancient conifer that was bare of leaves. Twice it had been struck by lightning, and the second time killed the tree. The crying was coming from that direction, and when Atal walked over, he saw an infant swaddled in linen lying against the trunk and wailing at the top of its lungs. It was a boy. Atal lifted him in his arms and tried to comfort him, but he continued to bawl as babies do who are hungry and afraid. Eventually though, he quieted down since, as you all know, my handsome fool of a husband has a way with squalling brats. But where was the child's mother? he wondered. Why was there no father nearby?

"Time passed, and the sun began to sink behind the mountains, and still no one appeared, so he headed home. Halfway there, Atal looked back, and when he did, he was astonished at what he saw. The baby's legs had stretched all the way from where he'd picked him up, which was almost a mile away. Atal threw his arms out, and the baby dropped to the ground and turned into a fawn.

"Atal had a magic touch when it came to growing things, resulting in a vegetable garden that was a wonder to behold, a panoply of plums, apricots, pears, grapes, of cucumbers sweet as berries, of lettuce, and cauliflower. From the branches of his pomegranate trees, you could hear birds chirping when the blossoms erupted like pink fireworks against the tangle of green leaves. Then when the fruits were ripe, their damp skins felt cold against your lips with the juice having a delicate sweetness that was both subtle and invigorating. He could usually be found there, either working the earth or trading produce to the villagers for grains and other necessities."

Perhaps, not so coincidentally, given that it was off-limits to us children, many of Gulapa's stories took place in or around this garden, which was located in Fort Jafar, a crumbling structure built by the British that stood adjacent to the adobe wall surrounding our village.

At each corner of the fort was a massive tower with their ornate iron grillwork. You couldn't climb to the top, although Khialo and I tried a few times, but what stairs there were, were nothing more than rickety wooden planks that trembled when you stepped on them. The way Gulapa described the fort, you'd have thought it was a beehive of activity, but in fact, no one ever went there other than her and her husband. The same was true of the crumbling mosque that was a short distance from the fort and stood behind high walls whose rusted gates were always locked.

Gulapa said that one time, a dead farmer had been left alone there overnight, but when his relatives came the next morning to bury him, his body was gone. "A shaitan from hell was to blame," she said, lowering her voice. "A devil who crawled inside his flesh and carried him away. Never leave a dead body alone. You hear me? Never."

I asked where the shaitan took him, and Gulapa shook her head. "Some answers are beyond me. Just remember this: Everything is alive, everything is breathing. Even the sand beneath your feet."

My imagination ran riot with her stories, not to mention her warning that if any of us tried to steal any of Atal's fruit or vegetables, a wraith would tear his throat out. "Go ahead," she jeered, the smoke drifting from her nostrils in ever-widening circles. "If you want to gamble with your lives, you're more than welcome to. Go on. I dare you." Which left us children in a quandary—should we sneak over when it was dark and tempt fate? We believed implicitly in what Gulapa said; all my friends thought that she had supernatural powers and could make the wind rise and the rivers flood.

So we'd go off by ourselves and mull over the issue, but when it came down to it, no one ever dared. Besides, Khialo would say, he didn't have to steal anything and risk getting killed. All he had to do was ask his father, so why should he get involved in some crazy scheme?

I didn't care. I was more interested in the wraiths, specifically the shaitan who'd entered the body of the dead farmer. "What did he look like?" I asked her. "How did he get in?"

"By twisting the man's head around and pulling it off." When she said this, she held her hands out like two claws and made a swift twisting motion.

"I bet you're making all this up," I said, but my voice faltered.

"Don't be smart."

"Well, what does he look like? Is he as big and tall as…as Droon?"

"My son? Twice as big. Bigger. With a scaly tail. And red pointed ears. Like a poisonous snake lying coiled up under a rock and just waiting. You can hear him sometimes if you're real quiet."

"What is he waiting for?"

"What do you think?"

"That he wants me to come closer," I whispered. "That he wants to kill me." I could feel my heart pound against my chest. "I hate that old devil, I hate him. And all those wraiths."

"Well, don't bother them, and they won't bother you. Now, go off and play. I can't sit here talking to you kids all day."

I thought about Lakhta who said that Gulapa was a know-it-all and that I shouldn't believe her stories, that she was only trying to scare me. "You see, *zwaia*, you are living in a world where the past is so alive, people like Gulapa sense its presence without understanding its meaning. That's why they make up all sorts of fables about it. But if you're not afraid, if you pay attention, you'll understand. There are no wraiths, but there are spirits from the past, our glorious past, when we were a great nation and a crossroads for the world. Go into the fort and take off your sandals so you can feel the stones against your bare feet. What are they saying? They speak if you can hear."

When I'd mentioned to Gulapa what Lakhta said, she had laughed mirthlessly. "To hell with the past, boy. It's dead. It's ancient history. Why should I worry my head about what happened a hundred years ago, eh? Better I should worry that our cucumbers are sweet, that Atal is happy, and my brats have a full stomach. Besides, like I've told before, you and that thick head of yours, that fort is haunted. There are devils there. What does that old crone know? Does she live here in Srakala? No. She lives in

Shabak. Is she one of us? No. Well then, who is she? Where'd she come from?"

I could have said Lakhta had crossed the mountains over the Khyber Pass, but Gulapa wouldn't have cared.

"Enough, enough," she said, snapping her fingers in everyone's face. "Don't sit there. All of you, be off!"

Meena and Sial headed home while Khialo and I went inside his house and listened to Afghan music on the radio. Later when I left, I went out of my way to pass by the mosque just to prove to myself that what Gulapa had said was absurd. But as I passed the fort, the stillness was broken by a *chunchana* as it flew from the north tower and perched on the mosque's minaret. It was as if, grave and stern, it'd been following me. A wave of anxiety washed over me. I tried to appear nonchalant, forcing myself to walk at a slow pace, but when I'd passed out of view, I ran as fast as I could until I was almost home, at which point I again assumed an air of insouciance. I didn't want anyone to see me. Especially Lakhta. She'd say I was being a baby after she'd advised me not to believe Gulapa and what she called her nonsense.

I used to think that Lakhta was the wisest person I knew. Although she had no education and could scarcely read or write, nevertheless, she always had an answer for everything. From the moment she began working for us as a nanny two years before, we'd been drawn to each other. The first time I met her, I'd wandered over to one of the springs in our fields. I was sitting with my feet in the water, leaning over to see if I could catch my reflection, when I was startled by a voice shouting, "Hey, boy!"

I sat up quickly and looked around. No one was there.

"Hey!" A woman came out from behind some bushes and said, "Look what I've got. Just for you." She was carrying a tray of tandoori cookies and a glass of fresh goat's milk. "Now," she said, placing the tray down and sitting next to me, "let's you and I get to know each other. I'm Lakhta. Your father has hired me to help your mother around the house. Let's see, I came from far away.

I have a two-year-old whose name is Bazgar, my little eagle, and another son, Azmoon, he's sixteen, a bright lad, he's going to be a pilot when he grows up. Then whenever a plane flies overhead, I'll think it's him. And I have an adopted daughter. Her name's Sandara, and she is a real beauty."

I reached for a cookie, my mind filled with images of flying in an airplane and looking down at all the people scurrying around like ants. "I saw a purple butterfly yesterday, and it flew all the way up to the top of a tree," I said and took a sip of milk.

She told me to make sure and finish it if I wanted to grow up to be big and strong. "The goat told me that this is just for you," she added. When I had emptied the glass, she said, "Okay, first things first. What is your name, and how old are you?"

I told her.

"Eight years old. I was eight once. A long time ago. For a whole year. And then guess what happened?"

"What?"

"I turned nine."

"Moor says that when I grow up, I'm going to be taller than my brother Jandol. Then I'll be able to ride my very own horse. Just like he does."

"Is that what your mother told you?"

"Yes."

"I used to ride a lot when I was a young girl. Not anymore."

"Why not?"

"You ask questions. I like that. So I will tell you. I have no horse."

"Why don't you use one of ours?"

"I don't want to."

"Why not?"

"Because I don't know them. Not yet anyway. I don't feel comfortable unless I've spoken to the horse and taught him to trust me."

"Are you married?"

"Of course, I'm married. How could I have two children and one adopted daughter if I weren't married?"

"Who are you married to?"

"A shoemaker named Samsoor. He's quite a looker."

"More handsome than Abba?"

"Your father? Let me see," she said. "Not more, not less. The same."

"Will he make me some shoes?"

"Do you have feet?"

"Yes," I said, sticking my legs out of the water and wiggling my toes.

"Well, finish eating, and I'll take you to our house and introduce you to my husband."

"Okay." I did as she asked and stuck a couple of cookies in my vest pocket. The next time I saw Lakhta, she was milking a goat in our stable. I asked if I could help, and she told me to hold the goat's beard to keep her steady.

"Lakhta, can I ask you something?"

"What?"

"Who owns these goats?"

"You do. I mean, your family does."

"Well, if we own them, why can't I bring them inside at night?"

"I don't think your parents would be too happy about that."

"Why not?"

"You've been around these farm animals all your life. You know that you sleep in the house, and they sleep in the stable."

"But it makes me sad for them."

"Why? There's no need to be."

"Does Azmoon go to school or Sandara?"

"Of course they do. When I save enough money, God willing, I'm going to send them both to the university in Jalalabad."

Lakhta continued tugging at the udders from which milk shot into the pail while the goat stood passively by, chewing the cud and gazing at me from her universe.

"Well, why doesn't God give you the money right away?"

"Ask Him. I don't know."

"But that's so unfair."

"Life's unfair."

It was the beginning of a deep and abiding relationship between the two of us. But now unable to stop thinking about what Gulapa said, for the first time I wasn't so certain that Lakhta knew what she was talking about. Gulapa sounded so sure of herself. I went inside, but before I could get the words out, Lakhta told me to go out to the shed and bring in some wood for the stove. When I returned, she fired up the oven, and the glow from the burning embers made her face glisten. She stirred the stew that had been simmering for hours, adding more water to the huge pot filled with vegetables from our garden and redolent with the heavy aroma of goat meat, which, when she was done, melted in your mouth. I always associated Lakhta with cooking, with lamb kebabs and beef stews and chickens marinated in lemon and garlic that were roasted until they were golden brown.

"Now slow down, and tell me what's the matter."

I repeated what Gulapa said and that I didn't know who to believe, and she asked me when was I going to learn the difference between make-believe and reality.

"But she said they were like horrible snakes just waiting to kill you."

"You are so gullible."

"What's gullible?"

"Someone whose head is screwed on backwards. Stop staring and close your mouth. When you're older and hopefully wiser, you'll see what I mean. Now go wash up, supper'll be ready in an hour."

"Where is everybody?"

"Well, let me see. Pamir, he's in Kabul working at the warehouse, and your father's at the mine near Tummanai. Your older sister Shamla's not coming, she's making supper for her husband for once. I hope he has plenty of bicarbonate of soda. Jandol's off doing God knows what, Sial's daydreaming about yet another far-fetched scheme of his, and Moor's over at your grandmother's—did I leave anyone out? Oh, Sandara's out back taking care of little Baz, and Meena is in her room trying to make heads or tails of her geometry homework, so don't go making a lot of noise."

"How do you know so much?"

"I have eyes in the back of my head. Let me finish, or I'll never get done. Why don't you go out to the garden and help Sandara. And don't forget to clean your hands before you come in."

"I think Sandara's so beautiful. The most."

"You and every other man in the village. They're just waiting for her to grow up."

No one knew where Sandara came from or who her family was. About ten years ago, right around when I was born, some villagers found her wandering in the fields; she couldn't have been more than five or six, and she was sick and hungry, just skin and bones, with no name, no history. Lakhta and Atal took her in and raised her as their own. As Sandara grew older though, it was like watching an ugly duckling turn into a swan. First of all, she was the smartest girl in our village. And second, she wasn't exactly beautiful, more exotic actually, but her eyes were hypnotic—green and luminous, with faint bluish shadows and heavy lashes. All the young and not-so-young men vied for her attention, but the word was she only had eyes for Droon, even though such a marriage was practically impossible.

Droon drove a truck for a cousin of his named Safi and worked for my father making deliveries, which put him in a totally unsuitable category for the man Lakhta—backed by Moor and Abba—wanted Sandara to wed, a man of breeding and intelligence, an educated man, one destined to rise up in the world. I used to watch her and Droon when they were together, but I didn't see anything out of the ordinary, although once, when

I asked her if she was in love with him, she said, "Ask me no questions, and I'll tell you no lies," which, at the time, I thought was the wittiest remark I had ever heard. From then on, whenever anybody asked me something, I said the same thing.

The patio in the back opened onto a garden where there was an elm tree that had been there for generations. Jandol had built a swing for the children, and Sandara was pushing Baz, who kept kicking his legs and shrieking, "Higher, higher!"

"Enough," she said after a while, and when the swing came to a stop, he scampered down and began playing with some wooden toys made to look like jungle beasts that Abba had brought back from Kabul.

I got on the swing and idly began pushing myself back and forth. "Guess what," I said to Sandara. "Today when I was coming home, I walked past the old mosque, and there was a blackbird staring at me with fiery red eyes that burnt my skin. But I wasn't afraid, not one bit." I pushed myself as high as I could, then lifting up my legs and lowering my head, I slowly coasted while the ground and the trees and the clouds rushed at me in a dizzying mélange of colors and patterns.

"Why would you be afraid?" Sandara said.

"Everyone knows crows are bad luck."

"I don't think that's true. It's merely something people make up."

"If that's so, why'd that old bird stare at me with those blood-red eyes?"

"Maybe it wasn't staring at you. Maybe you're making that up in your head."

"I am not."

"Anyway, it doesn't matter, you're safe here. See, not a single blackbird anywhere."

"Those birds are evil, and you know it," I said, coming to an abrupt stop.

"I don't know anything of the kind. Only people are evil. Nature is cruel but not evil."

"What's the difference?"

"That's something you'll have to find out for yourself."

"No, tell me."

"Well, the way I see it is that cruelty is born in the heart, and evil comes from the mind."

"I don't understand."

"It's the difference between feeling and thinking, you know, planning and simply…acting from instinct, from hunger."

"Stop teasing me," I said, not sure that she was.

I wondered if she was right, and then I rememberd something from when I was eight. I was outside playing near the old fort, and I saw a scorpion on the grass. It was covered with little baby scorpions. Moor had warned me never to touch one of them, but I never listended to anyone who told me what to do. I wanted to help the babies get them free from their mother before she ate them, so I got a couple of sticks, and applying them like a tweezer, I began pulling them off one by one. Suddenly, I felt myself being pulled backward by the collar. I turned and saw Atal.

"Are you crazy!" he said. "Do you want to get bitten?"

"I'm just trying to help."

"Help a scorpion? They don't need your help."

"They do, they do."

"Then you don't know an enemy when you see one."

"I don't have any enemies."

"Everyone has enemies, son, and if you can't tell them apart from frindes, you're going to be in big trouble."

Atal had been right. I was being bullheaded. I had forgotten about it until that moment.

Srakala was in the Hisarak District, a vast area of arid plains and inaccessible mountain ranges about sixty miles east of Kabul. In the summer the air was dry, and on sunny days you could see all the way to the snow-covered peaks of the Spin Ghar Mountains.

The village lay between the banks of two rivers, the Nawar Sind to the east and the Auzingianai Sind to the west, where the neighboring village of Shabak was located. The Nawar was not much of a river no matter what the season, but the Auzingianai was a different story. In spring and fall, when the rains came, it became unpredictable, treacherous. It was forever changing its banks, and you could never depend on the current that might appear slow and meandering until it suddenly became a rampage that washed away the temporary log bridges that'd been placed there. Flash floods were frequent, and at such times, it was impossible to cross from Srakala to Shabak, which meant that no one could buy meat from the butcher's, whose shop was in the local bazaar a mile west of Shabak.

When that happened, we would have to slaughter our own egg-laying chickens or buy fresh lamb from that jack-of-all-trades, the ubiquitous Shakar, who was also a potter and a blacksmith. When the rains didn't come, the rivers turned to mud and then dry sand, and people called them rivers of stone.

Because of our proximity to the mountains, the summers were mild and the nights were cool, and in the early morning you could sit under a pine tree and feel the freshness of the earth.

In the winter it snowed, and sometimes there were blizzards that made the roads impassable and rimed our windows. When the snows melted, the wind, harsh and angry, would come storming down from the mountains, and the windows would shiver in response. In February my father's father Emal Khan died, and my grandmother Bibi moved in with Shamla and her husband Kamkai, who were living in Minkhill, where he was a teacher at the local school. Shamla was expecting her first child and begged Bibi to stay with her.

Grandfather Emal was such a feisty old man; he used to say that I was the only one in the family he felt close to. He said I reminded him of himself when he was my age, always curious, always sticking his nose in everybody's business, which he counted as an attribute. He was the son of a general, and he and his offspring were wealthy landowners. It was an oft-told family legend that when he was a young man, King Zahir Shah asked him to serve in the Afghan army as his personal aide-de-camp, but he refused. "Imagine the audacity," Bibi would remark with pride in her voice, "saying no to the king."

But he and my father were forever at loggerheads, always butting their horns against each other, never agreeing on anything; if one said it was hot, the other said it was cold. The problem was that my father was an orderly man—or at least he tried to be—and my grandfather made up the rules as he went along. I wanted to tell him that I'd miss him, but children were not allowed to view the dead. If we did, it was said that a shadow would fall on us, and we'd be the next to die. Bibi presented a stoic face to the world and said it was God's will.

I thought about what she said, and that evening I asked Pamir who God was and where did He live.

"Never ever ask questions about God," he said. "You know what Mullah Kadoo says. If you do you'll go to Jahanam."

"The worst circle of hell? Why?"

"Go ask him, don't ask me."

"He's so creepy, he always spits when he talks."

"Well, don't stand so close."

"He's joking," Jandol said. "You know you can't believe those guys. They say one thing and do the exact opposite."

"'Listen to the mullahs,'" Pamir quoted that old cliché. "'But don't do what they do.' Remember the mullah who condemned the farmer for growing poppies, telling him that God forbad such evildoings. The farmer was so impressed he gave the mullah free land so he could plant his flowers. Well, you know what the mullah planted."

"Ah, but, Pamir," Jandol said, "the poppy is also a flower."

I didn't know what to think, but Pamir was almost an adult, so he must know what he was talking about. Besides, he was studying at Kabul University. I suppose it came down to the fact that none of us was a fanatic for in myriad ways, our way of life and those of our fellow villagers expressed a deep abiding faith in God and a connection to the land and to each other, without our being strangled by dicta. If God were everywhere, He was everywhere; we didn't have to do anything or go anywhere, nor did we have to attend prayer services five times a day. Instead of facing Mullah Kadoo's behind, we could kneel and give thanks wherever we found ourselves. It was such freedom, we felt, that allowed us to experience what true religion was about, namely a sense of the beingness in everything, a consciousness that existed throughout the universe. In this way, we lived our religion and valued our freedom.

Our lives, as those of our ancestors, were spent close to nature and to the land on which our livelihood depended. Most villagers were dirt-poor and struggled to eke out enough to feed their families. No gas or electricity, no telephones, no TV, no running water, usually no indoor plumbing, goats wandering loose, dogs, chickens, very few cars, houses made of mud, windowless dwellings that smelled of kerosene from the lamps, and until my father bankrolled it, no hospital. This was our village, our lives in this, our wild rocky country with its forbidding mountains and scrub-covered deserts.

In late spring, the winds died down and the rain ceased, and the sun turned into a riotous disc of fire. Waterlogged roads became accessible again while grass sprang up, covering the fields like a bright green blanket. Flocks of migratory birds soared on the breeze—*sharoo*, talking tuttis, and wheeling high above, birds of prey with their wings spread wide. Nature was bursting with life in a rhythm that turned each day into an adventure.

Jandol would pack a lunch and take me to the Ashrat Kala garden, which separated Shabak from Srakala and through which the Auzingianai ran. We'd have a picnic, just the two of us. I'd examine the different flowers and fruit trees, their colors, textures, and smells while Jandol would tell me what they were. Just to make sure I remembered, he'd spell the name for me then make me repeat it until I could say it properly. He was a great older brother. "When I grow up," I told him, "I want to be exactly like you."

Bands of nomads would pass by Srakala on their journey north to Ilband, their summer retreat on the lower slopes of the Hindu Kush Mountains. The villagers were glad to see them because they brought fresh butter, yogurt, cheese, and goat's milk in exchange for our grains and dried fruit. The women were so elegant with those little *khals* tattooed on their faces and their kaftans fluttering when they walked. Sandara wished she could travel with them, and Abba said that even though the people of our valley had settled several centuries ago, we had nomadic blood running in our veins. The only difference, Meena said, was that they were able to go wherever they wanted while we were stuck here.

"Don't forget," Sial added, "they don't have any papers, and we do."

"Papers? They don't need papers. They're free. We're the ones who need papers."

"You think that's so wonderful. Always on the move, never having a real home?"

"You call this a real home?"

"I agree with Meena, I think it's exciting," Sandara said. "Meeting different people, sleeping under the stars."

"My dear child," Moor said, pausing with her sewing needle in one hand and a torn sock in the other, "sometimes things look different when you take them out of the box."

"In other words, you have to think before you dream," Abba said.

"I suppose you're right," Sandara said in her soft musical voice. "But they lead such wonderful lives, seeing things, going places."

With a smile, Sial turned to Sandara. "Maybe you're right. At least they're not wedged into a corner forced to listen to people complaining all the time."

"Don't look at me," Meena said. "You're the whiner."

"Yeah, right," Sial said lazily. "This coming from the math whiz who thinks two plus two is eleven."

"Always this constant bickering between you two," Abba said. "Go outside and argue."

"We're not arguing," Sial said. "We're merely trying to understand a world we never made."

"We're trying to find ourselves," Meena said.

"What about you finding a husband?" Moor said, half-seriously.

"That's the last thing I want. Once you get married, you're caught for good, you can never live your own life. Not if you're a woman."

"You'll change your mind when you meet the right man."

"Never."

"You'll see. Wait'll someone appears with dark eyes and a way with the ladies. Then everything will be different."

"I wonder," Meena said. "I guess that would be…interesting. If it ever happens."

It was Sandara who introduced me to poetry—and I can still hear her voice as she recited the works of poets whose verses reverberated down the corridors of time, as precise and as moving now as they had been when first uttered. I can't say I understood much, but I liked how the words flowed. One time she showed me a bird's nest in our tree out back, and I climbed up so that I could watch the nestlings. When the mother saw me, she flapped her wings querulously and flew to a higher branch. From then on I'd periodically check out the nest until even the mother became used to me and paid me no mind. But then one day I discovered that the nest was empty and the birds were gone. When I told Sandara, she said it just went to show that every creature had its own destiny to fulfill. But where'd they go, and would they survive? I brooded about the fate of the birds until I decided that they probably knew more about surviving than I did.

Our village was on a hill, and our house was on the highest section of the hill. In most villages, everyone had their own hujra, a combination guesthouse and men's meeting room, but as I said, the residents of Srakala couldn't afford such a luxury, which meant that the only hujra was the one that my father's father had built next door to where we lived and which was used by all the villagers. With its own garden and surrounding walls, it consisted of ten rooms that opened upon a common area the size of a large living room. Although most homes had fireplaces, our house had one in every room. We were surrounded by a nine-foot mud wall with wooden gates at the front and at the back, where our patio faced the garden. The hujra was also enclosed within its own walls, but there was only one gate, and that opened onto our farmland, a huge spread fanning out around us for hundreds of acres. In addition to grains and rice, we raised goats, sheep, and cattle that were corralled in the grassy valleys at the base of the Tummanai Mountains, where they were tended by shepherds who lived with them throughout the year. This pasture was about a three-hour walk from Srakala, and Khialo and I, accompanied by my long-haired shepherd dog, Mamar, would hike over to see the newborn goats and lambs. Then on the way back, we'd pick *gogars* and give them to Moor, who loved mountain flowers. She said that they looked as if they had eyes that could pierce the soul.

Ours was a distinguished clan that included doctors, politicians, professors, and generals in the Afghan Army. We were the wealthiest family in the village, probably in the district, and many of the locals worked for us on our farm, which afforded them a livelihood they might not have had. In addition to Srakala, we had homes in Kabul, Jalalabad, and were in the process of building a house in Shabak, which was on the opposite side of the Auzingianai and larger and more prosperous than Srakala. Nevertheless, for every villager, no matter how wealthy, daily living was difficult, conditions were harsh, and work was harsh. Since there was no electricity, every meal had to be cooked fresh, especially when it was warm. If you wanted to bathe, you had to heat the water on the stove, which meant that by the time you had enough, it was always lukewarm, if that. I could go on and on.

What made everything bearable was that the villagers were like an extended family, each of us sharing the joys and hardships of our daily struggles with a sense of community that strengthened us and gave meaning to our lives. Since that time I have lived in cities of a million people and felt lonelier and more disconnected than when I was a youth in Srakala. I have learned that riches taken for granted—such as cars and TVs, gas and electricity, computers and cell phones, indeed, most artifacts of contemporary life—can never replace the simple human interdependence that I experienced in a backward village of one hundred inhabitants, fighting for survival in a far-off, war-torn country.

When I look back, I always remember that sense of continuity. So in a way, both Lakhta and Gulapa misunderstood something essential about our lives—it was neither the past that still lived in the present, nor was it lying moribund in dusty history books, nor was it the fury of wraiths and monsters. This aliveness stemmed from our interconnectedness to each other and to the land on which we lived. But it's hard to explain this to people in the West who've never experienced such a way of life.

My father was the owner of a company that dealt in the mining and distributing of *shamaqsudas*, a semiprecious stone used for costume jewelry and paperweights, among other things. He was frequently out of town, buying and selling as well as overseeing the mining operations. There were two—one near Tummanai and the other between Jalalabad and Kabul with about eighty employees. My oldest brother, Pamir, was studying engineering at Kabul University, and after school he worked in the main office, which was located in that city. My father drove around in a battered 1969 Volkswagen Beetle that had once been white and was now a dingy gray. Since the only place within a hundred miles to buy gas and oil was in Jalalabad, which was hours away from Srakala, he'd tank up there and fill as many containers as he could safely attach to the roof. It was only by the grace of God that he didn't blow himself up, and the car always smelled like a gas station. When he was away, my mother ran the farm.

School went from eight until one in the afternoon, six days a week with Fridays off, and ran from March until November, at which time the classrooms, lacking heating and electricity, became too cold and dark. That winter, the weather had been fierce, and now all of the rivers were running fast and furious with the melting snow. To reach the school, which was in Shabak, you had to cross the Auzingianai on a plank bridge that wasn't only high above the water, but lacked guardrails. My first day at school, when I saw the bridge, I stopped dead in my tracks. Sial and Meena were halfway over when they realized I wasn't following them. It took all of my courage and quite some time before I finally crossed over, holding my arms out for balance and moving slowly, one step at a time. I think if it'd been anyone else except those two, I'd have point-blank refused, but their jeering did more for my courage than any words of encouragement. Nevertheless, I fretted for hours about the return trip, which turned out to be a piece of cake as either the water had lessened or my courage had grown. That first crossing was such a victory, when Moor asked me what I'd learned in school, I went on and on about the bridge and how scary it was and what it felt like and how I wasn't afraid anymore until Sial told me to quiet down, it's not like I crossed the Nile. I didn't say anything because I didn't know where the Nile was.

At any rate, by the end of the first week. I could dance across, hopping on one foot. The funny thing was, a few weeks later on the way home, Meena slipped and fell in. Sial raced over to the bank, waded into the water until it was almost up to his waist, and clasped her by the arm. Boy, was she fit to be tied. For the next few days, I went around telling everybody that Meena had almost drowned in the Auzingianai, that she had been staring at the water, and one of Gulapa's wraiths leaped out and grabbed her. A scaly monster with claws and slatted eyes, with poisonous fangs and a forked tongue. Someone told Meena what I was saying, and she said I was a liar, that there were no monsters, and that she'd fallen because the bridge was so slippery.

"Why do you go around telling lies about Meena?" Sandara said to me. We were out on the verandah huddled together to keep warm as the moon lifted off from the shadow of the earth, turning the fields into insubstantial wisps like a land of smoke.

"I wasn't lying."

"She told you she slipped. And you go around making up stories about crazy ghosts. Now you're lying to me."

"I hate her, she's ugly and twisted. Like an old ugly twisted tree. Like the one in our schoolyard, twisted and ugly."

"That's a terrible thing to say. Won't you be surprised when that tree begins to blossom."

"That'll never happen."

"Don't be so sure."

"Do you hate me?"

"Of course not. I love you."

"But you're angry with me."

"I'm disappointed. I expect great things from you."

"What things?"

"Things."

"But you don't get along with Meena."

"That's not true. There are always conflicts between people. Besides, she isn't my sister. She's only my pretend sister."

At the end of March, we celebrated the Afghan New Year, a two-day celebration that included every village in the Hisarak and was being held in Srakala this year. By February, I was already counting the days until the festival. That year Sial, who was no whiz when it came to his studies, had gotten a B average for the first time in his life—the first and the last, as it turned out—and as a gift, Abba had ordered him a pair of hand-made leather sandals from Charsadda where all the best shoemakers were. This was quite a complicated process since Charsadda was two hundred miles away across the Durand Line, but Abba managed to get this taken care of through Droon and another driver friend of his, and the sandals arrived in time for the festivities.

Well, what can I say, the minute I saw them, I wanted a pair, and I went to Abba, but he said there wasn't enough time. I told Lakhta, and she said she'd ask Samsoor to make me a pair.

"He's as good—if not better—than any shoemaker in Charsadda or anywhere."

A few days later, when I went over to be sized, I asked Samsoor if I could watch him make the sandals. I wanted to make sure that he didn't skimp on the material and that he finished them on time. I was also afraid, what with the festivities coming up in a week, that someone else would give him an order and jump ahead of me. Not that I didn't trust him. Each day, I sat there while Samsoor worked, and it was fascinating; his thick fingers that always seemed clumsy were so dexterous, his stitching was spot on, and he used the best parts of flat tires for the soles. When they were ready, I thought they were the most elegant footwear I'd ever seen, including Sial's hand-made sandals from Charsadda, and I raced home to show them to him.

"Look what I've got," I said and thrust the sandals at him.

He was lounging in bed in his peacock blue pajamas, eating halva out of a porcelain bowl and studying himself in a hand mirror. He glanced at me, placed the mirror facedown on his bed, and said, "What now?"

"Look, look, look."

He sat up, took hold of the sandals, and put one hand in the right foot, and the other in the left. "Ooh," he said, moving his arms up and down, "your sandals are dancing."

"Stop fooling around. Look at the material, look at the stitching. Aren't they terrific?" He kept moving his hands and going "Ooh" and "Aah" in that sarcastic way of his until I pulled the sandals away. "You're such a fool."

"I'm a fool? You're the one that's the fool," he said and burst out laughing.

"What's funny?"

"You are. I have real sandals made by a real shoemaker."

"And what do I have?"

Sial reached forward and grabbed my sandals from me. "Look at them," he said, holding them from the straps and shaking them in my face "They're bigger than a Russian tank. The heels are made of old tires. And this leather? Where'd he get it from? A dead rat?" When I tried to take the sandals back, he held them too high for me to reach. "They're like clown shoes, like the kind Mullah Nasrudin wears." With that observation, he dropped the sandals to the floor. "What a jerk you are."

"You don't know what you're talking about." I said and stormed out. Moor asked me what was going on, but I couldn't answer her. My cheeks were burning. I was seeing the sandals as if for the first time, without the patina of romance obscuring my awareness. They weren't beautiful; they weren't elegant. They had tricked me, Lakhta and Samsoor, and I hated them. Now I had to listen to Sial who was like a dog worrying a bone—after supper when Lakhta left, he began making fun of me until Moor finally told him to stop it at once—or else.

"Don't listen to him," she said to me. "I think your sandals are beautiful."

"Don't lie," I said. "They're a piece of junk, and you know it."

"You just need to break them in, you'll see."

"If they don't break him first," Sial said.

Next morning when we left, it was still dark out. I put on the sandals, but they were uncomfortable, heavy, too big and too small, they pinched my toes, but I couldn't get the straps tight enough to keep them from slipping back and forth. On the way over, I took them off and hid them behind some bushes, thinking I'd get them on the way home, but with all the excitement that went on, I totally forgot, and when I did remember to return, they were gone.

The festivities always began with a contest to see who'd be the first to climb to the top of the tallest tree and raise the Afghan flag. The winner would then be crowned as the king of the festival and wear a garland of yellow flowers around his head like a crown; it was a great honor. The competition was fierce, and three years before, two contestants—they were brothers from Minkhill—had fallen, and one of them almost died; villagers still talked about it.

In the field south of the village were five oak trees, each about the same height, and already a crowd had gathered. For each tree, depending on its girth, there were two and sometimes three opponents. Jandol, Azmoon, and Droon were going to climb the same tree, but at the last moment, Droon pulled out. "I won last year," he said, coming up to me and Khialo. "So why rock the boat?"

Sandara heard what he said and asked him what boat he was going to rock. "Why, the boat of my achievement," Droon said, and he placed his hands on his hips. "I thus remain undefeated."

"Oh, look" she said. "The race is starting."

"It won't begin for a while. Not until Mullah Kadoo makes a speech about how great the Afghan people are. Particularly his own achievements."

"Well, what's wrong with that? It's something we don't hear that much of. All we ever hear is how we've been victimized."

"Personally, I'd rather be victimized than praised by that fool."

Indeed, at that moment, Mullah Kadoo's voice rose as shrill as a clarion, while he stood before us with his shoulders bowed by the weight of centuries of agonized longing. Sheepish to those above, contemptuous to those below, the moment he opened his mouth, he bared wolfish fangs, his greatest power over us that we never knew what to expect, the savage or the ruminant. It was his teeth that Sandara said gave him away—cruel, sharp, and the color of striated rust. Of course, once she'd pointed them out, all I could ever focus on whenever we met were those canine incisors, spittle-wet and serrated at the edges. He was overweight, scant-bearded, and at fifty-two, had been a mullah forever. He had small hands, small feet, and an overripe smile hung from his damp lips, lips that never were still, thin lips that puckered open and then clamped shut. The words flew from his lips; they flew around like crows and turned a bright morning dull. His words meant nothing to me. They just flapped around my brain in a dizzying, meaningless formation. What was he saying?

"Hence, our job is to mobilize and to fuel, to rectify and to bless, to incite and to protest, to pray and to protect, to praise and to probe. For Muslims the world over, our time has come, our future is near, and our past will never die—no, not for a thousand, not for a million years, not if the universe itself were to explode into oblivion. Our religion will ever dominate our lives in hovels as well as in presidential palaces and houses of parliament. Governors and kings, serfs and beggars, must follow its edicts." He paused to gaze at his audience. Only a few of the villagers were listening to him; the rest, including me, my family, and everyone we knew, were milling around, waiting for the tree-climbing race to start and wishing he'd shut up.

Undaunted, Mullah Kadoo continued. "God gave life and breath to the universe. And the earth and all the creatures that walk, talk, crawl, swim, and fly. God created bands of angels, He made the heavens, He made the sun, the moon, the stars, and galaxies. He made the rains fall on the dry earth and from the soil brought He forth the fruits and vegetables of His labors. And the fruit was sweet and the vegetables were nourishing for He had made them. And made He man from the dust of the earth into whom He breathed life, and He called this man Adam. And from Adam's left rib brought He forth Eve, and they lived in

Paradise. But when He ordered all the angels to bow down before Adam, Iblis refused, and as a result of this refusal came all of the sins of the world, for Iblis was banished to hell from which he wages constant war. And it came about that Iblis, disguised as a serpent, tempted Eve to eat from the Forbidden Tree, and she did as he asked, and she handed Adam the fruit and he took a bite, and they were both cast out from Paradise. But though our afflictions are legion and though they manifest in various forms and shapes, we who take heed of the teachings of Islam, we who obey the will of God, shall find that one day soon we can return to Paradise. And thus we must not waver—nay, not even if death stands before our door."

"I'd like to see what he does when death knocks on his door," Droon said, sotto voce.

In the interval of silence following his speech, the judge raised his hands as a signal for the contestants to take their positions. The onlookers moved forward and formed a dense semicircle around the trees. A hush fell on the crowd. Fifteen minutes later, he shouted, "Now!" Instantly, each young man began scrambling up the tree boughs. This initial stage was the hardest part of the race since the branches were generally too high to get a good hold of, and you had to hoist yourself up by sheer strength until you could wrap your legs around the branch. Once there, you reached up for the next branch and the next. Some of the men were as agile as monkeys, while others were unable to do more than hang for a minute before falling off.

Jandol and Azmoon began their ascent. Azmoon was stocky and strong as an ox, but Jandol was as wily as a ferret. At first they kept jockeying for position, one higher, one lower, and vice versa. But as they climbed and as the tree narrowed, Jandol balanced momentarily on one branch and leapt up, taking hold of the next higher limb. When he did this, the branch he'd been standing on splintered, and for a second he hung forty feet above the earth. Everybody held their breath until he was able to wrap his legs around the trunk and raise himself so that he was able to grasp another branch. Azmoon didn't even try; he was too heavy. Jandol was the first to reach the uppermost part of the tree, and he hollered at the top of his lungs, pulling off his *pakul* and throwing it out to the crowd below. It twirled round and round as it descended while everyone raced to catch it until it disappeared in a mob of reaching hands. From below, the flag was passed up from tree to tree until Azmoon took hold and handed it to Jandol. He secured the flag, and as it unfurled, gently flapping in the warm soft breeze, the villagers raised their arms and shouted, "Achariar! Achariar! Achariar!"

The musicians began to play, and the drummers pounded on their drums rhythms that came down from the ages in a fiery, unceasing thrust that vibrated through your body. Jandol and Azmoon joined us, and Moor, Bibi, and Meena threw their arms around Jandol, after which Sandara congratulated both of them. But when she turned to Jandol, he stared at her so intently that Moor took hold of his arm and asked if anyone were hungry, breaking the spell.

The musicians began to play, and people began dancing, and Moor and Abba made their way to one of the numerous cots that had been scattered around where they'd placed our picnic baskets.

The various smells of cooking were everywhere: beef being braised, lamb simmering with vegetables in huge pots, marinated spiced chicken being barbecued, and lamb kebabs skewered over open fires. For desserts there were pies, cakes, and sweets galore. My favorite was *jalebi*, where you mixed sugar and flour, added water, then placed the mixture in a paper cone, which you dribbled into a sizzling-hot frying pan until it splintered into something that looked like fettuccine, only it was bright pink, crunchy, and ambrosial.

By the time Khialo and I had sampled a little taste of everything, it was time for the egg rolling contest. We returned to where Moor and Abba were sitting, picked up our sacks of hardboiled eggs that we'd decorated the week before, and headed toward the place where the contest would be held, an area in which the ground fell sharply downward. A series of planks had been placed next to each other at a steep angle, and about ten of us lined up behind them, waiting for the signal from the ref to put an egg at the top of the plank and let it roll down the incline. Whoever's egg rolled the farthest got to collect all the others. Eggs were something of a delicacy, so the tension ran high.

Sial appeared, trumpeting about the superiority of his eggs, although naturally, he didn't let on that he'd boiled them in pomegranate skins after which he'd stuck in a syringe and filled them with something to make them heavier. When Khialo and I ran out of eggs, he asked us to wait under some trees so we could keep an eye on his winnings. He wasn't kidding, my brother; he proceeded to beat every other entrant until we had a pile of eggs spread before us. I began furiously devouring them as fast as I could; that'd teach that conniver a lesson. The minute Sial turned his back, I'd peel another one.

Khialo, who didn't like getting into rows, told me to cut it out, but I refused to listen, and when I offered him one, he said he wasn't hungry. I lay back in the grass with one hand behind my head while I finished yet another egg. Some were hard to peel; the shell would stick to the skin, and I'd get impatient and pull it off, and a big chunk would go along with it. Apparently, there was some trick to peeling an egg because when Lakhta did it or Moor, they came out perfect, whereas mine looked ravaged. I thought that was funny, and I turned to show Khialo my latest misadventure when I felt a stitch in my side. I took a deep breath, only that made it worse, turning it instantly into a sharp pain. I lay back down, and now the pain seemed to be all across my stomach, and when I sat up, I felt dizzy, with a rushing sound in my ears. I tried to stand, but the pain became so intense, I told Khialo to get Jandol. At that moment, everything went blurry, and voices sounded like they were miles away, and then it was black.

The next thing I knew, I was in the hospital hooked up to an IV drip, my stomach feeling as if someone had dropped a cement block on it. I was in the hospital for three days, and I never did find out what Sial put in those eggs—actually, I was afraid to ask him, afraid he'd tell me. When I came home, Sandara brought me some biscuits she'd made—with no eggs, she said since the very thought of one made me faint—and Khialo gave me a coloring book. He asked me if I'd met any ghosts while I was unconscious, that Gulapa wanted to know, but I didn't remember anything, I told him. Not even one?

Meena told him to stop worrying me about such nonsense, and they started bickering, but I didn't care. I was glad to be home, glad that everyone was being so sweet to me, making much of me while I basked in the attention, knowing full well that it wouldn't last.

"So, Jandol," Azmoon said, "what do you think's going to happen in Kabul?"

"It's too early to tell. We just have to wait and see." He didn't sound very hopeful.

It was the third week in September, the Sunday following Taraki's execution and Amin's grabbing of the reins of power, and we were out on the back terrace with Sandara, Droon, and Azmoon. For some time, Jandol and Sandara had been talking quietly, unaware that Droon was casting daggers at them so that when he spoke, his intensity caused them to look at him in surprise.

"You know, when anyone talks about the future, I want to punch their lights out. If we don't watch our step, we won't have a future."

"Well, I for one never liked Taraki," Sandara said. "The People's Democratic Party of Afghanistan? What people? What democracy? No one consulted me about anything. Not Taraki or Amin or Karmal."

"Why would they talk to you?"

"So they'd know what was going on."

"You think they don't? They're not stupid."

"But if we could tell them what our lives are like, how much we want to grow and learn and achieve, surely they'd listen. Instead of mouthing pretty words that mean nothing. How long has it been, how many years of struggle and fighting? A hundred, a thousand? Persians, Greeks, Arabs, Mongols, the British, now the Russians. When will it ever end?"

"It will end when we're all dead," Sial piped up.

"That will never happen. Never!"

"You are a woman of fire," Jandol said.

"Who, me? I'm only an ember."

"From embers raging fires have begun."

"So, Jandol, what do you suggest we do?" Azmoon said.

"Why ask him?" Droon said. "He's an idealist, a silverfish eating the binding of a book. But me, I'm a realist. I drive a truck every day, I see how business is run, how the money flows, where it comes from, and where it goes. I'm the one you should be asking."

"Well then, please enlighten us," Azmoon said, leaning forward with his elbows on his knees.

"It's simple. We have to learn to accept what is happening and to keep our heads low so they don't get shot off."

"Such an optimist."

"I'm only saying what everyone knows. Taraki was the latest in a long line. And Amin'll be next on the chopping block."

"Droon's right," Jandol said. "And don't forget, Amin's shadow is a thousand times worse than he'll ever be."

"The shadow that falls on us like a hungry vulture," Sial said.

"Forget the shadows and vultures," Sandara said. "It's Arab oil and trade routes. It's the Indian Ocean."

"Ah," Azmoon said, lifting his hands palms up and spreading his fingers, "the salt-sifted wind that perfumes the Indian seas."

"Which the Soviets want," she said.

"And intend to get," Jandol added.

"It's not like they haven't already taken over," Droon said. "Divide and conquer, ethnic against ethnic, Communist against Communist. How many arrested, how many fleeing to the mountains to escape the hangman?"

"We've no one to blame but ourselves," Jandol said.

"Oh, of course, we're the ones who started everything."

"We might not have started it, but it doesn't help matters to say it's the king's fault or the prime minister's."

"King Zahir should have kept better eyes on that cousin of his, Dawud. That whole takeover was a travesty, the quiet revolution, the bloodless coup. King Zahir never should have abdicated. He should have come back from Italy at once. He handed over Afghanistan on a silver platter. And us along with it."

"How could he have come back?" Azmoon said. "He'd have caused a civil war."

"I'd rather have a civil war than what we've got now." Droon's words only seemed to make him angrier.

"Who says Zahir was so great?" Sandara said. "There are no kings in Europe or India, you know. In some countries there's even elections whereby people vote for who they want."

"Our king might not have been great, but at least life was peaceful."

"Peace. But at what price?"

"It doesn't matter now, anyway," Jandol said. "Our way of life is finished. And I say rightfully so. It has served its purpose, and now we must move on. Face the facts, we can't live in the same way as our ancestors. It's impossible, we'll be mowed down. That's what history tells us."

"You're being judgmental, as usual," Droon said. "We live simple lives, we don't ask for much, mostly to be left alone, and automatically, we're the bad guys."

"We've been living with our heads in the sand, and now we're paying the price for it."

"That seems to be our role in life. Always paying for something we lose. Now it's our freedom. How much will that cost?"

"You can't live in the past," Jandol said. "You have to move forward."

"Who's living in the past? I'm not living in the past. What makes you say I'm living in the past? All I'm asking for is to be left alone. To be allowed to work every day. Always I have felt this…sense of betrayal. Never have I felt secure. Okay. So now I drive a truck. Hey, it's an honest living, right? Not much of one, admittedly, but one nonetheless. And maybe it will lead to better things, a better life for me and my family. Is that so much to ask?"

"It's what we all want, Droon," Jandol said evenly. "But look around you. You're healthy and strong, you're young, you have your dreams. But what about the others who aren't as young as you or as smart? What about them?"

"Who are you referring to?"

"To most of Afghanistan, brother. To those who scrape and stumble, who work their fingers to the bone and wind up with nothing."

"Yes," Sandara said. "Even if we had decent schools and universities, which we don't, who can slave twenty hours a day at a life-negating occupation and go to university?"

"We're a great nation," Jandol said, "in spite of ourselves, not because of it."

"Revolutions take time and money," Azmoon said. "Neither of which anyone has. Not that it matters anyway once the Russians take over. As it is, we already have a de facto Communist government run by Soviet puppets."

"We live like it's the Middle Ages," Jandol said. "When are people going to wake up?"

"And what if they do? Then what?"

"It's not a question of if they do. It's a question of what happens if they don't. And if they don't, I feel it's the end. I see nothing ahead but suffering and loss. Let's face it, the strong devour the weak. It has always been so. And we are weak."

"Afghanistan's like a juicy lamb kebab," Droon said. "Everyone wants a bite."

"According to Jandol," Sandara said, "Afghanistan's no longer so juicy."

"It's juicy enough."

"Go ahead," Droon said, "make jokes. Meanwhile, our immediate problem is how to keep those red noses out of our ass."

"Ah, but they have such long noses," Jandol said.

"Let them try to sniff mine," Sial said. "I'll show them."

"Boys, boys," Bibi said, thrusting her face forward. "Your language."

"I'm sorry, Grandmother," Sial said.

"You boys are so excitable. But you'll see. Everything will quiet down, and things will go on as they always have. Remember, nothing lasts forever. Be patient."

"But we've been patient," Sandara said. "We've waited, and what has it gotten us? Yet another invader."

"I was eight years old when the British forced us to leave Peshawar," Bibi said. "There'd been a series of armed skirmishes, and the British decided to empty the city. It was in the spring. That was when we left for Afghanistan, and it was raining, and the rain never let up. It went on every day, and you couldn't stay warm or dry. Our friends and neighbors, everyone we knew. There were no buses, no trains or autos. Our horse and wagon had been stolen by the British. So we walked. Me, my mother, and my grandfather, we were only able to take what we could carry on our backs. I remember that final night at home. A few weeks before, my father and my uncle had gone on one of their mysterious trips, and we hadn't heard from them. When morning came, British soldiers surrounded our house, and we had no choice but to leave. I never saw my father again. Later I found out from my uncle that they'd joined the resistance and that there'd been intense fighting in the bazaar and that the Story Teller's Street was in shambles, with heavy casualties on both sides. We never learned anything else.

"We crossed into Afghanistan by way of the Khyber Pass, and it was raining and cold, and everyone was dispirited, and we marched with our heads bowed. The winds were unpredictable. They came from every direction. They'd suddenly veer and come at you from behind, only to whip around and hit you in the face and make every step a torture. Above us, the sound of warplanes and helicopters. No one spoke, the straps from my pack cut into my shoulders, my grandmother was weak and frail in this world of rain and echoes reverberating around, the tramping of boots, the murmurs emanating from voices that rose and fell, and the rain that pierced through our clothing.

"At night we tried to keep warm, we tried to find places where there was some kind of outcropping. I was numb. I didn't understand anything. I only knew that we had to leave, and we were going back to Shabak. Everywhere there were refugees, many in worse condition than we were. What did I know about such a journey? I'd never done anything for myself. I'd been waited on hand and foot like a little princess.

"By the third morning I was sick and feverish, and I had chills. My mother tried to carry me, but I was too heavy. She sat down, she and my grandmother, unable to decide what to do. She held me against her. It was then that a handsome young man, a tall prince with piercing eyes and a sweet smile, he came over to us and asked my mother what the problem was, and when she told him, he lifted me up in his arms and carried me all the way to Jalalabad. Two days and two nights. I've always remembered him. I've always been grateful. Now I hear that he is a great man, that he leads his people, and that he is known wherever he goes. So you see, I didn't choose to leave Peshawar, but life made the choice for me, for me and my family. And when our journey was over, we found a place to live, and I married a wonderful man and had wonderful children."

"Bibi, what is the meaning of your story?" Sial said.

"The meaning of my story is that sometimes life comes along and pulls you out to sea. If you're strong, you swim. If you're weak, you drown."

"But things are different now," Jandol said. "The British are gone. Now we are eaten up from within."

"Within, without, what's the difference? You must bend with the wind, and when the wind is spent, spring up straight again."

Such proud women, I thought. Moor, Lakhta, Gulapa, that witch of a fabulist with her raven hair, her kohl-smudged eyes, her high cheekbones covered with a network of fine wrinkles, and Sandara, whose grace and elegance did not detract from her adeptness in confronting the inevitable. Our men too were warriors. Take Droon, quick-tempered, volatile, with hair that hung in tendrils across his forehead and his dark skin, clean-shaven except for his black mustache. Azmoon with his passionate thirst for knowledge. Jandol, Abba, all of us. Yes, we were survivors; we had no choice. Even if surviving meant being supple rather than swordlike, you couldn't remain rigid when dark winds whirled around you.

"I have told you boys over and over," Abba said sententiously. "It is useless to argue amongst ourselves for we can do nothing. My hope is that we will survive by remaining true to our ideals and by working hard. Not, that is, by hiding like victims, but by abiding in the face of momentous events."

"Enough talk," Moor said. "Enough problems. Let's have music."

"Yes, yes," Sandara said.

The sky turned magenta in the waning afternoon, and Moor lit two kerosene lamps, placing them on opposite ends of the terrace. Azmoon had brought his *rabab*, and he tuned the strings and fingered the stops, while Droon began lightly tapping a rhythm on his *tabla*. After a moment, they began to play melodies that had been familiar to all of us ever since I could remember.

I lost myself in the intertwining of their instruments that increased in complexity as musical phrases repeated themselves in a burgeoning crescendo that slowly dropped down to a lovely sound as soft as someone's breath until once again the drumming gradually increased, growing more intense, more driving. Droon began to sing, his voice thin, steely, hoarse, joined by Sandara's surprisingly powerful soprano, which rose higher along with Azmoon's deep baritone. Moor joined in, and the rest of us clapped our hands. They sang of Afghanistan, of the land that was our mother and our father, of snow that burned like fire and suns of ice, of wars and swords, of pride in our destiny, of eagles that soared over the wide sea of sand that gave birth to a country that was half as old as time.

Later that evening, as usual the men were in the hujra, their animated voices raised in anger, shouts, bellows of laughter. Even as the stars, in their inaccessible mastery, warn about the futility of endeavor against the illusions of time, still this passionate diatribe, this butting of heads like rams in a barnyard.

I was lying in bed while my mother and grandmother were talking together in the living room, their voices softly rising and falling in the soft night air.

"Did you see the way Jandol was staring at Sandara?" Bibi was saying. "His eyes were popping out of his head." She loved to needle Moor, mainly because my mother was so gullible.

"Now, Bibi, every boy of that age acts the same way. It doesn't mean anything."

"It's a sign he's ready."

"Ready for what?"

"Ready to sweep her off her feet and carry her away."

"I don't think so. Jandol's like his father. Practical. He's not about to sweep any girl off her feet. Not until his own feet are touching the ground."

"If you ask me, Jandol likes Sandara more than he lets on."

"Haven't you heard that Sandara's in love with Droon?"

"One hears lots of things," Bibi said with that teasing lilt in her voice.

"Well, it's true, and you know it."

"Imagine, a princess in love with such a buffoon."

"He's no buffoon. Droon is a fine, upstanding young man. And Sandara is no princess."

"Droon hasn't got two Afghanis to rub together. And you're wrong about Sandara."

"She comes from nowhere, Bibi. No one knows anything about her."

"There, you see, exactly like the princess in a fairy tale."

"Fairy tales can have terrible endings," Moor said. "Anyway, it's not Sandara I worry about. She's a woman with a head on her shoulders. She's not about to go off the deep end. It's Shamla and now Meena."

"Shamla's always so headstrong," Bibi said. "She just needs to settle in with her prince. Everything'll work out, you'll see."

"Kamkai, a prince?"

"You can't blame him for their problems. The poor boy thought he'd married a kitten and wound up with a tigress."

"Every unhappy woman has claws."

"Lila, the boy works hard, he's dependable. Shamla's no piece of cake."

"It's the same with Meena."

"She's so picky, she'll be lucky if she ever meets anyone," Bibi said.

"The girls nowadays, I don't understand what they want or what they think they'll get."

"It wasn't like this when we were young," Bibi said. "Was it, Lila?" Both women laughed softly. They knew each other so well, they could read each other's mind. "I never even met my husband, Miwand's father, until the night of the wedding. He sat with the men in one room, and I was with the women in another room. Two witnesses went back and forth sending messages from him to me and from me to him. I married a name, that's what I did. His parents chose me, and my parents agreed. I knew nothing about him. Nothing."

"When I first saw Miwand, he frightened me."

"I'm his mother, and he frightens me sometimes. What a mind."

"But you know what they say," Moor said, "the man is the head of the family, and woman is the neck. And the neck moves the head."

"It's hard to believe so many years have gone by. Can you believe it? So many years, so much has happened, it's hard to take it all in."

"When Shamla has children, she'll be happier. She's alone too much, and then she starts worrying and thinking."

"Woman is the tree, and children are the fruit. A tree that is leafless and bears no fruit will wither and die."

"Did you really think that Jandol was staring at Sandara?" Moor asked Bibi, and their voices faded into the softness of the night.

It was early morning, the best time to plant, and the air was a cold faint perfume. Droon and Azmoon led the way, and I followed close behind, clasping a bundle of branches and twigs we'd cut off from the pomegranate trees in Atal's garden. When we reached the Auzingianai, we found a spot close enough to the bank so that when the river was full, the roots would help keep the earth from eroding, but far enough away so that if the water did rise, the trees wouldn't be washed away. The earth was hard and the bank rose slightly before tumbling downward, and Azmoon and Droon took turns digging while I divided the branches and lined them up on the grass, five separate stacks about twelve inches in length.

They dug five equidistant holes a couple of yards apart and about a foot deep. Placing the branches into the openings, we held them in place and poured a little water and enough soil so that they'd remain upright with the ends just sticking above the ground. When this was done, we packed the earth into mounds that had a concave surface into which we poured more water. While we were working, the sun broke free from the mountains, and a glowing flare momentarily turned everything bright orange. It only lasted a minute.

"New trees mean new life," Azmoon said, standing up and brushing the dirt from his hands.

"It shows that we still have hope in our hearts," Droon said. "Jandol says I live in the past."

"He doesn't mean you live in the past," Azmoon said. "It's just the other way around. The past lives in you."

"Well, that explains everything," Droon said and laughed suddenly.

"It lives in all of us. We perpetuate the past, we immortalize it, we sustain it."

"Oh, so you agree with him?"

"I don't agree with him, but I understand him."

"Ah, you intellectuals."

"I just hope that these trees don't outlive the three of us."

"Don't look at me, brother. My rule is not to trust anyone."

"Hell, maybe the Russians will make some improvements. Things couldn't get worse."

"So long as they don't plunge us into a civil war."

"There is that to consider."

"If you want to know the plain truth, I try not to think about any of it. All I want is to—well, never mind what I want."

From then on, every week I'd go with a shovel and a pail of dried cow dung, and I'd dig the topsoil away and place the fertilizer around the branches. After that I'd fill the pail from the river and water the saplings. Sometimes I'd sit quietly and watch, but other times Mamar would follow me, tearing around like crazy, chasing squirrels or bounding into the water after the ducks. He would rush over to where I was, shake the water from his coat until I was soaked, and then leap away before I could grab him.

Really, the burning questions of politics and war, of invasions and Russians, of executions and warlords, most of what I heard went over my head, but the tension that everyone felt, the palpable disquiet, that cut right through me and made me afraid. I knew something was wrong, I just didn't know what, but I began having nightmares, and for once I was glad that I shared a room with Sial. If he heard me crying in my sleep, he'd come over and wake me and sit with me until I fell asleep again.

ON December 24, 1979, the Soviet Union invaded Afghanistan. They came at night. Amin and his entire family were assassinated, and Babrak Karmal, who had also been a deputy prime minister and had escaped to the USSR when Amin took control, was installed as president. He became a drug addict and an alcoholic, and in 1986, the Soviets removed him forcibly from office and replaced him with Najibullah, an operative for the KHAD (Afghan Intelligence), which was under the control of the KGB. Throughout this time, thousands of Afghans were being trained in Pakistan by the ISI (Inter-Service Intelligence) and in Iran under the QUED (Iranian Intelligence) to fight the Soviet hegemony. When they completed their indoctrination, they returned to Afghanistan and infiltrated various local cells of the resistance, taking positions of power. Funded and armed by the Saudis and by various Western nations, through the driving force of the ISI, they used mosques to disseminate their increasingly conservative, increasingly aggressive rhetoric.

In Shabak, Mullah Kadoo became a mouthpiece for them. Every time he prayed, he would cry out for jihad and for death to the godless. "We are waging a sacred war," he'd intone, and the insurgents—the freedom fighters, the Mujahideen, the Jihadists—are Holy Warriors whose goal was the freedom for all from the horrors of the infidels.

Kabul, city of apricots and icy winters, roses and dust; city of death and white horses; the column of knowledge and ignorance against jagged peaks; camels and trolley buses passing each other on streets without names; the Victory Arch commemorating the martyrs in the war for independence; ruins and white buildings; bakeries, teahouses, the great bazaar; a dance of plagues and lemons, of ghosts and kitchens buried in sand; one million inhabitants; the eastern terminus of the Khyber Pass, over which Alexander the Great and his army marched to the plains of India; the towering, snow-covered mountains of the Hindu Kush; the city "a vision of paradise in its mountain setting." January is the coldest month; in early April the rains begin and continue on through May. A city thirty-five hundred years old, fought over by empires, the capital of Afghanistan.

CHAPTER TWO

I KEPT THINKING HOW amazing it was that a mere three months after moving from Srakala to Shabak, we were on a bus heading to Kabul to begin a new life. I knew that men who'd been leaders in their communities were being stripped of their properties, their bank accounts frozen, their houses commandeered, while those with neither skill nor ability were placed in positions of power in which they wielded the scepter of life and death. But I never imagined such goings-on would affect us.

Then last week, Abba announced our imminent departure. He was concerned that with the Communists firmly entrenched in the king's palace, his jewelry business was in danger of being *liberated*, and to make matters dicier, he'd just invested a huge chunk of money in the operation.

We formed two groups—Abba, Jandol, and Sial took the car while Moor, Meena, and I went by bus. By taking back roads, Abba hoped to avoid the Communist checkpoints, which were placed along the main highways, where there was always the danger that both sons could be conscripted into the Afghan army. No one would bother Moor or Meena and me, so we'd be safe on the bus. Then at the last moment, Abba told Sial to go with us. He was afraid we might be robbed, or worse, that we needed some male protection, although if anyone asked, Sial was to say he was twelve—just to be on the safe side.

But though our parents were concerned about the danger, we were thrilled. Sial and Meena couldn't stop talking about the stores, the crowds, the excitement of life in a big city. Jandol's anticipation manifested itself in an alertness, a springiness to his movements that had been sorely missing lately. I was so filled with the wonder of Kabul, I couldn't even organize my thoughts beyond the present moment since each experience was new and had to be examined from every angle.

Although at the time, I thought our bus the most beautiful vehicle I'd ever seen, I realize now that it was a genuine dinosaur, Afghan-style: a showy four-wheeled behemoth whose exterior was decorated with splotches of Day-Glo colors overlaid with baubles, trinkets, and other ornamental frippery that made tinkling noises against the jouncing of the wheels. We couldn't find enough seats, so I sat on Moor's lap, and we squeezed in next to Meena while Sial stood with his arms around the overhead strap to steady himself since the bus kept bouncing on the rutted, mud-hardened road. When it stopped to let a family off, he nabbed an empty seat before anyone could take it, and I slid in next to him. Every few miles or so, we came to a grinding halt to pick up or let off passengers as we made the journey to Jalalabad, where we had to change buses for Kabul.

I'd been to Jalalabad many times where we'd stayed with my father's brother Baheer, who was a doctor, but I'd only been to Kabul once when I was six, and we spent the winter there while my father opened a larger office and warehouse. All I remembered was that at night, you could see a glittering array of lights surrounded by impenetrable darkness. Every light meant another face, another family, thousands of lives, and each one different, each mysterious. I fell in love with the panorama, and I'd go to sleep with tiny bands of electricity whizzing behind my eyelids.

As the bus sped across the Ashpan Desert, the countryside and the far hills seemed to be wavering in the brisk morning air, as if they were in motion, and we were standing still. I was about to say something to Moor, who was across the aisle from me, sitting quite still, but Meena signaled for me to leave her alone.

We drove through the Gandomak Desert, past the battlefield where the Afghan Army massacred an entire British regiment. The ruins were spread out against the sand, giving you a feeling of melancholy for things long gone, for battles lost and won. What the Russians thought when they drove by was impossible to ascertain. Probably nothing. But when we Afghans rode through this mass graveyard, whose heart didn't pound?

In Jalalabad, as usual, we stayed with Baheer, but even here, on streets beginning to be patrolled by Communist soldiers, the tension was high, and we were anxious to be off. Also, since Abba and Jandol had bypassed Jalalabad in order to drive directly to the mine, we had no idea if they'd arrived in Kabul safely.

The next morning, Baheer took us to the bus stop; there was no station, no schedules—riders simply hunkered down and waited, and we joined their ranks. When the bus arrived, it was one of those sleek blue models, much more comfortable than the one we'd been on, with windows that slid back and forth and cushioned seats. It was even air-conditioned.

For the entire trip, I sat with my face glued to the glass, not wanting to miss a thing. The distance was only fifty miles as the crow flies, but traveling on Highway 1 took hours, what with its narrow, unmarked, circuitous lanes that climbed up almost a thousand feet through the Kabul gorge, where it was flanked by towering peaks and jutting shards of rock. Whenever the road plunged down, it inevitably rose up, always becoming higher and steeper, with views that took your breath away so long as the bus didn't make a wrong turn and send you to a fiery death. Such accidents were not unknown. But our driver was the conservative type, who always allowed the heavily-loaded hauling trucks to pass us and who slowed to a crawl when the road became particularly twisted or precipitous.

At the military checkpoints between Jalalabad and Kabul, we were confronted by soldiers pointing AK-47s at us while from within their Humvees; officers of the Communist-led Afghan National Army kept a close eye on everything. The soldiers were typically Afghan, but you sometimes saw uniformed officers emerge from the wooden kiosks, the Soviet brass with their aviator sunglasses, their stomachs bulging over their belts, often with a cigar hanging from their pendulous lips. At every outpost our driver waited, frequently at the end of long lines of trucks and buses, many with their motors idling until the air became rotten with gasoline fumes. The guards would board our bus and go from person to person, questioning everyone with an intensity that was frightening. We were just ordinary people; we weren't terrorists. But if you acted the least bit suspiciously, or if your papers weren't in A-One order, you'd be detained, and the bus would take off without you.

When these guards came stomping in, Meena threw herself into Moor's arms, and Sial glared straight ahead; one time a young boy near Moor began to cry, and as his parents tried to comfort him, she told the man that he was upsetting everybody. The guard refused to acknowledge her; he just grunted and went on with his questions as if it was our fault for making him go through this tedious rigmarole. He finally exited, but as the driver closed the hydraulic doors, even before we'd begun moving, Sial came across the narrow aisle and told Moor that she was crazy talking to those men, that she was lucky they didn't pull her off the bus. You had to blend into the background so no one noticed you, he said. You couldn't stand out in any way. Moor said she was sorry; it wouldn't happen again. I was surprised at her meekness since I expected her to tell Sial to mind his own business.

At other checkpoints, we had to vacate the bus and wait forever while the guards searched through everyone's belongings.

"A bunch of illiterate thugs," Moor whispered. "They're just as afraid of us as we are of them."

By the time we reached the outskirts of Kabul, there were no more checkpoints. Later on, Pamir told me that the Communists were keeping a low profile in Kabul, but when I asked him why, he said, "Hey, who cares, right?" Yeah, who cared?

Our home was in Koti Sangi, a middle-class neighborhood of paved streets and neatly-groomed lawns located at the northeastern edge of the city. Abba and Jandol had arrived the day before, safe and sound, which was a relief, but they hadn't had a chance to turn on the electricity, so we dined by candlelight. Our new home. There still weren't enough bedrooms for me to have my own, which meant Sial covering every wall, with the likes of, among others, Dharmendra, Bruce Lee, John Wayne, and Yasmin Khan. The last face I saw at night and the first in the morning was the sensuous Indian actress Hema Malini, with her tawny skin and melon lips slightly parted, ready to throw herself into my thin, inexperienced, waiting arms.

In addition to electricity—no small convenience—the house had indoor plumbing and a modern bathroom with a working shower. What luxuries. That first night though, I had such a strange dream that when I woke, I felt as if I were being compressed by a vise. I couldn't articulate any clear picture other than some faint, abstract impressions of menace that remained with me even after I woke and seemed, in the months to come, neither to reveal itself nor to completely disappear.

Even though our country had been invaded by the USSR, at least in the beginning, other than the sight of Communist soldiers everywhere you went, life went on pretty much as it always had, and we quickly settled in. Abba went to the Ministry of Education where he got student IDs for Jandol and Sial, which would protect them from being drafted into the military. Pamir already had one, Meena didn't need one, and I was too young. He also enrolled us in various schools.

As the weather grew warmer that spring of 1980, we drove to the Old Kabul Bazaar, whose shops, stalls, and teahouses, stretched for blocks in every direction, crowded with people, so crowded indeed in certain sections you could hardly move. Modernistic glass structures that sold electronic equipment stood beside mud huts filled with used clothes; vendors pulled wooden carts overflowing with fruit and vegetables, hawking their wares; butchers held up live chickens.

Unlike many bazaars in Afghanistan, such as the one outside Shabak, women were allowed to shop here, though they were still in the minority. And what an array, male and female—I didn't know where to look first. Some women wore *tikrai* with long flowing silk scarves, some were dressed in burkas, while others wore Levis, tank tops, and stiletto heels. Many of the men wore the traditional *kamis partoog*, knee-length dresses over baggy pants, gold-stitched hats, and leather sandals. But there were almost as many in business suits and turbans as well as beardless youths dressed in jeans, green bomber jackets, and pointed cowboy boots.

Pashto music came from everywhere, the slow winding sounds of Pashtoo music, competing with Indian ragas, to create a cacophony that bounced against each other, filling the ear with their strains. We found our way to the Miwa Mindai Food Bazaar, had lunch, and Moor purchased some cooking supplies.

When it was time to leave, I hated to go and vowed I'd come back soon. On the way to our car, a group of Afghan soldiers elbowed past, and one of them, a youngish-oldish man with sunken cheeks, pointed ears, and yellow eyes, grinned at Meena, who pretended he wasn't there.

In the summer, we spent a lot of time at Lake Qargha, which was about half an hour away. Given that the lake was filled with jagged rocks, deflated soccer balls, broken bottles, and all sorts of other junk, I preferred to lie down at the water's edge, allowing the soft little waves to flow over me. I found this relaxing, especially when it was broiling hot out, and I'd spent the morning in a stuffy classroom with windows that wouldn't open, listening to a lecture on the "Benefits of Communism for Young People." Sometimes I'd build sandcastles on the waterline and watch as the tide inched in and gently washed everything away. Something about the gradual destruction fascinated me.

I'd never been to a movie before, and one afternoon, Sial took me to see *Ajab Khan Afridi*, a Technicolor extravaganza about the nineteenth-century eponymous Afghan hero. Overflowing with love, romance, and battles to the death, it took my breath away. We stuffed ourselves with popcorn and sat through it twice. By the time we got home, it was already dark, and Moor scolded us for staying out so late and worrying her to death, that it was a school night and we should've known better. At any rate, for the next week, that's all Sial and I talked about, although as I look back, I realize that for me, it was fun going to the movies, but for him it was more—it was everything. It stoked the embers in his smoldering soul in a way that life never did; it gave him his calling, his vision—it fed his dreams.

Every Friday when there was no school, he went, and when he returned, he'd sequester one of us—mainly me—and go through every single plot twist, scene by scene. His descriptions were so precise, it was almost like being there. I knew the stories of more movies that I hadn't seen than anyone ever. The truth is, I wanted to go too, but Moor said I was too young to go alone. Nor did she want to see my brains scrambled by fantasies that had nothing to do with real life. Even so, whenever Sial went, I'd beg him to take me, and sometimes he did, although usually he'd tell me to get lost, that he'd rather be alone. But I think that the reason he didn't want me to go with him was so that he could tell me the story of the movie.

Indeed, he talked so much about movies that Meena told him he was giving her a migraine headache. "The problem with you is you just want the easy life."

"Easy life, are you kidding? Do you know how hard it is being in the movies? I don't know if you are aware of it, but a star has to look good and remember his lines and know where the chalk marks are."

"What are chalk marks?"

"They're where you're supposed to go so the camera can follow you."

"How do you know all of this?"

"I read, I ask questions."

"You are such an idiot."

"*I* am?"

"Yes, because you don't know the difference between make-believe and real life."

"And you do, I suppose? Well, Meena, as a matter of fact, I do know the difference. Make-believe is fun, it's exciting, whereas real life is a drag. You know, like being with you. Nothing but boredom, saying the same things over and over, never getting anywhere."

"Oh, Sial," Moor said. "To hear you talk such nonsense. Besides, you couldn't be more mistaken."

"No one in this family has any ambition."

"That is not true," Meena snapped at him. "Pamir's at university, Jandol wants to go into politics, and I'm going to do something too, I'm just not sure what."

"I've decided I want to be a poet," I said. "Like Ghani Khan. To capture in words the hungry longings of my people and my country."

"That'll bring food on the table," Sial said.

"Well," Jandol said, "at least he'll have a table."

"What does that mean?"

"It means that Meena's right. You live in an imaginary world with imaginary tables."

"And you? What about you?"

"I wish I had an imaginary world."

"No, you don't. You're just saying that."

"You're right, Sial," Jandol said. "I am."

"You can make fun of me, but you will all be jealous when I'm famous."

"Why would we be jealous?" Moor said. "We'd be happy for you. We would rejoice in your success."

"If it happens," Meena said.

"It will happen, I know it will. It's…it's written."

"In your mind, you exist at the center of the universe," Jandol said, "but in the real world, no one knows you're alive."

"Well, they will."

"Sometimes I think you're all crazy," Moor said. "Each one of you has birth defects."

"Especially Sial," Meena said.

"Maybe it was the forceps," Jandol said.

"Don't listen to them, son," Abba said. "I'm glad you have plans for the future, dreams you want to fulfill. And you"—he turned to Meena—"if you want to attend university, I suggest you get better grades in school."

"Oh, Father, please."

"Now, where is Pamir?" Moor said. "He said he was coming over for supper."

"He's at the warehouse, a shipment's coming in," Abba said. "I forgot to tell you."

"Well, I for one am starving," Sial said.

Lila and Meena went out to the kitchen to begin preparing supper while Abba lay down in their bedroom with the radio on. The minute they left, Sial said, "This imaginary world business, what a bunch of crap. Sometimes you guys make me want to throw up."

As usual with him, it was best to keep your mouth shut; it made life much more pleasant even if he got on your nerves with all of his plans that never materialized. I thought about my own daydreams, mostly made up of images from Abba's extensive collection of books over whose colored illustrations, photographs, and engravings I would pore over. I'd make up stories in my head and pretend I was living in ancient times or during the Middle Ages; I'd be a nomad, a warrior, a king. I'd turn into a chameleon; I'd cross empty deserts, swim turbulent seas, slither up trees like a python. I'd go out in the garden with my box of plastic animals and spend hours playing with them. Sial used to say I was a useless daydreamer, but truthfully, not only was he just as much of a daydreamer as I was, but that he wanted to make his daydreams real, whereas I just wanted to have some fun. There's nothing bad about trying to manifest your dreams, but he usually wound up chasing one mirage after another. Poor Sial, spending his life trying to connect the dots. It reminded me of when I was a youngster in Kabul and how I'd gaze out the window at the glittering lights, each a tiny discrete glow to which I could find no common thread.

When did the situation in Kabul change? I can tell you, it didn't happen overnight. We're talking about small steps, incremental advances, as if you were shutting a cell door that had always remained open so that as the gap narrowed, you never noticed—not, that is, until you heard the click of the lock and realized that you were trapped. More than a year had passed. Abba, Pamir, and Jandol were working day and night to retrieve some of our money, and the rest of us were in school. Maybe it began with Moor telling us to come directly home from school, no dillydallying. She really meant it because Sial had gone with some friends to a movie one day, and when he came home, she hit the roof. Nevertheless, there was no specific date, but the atmosphere began to feel, I guess you could call it heavy, a denseness in the air you breathed that even I discerned, young through I was.

First were the rumors that floated around, nothing specific, nothing you could lay your finger on. You'd hear about someone disappearing, no one you knew and not a word in the papers, but eventually a friend of a friend. Others were jailed on trumped-up charges, robberies, beatings, a young mother raped and left for dead, Mrs. So-and-So's husband's in prison, and now they'd taken her home away. You couldn't go to the police—indeed, we heard of people who went to them winding up in prison themselves. Grocery stores began to run out of basic food items; lamb, sugar, and butter were hard to come by, and what was available cost an arm and a leg. It became too risky to go out after dark; people were mugged for a few Afghanis, with never any arrests. There'd always been a curfew, but no one had enforced it, but now, if you were caught outside between eleven to six, you'd better have a good excuse. You didn't know who to trust. There were informers everywhere, even people you knew your whole life, customers you'd done business with for years, whose wives and children had come to your house for supper. The tide, no longer a gentle movement but a raging storm, was razing our sandcastles.

Abba wasn't certain that he'd be able to hold on to his jewelry business. The amount of red (no pun intended) tape he went through was unending, making the simplest transaction a tedious, drawn-out war of nerves. At any time, the officer in charge could have his books audited, the slightest mistake capable of bringing the whole house down. Coupled with this were the huge sums of cash floating around that customers owed him. One hundred thousand dollars, and it looked like he might it lose all of it. My father's jewelry business had always been based on trust. Vendors would purchase stones on a monthly installment plan, but now they themselves were in such bad shape financially, they could neither pay him or move the jewelry. Abba understood since he was in the same boat himself, but it didn't help our situation. On paper my father was a wealthy man, but in reality, we had little enough cash on hand to take care of our daily expenses. Every day he and Pamir went to the different vendors, but always it was the same, promises, small payments, no offers to buy anything. At the same time, in Abba's warehouse and at the homes of various miners, there were crates packed with semiprecious stones that were worth a small fortune that just sat there.

The pressure from without increased that from within. Abba, determined to avoid financial disaster, as was usual with him when he was stressed, became emotionally remote. If you asked him a question, he'd look at you as if he didn't understand what you were saying. Pamir was so busy we hardly ever saw him. In addition to tending the store, he was often away at the mine, frequently forced to stay there for days at a time, which left him little time to pursue his studies. Jandol remained calm as did Moor, who could usually find something to interest her when she wasn't busy taking care of everybody. The bickering between Sial and Mean continued unabated, their angry voices adding to the edginess at home, though occasionally they'd appear arm in arm to say they'd made up their differences, and peace would reign temporarily.

Month after month we expected to get news from back home, but there was no regular mail, no phones, and the Kabul papers were controlled by the Communists. Moor was constantly worrying about Bibi and Shamla, who'd moved from Minkhill and were living in Jalalabad. She hoped that Kamkai was able to hold on to his job as a teacher, but who knew? To add to our fears, we heard on the Pakistani station that there'd been heavy fighting in the Hisarak district between the Communists and armed bands of partisans called freedom fighters. Just imagine, Sial said with pride, the Soviets have so much firepower, so many helicopters and tanks, but they can't stop the guerrillas from counterattacking. He said he wanted to join them. He'd sneak into the enemy's camp as silent and as wary as a mountain lion, just waiting to pounce. Meena warned him to make sure to find his chalk marks, which set off a shouting match between them. But really, each of us felt a sense of pride that our countrymen weren't taking the invasion lying down, that we were facing the enemy. Like David and Goliath.

As fighting increased throughout the countryside, the Communists in the cities, Kabul being the most important, began to tighten things up even more. You could be imprisoned for the slightest infraction of the law, laws that were becoming more draconian as the months passed. Like the curfew. Whereas in the past, if you were caught out after eleven, you'd simply be sent on your way with a warning. Now there was a good chance you'd wind up in prison, perhaps for months at a time. Kabul was turning into a police state, and there were pro-Communist demonstrations with thousands of rabid adherents, emotional firebrands, ready to drown you in a flood of rhetoric that swept away any sense of reality. The streets, bazaars, restaurants, and businesses of Kabul were under the radar of the KGB. You were constantly on alert. If you heard footsteps, if someone glanced at you in the wrong way, if you spoke too loud, you asked yourself, "Am I imagining things? Am I being paranoid?"

Every day, Abba and Moor hammered into us the fact that we were living in an enemy-occupied city in a land that was no longer ours. Invisibility was our only protection, silence our only shield. They didn't have to remind us of what happened to Mirwis or those two brothers from Jandol's class. Though Mirwis was a few years older than me, he was already fired up about the occupation and what could be done to free ourselves. He worked part-time with Pamir and occasionally came over for tea. I remembered him as something of a chatterbox. One day he was in his bedroom listening to the Voice of America on the radio, and some men from the KHAD came barging in and arrested him. Now no one knew where he was or if he was alive. Then a short time afterward, two of Jandol's classmates challenged the history teacher. She let them vent without responding, simply waiting politely until they were through before continuing with her lecture. But after recess, they didn't come back. On the third night, their father, Mudir Saib, went around the neighborhood asking if anyone knew where they were. He was distraught, but we couldn't help him.

Moor gave him tea and sweetened almonds. "Have something. Have you eaten? Here, drink this."

The man's hand shook when he lifted the cup to his lips. My father was standing with his back to the window, framed against an evening sky ablaze with stars, his eyes hawklike, his shoulders rigid, his entire body as still as a statue.

I was out in our front yard playing with Meena when a man knocked on our gate and asked me if Abba were home. I was about to say he was in Kandahar when Moor hurried over and asked the man what he wanted. He said he was a business associate, but when she asked him his name, he said he was sorry to have bothered her, that he'd come back another day.

We watched until he drove away, then Moor knelt down and took both of us by the arm. "The next time someone knocks on the door who you don't know, you get me or your father. If we're not here, get Pamir or Jandol. Don't say anything to anybody, you hear me? Nothing."

From then on, strangers kept dropping by at odd times, asking for Abba and once for Pamir. One time Meena was outside playing *tuka* with some of her girlfriends, and a man and a woman, both wearing black raincoats, stopped one of the girls and engaged her in conversation. Meena came forward and asked them what they wanted, to which the woman replied that she was thinking about moving into the neighborhood and that she had twin daughters her age. Meena stammered some kind of reply, and the couple eventually left.

Upon Abba's return from Kandahar the following week, we told him what was going on, but he said for us not to become alarmed. Everyone was nervous, he said, including the Communists, and as the months wore on, it seemed that he was right. Eventually, no one came knocking on the door, school went on as usual, and we lived our lives. When the weather turned cold, we wore embroidered jackets and sweaters Moor and Bibi had knitted for us, and the fruit stands sold pomegranates, oranges, and apples, and the bazaar was as crowded as in the summer. As December approached, I counted the days until classes were over for then I'd have the whole winter to read, to think, to make plans, to build sandcastles no waves could erode.

Jandol said the sky that night was particularly clear, but it was impossible for him to savor the view because of the racket made by a couple of helicopters that were circling directly overhead. He returned to the office where it was quieter, wondering what it would be like to float above the city in one of those things, to feel that sense of expansiveness, of freedom as you flew across mountains and strange cities far from everything you knew. If only Abba and Pamir would return from Kandahar. They'd already been gone for over a week, leaving him in charge of the business. Since most customers came during the day, the hours at night hung heavily on his hands. At least the lack of business was enabling him to finish a school paper he'd been putting off because of the complicated statistical analysis.

As he was trying to draw an acute angle, he became aware of a presence next to his desk. He hadn't heard the door open, so it was a little creepy, not to mention the fact that he hated it when anybody watched him working since the result was usually a whole bunch of mistakes. Faced with all these tedious angles and numbers he was carefully applying, he put his pencil aside with the intention of asking whoever it was to move away. He found himself looking up at a dark-haired youngish-oldish man wearing a pinstriped business suit.

"Are you in charge?"

"Yes. Can I help you?"

"You were recommended to me."

"I was? Or my father?"

"That doesn't matter. The point is, I would like to talk to you about a project."

"Let me get you a chair."

"Never mind about the chair," he said. "I need a more private place to talk about this. I don't want any interruptions. By the way, is there a phone I can use?"

"Yeah, there's one on my desk. You're welcome to it."

"No, no, I want a public phone. Much more private."

"A public phone? There's no problem, just use this one."

"No, no, it has to be public."

"There's a telephone booth down the road a couple of blocks away."

"Which way?"

"Make a left. Go two blocks."

The man hesitated for a minute, and then he said, "I'll be back shortly. I'd appreciate it if you'd wait. There's something important I want to discuss with you. An important project I'm involved in."

With this, he walked out. After he left, Jandol wondered if he'd ever come back or was it just some hallucination. He took his seat, once more facing the mass of digits dancing before his eyes. He opened the bottom drawer where Pamir hid his cigarettes, lit one, and went back to his angles.

Fifteen minutes later, the door opened. "Good, you're still here," he said. "Okay, now I have to talk to you, so let's get out of here. I need a more private place."

More private? "Where do you want to go?"

"I know a little teahouse down the road," he said. "Let's go there. They make their own almond baklava."

"There's really no one here. I could go next door and get some tea and biscuits."

"No, no, let's go to the teahouse. Put on your jacket, and let's get going."

"I can't leave, there's no one else here."

"Half an hour?"

The teahouse was overheated and crowded. He and Jandol took a table by the window, which was coated with steam, and the man ordered green tea and four almond baklavas.

"Is that all right with you?" he said. "Do you like almond baklava?"

"Sure. They're okay," Jandol said.

"You ever been here before? They're beyond okay. They're the best in Kabul. There are other places that have better walnut baklava, like Maliar Milmastoon, you know, next to the Polikhishti Mosque, but nobody has better almond baklava."

"Maybe it was the mullah's recipe?"

"I'm sorry."

"The British spy, the one who pretended to be the head mullah at the Polikhishti Mosque. Maybe he had something to do with the walnut baklava."

"Anything is possible."

"Excuse me, I didn't get your name."

"Call me Andrei."

"And who recommended us?"

"That's unimportant for now. The important thing is, we need people who are trustworthy and reliable. Are you the man for me?"

"I don't know, what do you want?"

"I need someone to help me, someone with a head on his shoulders who I can trust. In other words, someone who can keep his mouth shut."

"I understand the rules of business."

"I mean, you can't discuss this with anybody, not even your closest friends. Even in the most casual way. Do I have your word on this?"

"Sure. No problem. I'm very discreet."

"Good."

The waiter brought the baklavas and the tea, and Jandol's companion took out an expensive calfskin wallet from his inside jacket pocket. Jandol saw an inch-thick wad of paper bills. He started thinking, *This is okay, I'll be better than discreet. I'll be absolutely mute.* Andrei paid the waiter.

"I don't have much time. I don't want to wait for him to collect when we're done."

They drank their tea and ate the almond baklavas.

"Aren't these fantastic?" Andrei said.

Jandol nodded approval, wiping the honeyed crumbs from the corner of his mouth. *How secretive this guy is,* Jandol thought. But hell, let him praise these baklavas from here to Kandahar for all he cared. But what did he really want? After Jandol finished off the baklavas, he asked, "What kind of a project is this?"

"Big. Very, very big."

"What's my job?"

"To go here and there."

"Oh, here and—"

"There," the man chuckled. "It's easy money, brother, just a couple of days a week."

"But you still won't tell me what it is?"

"No, no, no, no, that's not the way we're going to operate. I assume you speak Farsi."

"I can manage."

"Can you read it?"

"I can manage."

"Okay, any other languages?"

"Pashto."

"I would expect that. Also, my friend, there's one important thing we haven't discussed yet, and that's how much are you going to charge. Now, remember, I'll be giving you a lot of business, and I expect a good price. So how about fifty Afghanis an hour. I don't want to quibble with you. Would you be comfortable with that?"

"Fifty?"

"An hour. Is it a deal?"

"Fifty's fine. Great. It's a lot of money."

"I know you're conscientious. Later on, if I need you to work more, I'll pay you an additional twenty-five over the fifty. Agreed?" Andrei extended his gloved hand, and Jandol shook it awkwardly, noticing that it was covered with a film of pastry flakes from the baklavas.

"There's one final thing," Andrei said. "Since this is such a long project, I'll expect you to put aside all of your other work. I will pay you, let's say by the week, every Monday. In fact, to show my good faith, take this as an advance." He handed Jandol three crisp new thousand Afghani bills. "What time do you usually get in the office?"

"Around eleven."

"I assume you don't work Fridays."

"That's right."

"From our conversation, you said you'd be working on my project during the week. Since today's Thursday, my man will see you Monday morning. He will tell you what to do."

"Your man?"

"Is that okay?"

"What time?"

"Between two and three. Three at the latest."

"I'll be ready. By the way, if something happens and I have to get hold of you, how will I do it?"

"If you have to contact me," Andrei said, giving him a card, "just call this number."

"Great," Jandol said, putting it in his pocket without examining it.

"Is there anything else you want to ask?"

"Between two and three on Monday, right?"

"That's right."

"Good."

"Okay, well, that's it. Good meeting you. I have to get going."

With that he left the teahouse, but when Jandol followed only moments later, Andrei was nowhere to be seen.

Back in the office, Jandol took out the man's business card and looked at it. All it had was a phone number—no name, no address, just a phone number in fancy embossed gold. *Strange*, he thought. But this whole thing had been strange. Three thousand Afghani bills in his hand, secret messengers, mysterious recommendations. At that moment, the phone rang, startling him; it was Sial saying Moor wanted him to close shop and come home, that supper was almost ready.

On Monday afternoon it rained, and Jandol stared out the steam-fogged window, but all he could distinguish was a blur of people racing up and down, their umbrellas ballooning in the heavy blasts of wind-driven rain. It was fifteen past three. So where was Andrei's assistant? He sat up straight in his chair and placed his palms on the smooth wood of the desk. A picture flashed in his mind of gulls flying across the ocean, their destiny a distant glimmer of chalk-white cliffs shimmering in the white sea air. So simple, so beautiful, and here he was getting involved in God knew what.

The statistical table was still unfinished, but it was impossible to concentrate. He kept glancing at the clock every two minutes, and each time his slide rule left the page, he lost his place. By five, with no private gofer arriving, Jandol decided the hell with it and focused on his paper. The next time he noticed the clock, it was quarter after six. Hardly any customers had come in all afternoon, and he'd stopped paying attention to the gusts that swept into the drafty office through the broken transom window. So when he heard his name called, he looked up in surprise. A man in his thirties with fine dirty-blond hair and broad shoulders and wearing a black raincoat was standing in front of the counter, holding a furled umbrella in his hand. "Where can I put this?"

"By the door," Jandol said, pointing to a blank space of wall. He watched as the man walked over, put the umbrella down, and turned back to where he was sitting. He took a chair facing Jandol.

"I'm supposed to give you something," the man said, and he extracted a legal-sized envelope from a black leather briefcase, placing it in front of him. Jandol reached for it, but the man said very softly, "I'm sorry, but I'm going to have to see some ID before I turn this over to you."

"What's that?"

"ID. Identification."

"You mean like my *tazkira*?"

"Yes. Some identification."

"What for?"

"I'm sorry, but I have to see some identification. It doesn't have to be your *tazkira*. Any kind of ID will do," he said, speaking even more softly and looking at him expressionlessly.

Who is this guy? Jandol thought, beginning to wonder if this humorless stranger in his fancy raincoat would whisk him off to some distant part of the country where he'd find himself confronting a homicidal lunatic in a crop duster. He extracted his wallet from his side pocket and dropped it on the desk. The man picked it up and examined it for a moment before handing it back.

"So now that you've seen my ID, I'd like to see yours," Jandol said, but the man didn't reply to his request.

"The work is extremely confidential. We wouldn't want it to get in the wrong hands," he said so softly that Jandol had to strain to catch his words. The man pushed an envelope forward, indicating that Jandol should open it up. Inside was a message that said he would get a phone call in the next thirty-six hours. He looked up at the man questioningly, but the man avoided his gaze. Then without another word, the man took back the envelope and snapped his briefcase shut. "It was nice meeting you," he said. "I'll be talking to you." He shook Jandol's hand briefly and walked out the door.

It had happened so quickly, Jandol began to doubt whether it had actually occurred, or was it something he'd made up?

On Tuesday the weather stayed miserable with an incessant downpour. Every time the phone rang, Jandol picked it up on the first ring, wondering if it were the famous phone call. It wasn't, nor were the other myriad calls.

Abba and Pamir returned that night, and Jandol slept in. When he came to work, Pamir said pointedly that someone was pilfering his cigarettes. Jandol told him he shouldn't be smoking anyway; it'd stunt his growth.

"Since when are you telling me what to do?" Pamir said.

"It's your funeral," Jandol replied.

"All this jibber jabber, I almost forgot. Someone called you earlier."

"Who?"

"They didn't leave a number."

"But who was it?"

"I don't know, they said they'd call back."

"Well, was it a man or woman?"

"What do you think?"

"I think you're a jerk."

"You know, that really hurts my feelings. Punk."

A truck pulled in front and stopped with the motor still running and Indian sitar music blaring. The driver entered, giving Pamir his order, and the three of them began carrying boxes out of the truck bed and placing them in the warehouse. As they were lifting the last one, the phone rang, startling Jandol, so that the box slipped from his hand and became stuck to a metal towing hook beside the tailgate. Pamir and the delivery man climbed on the truck and lifted the other end and proceeded to jockey it up and down while the phone kept ringing. When they finally pulled the box free, Jandol placed his end on the ground and raced inside, but the moment he picked up the receiver, the line went dead. He angrily slammed it down. Instantly, it began to ring again.

"Yes, yes!" he shouted into the mouthpiece.

"Calm down," Moor said. She only wanted him to go to the bakery and pick up a banana cream pie for dessert now that Abba was home.

That evening when Jandol told us about Andrei and the other guy and the phone call that never came, Abba hit the ceiling.

"I can't believe what you're telling me. After all I've warned you about, you start playing footsies with a Russian spy."

"I never said he's a spy."

"Well, what do you think he is?"

"I don't know. A customer. I don't see why you're getting so angry."

"You don't? Tell him, Lila. Maybe he'll listen to you. Our lives are in danger, my company is in danger, my finances are all over the place. And you agree to work with a stranger on some project about which you know nothing. Not only that, you take three thousand Afghanis as a statement of faith. More money than we've seen in a month."

"I agree with Abba, it was a very foolish move," Sial said.

"Did I ask your opinion?" Abba said.

"I was only trying to help."

"I don't need your help."

"I was only trying."

"This is between your father and Jandol," Moor said.

"Everybody always picks on me," Sial said.

"Not another word."

"I'm going for a walk," he said and stormed outside, slamming the front door.

Meena and I were transfixed. I'd never seen Abba this angry. Usually it was Moor who disciplined us, and she rarely raised her voice. Or Lakhta, who had no trouble expressing her feelings, the louder the better. But when Abba stepped in, it was usually with a calm demeanor, like a judge at a trial.

Feeling the power of his wrath, Jandol waited for the ax to fall in a silence that was literally deafening.

"What are you going to do when this man returns? If he returns, I should say."

"I don't know."

"Well, I do. You're going to give him back his three thousand Afghanis, and you're going to tell him, if he wants to do business, he needs to see me first, that I'm the owner of this company and not you, and that you do not have the authority to make such decisions."

"Whatever you say."

"Whatever I say? When have you ever listened to me or anyone but yourself?"

"Enough," Moor said. "Jandol was only trying to help."

"Such help I don't need. Don't you realize that it's me they're after? Or didn't that occur to you? Or the fact that once you started working with these people that they'd never let you quit."

"I said I was sorry."

"Sorry or not, you must extricate yourself from the situation. Apologize for your rash behavior and hope that's the end of it."

"I guess I screwed up all around," Jandol said.

"You know I don't often tell my children what to do. I feel it's my role as a parent to be a role model but not a dictator. If I tell you what to do, I myself face two dilemmas. One, you'll never learn how to make your own decisions. And two, if you don't listen to what I say, I will be angry. But as you know, this doesn't mean that I will not point out the errors of your ways or where you've gone off the path, as I have just done with you, Jandol, and will continue to do. That said, I want to point out something that might help you. Son, your challenge is not to worry about what you don't have. Anyone can do that. Sial is the perfect example, and where does it get him? He digs a deep hole, and when he can no longer climb out, who does he blame? His digging? No, he blames the hole. It is the hole that entrapped him, and not the other way around. He forgets that originally, there was no hole.

"We are facing difficult times, Jandol, but what seems to be destroying our dreams is capable of building our character. Inner growth is what your mother and I are concerned with, not how many laurels the world offers. Perhaps you can see what I mean. Now enough of this business. Your mother's right, let's allow it to rest."

The rain continued off and on for the next few weeks while Jandol walked around under his own cloud. Andrei hadn't reappeared, nor had the man with the fine dirty-blond hair. At some time, although he knew it was wrong, Jandol's curiosity got the better of him, and he dialed the number on Andrei's card. He let the phone ring forever, but no one answered. He tried it another time with the same result. The third time he lost his temper and tore up the card. Andrei never did come back. At the same time, he never left, by which I mean the paranoia he induced in all of us remained, usually in the background but still a constant factor that tightened or lessened, depending on the situation.

It was late winter 1982, and we'd gotten through the winter, but it had been a struggle. Meena and I hated school and the rah-rah about Russia and how they'd broken the chains of czarist tyranny and were bringing freedom to our country, etc. I think I just zoned out in a kind of stupor. If a teacher called on me, I just spouted out the party line, as did Meena, although they couldn't infect our math classes, which Meena found interesting but for which I had no aptitude. But everyone had their burdens and conflicts, I wasn't the only one, and their strength made things easier for me to bear. Besides, I'd begun reading on my own and in a manner I hadn't done before, experiencing the lyricism of Pashto poetry as it played on my consciousness.

Truthfully, I didn't understand much of what I read, but now and then, something astounding would leap off the page. What was really strange was that I was finding it not enough to take in the works of the great poets and thinkers that I wanted to express how I felt. Tentatively, I began to write, although simply trying to describe a ladybug crawling on a leaf or the way a woman's burka flew around her when it was windy exhausted my ability, and the results were pretty amateurish. However, the challenge when I did successfully give life to words on a page thrilled me to the roots of my being. I would be a poet, I decided. I would. I wasn't just, I don't know, just pretending, and a hundred years in the future, people would read my words. Well, hopefully. At least I had my sense of, if not humor, the beginnings of irony. Even at such a young age, it was impossible not to be ironic, considering the temper of the times in which we lived.

Just this past month, there'd been a cave-in at the largest of the mines, and although luckily no one had been hurt, Abba didn't have the finances to make the repairs, so it stood idle, as did the workers. On the other hand, what did it matter, given that conditions were so chaotic, not many customers were buying semiprecious paper weights, especially with the fluctuations in the value of the Afghani.

Not only Abba but many businesses as well were at a virtual standstill, such as the refinery outside Jalalabad that processed the ore, who were now demanding a sizable lump payment before they'd hand over the stones, even though they had previously accepted monthly installments. Abba tried to straighten things out while Pamir and Jandol tried to drum up more business in Kandahar where our largest distributor was located, but according to them, things didn't look good.

A light dusting of snow had fallen the night before, giving the city a magical sparkle in the elegant blue air. Moor, Meena, Sial, and I, scarfed and bundled, had gone to the Old Kabul Bazaar where we had lunch at a restaurant that specialized in Lebanese food—their chicken tabbouleh was fantastic, plus they gave you a free slice of chocolate cake for dessert. Afterward, we wandered around, each of us continuing to find the place fascinating—so much to see, to think about. I could've spent the entire day in the bookseller's section, going from store to store, stall to stall, lost among the volumes. How I loved the smell and feel of the paper, even those printed on cheap stock, but the editions on rag paper that you could hold to the light and see the ripples, they were the best, like the fresh smell of a forest at dawn. I chided myself for such fancies, but that's a pretty accurate description of how I felt.

On the bus home, with everybody talking at once and laughing, having some fun for a change, my imagination was still alive with the music of the words.

But the moment we reached our gate, which was hanging half-open even though Moor said she was sure she'd locked it, our happiness came to an abrupt halt. Someone had broken in. The front door was ajar, with papers and books strewn along the verandah, the pages torn from their bindings. Sial pushed the door farther open, and we peered inside. The entire interior was a disaster with glass everywhere, smashed furniture, cots bayoneted, and clothes slashed. Sial's posters had been ripped off the walls, and the model jet airplane I'd so painstakingly put together was lying on the floor in a hundred pieces. Moor's and Meena's clothes had been ripped to shreds, dishes broken, glasses. The kitchen walls were splattered with food that had spilled all over the floors, making it slippery and disgusting.

Unexpectedly, the gate banged, causing each of us to jump. Sial went out to look. "Only the wind," he said when he came back inside. "I locked it."

We slowly went from room to room, accompanied by the crunch of broken glass. Meena wept when she saw what they'd done to her prized doll collection.

"I'll find out who did this," Sial burst out. "They think they can scare us. Well, I won't let them. I won't. I won't!" His voice bounced from wall to wall and then collapsed into the silence that hung there waiting for us. "I'm sorry, Moor."

"We have to keep our heads," she said firmly. Then she picked up a plate from the table that hadn't been broken, gazed for a moment at its flowery design, and then placed it down. "Remember," she said, "dolls, dishes, clothes, papers—they can be replaced. People can't."

"I'm afraid," Meena said.

"No one's going to hurt you."

"Who could have done this?" I asked.

But we knew the answer. The Communists had become much more aggressive over the past six months.

"They were looking for something," Sial said.

"Let them look. There's nothing to find," Moor said. "Or is there?"

All three of us cried out no, that we weren't hiding anything.

"What'll we do?" Meena said.

"First, we lock the doors and windows," Moor said. "Then we get to work and clean up this mess. When we're finished, I'll make supper."

"What will we eat on?" Meena said.

"Let's see if we can find some dishes and silverware that they might've missed. Meena, start sweeping, and you boys separate the broken dishes from the ones that are still usable. If any," she said, handing Meena a broom and a dustpan.

The rest of us spent the rest of the afternoon until late that night cleaning up and disposing of things. Amid the mess, we had a certain amount of luck. They'd missed some of our clothes that were in the dirty clothes hamper, and some of Meena's dolls just needed to be restuffed. Also, a few of Sial's posters could be taped together. But Abba's books and the bookshelves, Moor's knickknacks and bric-a-brac, all garbage now. Thank God Moor had hidden her jewelry under a loose board in the closet. Most of her rings, bracelets, and earrings had been in her family for generations and were irreplaceable.

We kept repeating the same remarks over and over. If only Abba were here, Moor would say. If only he didn't have to travel so much. Because if he were in Kabul, this would never have happened. Yes, Sial would agree. With him here, no one would've dared to screw around with us like this.

"But he wasn't here," Meena said. "He's never here."

Nerves taut and lips dry, we ate our supper by candlelight with the curtains drawn.

CHAPTER THREE

"AH, THE BIG HEADACHE is back," Gulapa said, looking up and shading her eyes against the glare.

"I thought I was the little headache?"

"Well, Mr. Troublemaker, you've grown."

"You look the same," I said.

"I'll take that as a compliment."

"Of course."

Gulapa, Atal, and Droon were sitting under the pecan tree in their courtyard. The mud-brick walls still looked a little worse for wear, chipped in the same places and needing still to be replastered. Nothing new. Atal and Droon were smoking from a hookah, and Gulapa was holding a *chach*, sifting the waste from rice.

She continued to shake the tray, which made a shushing sound. "Khialo, look who's here. Hey, hey, hey!"

Khialo came outside, followed by an older boy he introduced as Tofan, and the three of us shook hands. Khialo had a tiny bit of fuzz above his lips and his hair was longer, but otherwise, he looked the same.

"What bad news are you bringing?" Gulapa said.

"Gulapa, be nice," Atal chided.

"I will if you'll stop blowing smoke in my face. Now come here, you mobster, and let me give you a kiss."

I bent down, and Gulapa pecked me on the cheek. The touch of her dry lips transported me back to when I'd been terrified by her stories about aliens who'd tear me apart if I didn't do exactly as she said. Ghosts no longer frightened me, only real people did. Yes, they were scary enough.

"I want to hear all about Kabul," she said, but before I could say a word, she began talking about how there'd been heavy bombing throughout Hisarak. The night Droon drove them in his truck to Gulapa's sister Natkai's house in Minkhill, there'd been so many shells exploding around them, they'd been frequently forced to drive off the road and hide, waiting until it was safe to go on until the next round of attacks. "It took all night to get there. I was sure we'd never make it. But at least this way we could get killed together. As you can see, we remain in one piece. Sort of."

"We are each in one piece definitely," Atal said.

"That's what you think," Gulapa rose to her feet, shaking the *chach* so hard the rice jumped up and down while she made rapid mincing steps. "Our valley is no longer our mother. Father Death is swirling around our villages, and our lives and our children's lives and their children's lives are worth nothing. Death is famished, death is ravenous. The walls are crumbling, the earth is weeping, the sky is black with crows. Such gifts. It's better to gouge out your eyes, eh?"

Placing the tray on the ground, she began to whirl in circles that kept increasing in tempo, clapping her hands and stamping her feet on the hard-packed earth. "I am dancing with death!" she shouted. "Come join me!" She burst out laughing.

Atal told her to stop it, that she was scaring the children.

"Children?" she said, continuing to clap. "Once the first bomb explodes, childhood is gone." Nevertheless, she took her seat and reached for the hookah. "All right," she said to me, "enough of this nonsense. Why are you here? Why did you come back? Was it because of what those bastards did to your house in Kabul?"

"Is there anything you don't know?"

"God gave me ears and eyes, so I shouldn't use them? Now start talking."

I told her that when Abba, Pamir, and Jandol returned and we told them what happened, he said we needed to leave immediately.

"But where should we go?" Moor said. It didn't matter where. Someplace where we'd be safe. Where was that? No one had a ready answer because no place was safe. A week passed. Two. None of us left the house. We kids didn't go to school, and Abba and Pamir didn't open the office. Whenever we heard footsteps, we tensed up. One time someone knocked and, when we didn't answer, continued to bang on the door. Finally, the person or persons left. We kept the curtains closed and the windows shuttered and only one small lamp burning when it got dark.

One evening Jandol went out for some food, but when he returned and saw our faces, he said, "Who died?" Moor said that he'd taken so long, they thought he'd been arrested. He offered to take me and Meena back to Shabak, but Moor wouldn't hear of it. "Not without your father and me," she said. But the longer we stayed, the crazier and more threatened we felt. No, it was impossible. We were virtual prisoners in our own home.

Abba finally made the decision that, money or not, we would return to Shabak. Such an insignificant village, we could lose ourselves there. The Communists probably didn't even know it existed. Anyway, there was nowhere else we could go. But no one must know what we were up to. Which meant that we would have to leave everything behind, what belongings that were still in one piece, that is. It was imperative that our neighbors think we were just going for a drive. Pamir would stay behind and oversee the business. Abba had an old friend who lived across the Kabul River, and he would make arrangements for Pamir to stay with him. With his student card, he'd be safe enough so long as he kept his mouth shut and didn't get involved in politics.

Abba warned him to focus on the business and school, nothing else. "Don't get into any arguments with any of our customers. If they can pay, they can pay. If they can't, don't antagonize them."

We waited while Moor spoke quietly to Pamir then piled into the car. No one was around, which was lucky. Also, by taking this route and that and by staying clear of the main roads, we managed the journey without having any problems with the checkpoints. Helping us also was the fact that the Afghan Army was more concerned about people coming to Kabul than leaving. This, in a nutshell, was why we returned, but whether we'd stay or not, whether we'd be discovered by the authorities, and whether Abba would be able to hold on to his business—these were all up in the air.

"So was it a robbery, your house, I mean, or was it the work of informers or the police?"

"We don't know. No one trusts the banks, they're all in the hands of the Communists, so everyone keeps their money at home. Not a wise thing to do. The thing is, Abba discovered that all of his papers, his notebooks, and his business documents were missing. There wasn't even a piece of blank paper left lying around. In the initial confusion, no one had looked through the wreck that had been his desk and his file cabinet until Abba returned and discovered what had happened. He realized that someone was planning something, some trap in order to steal his assets in the name of the state. Or, what was more likely, to blackmail us. Our hope is that it's the work of thieves or blackmailers. They can't blackmail us if they don't know where we are. Our plan is to keep a low profile and hope they don't find us, whoever it was."

"You made the right decision. You shouldn't have moved to Kabul in the first place. It was a stupid idea," Gulapa said, tendrils of smoke escaping her mouth. What a dragon. I had the strongest impulse to tell her to mind her own business, but I kept quiet. Abruptly she rose, brushed herself off, and put the rice in a bowl of hot water that was steaming on the outdoor stove. "Enough talk. It's time to make lunch. Khialo, Droon, get off your behinds and help me."

After we finished eating, Tofan said he had to go home, that his mother became frightened when he was gone too long. Khialo and I offered to help clean up, but Gulapa chased us out of the kitchen, saying she didn't have enough dishes for us to break. We went for a walk, passing by the Srakala cemetery with its mounds of newly-dug graves and following the Auzingianai until we were out in the fields. There was no one around, which made it feel eerie. I kept looking over my shoulder, expecting some of my friends to come running up. I don't know what I expected. Maybe someone would leap out and murder us. A blot of color caught my eye. Blown against the trunk of a tree whose gnarled branches held it in place was a flyer that was flapping back and forth. In blood-red letters beneath a man's corpse were the words "Gron Afghanistan."

How sad, I thought, pulling it off and thinking about the words. Beloved Afghanistan. My country. I held the paper in my hand until we reached the Auzingianai, and then I let it go, watching as it fluttered down into the water and was soon gone.

"Guess what?" Khialo said. "Droon and Sandara are betrothed."

"The beautiful Sandara with her almond eyes and smiles of many meanings?"

Khialo nodded yes, and I asked him when it happened.

"A few months ago. Currently, my dear brother is working his butt off trying to save enough money for them to find a place to live. He walks around in a daze. Of course, Azmoon wants to strangle him."

"I don't think Jandol's going to be too thrilled either." We both thought that was funny. "So when are Droon and Sandara going to tie the knot?"

"First they have to find the rope."

"Meaning?"

"Money, my dear friend. Afghanis, rupees, you've heard of them."

"Why don't they become nomads? Then they wouldn't need any money."

"Droon will never leave us. Without him, we wouldn't have a roof over our heads. Let's face it, if my father didn't work for your father, we'd be sleeping under a rock."

"What does Sandara say?"

"She doesn't care if they have money or not, but Lakhta and Gulapa said they had to wait."

"I'm amazed that they decided to let them marry in the first place. I thought they were dead set against it."

"This whole Communist takeover has changed all the rules. All we can hope is that sooner or later they'll go back to Russia where they belong, and we can relax."

"Dream on."

"No, really, I mean it. They shouldn't be here, and you know it. Why doesn't somebody do something?"

"I thought the partisans and freedom fighters were doing something," I said. "Hey, let's both of us join up and go live in one of their mountain camps. Want to?"

"Do I! But how? You know we're too young, too wet behind the ears."

"By the time this war is over, we won't be too young, I can guarantee you that."

Tofan lived alone with his mother, his father having deserted her for a younger wife because she couldn't bear more children. The father was a real piece of work. Tofan had pointed him out to me once on the terrace of a teahouse in the Shabak bazaar, a stubby, bearded, middle-aged man with bulky fingers wrapped around a cup with his pinkie sticking out. Tofan said he left them with nothing, although he was drowning in money, that he traded spices and had his own shop at the bazaar. It was a complicated situation. His mother was almost an invalid with some kind of arthritic disease, but the father refused to help, said he didn't want to have anything to do with either of them.

Their place was an absolute hovel. They just about eked out a living, mostly buying scraps from various vendors with Tofan doing odd jobs. He was ashamed but proud and fierce, quick to take offense. I met his mother, a kindly soul but not very bright, crushed by circumstances. I supposed that the Communists decided to let that particular rose wither on the vine when it came to sharing the wealth. But I felt sorry for both of them. For her I could do nothing, but for Tofan, both Khialo and I tried to include him in everything. It was strange because he was so hypersensitive. One thing in his favor, as far as I was concerned, was that Sial didn't like him.

"He should marry someone like Gulapa," Sial said. "That'd make a man out of him."

"She'd eat him alive," Lakhta said. "Starting with his ears."

"That's the whole point. What do you see in him anyway?"

"What do we see in you?" she said, impatiently brushing a strand of hair that had escaped her head scarf.

"Maybe you could make an effort to talk to him," Khialo said. "Get to know him."

"Maybe I will," Sial said. "Maybe I just will."

"You leave him alone," I said. "He has enough problems without you pestering him."

"Problems? Everyone has problems. What makes him so special?"

"Never mind."

"Tell me."

"He has a hard time trusting people, you know, making friends."

"I think he's ashamed to," Khialo said.

"Well, I don't blame him," Sial said. "I'd be ashamed too if my old man had left us high and dry without two rupees to rub together and a basket case for a mother."

"Speaking of rubbing things together," I said, "why don't you get lost?"

"I already am," he said.

"Wise guy."

Khialo and Tofan were waiting out by the gate for us to walk to school when Moor asked me to stop at the hospital pharmacy on the way to get a refill of cough medicine for Bibi, who was recovering from a cold. This errand took much longer than expected, causing us to arrive an hour late. The guard, an officious little prick I'd seen brownnosing the teachers, wouldn't let us go to our classrooms, instead escorting us to the principal's office. When we entered, he was standing next to an obese man in a rumpled suit who was precariously buttock-perched on the side of his desk, smoking a cigarette and scattering the ashes helter-skelter.

They stopped talking, and the principal said that he was a busy man, so what did we want? This was the guard's moment in the sun. Like the messenger in a play who hands prisoners of war to the king, he announced that we were an hour late for school.

"I see," the principal said. He thanked the guard, who nodded and left. "Well, what have you to say for yourselves?"

He made me so nervous I began to stammer out an answer that even to me sounded as if I were making it up. To confirm what I said, I held up the bottle. "It's for my grandmother. She's not feeling well."

"I see. Your grandmother. And you two? What did you need at the hospital?"

Khialo mumbled something while Tofan remained silent. "You," he said to Tofan, "the tall one. Cat got your tongue? I'm only going to ask one more time. Why were you involved in this nonsense?"

"I don't know."

"You don't know." He turned to the man on the desk. "He doesn't know."Then he asked me why I didn't pick up the medicine on the way home.

"It's too busy then, I thought it'd be quicker in the morning, but…there was an emergency, and they made us wait, and so—"

"You. The one in the middle."

"Me?" asked Tofan.

"Are you in the middle?"

"Uh—"

"Are you in the middle?"

"He means me," Khialo said.

"Look down when I'm talking to you," the principal said to Khialo, who immediately bowed his head. "Now, what did you need at the hospital?"

"I…I…um…I just tagged along."

"You just tagged along."

"We thought we'd have plenty of time."

"You thought you'd have plenty of time."

"We did. Have plenty of time, I mean. At first. I mean, they took our order and everything, but then…like he said, there was an emergency, and it took much longer than expected."

"Then why didn't you leave and pick it up later?"

"Well, they kept saying any minute."

"You two geniuses, get out of here, go straight to your classes."

Neither Khialo nor Tofan needed much persuading.

After they were gone, he said, "How old are you, boy?"

"I'm thirteen."

"Thirteen," the man on the desk said. "An unlucky number." The words fell from his mouth accompanied by clots of snot-inducing smoke.

"How's your father?" the principal asked. Taking a seat in his swivel chair, he rested his elbows on the arms, bringing his index fingers together to form a triangle above, which his icy glare was painful to the eye.

Ruffled, I said, "My father?"

"How much more money has he ripped off from the poor?"

"What's that?" the other man said.

"I know this one. The father's as rich as Croesus."

"That so?"

"Yes, a real Mr. Moneybags. Thinks he owns the world."

"The world's a big place," the man said, nonchalantly brushing lint from his sleeve. "Another one of those mullahs?"

"No, he's no mullah. The mullahs pretend to be honest. This one boasts about his thievery."

"My father is no thief," I said, gaining my voice as a rush of anger swept through me. No matter what, I wouldn't let them badmouth Abba. "He's a businessman. He's never done anything to harm you or your government. He's a simple man, a great man. He's—"

"Enough, enough," the principal said, chuckling. "You people have no more sense than pigs in a sty. I'm in no mood to listen to a litany of your father's noble deeds. After all, we are talking about a man who steals from the poor, from those sad souls who are unable to survive, who live in mud huts with no running water."

"Ask him if he's seen them," the obese man in the rumpled suit said. "I want to know."

"Well, boy, have you seen them?"

"Seen what?"

"I bet you know well what I'm talking about," the principal said.

"We're waiting."

"Yes. I mean, no. I don't know. Maybe."

"He's seen them for sure," the obese man said. "No doubt about it."

"I'm not so sure," the principal said.

"Look at him, look at his eyes, the window of the soul. You can always tell if someone's lying. He's seen them."

They stared at me. Finally, I told them I had no idea what they were talking about.

"He has no idea, no idea at all," the obese man said to the principal, who clucked his tongue. Didn't these guys have anything better to do than to needle me? What was the point of this interview? In that moment, I felt superior to both of them. How could men like these have taken over our country? Why, they were weak, not outwardly, but inside where it mattered. Like garden snails that crawl out onto the paths after it rains, ugly little things that cracked when you accidentally stepped on them.

"What do they look like?" the obese man asked.

"Sir, I'm sorry, I—"

"How about a visual," he said, placing his hands on either side of his head and cupping them so that they resembled horns, and in a flash, I realized that he was talking about the devil, calling Abba Satan, asking if I'd seen his horns. Before I could say a word, in a sudden updraft, the pull cord from the window curtain began tapping annoyingly against the glass. The man, noticing the direction of my eyes, turned to the principal, and they each shook their heads at the stupidity of the Afghan people as personified by me.

"It's no use," the principal said. "No use at all." The game was over. "Get out of here. But remember, I don't want any more trouble from you. Oh, and tell your teacher that I want a full report on your behavior. The next time you mess up, maybe a few months cleaning army latrines might straighten you out."

As I left, he and the other man returned to whatever they'd been discussing.

That day I maintained my usual air of cheerful blandness, which was turning into a rigid mask—or rather, the brick wall of my will was slowly being breached by all the lies I had to tell in order to survive, although fortunately as yet, none of the cracks was visible. But the surge just below the surface to tell those bastards to go to hell was growing in intensity.

After classes, I didn't wait for Khialo and Tofan; I didn't want to see anyone. But when I got home, five minutes after Moor left for Srakala with the cough syrup, I heard footsteps and soft rapping at the door. "It's open!" I shouted.

Khialo and Tofan stepped inside. "Can we come in?"

"We wanted to apologize," Tofan said.

"Yes, we're truly sorry," Khialo said.

"We should have stood up to those guys."

"Tofan's right. We should have told them to mind their own business."

"You know that's impossible," I said. "But thanks for saying so."

"Well, at least we could have explained it better," Khialo said. "About your grandmother, I mean."

"Where'd you go after classes were over?" Tofan asked.

"I wanted to put some mileage between me and that slaughterhouse of the mind."

"Of the soul," Khialo said.

"Boy, I'd sure love to have kicked that principal in the balls," Tofan said with relish. "One good kick."

"He probably doesn't have any."

"Let's face it," I said, "the best thing in these situations is to play dumb. Luckily in both your cases, it didn't take much acting."

"No matter what you say, we're sorry," Khialo said. "We're sorry the whole thing happened."

"In a way, the principal was right," I said philosophically. "I should've picked up the medicine after school."

"You didn't know how long it'd take. Besides, who thought they'd make such a big deal about it? Not to mention that idiot of a guard would be waiting like a spider. Did you see his expression when he saw us? He all but licked his lips."

"The place is a trap," Tofan said. "A mind trap. Nothing but a Communist recruitment center where you're fed the same pap over and over until it scrambles your brain and squeezes you dry."

"Brother, I couldn't agree more," I said. "But if I were you, I'd go easy on the metaphors."

"What?"

"I agree with you. Look, let's forget about it. Let's move on."

"We might as well face the facts," Khialo said. "The only way they're going to let go is if we make them."

"We?" Tofan said.

"Not you and me. Us. All of us. We must rise up against oppression."

"Khialo, I had no idea you were so…patriotic," I said. "I like that in you. I always thought you were a realist."

"I'm too young to be a realist. I'll wait till I'm twenty-one."

"You're a funny guy, you know that? Anyway, I wasn't being serious. If we didn't joke about life…Well, you know. It's how we survive."

Lakhta came in carrying a wicker basket, which she placed on the table next to the door. It was filled with tomatoes from our garden. Some were twisted while others looked like they'd burst if you so much as breathed on them. She removed her head scarf and raked her fingers through her thick black hair. "How are you boys?"

"We're okay," Khialo said.

"If that's so, how can I tell when you're not okay?"

"It's school," I said. "We were a few minutes late, and they made us go to the principal's office."

"A few minutes?"

"We had to go to the principal's office, and he threatened to draft me into the army if I didn't shape up."

"Then you'd best shape up."

"Clearly."

"School is such a waste of time," Khialo said. "I know what you're going to say, Lakhta, but we don't learn anything there. They don't teach us anything. It's just all this mumbo jumbo about how great the USSR is."

Tofan said, "It's like going to a funeral and dancing with the corpse."

"All of you had better watch your tongues. Remember what Abba said."

"What did he say?" Khialo asked.

"Oh, you know," I said. "The usual. That we have to keep our mouths shut no matter what. He's afraid we might attract the wrong people, but I'm telling you seriously, I'm beginning not to care anymore. I mean it."

"Well, I do," Lakhta said. "One word from you could get all of us arrested."

"I know, I know," I said, "Quit nagging me. I haven't said anything."

"My mother says the same thing," Tofan said. "The older generation."

"This has nothing to do with age," Lakhta said.

"Give me an AK-47, and I'll say anything I want, whenever I want."

"If you act like a monkey, you're no better than a monkey," Lakhta said.

"Another philosopher." I shrugged.

"Philosopher?"

"We're being devoured, Lakhta. Surely you can see that."

"Has any of you ever heard of the mountains of Chin Kwi Kaf?"

"What about them?" Tofan said.

Lakhta started her story:

> When the Chin Kwi Kaf Mountains burst upward from the earth with a barrage of molten ash, caves were formed, some delving down for miles into the depths. In one of these caves there lived a race of bloodthirsty creatures, the Deew Toraban—known familiarly as the Deews. Their only flaw was their inability to survive in the light. If they went outside during the day, they went blind, their minds splintered, and they endured an agonizing death. Their leader, Balaa, a swarthy brute with a heavy black mane and powerful, muscular arms, had a reputation for ferocity far beyond that of any other member of his tribe. He trusted no one, let no one near, and his only companion was an aged vulture named Kajir.

King Balaa was wily and unpredictable, apt to fly off the handle at any given moment, which, of course, meant that in his personal life, he was not happy. He was more than unhappy; he was miserable, but he had no idea why. Although he never discussed his personal affairs with anyone, one day he asked Kajir what the matter was.

"You can tell me, bald head. Why is that I have everything, yet I have nothing? I have strength, yet I'm weaker than an infant. My bed is as cold as a sheet of ice, my waking hours bedeviled with anguish."

"You need a wife," the vulture said, flapping his wings.

"Who do you have in mind? Not some loathsome Deews with her diseased esophagus who takes three hours to devour a chicken." He was referring to Gliza, who was always flirting with him.

"No one in particular," the vulture replied. "But I'll find someone."

"Let me think about it."

Balaa pondered Kajir's remarks, eventually deciding that any sort of venture was better than just pacing back and forth in his cave day and night. "Just remember," Balaa said, "I want one whose heart is light. Find me that someone, Kajir, and you will be handsomely rewarded."

"My greatest reward is but to serve my king."

"Well said."

That same evening, as Balaa watched the vulture fly off, he thought, *We shall see, we shall see.* The truth was, Balaa, for all his posturing, was a lost soul who didn't even know he had one.

Now far below in one of the many nameless villages that dotted the valley, a beautiful girl was born to a family of poverty-stricken farmers. Her name was Ghotul, which means flower of love, and wherever she went, birds flocked around her. They watched over her by day, and when she slept, Qwaing the owl guarded her against evil spirits. Also in this village lived Pari, the oldest and wisest woman in the entire countryside, renowned for her understanding of the language of the birds. When Ghotul turned sixteen, Pari asked each of them to give her a single feather, which she then sewed into a magnificent dress that shimmered when it caught the light. When Ghotul put it on, she was transformed, and like a shooting star that traverses across the empty void of space, a trail of brightness surrounded her.

For poor Balaa the weeks passed slowly, each hour, each minute, hanging heavily on his hands. He was more irascible than ever, and when he caught prey, he tore the carcasses apart with extraordinary ferocity. That summer the sky was a hot-white flame of endless days, with nights that were over almost before they began. He lost count of time, not that it mattered since, when darkness fell, he became hot, restless. Then about the time that Balaa decided the vulture would never return, Kajir reappeared. He immediately cut through Balaa's fury.

"I've found her," he said as he settled down onto his perch with much neck bobbing and fluttering. "She's perfect. A genuine beauty, one for whom great deeds are done, for whom wars are fought."

"You say you've found a great beauty?"

"Such as you rarely find."

"What makes her so beautiful?"

"She has an inner light that shines through her eyes. She's as graceful as a young doe, her hair glistens on the dullest day."

"Enough!"

"I could go on."

"You're a fool."

"I beg your pardon?"

"Tell me this, Kajir. Why would such a treasure want to marry me?"

"The human heart is deep and mysterious."

"What's that supposed to mean, you infernal bird?"

"It means if she chooses not to marry you, you can always throw her to the wolves."

"I could do the same with you. Where exactly is this gem?"

"A few days' journey. An easy trip."

"Ah, so close and yet—so far."

"When shall we leave?" Kajir said.

As Kajir predicted, their journey was uneventful. When they reached the village, he led the way to Ghotul's house, where, noiselessly as only the Deews can be, Balaa slipped in through an open window, cast a spell on the sleeping girl, and carried her away.

Qwaing saw what was happening, but his cries for help went unanswered, other than a neighbor grousing at the noise. Not caring about his own safety, without a moment's hesitation, he flew after them.

The next morning when it was discovered that Ghotul was missing, the villagers raised the alarm. They looked everywhere, but no one could find even a trace of her, not even Pari, who urged everyone to continue searching.

The mystery was solved when Qwaing returned, somewhat worse for wear, and told the villagers what had happened. She's as good as dead, everyone said. A meeting was held during which Uncle Elkh, the wealthiest landowner in the village, offered a generous sum to anyone who could bring her home safely, but the savagery of the Deews was well known, and no one raised his hand. The men were brave; they were not afraid of death in battle or from sickness, but to die at the hands of bloodthirsty maniacs, to be torn apart while still alive—no, it wasn't possible. The silence—compounded of guilt, fear, and anger—was palpable. Finally from the back a voice was heard. "Uh, I'll go."

Everyone turned around.

"What's that?" Uncle Elkh asked.

"I said I'll go!"

"Who's speaking?"

In the back a voice said, "It's me, Uncle. Hawad. I work in your fields and feed your livestock. All I need is a sharp sword and a swift horse, neither of which I own, and I'll be on my way."

"Come closer so I can see who's talking."

"It's me, Hawad," he said, coming forward.

"You? Don't make me laugh. How can you rescue Ghotul? You haven't a dime to your name. Never would I trust you with my priceless sword that has been in my family for generations."

"Don't forget the horse," someone added, accompanied by much snickering.

"It's true I don't own land," Hawad said. "But it is also true that what you eat is the fruit of my labor. Remember, Uncle, poverty's not a crime."

"Neither are false promises."

Everyone began talking at once until Pari pounded her staff. "Quiet," she said. "Come here, boy."

There was a hush in the crowd as he knelt before her while she placed an arm on his shoulder. It was like one flame reflecting the fire of another, and they remained this way for some time.

"I believe you, Hawad. You are honest and trustworthy. Old man, give him your precious sword, which is worthless compared to Ghotul, and a nag with plenty of stamina."

"You must be joking."

"It's either him or no one. Look around you, Uncle Elkh. Count the volunteers."

"Why does everyone call me Uncle Elkh? Whose uncle am I? Although I do come from a distinguished family."

"This is not the time to climb the family tree, Uncle. Save it for later," Pari retorted. "Now as I was saying, give him your best stallion and your sword. And you, boy, hold out your hand." Pari dropped a black oblong stone into his palm. "Make sure you don't lose this. When you rub it, it will start to shine until everything around you turns whiter than snow. In such a bright light, no Deew can survive. But it only lasts a short time, and you only have three chances. Don't forget. Three. So wait for the right moment. Quaing!"

"Yes, Pari." The owl flew over and perched on the arm of her chair.

"You shall be his guide because you know where they took her. But I do not order you, I only ask. This quest will be dangerous, and you might not make it back."

"Of course, I'll lead the way," the owl said and bowed.

"Then it's settled," Pari said. "Uncle Elkh, get the supplies ready. We've no time to lose. Hawad, you will start tomorrow at daybreak."

The next morning, the entire village came out to wish Hawad good luck, and he and Quaing left. Unlike Balaa and Kajir, who were used to rooting around in the dark, the one soaring, the other leaping and climbing, or even Quaing who could fly over the formidable countryside, Hawad's journey was a difficult, time-consuming endeavor. When the terrain became too risky for the horse, Hawad stabled him with some farmers and proceeded by foot.

Now came the most burdensome part of the journey: the ascent of the Chin Kwi Kaf Mountains. Indeed, had it not been for Quaing's directions, Hawad might very well have plummeted to his death. At dawn on the third morning, they reached the adit of Balaa's cave, which, because of an outcropping of jagged rock, had to be entered from above.

So while Quaing kept guard, Hawad climbed up and then dropped lightly down into the cave. It was pitch-black. In fact, it took quite a few moments for his eyes to adjust, during which he took out the black stone, which seemed oscillated in his hand. At first he thought the cave was empty until he heard a sound that sent shivers of fear through him. He found he was only inches away from a huge bird of prey perched on a skull, and the sound he heard was the rustling of its wings as it slept.

There was a doorway-like opening ahead, and Hawad crept through it. He found himself in a smaller cave, almost filled by a gaudy canopied bed that was draped on all four sides so that you couldn't see in. *Aha!* he thought. *The monster must be asleep*. He cautiously lifted a corner of the fabric, tightly gripping the magical stone, but the bed was empty.

Then just as he turned, he felt the breath literally knocked out of him by razor-sharp claws that tore his doublet in two and raked across his flesh. A struggle ensued between Hawad and Kajir, which was only stopped by a voice that reverberated throughout the cave.

"What's going on here!" It was Balaa, and his voice was deep and cold.

Kajir froze, Hawad sprang to his feet, and the only sound was his gasping for air. "I know she's here," he said. "I know that you've imprisoned her. You can't fool me. But you must let her go for you, sir, have no choice." With these words, he held out the black stone, and Balaa instinctively recoiled, throwing his arm in front of his face as if even the sight of it caused his insides to burn.

At that moment, Ghotul stepped out from behind his cloak, surprising Hawad so much, he dropped the black stone, which rattled on the rocky floor and came to rest at his feet. He quickly retrieved it.

"What have you to say for yourself?" she said.

"I have come to rescue you."

"Rescue me? Who says I need rescuing?"

"Pari, all the villagers. Uncle Elkh. Me!"

"You?"

"I."

"What business is it of yours or theirs to interfere in my life? Besides, I have no uncle."

"But you were kidnapped."

"Was I?"

"Have you lost your mind?"

"What if I have? Is it any business of yours?"

"Of course it is."

"And why is that?"

"Because I was sent here to save you."

"Do you really think you can overpower Balaa? Why, he could break your neck with one hand. So why don't you go back where you belong?"

"You think he's so mighty? All I have to do is rub this stone." He held it out for her to see.

"I am not impressed."

"You will be if I rub it."

"I don't think so."

"I do."

"Well then," she said, "rub your little stone."

Hawad hesitated. "What has happened to you? You've changed so. I hardly recognize you."

"You recognized me enough to come here."

"It wasn't necessarily because I recognized you as that I want to kill Balaa and free our valley from his tyranny."

"His tyranny is nothing compared to the small minds who rule your shallow world."

"You make me fear for your sanity."

"Your fear is no match for Balaa's anger," she said. "Or mine. Oh well, we might as well begin our test of wills. If you think you're going to achieve your goal with your magical stone, you've got another think coming."

"You seem anxious for me to destroy Balaa. Even if you profess to be happy here. I know why too. It's the black stone Pari gave me. You're terrified of it."

"Oh, you fool, your stone means nothing. It's useless, a child's toy."

"You're mistaken," Hawad stammered.

Throughout this dispute, Balaa had not said a single word, but his eyes, resting on Ghotul's face, burned with an intensity that made Hawad distinctly uncomfortable. No matter what he wanted to believe, there was such love in them that he averted his own eyes, his confusion becoming stronger by the second. "You've been hypnotized by that monster. You don't know what you're saying."

"That monster you're referring to is my husband. Our child is already growing within my body. I will never leave him, so you see, you've made this long journey for nothing."

As Hawad became more uncertain, he inadvertently rubbed the stone. When he realized this, he stopped immediately, but it was too late. A flame of light leaped from the stone, danced across the floor and walls, and came to rest on Balaa's shield. Hawad braced himself for the imminent explosion. The seconds passed. But nothing happened; it was as Ghotul had predicted. The fiery light bounced harmlessly upon Balaa, proving once and for all that it was simply the kind of magical black rock that could be bought at any novelty shop, the same as millions of other black rocks.

"Give it to me," Ghotul said, holding out her hand.

Reluctantly, Hawad did as she asked, and she in turn gave it to Kajir, who clasped it in his talons.

"Now, Hawad, what are you going to do?" Ghotul said in a friendly tone.

"What do you mean?"

"You poor boy, how can you return to the village? If you tell them the truth, you'll be ridiculed, no one will believe you. They'll think that you're not only a failure but a liar as well."

"I can't stay here."

"Why not? You are one of us now. More than you think. Don't stand there with your mouth open. No one is going to harm you."

"But Balaa's a…a… He's a killer."

"Is he? You and Pari, my so-called uncle, all the other villagers, including my family, are living in a world of illusion. Of daydreams, of fantasies. While my husband and his band of Deews have always lived in the real world. That's why they appear so ugly and ravenous to you. Once I was one of you. I too lived in a dream world. Until Balaa rescued me. Is that so hard to understand?"

"What are you saying?"

"I am saying that reality is greater than black stones and riddles, than imaginary creatures howling in a void of your own making."

"I must go back."

"Suit yourself. But at least dine with us, spend the night in our guest room. You look exhausted. And tell your owl friend Quaing to join us. I'm sure that he and Kajir have much to talk about. Then in the morning we can show you an easier route by which to return as well as plenty of supplies."

"Why would you do that?"

"If you have to ask, you will never hear the true answer."

More riddles, Hawad thought.

The next morning, refreshed and with their stomachs full, our two weary adventurers took their leave and made their way home. "Ah, Quaing," Hawad said to the owl as they reached the outskirts of the village. "Ghotul's right, no one's going to believe us. But how can we lie and say our journey was a failure?"

Hawad was too honest to make up some fable, but when he explained that Ghotul and Balaa were man and wife, everyone reviled him, especially Pari, who said he had failed in his mission and was making up some cockamamie excuse. She banished both Hawad and Quaing from the village and soon afterward shriveled up and died, a lonely old ghost. The man and the bird left the village where they were born, and where they went, no one knew.

Ghotul bore many offspring whose descendants gradually multiplied ten times over, beings whose soul was either beast or human, depending on how they were perceived, and from these descendants the human race was born. Ghotul taught Balaa that he had nothing to fear from the sun, and soon he and the other Deews began leaving their caves whenever they wanted with absolutely no harmful consequences. Ghotul and Balaa lived to a ripe old age, and when they died, the entire community of Deews as well as of villagers mourned their passing.

> The moral of this story is everyone creates his own prison. Or his own garden. And just as imaginary gardens can have real flowers, so can there be living inhabitants in imaginary prisons.

"But how could Ghotul fall in love with such a monster?" Tofan said. "That's ridiculous."

"Ridiculous? It's the whole point of the story," Lakhta said. "Balaa wasn't really a monster. It's just that everyone thought he was, including himself. But when Ghotul fell in love with him, she saw a tall, handsome, dark-eyed prince."

"But how could she see a prince if the creature was actually a monster?"

"Are you listening to me? The point is that we create what we see from our own minds. In her mind, he was a good-looking prince."

"Oh. A prince, yeah right."

"Wait a minute," Khialo said. "Are you telling us that no one has an identity of their own, that everything exists in someone's mind? But if the monster wasn't a monster, what do you call someone who lives in a cave, doesn't go out during the day, and spends every night killing anything that walks or crawls?"

"What do you think?" Lakhta said.

"I'll tell you what I think. I think the monster was a monster, and Ghotul should have had her head examined."

"You have no imagination," Tofan said to Khialo.

"At least I understand the story."

"I'm not so sure," Tofan said. "I mean, I see it differently. I think that Balaa existed in a state of potential and that how others saw him and how he saw himself determined whether he'd be a demon or a good guy. That's what I think."

"What is a state of potential?" Khialo asked.

"I think I know," I said. "Let's say you're inside a room with no windows and someone unlocks the door. Well, if the person who unlocks the door thinks you're a monster, you'll come out a monster. But if he thinks you're a handsome prince, well, you'll come out a handsome prince."

"That is patently ridiculous."

"Quit being such a wise guy," I said.

"Now, no fights, you boys. The point is the story's a riddle. It has many interpretations. It's supposed to make you think, to question things. Life is the same way. It asks you to question everything. Don't believe what someone says, not unless you can feel it in your heart and your mind. Well, dear ones, I am going to make a curry sauce with some of the tomatoes. So I can't stay here gabbing with you. For me, enough of fairy tales and back to reality."

We never did come to any conclusion. Khialo was as stubborn as a mule, and Tofan soon got lost in his own maze of explanations. When we parted, we were no longer speaking to each other, but the energy felt good. It occurred to me that this had been Lakhta's plan all along, to get us out of the doldrums.

The following morning, Khialo dropped by, and we went to the Ashrat Kala garden to pick mulberries for Moor and Lakhta, who were planning on baking pies with that thick buttery crust that melted in your mouth. Running through the garden was a shallow fast-running stream that angled its way to join the Auzingianai. We took off our sandals and waded across, climbing up the shallow bank where the air was redolent with the scent of newly-grown grass along with the musty bark of the acacias. It was as if the earth had awakened from a dream or I had along with the miniature fish darting around the rocks in the fast-running river. Or the spider struggling to spin its web, which had been torn in places and was fluttering so that each time it tried, it fell downward. I watched intently, keeping perfectly still because when I made the slightest movement, the web trembled, and the spider froze.

Khialo grabbed hold of the branch of a tree, hoisting himself up and doing chin-ups before dropping to the ground, turning a somersault, and springing to his feet, making boxing movements. Nearby were the mulberry shrubs, a profusion of them, and we started picking the berries and eating them by the handful with Khialo saying we'd better be careful, or we'd get the heebie-jeebies. He was such a worrier, just like his brother Droon. Now, if Azmoon had come, he'd have gobbled up as many as he could without a care in the world.

On the way back, we heard what we mistook for thunder but whose tempo became louder and more distinct until we realized it was the sound of drums. Apparently, some kind of dance was going on or a celebration, maybe a wedding, although that seemed improbable for certainly we'd have heard about it. It was coming from the Srakala side of the garden, and we turned in that direction. We emerged from the shelter of the trees at about the same time that columns of villagers came pouring toward the road to Shabak; they came from all directions—from Minkhill, from Nawar, from Gari in the south, and from the bare and barren hills to the east, hundreds and hundreds of people led by musicians beating double-sided Afghan drums and playing *surnai* flutes.

Men and women, each in separate groups, were performing the Attan, moving in slow sensual circles and waving multicolored flags as they spun around with arms raised while others cried out, "Achariar, achariar!" Some of the men carried World War I British rifles, some had long knives, others had shovels, axes, and hammers. There were women of various ages decked out in festive holiday attire and children running all over the place. Wide planks had been set up over the Auzingianai, shallow enough in some places for people to wade across. They were heading toward the main road south of the garden that led to the hospital and then to the Communist District Office.

We raced toward them, and when we reached their ranks, I asked an old man what was happening, but what he said made no sense to me. He started laughing like a crazy person, shouting that we were going to take back our country, beginning with the Wlaswali. His expression was rapturous as he whirled away from us with his caftan billowing out around him.

More villagers were arriving by the moment, many of my friends from school as well as neighbors. Catching sight of Atal and Droon, we both called out to them, but they were too far away to hear before being swallowed by the crowd. As the tempo of the music increased, the dancing grew wilder, becoming an unruly expression of years of pent-up emotions, the singing raucous, harsh, accompanied by the clapping of many hands. At first Khialo and I had been on the fringes, but soon we were enmeshed by the rapidly growing mob. We were swept along as if we'd been caught in the throes of a body that had no head but was an elemental eruption that existed regardless of consequence or purpose.

We had just reached the section of the road that wound past the southwestern edge of the garden when we saw the helicopters, three of them, followed by three jet fighters, one in front flanked by two behind. There was a stutter of rapid gunfire exploding with plumes of black smoke that flew into the sky. A whistling noise, another dull heavy explosion that shattered the ground, throwing up piles of rubble and debris. Again and again. The smoke cleared to reveal tanks with artillery guns coming directly toward us from the district office and shelling the ground with great spurts of fire. As the tanks fired in their direction, those in front stopped so suddenly they were knocked to the ground by those who'd been following. The earth shook with more rounds of ammunition being fired. When this happened, people began running way, with voices crying out, "Hide yourself! Hide yourself!"

Then more bombing, blast on blast, helicopters flying low amid the rattle of their machine guns, fire, mayhem, everyone searching for cover where there was no cover. No cover and no relief. The noise was impossible. You couldn't hear yourself think. The earth was blowing up around us. Terrified wails. Crying. The dispersal of the mob, people shoving each other out of the way, women crying for their children.

I motioned for Khialo to follow me, and we zigzagged back to the garden, expecting any moment to be blown to kingdom come, in a world that was exploding around us. It was too dangerous to keep running, and we piled under the low-hanging branches of a pomegranate tree that was surrounded by thorn bushes abutting a low shelf of rocks. At that moment, there was a huge explosion, much greater than any that had come before, so jarring it made my jaws ache, and the ground shivered under us. The noise was unbelievable; the earth around us convulsed, covering us with debris. Then another explosion followed on its heels and another, more fires raging out of control and pandemonium, people shouting, helicopters buzzing like gigantic hornets, the jets, the whistling sounds of rockets, the spitting upheaval of earth. Nothing but black smoke and dust and fire. Fire making our eyes tear. A saddled but riderless horse galloping past us. The howls of frightened children.

A tongue of fire shot up nearby with a roar; trees that'd been here for a hundred years burst into a million pieces with branches, boughs, and limbs crashing around us. We dug wildly so that we could insinuate ourselves farther beneath the rocky shelf, ducking down as best we could. We were in a holocaust, and everybody was going to get killed. Hours, days, years, broken promises, words unspoken or spoken. I'd been born here, would die here. It would never end because it never began. One moment so cold, my teeth chattered, the next sweating inside my clothes, unable to stop shaking. We remained immobilized with our arms between our legs, with nothing between us and what was going on except for the rocks, some twisted branches that scratched us whenever we moved, and a sorry pomegranate tree pendulous with unripened fruit, its branches hanging low to the ground. Khialo said something, but I couldn't make out what he was saying. Fiery branches were flying around us. No, it was too much. We were dead. This was death's kingdom. This was hell. Mind, soul, body, thoughts on fire.

Then it was over, but in a silence more ominous than the noise of the bombing; the only sound recognizable was my heart pounding in my chest. As sudden as it had begun. At first, we couldn't believe it. My body was tensed, waiting for the next onslaught. But the bombs were spent, the guns were silent, the air was thick with acrid smog, the odor of burning gunpowder, but nobody there—no corpses, no voices, no birds chattering. My teeth were chattering. I forced myself to take deep breaths. It wouldn't help matters if I passed out. I parted a branch, but all I saw was a thick wall of black smoke that burned my eyes.

We waited for what seemed like hours but was probably only a short time. When it remained still, Khialo and I gingerly stepped out from our hiding place. At first we didn't know what to do. No one was around; the road to Shabak was empty. *What had happened to all the people?* I wondered. We decided to separate; he would go back to Srakala and I to Shabak. If there were any problems with his family, he would come to my house, and if mine were hurt, I was to wait for him.

But when I reached our house, it was still standing in one piece, and I could see my family out front. My clothes were torn and stained, and I thought Moor would kill me, but the moment she saw me, she hugged me as hard as she could. When she stepped back though, she cried out that there was blood all over my face and head. I touched my cheek. It was sticky, and when I saw that my fingers were red, my legs buckled under me. If Jandol hadn't caught me, I'd have fallen. You can imagine our surprise when we realized it wasn't blood but juice from the mulberries.

Jandol told us later that villagers had decided to take over the District Compound in Shabak, which they insisted upon calling the Wlaswali, thinking it'd be a cinch. Why they thought so, he had no idea. "Well, probably they didn't think it through," he said. "They just followed their feelings. No organization, just spontaneous combustion, and most telling, no leaders, simply angry voices, loud and impassioned, resulting in an uprising with no brains behind it, less than useless. What were they planning to do, hold hands and dance around the community office?"

The next day, the district governor called a meeting with the village elders that was held in our hujra. He arrived two hours late accompanied by his personal bodyguards. Without any preamble, he said that his intention with this show of strength had been to frighten us but not to harm anyone, merely a warning that if any disturbances like that ever occurred again, it would be a different story altogether. He reminded us that one tank was capable of leveling every village within a fifty-mile radius. He didn't speak for more than fifteen minutes, answered no questions, and concluded by saying, "Remember, we can crush you in our fists without even dirtying our fingers. Every one of you. Every home, every mosque. Don't make us do it. Good day." A real charmer.

After he left, the elders and many of the villagers stayed behind, their talk going on through the night, the result of which was that they concluded it was best not to antagonize them, at least not until we had our own tanks and our own ammunition. *What geniuses*, I thought when I heard about it on the following day.

But that was what we did. We waited, trying to ignore the rumors that sprang up since no one knew what was real and what was made-up. I kept a low profile, particularly in school, although Jandol said more than once that it was impossible with things the way they were to come out shining, no matter how hard you scrubbed. Here we'd hoped to escape the turmoil by returning to Shabak and instead found ourselves going from the fire into the frying pan. At least in Kabul, we could have hidden ourselves among the millions of inhabitants as the population nearly doubled after the Soviet invasion. But here, such anonymity was impossible. As of now, the Soviets ran the government, the schools, the districts, the police—everything was in their hands. They'd fanned out across the countryside and were everywhere and knew everything thanks to their vast system of spies. In the meantime, we were left in a country that had been conquered by forces who neither spoke our language nor knew anything about our culture, nor cared either. Our lives would be on hold as long as they remained. Make plans? Impossible. Do something productive? Yeah, sure. What? So when our elders bid us to wait, we had no choice but to do what they recommended, even if we weren't sure what we were waiting for. Well, that wasn't true. We were waiting for a miracle. We were waiting for those millions of sparks that still lit our individual souls to combine into a conflagration.

Unbelievably, in the near future, such a firestorm would be unleashed, one that became impossible to control, one that threatened to destroy the very existence it had come to protect in a way the Russians could only dream of. This was made possible because they came from within our ranks whereas the Soviets were foreigners. I'm talking about the Mujahideen and later the Taliban.

If the Soviets might push Afghanistan into the future, the Mujahideen (transfundamentalist fighters, jihadists) would do the opposite and take it back to the past. Born out of the upheaval of feuding Afghan warlords, the various bands of the Mujahideen were formed to defeat the Soviets. Many of these bands were made up of trained guerillas who had fled when the Communists invaded and wound up in refugee camps in Pakhtunistan, Pakistan, and Iran. Officers from the Pakistani ISI and the Iranian QUDS recruited them and brought them to their respective countries to be indoctrinated in the strategies of combat. Led by warlords and *mavlavis* who themselves had been carefully handpicked by the ISI and QUDS and with their forces increased exponentially by Muslims from other nations, the Mujahideen factions were organized as well as armed with the latest weaponry, although the different groups remained highly divisive.

One of the main objectives of Mujahideen forces in our part of the country was to block the Jalalabad-Kabul highway and lay siege to both cities. To accomplish this, they set up mountain camps in the Hisarak District, which meant that they were continually crossing back and forth through Shabak and Srakala. And as the attacks of the Mujahideen increased in intensity, with month after month of persistent assaults, the Soviets realized that they could neither dislodge them nor overcome their guerrilla tactics. Although pitched battles would continue throughout the countryside for years to come, the Russians withdrew their forces to the larger cities, and Kabul became the de facto center of the Communist government.

With the Mujahideen causing serious casualties to the Soviets, which made the cost of the war prohibitive, in 1989, they withdrew from Afghanistan, at which time Najibullah was overthrown. However, the different groups of the Mujahideen were unable to establish a united government, and after years of devastation, a village mullah named Mohammed Omar organized a new armed movement with the backing of Pakistan. This movement became known as the Taliban, the Arabic word for "student," which refers to the Saudi-backed religious schools known for inculcating extremism in its students. In 1996, the Taliban seized power.

CHAPTER FOUR

They say you can get used to anything. Maybe they're right. Maybe they never had to. Machine guns, cannons, fire, helicopters, jets, soldiers pursuing each other down village roads, sometimes passing so close their hurried footsteps matched your heartbeat, their commands seeming to come from your own lips. Then waves of black-goggled Communists in Humvees hurtling past, escorted by tanks, and not a day going by that you don't hear about some new atrocity, each worse than the last: rapes, executions, families slaughtered, this from both sides, the Soviets and the ever-increasing presence of the Mujahideen. Uncertainty and fear—these were our companions, even hope, for impossibly, days even weeks went by when everything was peaceful, and we were able to return to a semblance of normality. It was during such periods that we began to wonder if both armies had come to some sort of truce. Oh, but that was impossible. How could they have?

The seasons that year were equally unsettled, and when spring came, the sky was blanketed by silver-gray clouds, sometimes in dense formations, sometimes in delicate tendrils strung out like smoke from a distant fire. On those rare occasions when the sun broke through with momentary warmth, I'd take long walks with Lakhta's son Baz, who loved to go exploring, as he called it. He tried to keep up with me, meanwhile asking me a million unanswerable questions. My favorite time to take such hikes was right after a storm when the light cast on the fields gave depth to each stalk of wheat, and in the crystal clear gusts of wind, the desert was like an ocean of sand. At such times I could feel nature burgeoning with new life until the sun sank and darkness shrouded the countryside, whereupon it felt like something were dying, as if the Auzingianai, with its murky water, were reaching out to draw me in, those phantoms of the river Gulapa warned us about, ready to cradle me in their frozen embrace. Still, despite such ideas, I continued to make plans.

I couldn't just give up. I couldn't be like some of the village women who went around in black and told everyone they were in mourning for the lives that had been taken. Nor could my family simply leave everything behind as many did and move away, turning Shabak and Srakala into ghosts.

I remember one warm flower-scented evening in June with a full moon turning the earth into a lunar landscape almost as clear as day. The comforting sounds of village life were coming through our open windows, dogs barking, women talking, children playing soccer, their shrieks of laughter or anger piercing the soft breath of the impending night. We'd just finished eating and were resting in that space separating the busy furor of the day from that of withdrawal and sleep. Meena was carrying a handful of plates into the kitchen when a sudden silence fell. I'd placed a book I was reading on the window ledge, and on a swift draft, the pages began fluttering, but before I could move it away, there came a whistling sound followed by an explosion that rocked out house to the very foundations, I thought it was going to come crashing down around us. I hadn't even time to pull my hand back. Meena swerved toward us, and the dishes smashed on the floor, and she ran over to Moor.

Eyes wide with anxiety, bodies taut, minds on fire with questions, we looked at each other. More whistling, bombs exploding around us, a never-ending dance, the end of the world, of our world. Abba pulled me away from the window and motioned for us to sit on the cot in the living room, farthest from the windows. There was nowhere else to go since we had no basement. Jandol and Sial closed the shutters, and Lakhta raced inside, pulling Baz after her. We tried to maintain self-control in the face of the explosions from the guns, sweeping fires that came flying toward us, a barrage much greater than anything I'd ever experienced, the vibration so powerful, our house was inundated by flying debris, our windows shook under the impact, and the one in the kitchen shattered. In a moment of silence, I heard scratching at the back door and opened it a crack. It was Mamar. I let him in, and he jumped on me and almost knocked me over. I petted him, but he continued pacing in circles. Jandol was sitting in between me and Sial, and he put his arms around our shoulders. When the bombardment grew heavier, he pulled us toward him, and his heart was pounding. On and on, the tanks with their guns answered by machine-gun fire, the rapid stutter of machine guns followed by more shelling, an endless courtship that continued throughout that night, hour after hour, minute upon minute, a night in which time stood still. The reverberations kept blowing our candles out, and the only illumination came from a small kerosene lamp whose leaping fire was also threatened. The noise was so terrific conversation was impossible. I just wanted to run away somewhere safe, but there was nowhere to run to, no escape, no way out of this. We were trapped, and whether we lived or were blown to bits was based on luck; nothing but luck could protect us. Funny, when you thought about it, all the money and time and power and fear wrapped up in religion, but when push came to shove, it was only luck that could save you, and luck was nothing to rely on. Luck was too capricious.

The hours stuck to us like glue. You'd glance at your watch, but the hands wouldn't move. I don't know how long we stayed there. My stomach hurt, and I needed to pee. I made my way to the bathroom on shaky legs and had to hold on to the wall. I returned to my place on the cot breathlessly, as if I'd run up a flight of stairs. I lost track of time. Everything was a blur.

I must have fallen asleep because I struggled up from a suffocating darkness into a world of absolute quiet. It was getting light. What was going on? Who won this battle? We kept waiting for it to recommence, but after a while, we cautiously stepped outside to find our neighbors doing the same, what neighbors we still had, what with the number of evacuees. Word came that the Mujahideen had razed the district compound and that the Soviets had attacked in force but had been forced to retreat. Astonishing news that the Russians with their firepower had lost such an important clash of arms.

A group of villagers made their way over to the compound to find nothing left but rubble. The school and the hospital were also damaged in places, their walls charred, most of the windows broken, but they were still left standing. Our relief was short-lived, however, because a few weeks later, both buildings were burned to the ground by extremists among the ranks of the Mujahideen, who were themselves pretty extreme. To add to the carnage, the Communist district governor and his brother were stoned to death, their unburied bodies left exposed to the indifferent eye of the hot summer sun.

Within the next week, great numbers of the Mujahideen began arriving, singly, in groups, by foot, by horse, our victors, our saviors, until both Shabak and Srakala were overflowing, and the surplus continued on to Minkhill and Nawar. They marched through our villages, firing their rifles into the air, and shouting for the glory of Allah. "Allah-Hoo-Akbar, Allah-Hoo-Akbar, Allah-Hoo-Akbar! God is great! God is great! God is great!" They set up camp in our hujra and in the surrounding fields, men of different countries who spoke different languages, their conversations carried to us by the still night air. European and American photojournalists sometimes accompanied the fighters, and once, one of them took a picture of me and Khialo and promised he would send us copies.

Every village was taken over by a different warlord, ours setting up his headquarters in a vacated house across the road from where we lived. It didn't take us long to realize that we were merely pawns in a game in which our lives meant very little to either side. Instead of the Communists, it was the Mujahideen who'd knock on your door in the middle of the night. They'd read a quotation from the Quran, accuse you of being an infidel, and either arrest you or leave your body hanging from a tree, in either case grabbing every possession you owned. Brutal laws were enacted, rules, regulations; every day another was announced until you lost track. You couldn't listen to music, you couldn't dance, you dared not laugh. Women couldn't go outside unless they were accompanied by a male family member or a husband. They had to wear burkas lest they arouse an animal sexual heat in men. Every male had to attend religious services five times a day. The punishment was swift to those who failed to follow orders. Death. No questions asked. Two women from Kabul University who'd come home on holiday to Ragha, which wasn't too far from Shabak, were seen by the Mujahideen walking arm in arm. They were arrested and stoned to death.

In addition to the majority of the Mujahideen being cruel, we soon discovered they were greedy as hell and stupid to boot. Let's say the warlord of your village sent someone to your house to collect a religious tax. The next day another warlord from another village might send someone else to collect the same tax. You couldn't tell them you already paid. They'd say, "Paid who? Not to me." How could you respond to such polemics?

Even Sial and Meena kept their mouths shut. Gulapa told us that a bunch of them came to her house looking for valuables.

Atal tried to intervene, but she said to let them. Maybe they'll find their God. Sial said that their God was in our wallets, but she said, "In my house? You've got to be kidding. The only valuables I have are in between my legs," to which Bibi replied that Gulapa had no more sense than a rabbit.

Rumors sprang up about a man with no first name, known only as the Major. Villagers feared him. He was famously quoted as saying that he was very compassionate. "I would be sincerely sorry if my neighbor's children were torn apart by wolves." Some said he was a spy, others that he had been about to be executed when the Communists invaded and freed him, while still others maintained that he had been with the insurgents who captured a squad of Communist soldiers in the Tummanai Mountains and executed all of them. This when he was an unknown foot soldier. Once we saw him in person ambling around Shabak, a trim, neat martinet with a thin moustache, trim beard, and short hair combed straight back from his narrow forehead. We never did find out was his name was, only that he was from Lahore, or so people said. Others maintained he was born in Multan. Who knew. Maybe he was from Timbuktu?

The exploitation going on was brought home to me in a personal way. Khialo and I were at the bazaar when we heard angry voices. A couple of mullahs in white robes, their beards sprouting from their faces like porcupine quills, were reviling a shopkeeper over the price of a bag of rice. We joined a gathering of spectators who were observing the contretemps. The shopkeeper kept nodding his head, pressing his palms together, and pleading with the mullahs. He was a poor man, an old man; he had to make a little profit in order to feed his grandchildren whose father had died fighting the Soviets. In the middle of this, one of the mullahs lifted up the fifty-pound bag of rice and threw it at the man, knocking him to the ground. The other one pulled out a pistol and fired three shots directly into the bag, after which they sauntered off. Except for me and Khialo, the rest of the crowd dispersed as well. The show was over. God must have been on the shopkeeper's side because the bag of rice had saved him. We helped him to his feet, but he hardly paid any attention to us; he was too plagued with the fear that they'd come back and arrest him. What was he going to do? Who'd take care of his family? Arrest him for what? I said. For trying to cheat God. That's what they said, that he was trying to cheat God. I didn't know who I disliked more: those two bullies or this craven old man begging for his life. One thing became crystal clear though: all of us, me included, were only one step away from disaster, one that could occur at any time and for no discernible reason.

I was growing up, beginning to understand the meaning of my experiences, my bouncing thoughts less apt to bleed into each other like a madras shirt left out in the rain. I grew taller; my voice changed and, in moments of excitement, was apt to crack. Even though there was no school, one of the few pleasures for which I thanked the Mujahideen, I did more reading on my own than I ever had in class, choosing what I wanted from Abba's extensive library, predominately the works of various Pashto poets as well as Afghan history and books about plants and wildlife. I was also teaching Baz to read and write. Eight years old and smart as a whip, he reminded me of Khialo at that age, but my teaching skills were not the greatest, given that I still knew very little, if anything, about the world at large. Much of my knowledge was like the ellipses in a quotation, where you never knew if what was left out contradicted the meaning of what was revealed.

As the ellipses began to be filled in, I realized though that I was leaving my childhood behind, that I had to forget about childish things and learn to act like a man, to view the world for what it was, the good with the bad, and to make my decisions based on that knowledge. A way of life that had existed for centuries was being brought to an abrupt disastrous halt, and it was up to me whether I'd forever mourn its passing or plan for the future. But it wasn't in my nature to cry over the past, and

I recalled what Jandol once said about how we were living like our ancestors, how we needed to move with the times. Well, I decided that's what I'd do, but I'd always remember the charm of village life, of our sense of community, whether it came to birth, death, sickness, marriage; of the soft summer air and the rains that came in spring; holding a newly born calf in my hands; riding my horse across a desert waste that stretched away in every direction. How, when it snowed, Khialo and I would make sleds from scraps of lumber and toboggan down the steep slopes that surrounded Srakala. The afternoon when Russian military helicopters appeared, and the sky turned bright red. They were dropping thousands of flyers printed on red paper that said "Join the revolution! Support freedom!" Khialo and I raced after the flyers and gathered as many as we could until the choppers disappeared. Gulapa said they were flowers for the dead, that our village was a corpse covered with red flowers.

"Don't forget the snakes from Pakistan," Droon said.

"Or the scorpions from Iran," Azmoon added.

"What's got you two so riled up?" Sial said.

"Red poppies falling from the sky!" I shouted.

"Well, keep it down. I'm trying to read."

"You and those stupid movie magazines," Meena said.

"Children, children," Bibi said. She was knitting a jacket for me and asked me to stick out my arm so she could measure me. I asked her when it would be ready, and she said before winter. "What year?" I asked. I knew I'd be lucky to be alive by the time she finished.

I would always remain scornful of the village elders and their flocks who continued to gather in our hujra because it was always the same—that though this was no way to live, we still had to wait. And the arguments—that the West was sticking their nose in our affairs; that it was the Red Army; that it was Pakistan and Arab oil; that it was religion and God and Iran sniffing around; that it was atheism and what came with it; that we were surrounded by our enemies but were not yet ready to fight them; that we might as well accept conditions, that they were sure to change, to improve. I didn't want to listen to whining old men. I wanted to be inspired, to hear words of hope, of optimism. But wherever I turned, it was the same.

Afghanistan was being ravaged by men with dirty, matted beards, men with low foreheads and missing fingers who took our pulse with an AK-47, men who left us hopeless and in despair, even if we referred to the Mujahideen as holy warriors. One time a group of them were encased in a cloud of chars with its unmistakable odor. They were weaving across the road, snickering, pounding each other on the back, calling each other brother. Khialo and I were following them when Droon blocked our way, herding us into a courtyard and closing the gate.

"Are you guys crazy?" he said. "Do you want to be get shot?"

"Nobody's going to shoot us," I said.

"We're just having some fun," Khialo said.

"Well, those guys have a limited sense of humor."

"We're not doing anything to them," Khialo said.

"That's what the flea thinks when it bites the dog."

"Huh?"

"They're parasites, little bro, with sharp incisors."

"Well, if that's the case, why doesn't somebody get some flea powder?" I said.

"We might poison ourselves by mistake," Droon said.

"I'm serious," Khialo said. "When will we be able to live a normal life?"

"*Inshallah.* When God wills."

"And when will that be?"

"Who can say?"

"Well," I said, "I for one am not going to spend my entire life being kicked around like a soccer ball."

"One of these days you're going to have to learn to accept reality," Droon said.

"One of these days you're going to have to learn to mind your own business."

Yes, I would always remember those days, but I wouldn't leave my heart among the fading embers of a fire that had been stamped out. I wasn't sure if it were a strength or an inability, but I knew I wouldn't or couldn't. With that knowledge came the springing forth of my rebellious nature, a part of my personality I hadn't been aware of until recently, but definitely a part that had been growing stronger until it boiled over. This resulted in my speaking my mind, and the more I did, the surer I became. It was not my role to keep my mouth shut or to try to ameliorate conflict. It was my role to cut through all the tangles and discover a clear way to the truth of a situation. I certainly wouldn't egg my fellow man on to acts of stupidity the way that Sial often did—he seemed to get great pleasure out it—since I'm basically an easygoing, accepting guy. But on the other hand, I wouldn't simply absorb what I was being fed without first examining the contents. To swallow ideas without understanding them was really no different than my peers who allowed themselves to be brainwashed by fools and fanatics.

The path, gently descending through gnarled trees, past prickly briers that caught at your clothes, dropped sharply toward the riverbank, leading to the sheltered area where we'd planted the pomegranate trees. As Droon strode forward, he slipped on some damp leaves and would have fallen had Azmoon not caught him by the arm. I held on to different branches, sliding forward from the shade into the sunlight, the contrast always so startling. There was no one around, which made it feel as if you were on your own private island. Our trees had survived bombings, floods, droughts, and their flowers were about to unfold. I couldn't wait until autumn when the pomegranates would be ready to be picked. The first yield. Something I had planted with my own hands from the twigs of a tree.

"We're going to have a great crop," I said.

"If there's no spring floods," Droon said.

"There are always floods," Azmoon said.

"Maybe we'll have a drought," I said.

"Maybe," Droon said. "Anything is possible."

"Better a drought than a storm," Azmoon said. "It's the rain that kills them."

"Yeah, it's the rain that does it."

"Too much rain, and you might as well hand in the towel."

"The trowel, did you say?"

"Whatever."

"Well, they look healthy to me," I said.

"We just have to wait," Droon said.

"Yes, we'll have to wait," Azmoon said. "You can never tell."

"It's better not to plan. Just to go with the flow, as they say."

"It won't be long. You'll see."

I decided that when it was warmer, I was going to come here with my notebook. Perhaps my poems that came to life on the page would be as wild as the pomegranates growing among the brambles. The thorns were sharp, but my poetry would pierce not the skin but the soul. A harsh cry, the words distorted by a megaphone, shattered the glassine-like air. It was time for afternoon prayers, attendance at which was now being rigorously enforced by our new masters upon pain of imprisonment or even death. On the road that led to the Shabak mosque, we ran into Tofan at the same time that a company of insurgents appeared in mufti with backpacks and PK machine guns. About forty or so, two abreast, leaderless, like two pythons with no head. Instead of taking the road though, they were snaking through a field of tomatoes that were just beginning to appear on the vines, tiny red sparks of life being heedlessly snuffed out.

"Hey, look what they're doing," I said. "They're killing everything."

"Forget it," Azmoon said. "There are worse injustices."

"Azmoon's right," Droon said. "You don't want to get in trouble."

"You guys give me the creeps."

"Better us than them. It's much safer that way," Azmoon said.

"Come on, Tofan," I said, walking ahead and pulling him after me. "We'll be late."

Everyone was already seated, and we took our places in the last row just as Mullah Kadoo began the service. I followed by rote, my mind still on those pomegranates, how they'd be delicious, maybe even seedless, how I'd cut them open and the juice would trickle down my chin. Moor would say, "Be careful, you'll stain your shirt." I envisioned Atal's delicious tomatoes, with the skin so taut when you bit into one, the juice squirted into your mouth as sweet as an apple. That had been long ago. The towers of the fort beneath which he'd planted his vines had been strafed by the Russians, leaving rubble everywhere. Atal's garden had been demolished, and though he kept promising he'd plant another, so far he hadn't.

"That guy is a God machine," I said outside the mosque after prayers were over.

"Just think," Jandol said, "Kadoo, who used to be thankful for our leftovers, now rules the roost. Isn't life amazing?"

"Don't forget the Major," Droon said.

"The whole world's upside down," Azmoon said. "It's crazy."

"Who's the Major?" Khialo asked.

"Oh, another prince of darkness," Droon said. "They say he's a Paki spy."

"What's he got to do with Kadoo?"

"Birds of a feather," Azmoon said.

"Pooping on our heads," Droon said. "That's what they have in common."

"Except the Major shits bullets," Jandol said. "And Kadoo's just an old windbag."

"With an answer for everything," Azmoon said.

"You guys have it wrong," Tofan said. "About Kadoo, I mean."

"How's that?" asked Droon.

"He's a seeker after wisdom, and his speech reflects that… search," Tofan said. "They remain in your memory long after the events they describe are forgotten."

"What events?" I said.

"You know."

"How can I when he talks out of both sides of his mouth?"

"In other words, what he says has no relation to any event," Jandol said.

"Other than the ones in his head, you mean," Droon said.

"I see you like to hear yourselves talk," Tofan said.

"If there were no words," Azmoon said, "where would we be?"

"Our meaningless lives would be meaningless," I said. "Chaos would reign."

"It already does," Tofan said.

"Maybe we shouldn't talk," Sial said. "Maybe we should growl at each other like tigers."

"As if you didn't do that already," Tofan said wearily. "That's why Mullah Kadoo's voice is so significant, why his words are so transcendental, so luminous."

"Tofan, what's gotten into you?" I said, "You're beginning to sound weird."

"He always sounds weird," Sial said under his breath.

"Nothing's gotten into me," Tofan replied, studiedly ignoring Sial. "It's the other way around."

"How's that?"

"It comes out of me."

"It comes out of you?"

"How can anyone know what to believe unless it comes from inside?" Tofan said. "I mean it."

"You're wise beyond your years," Droon said.

"He's wise beyond our years," Azmoon said. "A paragon of virtue."

"I wish that were true," Tofan said, resting his eyes on Abba, who'd been talking to Atal and had just joined our circle. "Yesterday, there was a *mavlavi* at the mosque. From Dewbandi. We talked for hours."

"You spent hours talking to a *mavlavi*?" Sial said.

"Quiet, son, let Tofan finish," Abba said.

"When this man spoke, I felt a chill run down my body. It was like he knew exactly what I was thinking and feeling. He knew that I wanted to believe but that I couldn't, that everything inside me had died when my father abandoned my mother and me and turned us into vagrants, scratching the walls for a living. He said that God understood how I felt. That He had a special place in His heart for those who suffer."

"He must have a big heart," Droon said.

"Even if it's the size of a soccer field, it couldn't fit everyone inside," I said. "Not in a million years."

"He said that if I open myself to God, then anything is possible. I asked him how he could be so certain, and he told me to read the Holy Quran, not with my eyes but with my heart. He spoke about the Archangel Gabriel who visited Mohammad, peace be upon him, in the cave at Hera, of how the Prophet couldn't read or write but was able to memorize Gabriel's message and transcribe the Holy Quran."

"But certainly you've heard this story before," Azmoon said.

"It doesn't matter. It was as if I were hearing it for the first time. What I mean is, he brought it to life for me. He made me see the how the Prophet's soul was consumed by love, that the Archangel Gabriel was a being of light like the swirl of an ocean wave upon a depthless sea."

"This is getting too deep for me," Sial said.

"Sial, enough," Abba warned.

Tofan smiled gratefully at Abba and said, "Everything I've been taught has been erased like chalk from a blackboard. I see a different direction to take, one where I can learn to forgive, where I can once again feel I have a past and a future. With this *mavlavi*, I felt the presence of something outside myself, something greater than I am."

"You'd better make sure and keep one eye on his hands," Sial said.

"His hands?" Tofan said. "What's this, Sial, another of your jokes? Do you ever take anything seriously?"

"I take the ruination of my life seriously."

"The *mavlavi* said that we create our own problems by falling under the spell of infidels, that we're weak and lazy."

"Why is everything always our fault?" Droon said. "Does no one else ever accept any of the blame?"

"I'm simply telling you what he said. That the infidels must be punished so that we can cleanse our souls and take God into our lives."

"The *mavlavi* sounds like a real gem," Droon said. "Actually, Jandol, the guy sounds like you. Isn't that what you think, that we're weak and lazy?"

"I never said we're weak and lazy. I said we're blind and deaf."

"The truth is, we are blind and deaf and weak and lazy," Tofan said. "But it's not our fault. We have lost contact with God."

"This *mavlavi*, of course, knows what we need to do," I said.

"Anyway, he recommended some books for me to read, but they were in Arabic. I asked him if he had any in Pashto, and he said he didn't, but that he'd teach me Arabic. He called it the language of God."

"Of course, naturally. And we speak the language of the devil, right?" Droon said, tightening his teeth.

"Why are you so hostile, Droon?" Tofan said. "So closed off?"

"I?"

"Let him alone," Jandol said. "He's had a rough morning."

Droon had been making a delivery and had gotten caught up in a skirmish on the road between Shabak and Jalalabad and had to spend the night in his truck. But the conversation trailed off, and we took our leave. I went with Khialo and Droon.

"Fanatics are like cobras," Droon said when we were out of earshot. "Ready to poison you if you get within striking distance."

"Tofan's no fanatic," Khialo said. "Why do you call him a fanatic?"

"I meant the *mavlavi*. But maybe Tofan too. He has the makings of one. Did you hear the way he spoke? Such rapture! He'd forgive the mullahs any abomination so long as it was done in the name of Allah."

"Well, he was excited."

"I wonder if that *mavlavi* can really read minds?" I said.

"*Mavlavis* don't read minds," Droon said, "They own them. They don't want you to think, if you think they can't control you. They just want you to do what they say."

"You're reading too much into this," Khialo said.

"Yeah?"

"You know he and his mother are penniless. He feels trapped."

"He's a strange bird, no matter what you say."

"What do you mean, strange?" Khialo said. "He's not strange."

"Well, kid, he gets on my nerves," Droon said. "There's something about him, I can't lay my finger on it."

"No, no, you're wrong," Khialo said, his voice rising.

"Okay, okay. But he's your friend, not mine, and if you'll be so kind as to keep him away from me—"

"He's a lost soul. He's trying to find himself."

"I believe you," Droon said. "But enough about Tofan. I'm getting bored with the subject. Let's talk about Sandara and how beautiful she is, how smooth her skin is, and how glistening her black hair as it cascades down her back."

"You nut," Khialo said.

Droon's truck was parked outside his gate with its dazzling array of mandalas, dancing girls, white-robed nomads, orange fenders, the red hood, the blue roof, the rows of pentacles and stars along the sides. "Isn't she a beaut? I love that hunk of machinery."

"Too bad Safi's the owner," Khialo said. "Especially when he gets in one of his tizzies. You should see him, he practically turns purple."

"Did I say I loved Safi? Did you hear me say that? But you're right, he's quite the dictator. You'd think the truck was made of gold the way he carries on if he sees the slightest dent."

"One of these days he's going to keel over."

"Then it'll be good-bye Safi," Droon said. "And good-bye truck."

"Hey, if he does keel over," I said, "you can buy the truck."

"I would, except for a minor problem. You need money to pay for trucks, and I don't have any. Everything I make goes to feed the family. Ah, hell, who gives a damn? Once Sandara and I tie the knot, I'm jumping behind the wheel, and we're going to take off for parts unknown."

"I thought you said it was Safi's truck," I said.

"I'll send him a postcard."

"Quit pulling my leg."

"Well, okay, the hell with the truck. We'll hop on a bus. Maybe I can become a bus driver. Sandara is a queen, you know, a beautiful queen. She deserves the best a husband can do for her."

"Queens do not marry bus drivers," I said.

As Droon opened his gate, he turned toward us, and I caught such a patina of youth in his expression that I hollered, "Achariar!" Lakhta said of him that he was the future of Afghanistan, and the impact of her words struck me forcibly when he too returned my shout. "Achariar!" Then Khialo and I took off to drum up a game of soccer with some of the village boys.

It was the last week in April, and we'd just finished breakfast, and I was outside in the garden working on a poem that I'd modeled after some verses by the great Khushal Khan Khattak. In attempting to create something that equaled the fervor of his vision, I was winding up with high-sounding phrases that were simultaneously empty and congested. I needed powerful down-to-earth images, something that hadn't been expressed by the great genius of Pashto poetry, but I didn't have the vocabulary. I was in the midst of flipping through Abba's dictionary when Khialo came by.

"So guess who's ringing heaven's bell," he said, dropping down next to me.

"What's that?"

"Guess who's here."

"Who?" I said, closing my notebook and stashing it away while Khialo affected not to notice. "Well?"

"Guess."

"Give me a hint."

"She's as ugly as monkey, and he's a jerk."

"Can you be more specific?" I said, but I knew who he meant, and Khialo knew I knew and said to me to quit horsing around.

"Okay, okay. Shatoo Khola and that lamebrain assistant of hers, Mohammad Din."

"Be nice. They're man and wife now."

"No!"

"And they're setting up shop in Srakala."

"After what happened the last time they were here, I never thought I'd see them again."

"Well, here's your chance," Khialo said.

Shatoo Khola, a self-professed curer of whatever ailed you, practiced her form of folk medicine in many villages but had left the Hisarak District under a cloud of suspicion five years before and hadn't been back since. The cloud she left under was definitely heavy—the death of a neighbor's five-year-old son she'd been treating for snakebite with one of her potions. The boy had a series of seizures and died. Nevertheless, many villagers swore by her remedies, choosing to see her when they were sick instead of a regular doctor. This in spite of the fact that Shatoo was Iranian and spoke mostly in Farsi with a smidgen of Pashto, which made her diagnoses a sometimes unpredictable affair. Moor and Bibi thought she was a scam artist who always had her hand in the till. I didn't trust her either, but as I said, the villagers believed she was a true magician when it came to their health.

At any rate, the same was never said about her husband, whose intelligence was like a snowy day—cold, harsh, and dropping below thirty. Whereas we knew little of Shatoo's background, Mohammad Din was from Shabak. He came from a family of twelve siblings, most of whom had left for points unknown. A rail-thin youth, his mind was usually off in some distant galaxy so that when you asked him something, he'd change the subject or more often misinterpret what you were saying. His only saving grace was his ability to communicate with animals. With only a few words, he could calm down a recalcitrant horse, and mules, those balky creatures, ate out of his hand. It was uncanny. Even Mamar, who could be ferocious, followed him around, wagging his tail.

"Who's back? Sial asked, coming out to the front porch with a cup of chai.

"Shatoo Khola," I said.

"Who's Shatoo Bhola?"

"Khola. You don't remember her?"

"I don't know, maybe I do. What about her?"

"She's back. She's here. And Mohammad Din's with her."

"I thought she was dead."

"Very funny. Well, she's back. And guess what? She has two donkeys, a goose, a dog, and a new husband who's old enough to be her son. I think you know him too, Mohammad Din?"

"We're going to go snoop around," I said. "Want to join us?"

"Forget it. I've got better things to do than spy on my neighbors."

When Khialo and I reached Shatoo's house, she was inside unpacking, and Mohammad Din was in the front yard, unloading supplies while the donkeys waited patiently, flicking their tails against the flies and paying no attention to the incomprehensible foibles of men. Mohammad Din was as scrawny as ever with scraggly tufts of hair on his skeletal face, not enough to be called a beard, and a head of thinning hair that grew to his shoulders in scant dangling wisps.

I went over and was about to shake hands when he grasped my right hand, holding it in both of his in a formal Islamic greeting. As he did so, his cologne almost made me gag. What'd he do, bathe in the stuff?

"So, Mohammad Din," I managed to say, "you've come back."

"I am not Mohammad Din."

"I beg your pardon?"

"I am no longer Mohammad Din."

"Who are you?"

"I am Sadr-Ull-Din Imam Parast, the beloved husband of my beloved wife Shatoo, the healer, and we go wherever God sends us." His breath smelled of raw garlic that was only partly concealed by his perfumed beard. He released my hand, and I stepped back while he clasped Khialo's and went through the same rigmarole. "So what can we do for you? Are you sick? Do you need an appointment?"

Khialo started to ask a question, but he interrupted him immediately. "Mohammad Din does not exist. Imam Parast stands before you."

Shatoo came out to help her husband unload, and he introduced us. It was easy to see who was the gourmet in the family. Boy, had she put on weight. Her hair was dry enough to light a match on, dyed an unnatural coal black, and emphasized the catastrophic dimensions of her puffy, chinless, hawk-nosed face.

After helping them carry in the rest of the packages, Khialo and I left. On the way, the wind grew brisk, its fitful gusts causing the leaves on the trees to turn back and forth, green then yellow then green. With the flicker of the leaves so began the time of Shatoo the healer.

Word got around, and pretty soon, she had a thriving business, villagers throughout the district consulting her with their various health issues, love issues, money issues, you name it. Such a kindly soul, she helped them out of the goodness of her heart, reluctantly asking but a modest fee—the higher the fee, the greater the goodness. Imam Parast went around telling people that Shatoo was on a first-name basis with those who had died in the ever-present fight against the infidels, that her soul was a deep well filled with wisdom, and that only she could pull up the bucket; his words were always accompanied by the cloying aroma of that heavy perfume he doused himself with. Villagers didn't need too much convincing. What did they know about such matters? And in fact, they began to refer to her as the Amazing Shatoo, the Generous Shatoo, the Angelic Shatoo, with usually a line of people at her gate waiting to see her.

Her supply of homemade medication—vials, bottles, jars, creams, roots, crushed leaves, tinctures, teas—was as prodigious as the menu in a Pakistani restaurant. But though her consulting room shelves were stacked from floor-to-ceiling, the pièce de résistance was her collection of what she referred to with awe as her *magic water*. These had been collected from relatives, from friends of relatives, from the enemies of friends of relatives, from the husbands of dead women, from the widows of dead husbands, from children who had survived cholera, from the elderly whose kidneys were failing, and from other myriad unnamable sources. Quite a collection, each used for a specific medical problem. In fact, she warned, to use one for the wrong affliction could have severe consequences. "The most severe," she told the villagers, who oohed and aahed, murmuring among themselves that the wise Shatoo surely knew everything about curing illness, that she could see into the heart of a malady in a way that was beyond the scope of mere mortals.

But I have to admit that with the hospital destroyed and the Communist doctors gone off with the army, we had no one else to help us, although in serious cases, patients continued to go to Jalalabad.

A few times Khialo and I tried to talk to Imam Parast; we wanted to know more about Shatoo's formulas, but it was pointless. He was as wily as a silver fox. Besides, she kept him on a short leash, meaning he was often gone on mysterious trips, sometimes lasting for weeks, to gather medicinal supplies, very hush-hush, which only piqued our curiosity to the point that Sial once asked him straight out what he was up to. But my brother fared no better than the rest of us for Imam Parast's reply was as enigmatic as ever, proving beyond a doubt that the new imam and the old Mohammad Din were one and the same person. Sial called him a loser and walked away. I could see that the antipathy was mutual, although Parast refused to admit it, except through the facial contortions he exhibited when they met, a mélange of scorn, fear, and superiority that chased each other around his lips and flattened his eyes.

The only one of us who liked either of them was Tofan. We were surprised when we heard that his mother had been seeing Shatoo, whose remedies had been successful enough for her to leave her bed for the first time in months and that the treatments were being paid for by the *mavlavi*. Indeed, Tofan had become so chummy with him, we hardly ever saw him. Eventually, Tofan stopped coming around altogether, following which, when we saw them walking arm in arm, Tofan would either ignore us, or they'd deliberately change direction and hurry off. We never found out who this *mavlavi* was, which was odd, given how small our village was and how everyone knew everyone else. But those two stuck together and ignored everyone else.

We all felt sorry for Sial and gave him a lot of slack because he was having a hard time adjusting to the Mujahideen. The noose that was tightening around our necks was really strangling him, even as he told everyone that he was as free as a bird, to which Meena once said, "He'd better not mistake his mirror for the sky. He might fly into it and break his neck." The problem was time hung heavily on his hands. Unlike Jandol, who could roll with the punches, Sial's universe was a house of cards—any sudden movement, and everything went flying.

My present was the future, Abba and Moor's present was the past, but Sial's future was the present. So though he went around saying how free and birdlike he was, he spoke with such urgency, the tone totally belied his words. At other times, he'd be practically pulling his hair out. He was seventeen, soon he'd be eighteen; it was time for him to make his way in the world. Instead, he was trapped like a rat in Shabak, so he often said no school, no education, nothing going for him, nothing to look forward to. What could anyone say? Which is why we gave him plenty of rope, but it didn't make our living conditions any easier. Especially when Meena goaded him on, which she seemed to enjoy.

For her part, Shatoo flourished, but it was not to last much longer. Actually, it was Sial who drove the first nail into her coffin, and not through his own doing. He was helping Atal shoe a donkey when the animal kicked him in the head, knocking him unconscious. No one was home, and not knowing where else to go, Atal laid Sial across the back of his horse and took him to Shatoo's clinic. She was in the process of dabbing the head wound with her magic water when Khialo and I, hearing about the accident from one of the farmhands, came rushing inside. We were immediately engulfed by the sweet smell of incense. Didn't they ever open a window? We watched in silence as she covered the wound with chewing tobacco, layer upon layer, until it was inches thick. She opened a porcelain container and, with her bare hand, scooped out some moist horse dung. It stunk to high heaven. She placed it on the tobacco and tied everything in place with cotton strips. She had just finished fastening it together when my mother and Lakhta appeared.

"What happened?" Moor said, stepping over to Sial and looking over at Atal. "Tell me what happened."

Atal explained what had happened and began to apologize, but Moor didn't care whose fault it was. Sial still hadn't regained consciousness. His skin had a pale, bluish tinge, and the cotton wrap was discolored with blood and oozing dung, which continued to give off a creepy smell. Moor stroked his arm, careful not to jar him, gently lifted his head, and unwrapped the strips. She interrupted Atal, who once again was saying how sorry he was, to ask Shatoo for some fresh cotton, rubbing alcohol, and clean bandages, and Shatoo went into another room and came back with the items. Moor swabbed the wound until it was clean then pressed a dry cloth over it and bandaged it tightly enough to stem the bleeding, but not too tight so as to constrict the blood vessels. Shatoo stared at us with her predatory eyes, her fingers opening and closing as if they had a life of their own, like the wiggling of baby mambas. No one said a word to her, and she didn't speak to us, but on the way out, Moor slipped her some Afghanis, patted her on the shoulder, and thanked her for helping.

Atal carried Sial out and, as before, laid him on the horse's saddle. On the way, I asked Moor why she gave Shatoo money, and she told me not to ask so many questions; she knew what she was doing. When we got home, we put Sial to bed, and that night, one or another of us kept an eye on him. You can imagine our relief when he woke up the next morning with a searing headache but alert and aware of his surroundings, even though he didn't remember what had happened, which was to be expected.

Moor and Lakhta fed him warm soup, and Gulapa came over in the afternoon and sat with him. Sial was lucky because the accident didn't leave much of a scar, but for the next year, whenever the weather was extremely hot, he'd have moments of dizziness and had to lie down until it was over. Eventually, these spells vanished. When you got down to it, my brother was a tough guy.

But a nail had been put in the coffin. Moor couldn't get over the mess that Shatoo had placed around Sial's head and kept wondering what would have happened if she hadn't come when she did. Curious about the money, I asked Abba the reason, and he said it was always better to leave an enemy feeling guilty rather than angry. Word got around; Khialo, Sial, and I made sure of that. You might ask why we went to such lengths, but bear in mind that we Afghans are a proud and ancient civilization. Abba was chief of the Jabarkhil Tribe, a subtribe of the Ahmadzai, which is made up of thousands of nomads who continue to roam throughout the country. I am thus descended from a long and illustrious line of ancestors. At some point in the nineteenth century, my forebears settled in Hisarak so that we now had land and property and Afghan ID cards. But millions of nomads remained undocumented and thus stateless, nonexistent beings with nothing to be proud of except for their heritage.

For Afghans, our country is a garden whose ethnic tribes are like flowers with strange, exotic colors and perfumes that take your breath away. We were a land of diverse groups—Turkmen, Baluch, Tajik, Uzbeck, Hazaras Pashto—who had lived side by side for centuries but were now being taught to mistrust and hate each other. A poor but hardworking people, a proud people, stripped of their rights, injustice eating away at us like ravenous voles, conflicts generated and funded by foreigners and executed by holy criminals. Tyrants who misuse religion in order to carry out their objective of domination.

Shatoo was one of those who would fatten themselves at the expense of the Afghan people, really a nobody, less than a cog in a gigantic machine. But sometimes one cog can destroy an entire engine. We didn't have to say that to each other; we knew it. Oh yes, we would finish her off, her and that fool husband of hers.

Nail number 2 was a man named Zargual who worked at my father's grain mill. He developed a sty in his right eye and, against our advice, consulted with Shatoo, who began treating him. As we expected, her remedies were unsuccessful, and the inflammation increased to the point where he was having vision problems. He came over one day looking awful, with his eye red and swollen. Moor asked him what Shatoo was giving him, but he said he didn't know; it was an elixir with a strange smell. He said she got it from the kind oldest woman in the village of Nawar. Why Nawar? He didn't know.

Abba offered to drive him to the hospital in Jalalabad, but Zargual was afraid of doctors and refused, adding that if he went in he would never come out, which was what had happened to his wife. Moor said that he was being absurd, but he said that Shatoo assured him that she could cure him and that often diseases worsened before they got better. In fact, she said it was a good sign because it meant the toxins were boiling out of his body. Moor asked him how much these visits were costing him, but Zargual said that health was more important than money.

A month went by with no improvement, and now his left eye was developing a sty of its own. Shatoo told him that she had one last hope: her aunt, whose generosity was fabled, had recently celebrated her ninety-fifth birthday. She refused to drink water, which she felt was poisonous to the system and consequently was a pure acid factory, in whose body no disease could survive. Well, it turned out that this very acidic aunt produced an infinitesimal quantity of magic water, which was powerful enough to kill the poisons that were causing Zargual's eye inflammation. It was expensive, but Zargual was desperate and agreed to pay whatever she asked.

Shatoo sent Imam Parast to collect the solution from her aunt, and when he returned, she mixed it with a few drops of holy water that had been donated five years before by a very famous and revered imam whose name she was not at liberty to reveal.

She held the vial and shook it vigorously while intoning a prayer in Farsi. Before handing it to him, she had Zargual wash and dry his hands three times. Then she lit incense and candles, and they prayed together in honor of this divine gift from his Holiness. Zargual went home where, as per her instructions, he placed ten drops in each eye. She said it might sting a little but not to worry because that meant it was working. He was supposed to do this five times a day, and she promised that within three days his eyes would be free from infection.

Zargual did as she said, but the pain was so intense he stopped the treatment and made his way back to Shatoo, at which time she lost patience and said that obviously he hadn't followed her instructions. Her final recommendation was for him to kill a scorpion and grind it to a powder, make a compress, and place it on both eyes for one hour every day for two weeks. He would have followed her directions, but on the way home, he blacked out, and someone brought him to our house.

That fainting spell was the luckiest thing that could've happened to him. Abba took him to an eye specialist in Jalalad who'd been recommended by Baheer, and the specialist said Zargual should be thankful he hadn't blinded himself pouring those weird concoctions in his eyes. He explained that styes were infections that needed to be treated with antibiotics. Within a short time, Zargual was back to normal. But he was too embarrassed to say anything to anyone, even when Shatoo claimed that it was her treatments that had cured him.

The third nail was hammered by yours truly, with a little help from Khialo and Sial. This from me to them. "So Mohammad Din asks me to follow him—"

"Imam Parast," Khialo said.

"Don't interrupt. He leads me to a shed they have out back, and in the corner of the shed there's a hawk on a wooden perch on top of a metal pole. The hawk has leather straps on its legs, and they're connected to a long leather leash. On the other side, there's a cage filled with lots of little birds. Also, the place smells from here to high heaven with bird shit everywhere. Well, what he does is, he goes over to the cages with the small birds and opens the cage door, and about four or five birds fly out. It doesn't take long. The hawk seizes the first one and then another and tears them apart. Pretty soon there's nothing left except for a few feathers. So then Parast says to me that now, those little birds can fly around heaven, and when we die, we will dance to their songs. I'm telling you, the guy's sick. Well, I've had enough of him and that shrew he married. Tonight I'm going to sneak in there and free those birds."

"You're going to what?" Sial said.

"You heard me."

"Want some help?" Khialo said.

"Great. What about you, Sial, how about striking a blow for freedom?"

"What's the point? He'll only get another hawk."

"Well...we'll free that one too."

"It's ridiculous."

"You're wrong," I said. "There's things you can change, and there's things you can't change. Like we can't do anything about the war, but we can do something about those poor birds."

Khialo said, "I'd like to find out what's in those magical bottles of hers, that's what I'd like to know."

"That gives me an idea," I said. "Let's kill two birds with one stone."

"Very funny," Sial said, but at least he was still listening.

"After we free those birds, let's steal some of that holy water."

"But how will you find out what it's made of? You're no expert."

"We'll face that bridge when we come to it."

"I bet it's something poisonous," Khialo said.

"So, Sial, are you in or out?"

"All right, but if we get caught, I'm telling everybody it was your idea. That I was just along for the ride."

"I don't care what you tell them. Besides, if we play our cards right, we won't get caught."

We shook hands solemnly, swore eternal brotherhood, and I told them my plan. Which was why, seven nights later, the three of us were waiting for Parast outside the Shabak mosque after evening prayers had ended. Finally, he appeared along with Tofan, the famous *mavlavi*, and Mullah Kadoo. Framed in the doorway, the *mavlavi* was deep in conversation with Mullah Kadoo, who kept nodding his head, a fulsome smile plastered on his nonexistent lips. At last, Kadoo and the *mavlavi* went inside while Parast and Tofan headed toward Srakala via the Ashrat Kala garden. As per my instructions, having ascertained that this was their usual route, Khialo followed them. Before they crossed the Auzingianai, he caught up with the pair, saying he wanted to ask Parast a question that had been preying on his mind.

"I am a seeker," Khialo said. "I need guidance. I have wandered from the spiritual path." When Parast spoke, Khialo pretended to be swayed by his comments, swayed to the point where the great imam lost all sense of time (luckily) as he and Tofan went into a lengthy tautological argument, each interrupting the other, each proclaiming in his own way that for any man of intelligence, the glories of following the spiritual path were infinite. And numberless, Tofan added. The object was to keep them talking as long as possible. We figured we'd have half an hour, perhaps even more, enough time to do the deed and escape without being discovered.

At the same time, Sial tapped on Shatoo's gate, saying that he needed to see her about a personal matter, one that he was too embarrassed to discuss with anyone else. At first she was extremely wary, aware no doubt of Sial's contempt. Her tone of voice, when she said she only existed to help mankind, was edgily suspicious. We'd figured on that. He said he wanted to thank her for helping him when he was injured, that it was her medicine that had cured him, no matter what Moor or Lakhta said; after all, they weren't doctors like Shatoo. After a little more maneuvering on his part, she invited him inside where she prepared some kind of tea, which had the same flowery aroma that twirled around Parast.

After sitting in silence, Sial, with much hemming and hawing, attempted to reveal the nature of his problem, one that had begun when he was ten and had, over the years, worsened to the point where he could no longer call his life his own. Given that they basically spoke different languages, Sial's tale of woe included many euphemisms, nods, and hand gestures, one of which shocked the great Shatoo enough for her to take a sharp intake of breath and quickly rise to her feet.

As soon as the two of them went inside, I sneaked into her courtyard and went around back to the consulting room where Shatoo kept the vials locked in a wooden chest. This studio, principally an add-on mud hut attached to the main house with its own separate entrance, caused us the most concern, namely how to get in without Shatoo knowing. Actually, how to get in period? This is where Khialo stepped up to the plate. "Don't worry," he said. He'd take care of everything, which he did; the door was unlocked, and I entered. Later he told me that the night before our little escapade, he'd jimmied the lock with a screwdriver. The magic water was kept in a heavy oak chest. I had brought a hammer and some rags with me, and I covered both the hammer and the lock with the rags to muffle the sound and smashed repeatedly at the lock until it sprang open. Then I lifted the lid, took one of the vials, replaced it with another we'd made that was filled with tea, and reattached the lock, hoping it wouldn't fall apart but realizing that if it did, so what? So nothing.

With this part of the plan over, I went to the woodshed where the birds were caged and propped the door open with a shovel. Once inside, I moved the cage with the little birds to the doorway and unhooked the opening. What a sense of joy I felt as they soared away. I wondered how many would survive. They were young, and the world was cruel. Next, the hawk, which had a hood over it. I carried perch, pole, and hawk to the doorway. Standing behind the hawk, I lifted the hood then picked up the scissors and carefully cut off the leg straps. Once that was accomplished, I jumped back and watched. That stupid bird didn't move. It simply stared. *Go on and fly away*, I thought, clenching my fists. *I've got to get out of here*. I didn't realize it at the time, but the hawk needed an updraft of current in order to lift off the ground. But the air was completely still. Suddenly, the hawk stretched its neck and flapped its wings and, with a swift whir, headed up into the skies.

The morning after our coup, Sial and I were out on the verandah when Khialo appeared, and as we were going over the events of the previous night, we heard angry voices coming from the kitchen. Inside, we found Lakhta tearing into Baz, who was hollering at the top of his lungs.

"This is where we eat," Lakhta hissed, holding Baz by one arm and beating him with the other. He was kicking at her, trying to bite her hand. Finally, she hauled off and slapped his face so hard, his neck snapped back, and he flung himself down to the floor. "You're like a dog that hasn't been housebroken."

"What's going on?" Sial said.

"You keep out of this."

"You're giving me a headache."

"Well, take your headache somewhere else. This doesn't concern you. This is between me and Baz."

"Lakhta, calm down," I said. "What'd he do?"

Instead of answering me, she thrust the vial under my nose. "Smell this! Go on, smell it!" Then back to Baz. "Oh, you're such a bad boy. I can't believe it. I come in here to make a wonderful breakfast for everyone, and what do I find. This! Oh, I can't think, I just can't think. What got into that mind of yours? The smell's enough to make you want to throw up. At first I couldn't figure out where it was coming from, but it didn't take me long. When I pulled up the stopper, I almost fainted. I mean it, I almost passed out. Who would do this? What kind of joke is this? That's when

I see my little brat hiding under the kitchen table with that goofy look of his, and I yanked him out and…and—oh, I don't know what to say or what to think! Were you brought up in a pigsty, you little rat! I didn't have to ask who did it. The minute Baz saw me with the bottle, he tried to run away. Oh, you snot-nosed hooligan!" She raised her hand, and he curled into a fetal position. But Lakhta ran out the door to the garbage area with the three of us racing after her.

"Wait, wait, what are you doing?" Khialo cried.

"I'm dumping this, that's what I'm doing."

"You can't!"

"Oh, can't I?"

"It's not yours or Baz's. It's mine."

"What'd you say?"

"It's mine," Khialo said, holding out his hand. "Give it to me."

Lakhta turned to face him with one hand on her hip, the other holding the bottle. "This is yours? You're telling me that this… thing…is yours?"

"Yes, it's mine. So give it to me."

"What is this, some kind of sick joke?"

"It's not a joke," I said. "Khialo's telling the truth."

She whirled around to face me, and for the first time since I knew her, Lakhta was at a loss for words. "I can't believe you did this," she finally said.

"Did what?" Khialo asked.

"As if you didn't know."

"Just give it to him," I said. "I mean us."

"So this is yours?" she said to Khialo and me. "This horrible sample is really yours?"

"Yes, it's ours, I tell you. Ours. Mine. His."

"Well, which one?"

Both Khialo and I said, "Mine!" simultaneously.

"You're telling me that you both peed in this bottle and left it on the kitchen table and now you want it back?"

"Hey, what's that about peeing?" I said. By this time we were all shouting at each other. It was quite comical really, although at the time it wasn't.

"I want to hear you say it. I need to hear you tell me that both of you took a leak in this small bottle and left it for me to find."

Moor and Meena came outside, and when Lakhta apprised her of the situation, she said, "This time, you boys have gone too far. Shame on you!"

"Sial, say something," I said.

"They didn't pee in that bottle," Sial said, a flush spreading across his cheeks. "No one did."

"Well, how did it get in there?" Lakhta said, still holding vial. "By magic?"

"I'm telling you, no one peed in that bottle. It's medicine."

"For who? A lunatic?"

"Take a whiff, go on, I dare you," Lakhta was again taking off the stopper and holding it in front of our faces, and each of us took a sniff. It was urine, all right. The odor was unmistakable. We were nonplussed.

"We're waiting for an explanation," Moor said.

"I suppose you think it's funny," Lakhta said.

"I don't think anything," I said.

"Anyway, it's not ours," Khialo said.

"So now it's not yours," Lakhta said. "What a clever reply."

"It's not."

"Well, whose is it?"

"It's Shatoo's," Khialo said.

"Shatoo peed in this bottle and left it on the kitchen table?"

"She didn't leave it on the kitchen table," I said. "We did. But it came from her pharmacy."

"It's her magic water," Khialo said. "It's what she uses to cure people."

"We stole it," I said.

"You're telling us," Moor said, her soft voice more alarming than Lakhta's hollering, "that you went into her pharmacy and stole it?"

"Something like that."

"Why?"

"We didn't exactly steal it," Khialo said. "We borrowed it for testing."

"Yes, for testing," I said. "We're going to return it. So technically, it's not stealing. You see?"

"Well, you can save yourself a lot of trouble," Lakhta said. "It's full of pee. Someone took a leak in it."

"Boy, no wonder Zargual almost lost his eyesight," Khialo said.

"It's a good thing he didn't lose anything else," Lakhta added.

"What a liar," I said. "A thief and a liar."

"Who's a liar?" Lakhta said.

"Shatoo. I'm telling you, that's the magic water she's always bragging about."

"Wait'll people find out," Khialo said.

"Yeah," Sial said. "Wait'll we let it out what her magical bottles are filled with."

"You'd better put this back where you found it," Moor said, "before you get in trouble."

"Oh, my poor Baz," Lakhta said, returning to the kitchen to find him holding onto a leg of the kitchen table with his thumb in his mouth, sniffling and hiccupping. She sank to the floor next to him, trying to turn his face her. "Can you ever forgive me? I was a fool. A stupid fool."

This brought on more tears, but he did turn around and, after a moment, put his arms around her waist, his chest still shuddering in great gasps.

When she found out about it, Meena said we should get the kids to pee in bottles and make our own holy water, but Jandol said it'd be better if we spent our time on constructive things and not some idiotic scheme that wouldn't get us anywhere.

At any rate, a few weeks later, with gossip swirling around her fanned by all of us, Shatoo announced that it was time for her to move on to another village, that others needed her, and one morning, both she, the two donkeys, the goose, the dog, and the husband who was young enough to be her son disappeared—for good I hoped.

Lakhta treated Baz like a prince, making him special dishes and telling him stories about his favorite historical figure, Malala, the Afghan Joan of Arc, who spurred the ghazis to defeat the British at the Battle of Miwand. According to Lakhta, the moral of the story was a woman's work was never done, although I don't see how that helped Baz. This went on until Baz did something, I forget what, that annoyed Lakhta, and life returned to normal.

But Khialo and I had our own little revenge; it was sweet, it could have been sweeter, but you don't want to overindulge. This was right before they left. Khialo and I were out fooling around when we happened upon the white-turbaned Imam Parast dozing under a chinar tree. I told Khialo to follow me, and we went to a nearby rice paddy where I scooped up some mud and squeezed the water out until it looked like a bowel movement. Imam Parast was still sound asleep. Khialo hiked up his caftan and gently pulled open his drawstring pants while I placed the mud almost touching his butt. When we were finished, we lay down next to him and waited.

He must have sensed our presence because he soon stirred, although when he saw me and Khialo, he asked us what we wanted and added that this wasn't a good time to delve into the mysteries of theology.

"But we've been waiting for you. You're the only one who can help us," Khialo said. "And you were so helpful before."

"We have a question about heaven," I said. "We want to know where it is. I say it's in the first sky, and Khialo says that it's in the seventh."

"It's in the first."

"The seventh. I can prove it."

"How."

"I need a pencil and some paper."

A contemptuous expression fell upon Imam Parast's excuse of a face, as if a curtain that was supposed to open the first act of a play had instead closed just as the actors were making their entrances. He sat up, but when he did, he instantly stiffened, his eyes grew wide, and his lips twisted into a look of urgency that was priceless. Khialo and I continued bombarding each other with questions, but Parast didn't pay us the slightest bit of attention. In fact, he didn't move a muscle. You could tell he was just dying for us to leave so that he could see what was going on, but we seemed oblivious.

Unable to wait another second, he surreptitiously reached back in order to feel his pants from the outside. When he did, he instantly pulled his hand away. Finally, after we couldn't take any more, Khialo and I said that we had to go and thanked him for his time, but the second we turned, he jumped to his to feet as if he'd been struck by lightning, untied his pants, and slid his hand inside. When he bought his hand out, he stared with astonishment at the mess and tore his pants off and used them to wipe himself clean, which left him in the compromising position of having no pants to wear. It was quite a sight, Parast standing with his shortcomings exposed for everyone to see, definitely a picture worth savoring. I couldn't wait to tell Sial, but when we got back, he was out, and so much happened, I forgot about it. It wasn't until later that I remembered, but by then the humor was gone.

We'd only just entered when Lakhta came over, telling us that Azmoon had gone off to fight with the insurgents without breathing a world to anyone save her, Samsoor, and Sandara. They had begged him to stay, but he wouldn't listen. Now he was gone, and she didn't know what to do.

We found it hard to believe. Azmoon hated war and violence; he was a scholar like Jandol, not some crazy hothead going off half-cocked. If anyone were to enlist, it should have been Droon, who was as stubborn as that mother of his and equally fiery. But Lakhta said right after the bombing of the District Compound, Azmoon began hanging out with some school friends, and they convinced him to join up. He said they told him that it wasn't enough to let others do our fighting, that we had to face the enemy too. They said they wanted to form their own little unit. Right up until the last moment, she and Samsoor thought he'd change his mind. But two days ago, before the sun rose, there was a tap on their door. It was those so-called friends of his coming for him, and Azmoon slipped away. There were so many things she'd wanted to say to him, but the words wouldn't form, and now it was too late—he was gone. Moor tried to comfort her by saying that Azmoon was a smart guy, that he'd be all right. Abba wondered what would happen to our young men, what with Droon's delivery business at a standstill, Jandol unable to attend school, and now Azmoon off with the insurgents.

"We just have to go on," Abba said. "Each in his own way. What other choice do we have?"

"There is no other way," Moor aid.

"He's not your son," Lakhta said.

"You're wrong," she replied. "He is our son. They're all our sons."

CHAPTER FIVE

In June I turned fifteen, and now it was September, and the weather was mild even as the leaves of the wild peach trees trembled in the occasional wintry gusts. The rain turned the fields soggy brown, and on dry days the air became clotted by the dust that whirled in from the desert. Some nights, an icy chill could be felt, and when we awoke, our windows would be rimed, and the branches of the trees felt icy to the touch. When we breathed, smoke came out of our mouths, but as the morning wore on, the cold air quickly dissipated until it felt like spring. Meena, Sandara, Sial, and I were at Lakhta's, amid the usual miscellany of leather being tanned, sandalwood incense, and the hammering of Samsoor busily repairing the soles and heels of the Mujahideen.

"I don't know, Sandara," Meena was saying. "I want to do something with my life, something significant. I don't want to wind up like Shamla. Saddled with a husband she despises and another baby on the way."

"But you will do something, Meena, you will. You just have to be…to be patient and wait. This war won't go on forever, it can't. When it's over, things will return to normal, I know they will. Look at the sun, see how it's still up in the sky. Or the garden, how the flowers lose their petals, but in the spring they grow back." She turned to me and Sial. "Isn't that true?"

"Don't look at me," Sial said and shrugged.

"But, Sandara, what if our lives never return to normal?" Meena said. "What if the fighting never stops? What then? It's funny, I used to think it would, but I don't anymore. People will go on killing each other until there's no one left. No one at all. I know what I must sound like, sixteen going on sixty."

"I used to feel that way when I was your age," Sandara said. "As if the whole world was coming to an end and me along with it."

"And now?"

"Now when I wake up in the morning, I can't wait to get out of bed."

"That's because you're in love. But I'm different. I don't want to get married, at least not yet. Maybe never."

"You're just going through a rough period," Sandara said. "Everyone is. The way we live, it's no wonder you're upset. Who in their right mind wouldn't be? But you're wrong, this war won't go on forever. It can't. And then you'll change your tune. You'll begin to enjoy life, whether you get married or not."

"She wants to become a lawyer," Sial said. "Can you beat that?"

"What's wrong that that?" I said.

"What's wrong?" Sial said. "In what school? The University of Make-Believe?"

"You should talk," Meena said. "What about your so-called acting career? I thought you were going to be a worldwide star, the toast of Afghanistan."

"Well, I am toast, after all. Everyone is. Only the toast is burned."

"What's that supposed to mean?"

"It means that none of us has a chance for success, so why even try? Let's face it, we're lucky to be alive."

"Poor Sial," Sandara said. "You know you don't believe that. You have your whole life ahead of you."

"Do any of you live in the real world? Or are you blind as to what's going on around us?"

"Of course we're not blind," Sandara said. "But you can't give up hope. Otherwise, you're lost."

"You're wrong, Sandara," I said. "You're wrong, and Sial's right. Hope's an expensive illusion. There's only reality, and you'd better learn how to deal with it, or else. The truth is, you have to give up everything you believe in, everything you want and hope for. If you don't, it's curtains. If you don't, they'll get you."

"Who?"

"They. Them. The world."

"Besides, Meena," Sial said, "you change your mind so much, I never know when to believe you."

"I haven't changed my mind about you. I still think you're a jerk."

"Now, Meena," Sandara said. "You know you don't believe that."

Sandara's eyes drew you in, aqua-blue in contrast to her sleek hair that fell below her shoulders, smooth tawny skin, high cheekbones, eyebrows that slanted like wings above her eyes, her way of moving, her voice deep and soft, her full earthy body. Ever since she became engaged to Droon, she'd been decorating her feet and hands with *nakrizi* and darkening her eyes with *ronja*. Abba said that she was like a wildflower blooming in a hot-white desert under a pure blue sky. She told me once she wanted to have eight children—five boys and three girls—and laughed when she saw my horrified expression. "Close your mouth," she said. "The flies will get in."

But months went by, summer burned into autumn, autumn into winter, and still no wedding, until out of the blue, Gulapa announced that the wedding would occur in December. That's when her son Droon would marry his beloved Sandara.

So we talked back and forth and, as usual, not only got nowhere but became more entrenched in our various opinions. On the way home, we continued to egg each other on, but our bantering came to an abrupt halt when we reached our front gate.

"Will you take a gander at that," I said.

Our place was crawling with Mujahideen fighters—on the verandah, in the garden, around the hujra and the fields that lay beyond the walls of our house, the air thick with the sandalwood aroma of chars and the soft sighing sounds of men's voices at the end of a busy day. Abba was standing by the front door talking to an officer, and I boldly made way over to him while Sial hung back. Striking an aristocratic pose, Meena, her head held high, stared straight ahead as she marched inside the house. I studied the officer who had a thin, narrow intelligent face, narrow almond eyes behind gold-rimmed glasses, and weathered skin that was pitted by acne scars. When he turned to me, his pupils were so dilated you could see to the very bottom of his mind. It was like looking into a pool and seeing some strange creature staring up at you.

When Abba introduced us, I could feel myself growing hot all over. It was the Major.

"This must be your son," he said, his voice a thin high-pitched murmur. He asked me my name and age, lightly gripping my shoulder with a hand from which the tips of the two middle fingers were missing, leaving the knuckles thick and misshapen. "Masha-Alah, Jazakallah," he said in Arabic. "What a handsome son you have. I have never seen such eyes. They're like olives, black and salty. He will grow up to be a fine freedom fighter." He scrutinized me with an intensity I could feel spreading through me. "What fire I see in you. Do you understand, son, the fire within you? Is it burning in sorrow for the land in which you were born and which has been taken from you? I feel that fire myself. It is the fire of a good Muslim, and it is what keeps me alive. But the fire has to come from your soul, from your innermost being. If it doesn't, then it will quickly burn itself out and leave you walking, a ghost with neither friend nor home. Is this fire of yours a deep fire, and does it inform all of your actions? Only you know for sure. Only you." He removed his hand from my shoulder while his smile became more insinuating, as if we two shared a bond unknown by the rest of the world.

"He's just a boy," Abba said. "Give him time. Right now he's too young, not even fifteen. So what does he know?"

"Ah, the young. They grow up so fast nowadays. When I was a boy, life was different. You spent years listening from your masters, but your vacations were made up of endless days when you swam in rough seas whose waves lifted you up in their arms, a weave of spray obscuring the sands, when you visited strange cities where the sun never set, when you sailed on rivers that flowed for thousands of miles, winding up on the shores of nations you'd never seen but only imagined. But one must move with the times, eh? As I perceive that you have done, you and the rest of the villagers. What use to flail against the current? One moment you are wading by shore, and another you're pulled under by a rogue wave. Is it then the fault of the wave, your hopeless struggle? Perhaps you shouldn't have been there in the first place?"

"I agree, one must move with the times," my father said. "Of course, the times seem to move according to their own rhythm."

"That is always the case. Even for such a good-looking boy as you have."

For an awkward moment, no one spoke. Actually, I'd never heard anyone tell me I was handsome—well, other than Moor when she wanted me to do something—and I was embarrassed.

"No sacrifice is too great in our war against the infidels," Abba said, holding out his arms with his palms held up. "I wish there was something I could do, but as you can see, my boy is not yet old enough, and I am no longer young."

"Ah, but that is unfortunately always the case. Wars are made by old men, but they are fought by the young. But what can we do? To whom can we turn if not to the young? All I can promise them is that if great sacrifices are called for, then great rewards are given, if not here then in heaven. I myself am blessed with two daughters, both of whom are studying at the National University of Computer and Emerging Sciences in Islamabad. The oldest, Rani, is quite a beauty. She is studying geographic information systems, and Nasreen, the baby, well, she's not a baby anymore, is in the engineering department. Her dream is to design bridges. As you can imagine, I have my hands full." He took out his wallet and showed us a photograph of his family. "I took that last summer. We were in Gilgat, staying at a hotel near Lake Saiful Muluk. Have you ever heard the story of the lake? A young wanderer from a distant land went swimming one day, and an angel flew down, and they fell in love. The angel held him in her arms and lifted off into the wind. No one ever saw them again. But their beauty left a glow on the lake, which is why it's called Saiful Muluk."

"A beautiful story," Abba said.

"There is much beauty in the world. Just as there is much misery. Loss and victory such as we face in our war against the Soviet hegemony."

"I know we will triumph in the end. I have faith. Especially now, especially with men such as yourself leading the fray. But tell me, Major, how long will it take before our enemies are sent packing?"

"I will tell you, my friend. When everybody picks up an AK-47 and joins us. That's when this war will be over. Every Afghan, whether he chooses to or not, whether he knows it or not, must be a fighter for freedom against the oppressors that poison our minds and slaughter our children. And though it might not be today or tomorrow, one day we will prevail. Mohammad, peace be upon Him, will come to our aid in this our hour of need. Let me tell you a little anecdote. I mentioned rogue waves. Well, when I was a boy, we were in Karachi at a resort called Seaview. It's on the Arabian Sea, and the sand is as white as a field of newly-fallen snow. It was early in the morning, the beach was half-deserted, and I noticed a young boy, he couldn't have been older than your son, wading close to shore. Well, one moment he was walking in the sea but the next, he was flailing in the grip of a powerful riptide that pulled him under. People raced forward to try to save him. A woman cried out. It must have been his mother. Everyone thought he was lost. But then he washed up ashore half a mile down from where we were, gasping for air but alive. He was able to survive because he didn't fight the tide. He swam at an angle. That boy is Afghanistan, and the undertow is our enemy."

Abba must have appeared baffled by this anecdote because the Major, after having grinned conspiratorially at me, turned to my father and said, "We are not yet ready for a frontal attack, which is why we move at night, attacking from behind and within. We are embroiled in a holy war, but we are small like David, and the enemy is huge like Goliath. As did the resourceful David have to use his wits to defeat an enemy greater than he, so we too must do the same in order to succeed. The whole Muslim world is watching. We cannot fail. Even if every man, woman, and child dies in the struggle."

"We keep hearing rumors that you're heading toward Kabul. Are those your plans now?"

"Now? Today, this hour? To tell you the truth, I cannot think beyond food and chai and a soft cot to lie on. Perhaps you might take me to the hujra. We've been marching for weeks in this accursed weather, and my men are tired and need to rest. These godforsaken mountains, so grand to see but so inhumane to those seeking to cross them. That's what this country is, a land that is beautiful from far away and cruel close up. Funny that so many want it."

"Powerful words from a passionate man," Abba said and turned to me. "Go inside and tell your mother to get supper ready. The Major has been good enough to join us, but his men need to eat too, and we need to fix up bedding in the hujra."

By the time we'd finished eating, it was dark out. Throughout supper I found the Major not only not frightening but increasingly thought-provoking, his stories, his plans, his hopes filling my imagination—and not only me but also Sial and Meena as well as Moor, although Abba and Jandol were more reserved.

The man was a dealer in dreams, a purveyor of heroics; why, I could have listened to him all night. I also noticed how he gazed at me when he was speaking, as if my reaction was the most important thing in the world to him. He made me feel that I was somebody, a sensation I distinctly liked.

When he left for the hujra, Lakhta came out from the kitchen and asked if anyone had seen Baz. We glanced back and forth at each other, but no one had. We were still under the spell cast by the Major and didn't want to be bothered by household problems. How many times had Baz stayed out past his bedtime? Couldn't she control him?

"I didn't realize how late it was," she said. "If that boy's playing in the garden after I told him not to, he's going to go without supper. I warned him."

"Ah, well, let him have his fun," Jandol said. "Soon enough for him to carry the world on his shoulders."

"Besides, you know how he is," I added. "He gets interested in something and loses track of time."

"But it's so late. I'm telling you, that boy's just like Azmoon, neither of them has a brain in their body. They'll believe anything anybody tells them."

Abba asked her if she wanted us to go look for him, but Sial said that when his belly was empty enough, he'd show up. After half an hour, Lakhta decided to run home and see if he were there. But she returned twenty minutes later. No Baz. In fact, Samsoor thought he'd been with us. At this point, Abba said we'd try to find him, and while Moor and Meena waited at home in case he came back, which seemed more than likely, he brought out flashlights and kerosene lamps, and we went out to search for him. Having split up, we went from neighbor to neighbor, but no one knew anything, although they did offer to help. We fanned out in different directions calling Baz's name, our shouts growing fainter as we spread apart.

Jandol and I circled around the perimeter of Shabak where the land was flat, but we saw nothing, no one, just a motionless sweep of sand, debris, and bushes. There were poisonous snakes hidden behind the sparse foliage that you had to watch out for, and once we thought we saw Baz, but when we got closer, it turned out to be a pile of dark shale. We headed toward where the Wlaswali had been and then across Shabak to the Ashrat Kala garden.

As the night wore on, the weather turned chilly, and in the black garden—more a forest really—a damp fog descended, blurring all of the vegetation so that even the flashlights weren't much help. There wasn't a sound, everything muffled in the cold mist. I was so focused on locating Baz that I lost my sense of direction, and when I turned around to ask Jandol which way to go, I discovered that I was alone. I continued searching, trying to keep a straight direction and somehow wound up beside the Auzingianai River, where I was able to get my bearings. I headed in a southerly direction through a nightmare forest that was silent and ominous, the only movement that of the river as it flowed darkly past.

As the sky gradually lightened and the mist thinned, I reached the place where the Nawar and the Auzingianai conjoined to create a narrow rapidly-moving channel hurtling between steep mossy banks. Hearing voices, I came upon a group of our neighbors standing around in a loose circle and speaking in agitated whispers, Jandol among them. I went up to him, and he nodded toward what looked like a spot of color. It was Baz lying half-submersed on edge of the river with his legs in the water and his body covered in muddy debris. Droon was beside him feeling for a pulse, but he shook his head, after which he carried him to where the grass was dry and laid him down.

It broke my heart; it broke all of our hearts. How could this have happened? He knew this garden like the back of his hand. How could he have slipped into the water? For certainly he must have fallen in, been dragged under by the current, and deposited here. And now he lay on the cold ground with only the burbling of the river to punctuate the unearthly silence. It was overwhelming; it made no sense.

Jandol said we needed to find Samsoor, and he took off while the rest of us waited. When they returned, Samsoor carefully lifted his son up in his arms, and shortly after, we began the long walk back to Shabak. Someone had to warn Lakhta, Jandol said. We couldn't just walk in on her like this, and he told me to run ahead and get Moor.

We came to a halt at Samsoor's home, and he carried Baz inside and laid him down on a cot in the living room. Moor, Sandara, and I were with Lakhta, who cried out when they entered, falling to her knees and embracing Baz as if she'd never let him go. Removing her head scarf, Sandara brushed off the mud from his face and kissed him on both cheeks.

For the Pashto, death requires certain procedures and rituals that need to be adhered so that the final journey will be a peaceful one. In the morning, after the Major and his men departed, Moor went over to help Lakhta and Samsoor prepare Baz for burial. They sponged off his body and cleaned him up. When he was dry, they put mascara around his eyes, spread cologne on his arms and legs, and covered him with a white muslin sheet. Since it is the Pashtoon tradition to bury a body as soon after death as possible, the following day the funeral was held. Word must have gotten around because there were hundreds of mourners from every village in the district. It was a simple ceremony, with Mullah Kadoo reciting some appropriate verses from the Quran and commenting upon Baz's spiritual path. For once Kadoo seemed to be genuine, his words down-to-earth for even he had loved little Baz. But I was distracted; something was bothering me, something about the manner in which he had died that I couldn't lay my finger on, just this feeling I had that something was off-kilter.

When Kadoo was finished, the mourners made their way to my house where Moor and Sandara, with the help of other villagers, set up an elaborate buffet. After everyone had filled their plates, the men carried theirs to the hujra, which was still somewhat disheveled after the Major's men had left, while the women remained in the house.

Moor and Sandara made a large pot of *halwa* that they served with warm milk for the soul of Baz, and as part of the ritual, throughout the day, each member of my family brought bowls of soup to different villagers, going from door to door.

That evening, Moor made up a plate of food and sent me and Meena off to Lakhta's. We found her lying on a cot in the dark in the living room, and as Meena lit a candle, I placed the tray on the cot and said that Moor had sent it.

"I'm not hungry. Put it in the kitchen. I'll eat it later."

I did as she asked. "If there anything you need, just ask," I said.

"I don't need anything."

"Moor said she'd come over later," Meena said.

"Where's Samsoor?" I asked.

"Out somewhere. I don't know. He has to collect himself. He'll be home presently."

"You're sure you'll be all right, that you don't need anything?" Meena said.

"What I need you can't bring me. No one can. When death comes, everyone's helpless. Rich and poor, king and slave, no one can do anything. It's not in our hands. It's in God's hands."

"You know what Gulapa says? She says that God kills those first who He loves the most."

"She should know. Now, go home, both of you. I love you, but I need to be by myself. In this way I'm like Samsoor. Oh, don't worry, my back is strong like an ox. I'll survive. But the only way out is to go in, and I need to do that. I need to reach inside, but I can't do it unless everyone leaves me alone. Do you understand?"

"We understand," Meena said.

"But if you find you need something—anything—send Sandara over," I said, and we slipped out.

Baz's death affected every villager. Lakhta went around pale and listless, and Samsoor was more silent than usual, even as his shoemaking shop, which had recently picked up business thanks to the Mujahideen, went all to hell. Sandara tried to help, but it was a difficult situation. Suddenly, Lakhta and Samsoor were childless, with Azmoon's joining the resistance and Baz's drowning. But life goes on and time leaps forward, and one day Lakhta showed up to help Moor prepare breakfast, and slowly things began to return to normal.

In our garden were many fruit trees, and in their branches birds built their nests. I used to like climbing up and watching them. Not long after the funeral, I climbed up an apple tree that was bursting with green apples, and midway up, I spotted a nest of sparrow chicks. I scooted halfway across a wide branch, reached over, and pulled one of the baby birds out. Cupped in my palm, it made a tiny whistling noise, and I whistled back. The mother, flitting up from below, fluttered from one branch to another, in constant motion, but when I returned the baby, she immediately flew back into the nest.

As I was climbing down, I heard a high-pitched hiss. It was a neighbor's cat. A fledgling had fallen from one of the nests, and the cat was about to pounce on it. I jumped down to the ground shouting and waving my arms, and it scampered off. I picked up the wounded chick and brought it to Lakhta, who was in the kitchen with Moor, preparing supper. I handed the bird to Lakhta, and she dabbed the wound with hydrogen peroxide until it was clean. It was best to let it heal naturally, she said, and we made a nest out of newspaper clippings and towel strips, which we placed in a wooden box near the stove.

The bird continued to cry with its mouth wide-open, and Lakhta said it was hungry. She put a few bread crumbs on her tongue and held the chick until its tiny beak was inside her mouth, and the little creature started eating.

For the next week or so, we both took turns feeding it. If I thought the bird was thirsty, I'd pour some drops in my hand and hold it so that its beak touched the water. The bird needed to be fed every few hours even at night, but I didn't mind. I called the bird Chi Chi, and I loved to just lie by his box and watch him. But everything came to an end a week later when Lakhta said that it was time to set the bird free. I carried the box into the garden, near the same area where I'd found him, and I scooped him up and opened my palm. The little bird flapped its wings and flew around and then alit on one of the branches. It only stayed there for a moment and then fluttered away. I thought about the birds I'd freed from Parast's cages, but this was different. It was exciting just to let them go, but Chi Chi was my bird, I'd saved his life, and now he was gone.

"Don't look like that," Lakhta said. "Cages are prisons."

"I know," I said.

"What do you know?"

"That cages are prisons, and no one wants to be imprisoned."

"You'd have had to keep it in a cage until it died, or it would have flown away."

"But why do I feel so sad?"

"Life is sad, and you feel it."

I understood. Birds were meant to fly. You couldn't keep them; it wasn't fair. Later that night, when I was in bed, I heard a child laughing, and he sounded exactly like Baz, but when I opened my eyes, the laughing stopped. Maybe now that he was dead, his soul was free. Just like our little wounded bird. Oh, I hoped so, I really hoped so. Then everything would make sense. Oh, if only that were true. If the soul was a bird and the body was a cage, wouldn't that be remarkable? Then death wouldn't be scary, and life and death would be friends instead of mortal enemies. I hoped so, I truly hoped so.

But still there was something that bothered me about Baz, something I couldn't put my finger on. I could see the scene as clearly as if I were there: the water rippling against the bank, a slight breeze, not enough to rifle the leaves, mist that seemed to be hanging from the trees, and my neighbors huddled together, staring down at the water where Baz's body lay. There was that cloying aroma, like some powerful flowery perfume that was borne by the air or that arose from the earth, a sickeningly sweet fragrance that smelled like rotting flowers. Maybe it was the odor of death; maybe that's what was bothering me. Baz had been there long enough for his joints and muscles to stiffen. I didn't know.

I finally decided that it didn't matter whether something bothered me or not. Baz was dead; nothing could bring him back. When people died, the living either went on living, or they died too, and I was sure that the dead wouldn't want this to happen.

Things returned to normal with the constant influx of insurgents day and night, of extra work for Moor and Lakhta, extra cleaning up of the hujra, which the fighters never bothered to help with, occasional sorties and the sound of gunfire at night. The daily struggles that turned molehills into snowcapped peaks.

As with anything in which Gulapa was involved, there were unforeseen difficulties. Now, according to Atal, in spite of the ban by the Mujahideen, she was planning to have live music at Droon and Sandara's wedding, which was to be held in our hujra. "They'll slice her head off and serve it on a platter," Sial said. "And ours along with it for allowing her to." No one was amused by this observation, least of all Atal, who said that she refused to listen to reason.

Jandol and I, offering to help, accompanied him to Srakala, only to be caught by an unexpected thunderstorm that rapidly churned the dry dusty roads into muddy quagmires, giving my brother and me an eerie sensation that Gulapa controlled the weather. We were soaked by the time we reached their home, whereupon Atal left us at the gate and said, "I'm going to Shakar's. You two talk to her, I give up."

Gulapa was in the middle of mending the seam on a blouse, surrounded by various fabrics piled haphazardly on top of each other, halfway to the ceiling. It looked as if she had enough material for a hundred weddings, but how would she ever get things ready in time?

"Grab some towels," she said. "Look at the mess you're making." As we dried off, she gestured toward the swatches of material. "So what do you think?"

"They're beautiful," Jandol said, somewhat inadequately.

"So what brings you two little busybodies here?" Gulapa said, picking up her sewing. "I hear Atal's been running off at the mouth again."

We both looked at each other. Did that woman ever miss anything?

"He did say something about you wanting to have music at Droon's wedding," Jandol said, diving right in.

"And?"

"We think it's wonderful. Considering."

"Considering what?"

"Oh, you know, the state of things. Conditions."

"Conditions. Exactly what did Mr. Big Mouth say?"

"He said he'd like our heads to remain connected to our bodies," I said.

"You know what conditions are like," Jandol said, trying to sound reasonable.

"Conditions? Do you think I care about conditions? You can just tell Atal and all the other busybodies that my mind is made up. I'm going to have guitarists and flute players and singers. Lots of them. I'm going to get the biggest drum in the district too, and I'm going to beat it so loud that the whole district will shake. That is my final word on the subject."

"In our hujra," Jandol said. "Rabapi will never allow it."

"What does Droon say?" I asked. "Or Mullah Kadoo?"

"Droon's head's in the clouds, and Mullah Kadoo's, well, let's just say, it's in the opposite direction."

"But will Droon think it's such a great idea?" Jandol said. "When he comes back to reality, I mean. He surely doesn't want any trouble on his wedding day."

Gulapa began jabbing the sewing needle into the material, and her voice was as sharp. "He will say that we must have music to celebrate, that's what he'll say."

"But supposing he doesn't say that?" I said.

"Not have music at his wedding? Songs he's loved since he was a baby? Songs I heard when I was a little girl, that my mother sang before me and her mother before her?"

"Don't forget the mullah," I said. "No matter where his head is."

"What about him? That shrunken lemon. I'll stick some Afghanis in his pocket, that'll shut him up."

"Right. You know he's hand in hand with the Mujahideen warlords."

"Yes, you're taking an awful risk," I added.

"I'm not afraid. My ancestors will protect me."

"How?" Jandol said.

"You ask too many questions, both of you."

"Well," I said, "we don't want Droon's wedding day to also be his funeral."

"Always with the words," Gulapa said. "No wonder you're a poet."

"This conversation is ridiculous," Jandol said. "Abba will never allow it. Or Moor."

"Then I'll hold it here in Srakala."

"The hujra is not big enough, and you know that. Besides, what makes you think that Abba will let you do it here?"

"I'm busy. Go away. Torture someone else."

We went round and round but got nowhere, so we dropped the subject and nestled in her colorful cocoon, accompanied by the comforting sound of the rain pattering against the roof, and waited for it to let up. My eyes fastened on the drops that flew against the window in a torrent of changing patterns. Drop upon drop. I wondered if, like snowflakes, each was different. They looked the same. When the room lightened, Jandol said, "It looks like it's letting up. The sun's coming out, and we have to be on our way."

"Good. Now you can both go home and leave me alone. I have work to do."

At that moment from down the street, we heard a familiar high-pitched screech, something between a scream and a roar. "Banjari, Banjari, *Banjariii*!"

"Ah, so that good-for-nothing peddler has finally arrived," Gulapa said. "Come on, let's go pull his excuse for a beard." She put aside her sewing, covered her head with a shawl, and the three of us went outside and joined a group of neighbors who were also waiting, mostly women and children.

"Banjari, Banjari, *Banjariii*!" We heard him before we saw him, not that there was so much to see when he finally did appear. Just an old man leading a heavily-laden mule who looked like it had seen better days.

"Get a load of that donkey of his," a young woman said and pointed. "Where'd he get that old nag!"

"You should look so good with fifty pounds on your back," Gulapa said, waving at the peddler, who stopped in front of her and proceeded to unload his wares, spreading them on a ragged Oriental blanket that he placed on the wet stony road. Soon he was surrounded.

"What took you so long?" Gulapa asked.

"Ah, life is hard and the road is long."

"A philosopher," she said, turning to the others. "We have a thinker among us. Now you listen to me and listen good. My son is getting married, and I want you to make me look young."

"First you must feel young."

"I already feel young, but as you can see, it's not enough."

"If you don't look and feel young, then who else should?"

"Did you bring some good nakrizi plants?"

"Nothing but the best, my lady. Nothing but the best." He bowed to the crowd. "Youth loves youth. But age and wisdom cannot be denied."

"For a man, age and wisdom are ornaments," Gulapa said. "But for a woman, they are disastrous."

"It's the other way around!" a young man shouted, and the women giggled among themselves. "Smart men have big potbellies and die at fifty."

"Who can afford a potbelly?"

"I hope you don't mean me," Banjari said, caressing his ample stomach.

"Don't worry," Gulapa said. "Your stomach's in your pocketbook."

"His heart still beats," said a woman.

"How come it sounds like a cash register?" asked another.

"Banjari, Banjari!" The peddler held up some scarves for everyone to see. "Banjari for the wedding guests. And chewing gum and candy for the little ones. Come one, come all. Banjari!"

One of the boys said he wanted a pack of bubble gum and held out his hand. The peddler pulled out three packs, but when the boy reached for them, he yanked his hand away. "Life is not cheap, even here in Afghanistan."

The boy dug in his pocket and brought out a handful of change.

"Ah, you are a prince among men," the peddler said, quickly pocketing the coins and giving him the gum, plus a chocolate bar. "Never say that I am a greedy man. And now, young lady," he said to Gulapa, "how can I help you? What miracles can I perform?"

"Don't ask for too much," a neighbor said.

"Don't listen to her," Gulapa said to the peddler and bought the nakrizi and a half dozen green bracelets made out of plastic along with two pairs of shoes to match, one for her and another for Sandara.

"What do you think, little ones?" she said, extending her arms and shaking the bracelets. "It will match the color of my dreams, eh?" She turned to the other women and said, "For this wedding, no misery and no black."

"I look good in black," one said.

"My dear, you looked good in black forty years ago," Gulapa said. "Anyway, Droon's wedding is going to be a day of brightness. Enough sadness. It will be a great day. Music or no music." When she said this last phrase, she smiled sardonically in our direction.

Jandol and I were about to leave when I spotted Tofan's mother fingering a shawl and looking faded and lost. Jandol and I went over to her, curious to know what Tofan was up to since we hadn't seen him for weeks.

"Don't ask me," she said. "He's gone."

"Gone?" I said. "Are you serious?"

"Yes."

"But where did he go? And when?"

"You remember the bombing that went on? It was right after that. He just sprang it on me one night. The next morning he was gone."

"He never said anything else?"

"Never. The boy's full of secrets. Just like that father of his. He also left without saying where."

"Did he go by himself?" I said. "I bet he didn't. I bet he went with the *mavlavi*."

"What *mavlavi*?"

"You never met him?"

"I never knew any of Tofan's friends."

"He wasn't a friend," Jandol said. "He was a teacher. From the mosque."

"I don't remember any teacher."

"Well, it doesn't matter."

"No, it doesn't matter. Nothing matters."

We talked a little more and then left. On the way, Jandol said that Tofan's mother was a strange woman. You never knew what she was thinking.

"Did you notice her eyes?" I said.

"It was impossible not to."

"Have you ever noticed, she never looks straight at anyone. She always looks to the side."

"Yes, you want to make eye contact, but you never can. She won't allow it."

"Tofan's the same way," I said.

"Is that so? I don't really know him too well."

"You can never really figure out what he's thinking. Or her for that matter."

"Especially when you compare her to Gulapa."

"I know. Gulapa's eyes are like x-rays. They bore into you."

"They certainly do. Why, she could tell why we'd come the minute we stepped in the door."

"Gulapa's a fighter," I said. "When she dies, it'll be with her hands around someone's throat."

"Hey, don't say such things, brother. It's bad luck."

"I was just joking. Actually, I feel sorry for her. Tofan's mother, I mean."

"I know what you mean. But what we can do? We have enough on our hands as it is."

"First Azmoon and now Tofan," I said. "Who'll be next?"

"Let's just make sure it's not one of us."

"What about Sial?"

"Well, now that's a different story," Jandol said.

"Tofan's so gullible. Same with Azmoon."

"I agree. I think it's because they're looking for something outside themselves. When you think about it, isn't that what Tofan said the last time we saw him, how you had to change internally, and yet that's not the path he chooses to follow."

I have to be honest, there's something I don't trust about Tofan, but I can never lay my finger on it."

"What do you mean?"

"He's always watching you when he thinks you're not looking. I tried to talk to Khialo about this, but he gets so defensive whenever I mention Tofan. It seems like Tofan's his special project or something."

"Anyway, we probably won't see either of them for a long time. If ever."

The day before Sandara and Droon's wedding was Meena's birthday, an event rarely celebrated by the Pashtoon, but nevertheless, both Shamla and Bibi had come from Jalalabad, leaving Kamkai to care for their two children, so the house was a whirl of activity. Lakhta baked banana cakes, and Moor made carrot *halvah*, and for supper we had a special lamb curry, very spicy, just the way Meena liked it, tender on the inside, charred on the outside, and hot enough to burn your mouth off. Her girlfriends, Muska and Shaista, brought her a hand-painted porcelain doll dressed in a silver-embroidered caftan. Khialo gave her a bag of candied dates and apologized for Gulapa and Sandara, who were too busy to come; also Droon was somewhere between Shabak and Kabul.

A couple of days before, Safi had gotten a large grain order; it was a ten-hour trip in each direction, and presumably, they were on their way back that very afternoon. Khialo was in a crazy mood, and he picked up the doll and started cavorting around the living room, until he came face-to-face with Meena, whose humorless glare stopped Khialo in his tracks. She snatched the doll from him and said it was high time he acted his age.

Supper was festive. Midway through the meal, perhaps still smarting from Meena's earlier rebuff, Khialo said, "Tell me, my sweet birthday girl, what are you going to wear to the wedding? Something stylish, I hope?"

"I haven't decided yet."

"But the wedding's tomorrow."

"Why do you care what I wear?"

"I was just wondering. There's nothing wrong with that, is there?"

"What are you going to wear?"

"White with a red vest. Like fire on snow."

"Oh, Khialo."

"Meena will wear something elegant," Moor said. "I can promise you that."

"Maybe she should wear black," Sial said.

"Yes, dear," Shamla said. "Black brings out your black eyes and tawny skin."

"Maybe you should both put bags over your head," Meena replied. "That way you won't scare everybody."

"I'm serious," Shamla said. "You look beautiful in black."

"She can't wear black," Khialo said. "My mother specifically said she wants everyone to wear cheerful colors. If she said it once, she said it a thousand times, 'No black at Droon's wedding.'"

"I'm going to wear something to…to knock your socks off," Meena said to Khialo.

"What if he's not wearing socks?" Sial said.

"All of you, stop being such comics," Moor said. "Finish eating and let your sister alone."

"Anyway, they're not so funny," Meena said. "Not in the least."

As we were lingering over our tea, Moor nodded at Abba, who left the room. "All right, Meena, darling, now close your eyes," she said. "We have a surprise for you!" Abba came back and placed a box in front of her. She tore off the ribbon, and her eyes lit up when she saw that they'd bought her an acrylic paint set just like the one she'd seen at the art store when we were in Kabul. "Oh, Moor, Abba, thank you, thank you! I love you!"

Khialo and I looked at each other, both of us amused in our boyish superiority by the sentimentality of the scene, amused but touched. *Family*, I thought. What else was there? You took the good with the bad, you had to; they were inseparable, and you rolled with the punches. Light and dark, night and day, wrong and right, relationship was a dyad; nothing existed purely as itself without connection to something other than itself, and this adherence was epitomized by the family, by all the families.

Abba tapped on his glass for silence. "Now that you are growing up, Meena, now that you are leaving your girlish days behind and embarking on adulthood, perhaps you fear you're alone in a dark wood with no one to help you choose which direction to take. You might be asking yourself, which leads to fulfillment and which to an abyss? I want you to remember that your mother and Bibi and I, as well as your brothers and sister, will always be here to love, guide, and protect you. But the path that you follow must be of your own choosing. In that choice you might look to us for advice, but in the final analysis, your way must come from you and only you.

"When you create a picture, Meena, it is your way of interpreting reality, which you see, not as an abstraction, not as a thought in action, but as a series of brilliant images which evoke thought. Our hope, Moor's and mine, is that this paint set can help you express your feelings, just as your brother is learning to do with words, and that in this way your path will become clear to you.

"As you well know, our lives have changed dramatically over the past few years and in ways that we never imagined possible. Much has been lost, there is no surprise there. We have lost our security, our roots have been ripped from the earth, our garden of prosperity uprooted. No longer is the future simple or straightforward as it once was, particularly for you who are on the edge of it. What was once a fruitful field is now a steep precipice. But we have gained something too, and maybe what we have gained is, in the long run, greater than what we have had to give up. For in having to rely on our own fortitude, in deepening equanimity, we have learned how to cope with our many challenges, we have learned how to bolster our strength and our courage and to leap over our many obstacles that bar the path to freedom. Though you may not realize it, such gains are invaluable. For you, my daughter, those are the gains that will be an integral part of your psyche for as long as you live. For certainly they will come in handy when you make your way forward."

Following upon Abba's toast, each of us said a little something, beginning with Bibi. It was a moment purled from the skein of daily life to show a girl dancing on the shores of the mind, obliterating the devastation wreaked by storm, her movement glazed by the winding of the desert sand, white like the icy peaks that guarded our country, and each of us was touched, each moved, this acknowledgement that was invisible, and yet not even death could tear apart of a dancing girl, a sister I thought I knew but saw really for the first time.

Indeed, so enrapt were we that it took a moment for us to realize that someone was insistently rattling the front gate. Finally Shamla, with an expression of irony, went out to see who it was. It turned out to be a neighbor. There'd been some kind of accident, and Droon was hurt. How bad, no one knew. We looked at each other in alarm and then hurried over to Srakala, where we discovered a crowd of villagers milling around Gulapa's house. Abba told the rest of us to wait by the front gate while he, Moor, and Bibi went in to see what was happening. I looked for Jandol, but he'd been swallowed by the throng.

"Hey, what are you guys doing up there?" It was Shakar. A couple of kids had climbed to the roof of Droon's truck and were jumping up, trying to grab hold of a tree branch. "Get off there, you little punks!" He was leaning on the hood holding a lantern, whose flickering light cast eerie shadows on his face, giving him the expression of a devil. "What a time to be screwing around."

"What happened? Is my brother okay?" Khialo asked, but Shakar had stepped away, leaving us surrounded by a bunch of village kids.

"Did you see the body?" one of them said to Khialo in a breathless rush.

"What body?"

"I've never seen a dead man," said another.

"I saw a dead body once."

"Oh, you did not."

"Did so."

"Who?"

"A soldier, and he was lying right in our garden. Dead as a doornail. His whole head was blown off."

"Who's dead?" I said.

"Droon! He was murdered!"

"What'd you say?" Khialo said, seizing the boy's shirt.

"They just brought him in."

Khialo elbowed his way through the mob with me close behind him. His living room was packed with villagers, the air thick with smoke from the kerosene lamps whose smell merged with that of too many tense bodies crammed together in too small a space. Even with the door and windows open, the heaviness in the air wasn't dispelled. Droon was lying on the cot with his head in Gulapa's lap, and she was tying the customary white ribbon around his forehead while Atal bound his feet together. Her face was ashen, but her eyes were like two burning embers.

Khialo flung himself at Atal, who held him, and I could hear his muffled sobs. I wanted to cry too, but no tears came. Instead I thought, *First Baz and now Droon*. But Droon couldn't be dead; he was too full of life. Only he was dead. He was dead and Baz was dead. I was living in a dead land. No, he couldn't be dead. He was getting married tomorrow.

No one spoke, but there was a murmur in the room that rose and fell, a lament that sounded inhuman. I remembered the little puppy Sial found when I was seven who died of distemper and how horrible that had been. We hadn't even given him a name, and without warning he was dying, foaming at the mouth, going into convulsions, constantly whimpering, but you couldn't go near him; there was nothing you could do. Finally, Abba went out back and shot him, and we buried him in the field and said an incantation. I didn't understand what was going on, not then and not now. Especially not now. I could only stare at the body on the cot. Jandol and Meena came up and stood beside me.

"Tomorrow was supposed to be his wedding," Gulapa said to Moor, who put her arms around her. "I just put the finishing touches on my dress. It's so pretty. It's burgundy, and I have a silver shawl to wear over my hair. I made everything myself. Including Atal's silk turban. Did I show you his turban, how it caught the light? Droon brought the material from Jalalabad. And my shiny green shoes that I've never worn." She raised her fist. "What kind of God brings such misery to people? Now, I'll have to dye everything black. And I didn't want to wear black tomorrow, I wanted everything to be…to be memorable. Children, what do they bring? Sorrow. Pain and sorrow. No, there's nothing worse than losing a child. He should be at *my* funeral, not the other way around."

Atal tried to comfort her, but she waved him away with an angry shake of her arm.

"What about Sandara?" he said. "Has anyone seen her?"

"I thought she was with you," Gulapa said.

"I haven't seen her."

"Oh my god," Gulapa cried out and would have risen, but Moor held her firmly.

"Jandol will find her," Moor said. "You stay where you are."

Without a word, Jandol took off with Sial at his heels.

A few moments later, Safi came in and stood in front of Gulapa, nervously twisting his *pakul*. Everyone fell silent. "It was a sniper," he said. "It was about five in the afternoon. We were driving back from Kabul on the Maipar Road that runs through Tangai. You know, that narrow road outside Surabi where the outposts are? We heard machine-gun fire. And then before you could even think, there were shells everywhere. Explosions. Gunfire. 'Let's get the hell out of here!' Droon shouted. He was behind the wheel, and he floored the accelerator. I thought to myself, 'This is it.' We were carrying containers of kerosene and gasoline that we'd exchanged for the grain—one spark and they'd have blown us to kingdom come."

Gulapa was staring at Safi with those burning eyes of hers, but he couldn't meet her glance.

"The road was empty, there was not a car in sight, just us, like a red-hot moving target. Finally, everything cooled down, and we managed to get away. What a relief! We began laughing like two hyenas. We were just roaring, I couldn't even catch my breath. And that's when it must have happened. At first, I didn't realize anything was wrong. But the truck suddenly veered to the left. I hollered at Droon to watch where he was going, but he was slumped against the door, so I grabbed the steering wheel and pulled the truck off to the right shoulder. When we came to a stop, I said, 'What the hell are you doing?' Then I saw he wasn't moving. I tapped him on the shoulder, but he didn't respond. It's funny because there was hardly any blood. It was only later that I realized he must have died instantly." Safi paused and continued to twist his hat. "It must have been a sniper. As I said, there was hardly any blood. At first I thought he was pulling my leg, you know what Droon was like, him and his practical jokes, anything to get a rise out of a person. But he was gone."

Neither Gulapa nor Atal said anything. What was there to say? Questions would come later when they could think clearly. Painful questions that would demand answers, even though no answers would ever be forthcoming.

Presently, Sandara came in followed by Jandol, but when her eyes fell upon Droon's body, she slumped against Jandol and would have fallen if he hadn't put his arms around her.

And so, on an autumn afternoon of perfumed breezes and joyous songbirds, Droon's wedding day became the day of his funeral.

Referred to as the city on the frontier because of its strategic location near the eastern end of the Khyber Pass, Peshawar (emphasis on the second syllable) was formerly the winter residence of various Afghan kings. Like Kabul, the city is more than two thousand years old. It is in Pakhtunistan, which is controlled by Pakistan, and across the Durand Line from Afghanistan. Predominately Pashtoon, its population increased significantly as the result of the influx of Afghan refugees displaced by the Communist occupation and the ensuing civil unrest.

In 1988, hundreds of thousands of refugees had immigrated there, during which Peshawar became the military and political center of anti-Soviet forces. Enemy agents often infiltrated these organizations, which led to eruptions of violence on the city's streets. In addition, although the Durand Line was a porous border with much traveling back and forth, it was also carefully monitored by the Communists, by the Mujahideen, and by the ISI. Armed deserters and thieves also scoured the area.

PART II

CHAPTER SIX

MEENA SCREAMED. "WHAT'S THAT!" She seized hold of Sial's arm.

"Quiet down," he said. "You want to get us killed?"

"I'm sorry, I'm sorry, but look!"

"Meena," I said when I reached them, "what are you—" Then I too saw. Right in front of us, on a pile of snow smeared with blood, lay the half-eaten corpse of a donkey with its entrails exposed and its eyes frozen open.

"Don't look," Jandol said, waving us on. "Keep moving, keep moving. It's going to be light soon. We have to get to Tummanai."

Earlier that evening we'd left Shabak—our aim was to resettle in Peshawar—but we had to travel after dark, what with the continued threat of Russian helicopters, to say nothing of Mujahideen spies. The Soviets would gun you down, but with the insurgents, you never knew what to expect. They might leave you alone, or they might enslave the women and shanghai the men. We had to avoid the larger villages and the busier roads, which was why we were taking a roundabout route, going up the mountain to Tummanai where we'd hire a local guide to show us the way east: most of the villagers knew the mountains paths like the back of their hands. Our plan was simple but risky: Tummanai was about a seven-hour hike, but we'd take two mules to carry the heavy stuff, so that part shouldn't be too difficult.

For a couple of weeks we'd stay with Mirdin and his wife Miriam and their three sons, each of whom worked for my father as shepherds. Then we'd make our way to Taramangal, a small village just the other side of the Durand Line, about a five- to six-day hike through forests and across mountains, on hidden trails and narrow paths. The most difficult part of the journey would be crossing the Durand Line, but we'd deal with that when we came to it. From Taramangal, it was only a four-hour walk to the bus stop where we could catch the express to Peshawar. Once in Peshawar we would stay with Bibi's cousin Zakria until we found a place of our own.

The events that began with Shatoo and ended with Droon's death were catapulting us from our home and our way of life. Any lingering hope that the insurgents would save us had been extinguished with Droon's death. Who could forget his funeral with everyone looking like ghosts? Who could forget Meena's friend Razia forced to marry a man old enough to be her grandfather? The village elders were afraid to open their mouths even as friends and relatives were imprisoned, or worse, executed on flimsy grounds via hasty military tribunals. Each week, more Mujahideen bivouacked in Shabak and Srakala, which meant, in addition to the increased brutality, endless hours of cooking and cleaning for Moor and Lakhta, especially now with the exodus of half the population of both villages.

It was Khialo who burst in with the news, and from that time on, nothing was the same. Someone had told Gulapa there was a rumor that the Major had his eye on our properties, that although he hadn't as yet made any overt moves, he was going around telling everyone that he suspected us of being infidels. Abba made his own inquiries, which then led to the mad scramble to escape before we were arrested. Everything had to be done in secret, which meant not telling Gulapa, who would never forgive us, I was sure, or Sandara, who still walked around as pale as the flowers that she placed on Droon's grave. But Lakhta? Exactly how could we hide the truth from her?

I pleaded with Abba and Moor to be able to confide in her, but I finally had to understand that the less she knew, the better. That way if she were questioned by the police, she'd have nothing to hide. Of course, we couldn't disguise the fact that we were going somewhere, but we told her that Abba was taking Moor and Meena to Jalalabad to stay with Shamla, who was pregnant for a third time and who wanted Moor to be with her when she gave birth. The sad part was, unlike our move to Kabul, there'd be no coming back; when we reached Peshawar, that'd be it. So not being able to say good-bye was heartbreaking for each of us even, and we had to keep reminding ourselves that there were moles everywhere, and I'm not talking about strangers but people you'd known your whole life, who were more than willing to give information as a way to get in good with the insurgents, maybe collect a small reward.

It was snowing when we reached Tummanai, but Mirdin and Miriam were great. They thought nothing of being awakened at three in the morning, and when we explained the situation and the dangers involved, they insisted we stay with them and led us to a small mud structure next to their own home. No electricity, no kitchen, no bathroom, no furniture, a two-burner kerosene stove, a couple of kerosene lamps, and an old-fashioned paraffin heater. Our temporary lodging. We'd settled in when Mirdin brought in some cots, followed by Miriam, who carried a tray with steaming-hot milk tea, fresh-baked bread, home-churned butter, and half a wheel of goat cheese that had been softened first. We hadn't realized how hungry we were and how disoriented we felt, but once we'd eaten, our spirits rose. All that night and throughout the next day, the snow continued to fall until the village was buried in deep heavy drifts. It looked like we might be staying longer than we'd planned, at least until the snows melted and the trails became passable.

The first thing Moor did was to organize everything—where we'd sleep, where we'd store our perishables, keeping eye on the heater, tethering the mules, unpacking our clothes, assigning individual tasks. But more importantly, she set the emotional tone for the entire experience, really for the entire journey. Her optimism in the face of every obstacle, her sense of our triumphing against insurmountable barriers, imbued the rest of us with courage, even Abba, and she accomplished this without a lot of talk, no fiery speech, no pep talk, but in her quiet way, although on that first night she complimented Abba.

"Well, Miwand," Moor said that first morning as we were breakfasting on the remains of the food Miriam had brought. "We've completed the first part of our journey, just as you said we would. What would we do without you? You're the rock upon which this family stands." The rest of us looked knowingly at each other. Abba was the king, but Moor was the boss. It was like that old saying, "The man is the head of the family, but the wife is the neck, and the neck moves the head." That's what our family was like. Maybe every family. But Moor would take no credit for it; she would give the laurels to her husband and to her children, meanwhile downplaying her own contributions.

"Now, the rest of you, finish your meal. We have a lot of work to do. Let's see, we have enough to eat for a few days, but we need to find out where we can obtain more food. And I want to borrow some cleaning utensils from Miriam. This floor looks like it hasn't been scrubbed in years."

"We're going to need firewood," Jandol said. "It's going to be freezing tonight."

"Tonight?" Sial said. "It's freezing now."

"Well, let's get a move on," Moor said. "Meena, finish your breakfast and help me unpack."

"I hate goat's milk," Meena said, scowling.

"Me too," Sial said.

Hearing them complain, I drank my entire glass with gusto, rubbed my stomach, and said, "Yummy."

The days passed, freezing cold, snowy, sometimes dry fierce winds sweeping down from the mountains, then a lessening, a brightening, which, as the weeks went by, became longer-lasting, although the weather remained considerably more intense than it was in Shabak, which was sheltered by these very heights.

Following Moor's example, each of us kept busy in our own individual way. I took out my notebook and wrote poems about the summer, Abba read his philosophy books; Sial sat with his comics; Jandol was active, repairing the roof that leaked, gathering firewood, helping Mirdin with the animals; and Meena and Moor kept house.

One morning when the sky was bright enough to cast a bluish hue over the frigid landscape, we made our way to the holy Garda Tsirai tree. According to villagers, the tree not only had the power to cure the sick but to ward off evil forces, so that when Russian fighter planes flew overhead, what they saw below was a dense fog. It was said that if you had yellow fever, you went to the shrine of Gardi Ghows in Jalalabad; if you wanted to succeed in love, you went to the grave of Mehtarlam Baba in the Laghman Province; if you wished to have children, you visited the burial site of Peer Baba; but if you sought true spiritual enlightenment, you prayed at the Garda Tsirai tree.

At first I thought we were the only ones there until I noticed an old woman in a heavily embroidered shawl who was bowing before the tree. She looked so much like Lakhta—the same curly black hair, the same heavy brows, high cheekbones, dark-fringed eyes, aged anywhere from forty to sixty—I almost went over to her. Oh, Lakhta, how I wished she was here with us. I missed her so much.

"I don't get it," Meena said, oozing disappointment as we stood before the tree, around which devotees had placed various good luck charms, candles, and sticks of incense. "It's just a tree. Nothing to write home about."

"Not that we have a home," Sial said.

"Always with the quick answers," Abba said.

As to the tree, in fact, Meena was quite mistaken. Long before, lightning had split the bole almost in half, so that one side was lush with cones and needlelike leaves while the other, in stark contrast, lifted gnarled lifeless branches that trembled beneath the bone-white sky like broken fingers. This duality, this sense of life and death as originating from the same source, gave the tree a mythical underpinning that called to those with a mystical beat.

"Well, Meena," Moor said, smiling at her daughter, "what did you expect?"

"I don't know, something bigger. Grander."

"Dream on," Sial said. "You know as well as I that this tree that people rave about is only that. A tree. Isn't that right, Jandol?"

"You lack discernment," Abba said. "You close off your minds to new experiences. I wonder how that serves you?"

Now it my turn to be surprised. "But you don't believe in any of this mumbo jumbo, Father."

"I don't and I do."

"Well, which is it?" Sial asked.

"Perhaps it's both."

"But how can that be?" I said. "Either you believe or you don't. You can't have it both ways."

"Let me explain," Abba said. "Like the rest of you, I don't believe that this tree—or any tree, for that matter—has magical powers. But people believe it does, and if it helps them, then what's the harm? And who knows? We could be wrong. There are mysteries that have confounded man since God fashioned him from the dust of his imagination, molding the clay and then imbuing it with the spark of life. If it turns out that the tree is magical, more power to it. If not, well, I'm not disappointed."

"The harm," I said, "comes from people's delusions. If they think that a magical tree is going to confer special powers on them, then they won't try to do something on their own. They'll just sit around waiting."

"People are like fish," Sial said. "You catch one and put it in a bowl of water, and the fish thinks it's back in the ocean."

"Now, everyone, hush," Moor said. "Show some respect."

As more visitors arrived, we continued talking in low voices while Meena ran her fingers along the striated bark, flaking off the trunk. She then wrapped her arms around the bole, resting her head against it with her eyes closed. When Sial asked her what she was doing, she told him to be quiet, that she wanted to see if she could hear the voice of the tree. We didn't stay too much longer since the sky was beginning to cloud up along with a rising wind that presaged more icy rain.

On the way home, we passed by a narrow waterfall that fell from a great height, along the sides of which descended tiers of ice crystals whose shards reflected the light in such a way that it was transformed into a rainbow. Beyond, the mountain peaks glimmered, one after another, as far as the eye could see, those vast ranges that crossed from Afghanistan to Pakhtunistan. Being so close to them, it was as if they had flung themselves up from the young molten earth, trying like the Garda Tsirai tree to reach something that forever eluded them.

Here we were, small and insignificant, comparatively speaking, yet our dreams were as great, if not greater. For our dreams encompassed these very mountains even as they seemed to mock our existence, particularly Tummanai, with its desultory scattering of mud huts and steep mud-washed roads, about to topple into oblivion.

It was lucky that we'd left Shabak at the tail end of winter; otherwise, we'd have had to remain in Tummanai of months instead of weeks. The snow stopped, the sun came out, and before long, green shoots began springing up that gave the mountain village a fresh, exciting ambience. But more than that was the optimism it instilled in us. Pretty soon, the waterfall I mentioned came roaring down from the cliffs above, melting the ice crystals and turning the little stream it fed into a swiftly moving torrent.

Some of the villagers raised goats and sheep whose offspring would run around inside their enclosures. I'd make clicking noises to get their attention so that they'd come up to me until they lost their fear. Villagers were so poor many of their children had never tasted candy, and since we'd brought bags of sweets, I began passing them around, an act that turned me into the most popular kid in town. I'd make up stories about Shabak, about Atal's gardens where there were giant oranges, figs, and apple trees—and aliens. Gulapa would have been proud of me.

Aside from the inconveniences, the petty quarrels with my siblings, the complete lack of privacy living in such close quarters, I began to see my family differently than I had previously. Take Sial. He wasn't a spectacularly self-centered, self-driven, egotistical narcissist. It was really the other way around; his sense of worth was fragile and easily breached, which was why he was so hypersensitive. Too bad though that he masked his uncertainty in such an aggravating way. Poor Sial. I think he'd have been happier never leaving Shabak where he could spin as many daydreams as he wanted, meanwhile always blaming his circumstances for their lack of fulfillment.

One night I was listening to a musician on the radio playing Pashto songs that were practically indiscernible over the static when a slur of black flapping wings filled the room. A murder of crows! I shouted at them to get away, but there were too many, their cries harsh, raucous, filling my mind until I couldn't think. The scene changed. Soldiers in the thousands with steel-tipped boots storming across a wilderness of skulls, the pleas of a conquered nation flung down the centuries, the clash of sword upon sword, then bullets, bombs, the shouts of victory and of defeat, an unending onslaught. Again, the scene changed. Birds of prey were swooping down toward me. I tried to run, but I couldn't move. I made a superhuman effort and shot toward the light...

"Son, wake up. You're having a nightmare."

"What!" I awakened with a start, my heart pounding in my chest.

"Wake up, you're having a bad dream." It was Moor. It took me a moment to shake away the pictures that were going through my mind.

"I was dreaming about horrible birds. They were trying to peck out my eyes. It was so dark and cold."

"It was only a dream."

"It felt so real."

"They feel real, but they're not. That's why they're called dreams. You're nervous about leaving tomorrow, that's normal. Just close your eyes. Everything'll be fine."

"I don't think I'll ever be able to sleep again," I said as I fell back on my pillow, and the next thing I knew, it was morning.

"What were you crying about last night?" Sial said. "You woke me up."

"It was nothing," Moor said. "Just a bad dream."

"Yes," I said. "Everyone dreams. Even you."

That morning Mirdin and Miriam invited us to share their breakfast, which consisted of *roht*, a sweet round flat bread, freshly baked, creamy yoghurt sweetened with homemade apricot jam, cream cheese, and green tea. Abba said that the color of the tea was like the glow of the mountains as the sun surged over the snowcapped peaks. He thanked them for their hospitality, and Moor asked them to join us for breakfast.

Afterward, Abba asked Mirdin to step outside for a moment while the rest of us helped Miriam clean up. We'd just finished when Abba returned, saying that Mirdin had agreed to be our guide. In fact, he said he wouldn't let anyone else take us to Taramangal. Everyone started talking at once until Abba said, "He thinks we need to wait another couple of weeks, to make sure that the snow has melted and the ground is firm."

We groaned when we heard this, but indeed, this was good news given that there was no one more qualified than Mirdin if you were stranded on a mountainside during a blizzard.

The weather was so unpredictable, it was actually three weeks before we left, dressed as nomads with our two heavily-laden mules led by Mirdin. Our only weapon was a British World War II Sten gun with no bullets, which Sial offered to tote until he lifted it, at which point, realizing it not only weighed a ton but was basically useless, he changed his mind, and Mirdin tied it to one of the mules. Our protection had to be by stealth; there was no way we would succeed in any confrontation with either the Communists or the Mujahideen.

The trail wound through a forest of evergreens that became thicker before giving way to an open space where the ground dropped sharply, then rose onto a series of increasingly steep ridges, one after another in an endless chain. At one point, we had to cross a narrow path that edged a precipice, from which, as we gingerly stepped forward, rocks flew off into empty space, along with the echoes of our footsteps.

Meena said she was afraid, and Jandol tried to reassure her. We went single file with him leading and each of us holding on to the shoulders of the person in front, while Mirdin brought up the rear with the mules. "Keep your eyes straight ahead," Jandol said as we started. "And don't look down." Not that there was much to see other than the darkness itself, whose invisible immensity had about it the sensation of absence as a palpable force.

Once accomplished, Sial threw himself down on the ground while the rest of us more or less followed in kind. We wanted to rest, have a bite to eat, some chai, but Mirdin said absolutely no cooking; someone might see the smoke. After too short a time, he said we had to move on, that it was too dangerous to stay where we were. For the entire journey he kept up a killer pace, turning what at first had seemed to me like a great adventure into a brutal trial of will power. Keep moving, keep moving, don't lag; if we get caught, we'll be shot. So on we trooped, usually on trails that were little more than loose debris and rocks whose sharp edges slid from under our feet. Or on places where there was no trail, where we'd have been totally lost if it hadn't been for Mirdin's unerring eye. He knew the exact locations of the various rivers and streams in the region so that when we came to one, he'd lead us to a shallow section or to a bridge, always makeshift, always slippery, much worse than the ones over the Auzingianai but passable.

Because of the recent rains, a large part of our journey was spent slogging through muddy quagmires that made it impossible to keep our shoes dry, and they made squishing noises when we walked. There were ravines that we had to climb down into then clamber out by grasping at roots and tree branches; there were the dry beds of mountain streams so boulder-strewn, we had to constantly watch our step or risk breaking our necks; there were patches of snow, some knee-deep, that we tried our best to avoid. Once we had to help the mules climb up a particularly steep bank, with half of us pushing and the other half pulling. That took strength and ingenuity, believe me.

As the cloudy sky lightened, Mirdin said how lucky we were that the sky was so gray, which meant that there'd be few, if any, Russian helicopters passing overhead. Along about this time we heard gunfire, followed by a series of explosions, most far away but some uncomfortably near. We hurried on even after the firing stopped for it had left in its wake a silence that was equally unnerving. When the sun broke through the clouds, Mirdin herded us into a thick grove of trees, and we set up camp. But like before, he said no fires, so we dined on cold chai, cold eggs, and figs, and then sleep hit me like a sledgehammer the minute I wrapped myself in some blankets and lay my head down on my backpack.

When I woke, for a moment I had no idea where I was. After a hasty meal, we began our march and continued until dawn, unobserved, in a friendless land of snow and rock, of cliff and precipice, where men in helicopters or on patrol or in hidden mountain lairs stared through binoculars, ready to pick you off one by one. Fortunately, no one saw us, no one met us, no one knew we were alive.

Moor handed each of us a small paper bag containing mixed roasted nuts whose salty flavor took my mind off my feet, but that extra bounce only lasted a short time before fatigue and hunger took over. We never rested enough, and believe me, once you sat down, it was doubly hard to get started again. I felt as if I were walking in my sleep, that my legs weren't mine. Meena and I took hold of each other's hand so that if one of us fell behind, the other could help them.

Toward morning, we left behind the Tummanai mountains, emerging into a grassy swale that leaned toward the Azra River. From here we would follow the river until we reached the mountain range known as the Lakarai, on the other side of which was the Durand Line. But even though it was still dark, we were too close to the villages that dotted the lush countryside to think of stopping. We continued walking, with Mirdin admonishing us to hurry for even though we were shielded by the heavy foliage, tiny stick figures, the farmers, could be seen working in the fields.

On the second night after this, we found ourselves at a point where the river curved to the northwest, away from the direction we were going and toward a series of forbidding summits.

"Do you see those mountains?" Mirdin said, indicating two peaks that towered over the others like twin minarets, seeming in the hazy distance to break out of the obscurity of drifting clouds. "The one on the left is Tora Bora. It's one of the main strongholds of the Mujahideen. They say there are hundreds of caves and tunnels for them to hide in."

He allowed us a brief glance before waving us forward and away from the mountains. Even though it was light out, we continued for two more hours until he had us come to a halt beside a rickety fence, behind which were a scattering of mud huts, half hidden by vines and shrubbery. Mirdin told us to wait, and he opened the gate and rapped on the door of the largest hut, and an old man and woman came around from the side, both carrying wicker baskets filled with potatoes and onions. They placed the baskets down on the ground and greeted Mirdin, who brought them over to us. They were friends of his, and when Mirdin asked if we could stay until the evening and offered to pay, they refused his money and welcomed us as if we were old friends.

The woman led Moor and Meena into her house, while the man took the rest of us to the hujra, merely a slapdash lean-to with a roof of straw. Supper was the best meal I'd had since we left Tummanai, boiled beef with vegetables over Jasmine rice dripping with butter, warm bread, milk from a cow and not a goat, and for dessert we shared our figs. Afterward, I went to lie down for a minute, and the next thing I knew it was late afternoon.

Time to move on. I was beginning to learn how to pace myself. The trick was to allow yourself to respect the initial fatigue, not to push, simply to wait until you got your second wind, at which point, as the energy filled your lungs, you might find yourself almost running. The smell of the mountain ash was invigorating as well as the cold air that had in it no hint of spring, but that still added a lightness to my step.

When we reached the foot of the Lakarai, we skirted toward the south until Mirdin brought us to what had once been a thriving village before it had been bombed by the Communists. Most of the mud huts had been destroyed, but one in particular, although the front wall had been demolished, was covered by rugs tacked to sheets of plastic that were attached to the sides. Our home for the night.

Mirdin had apparently stayed here many times before since he seemed to know his way around. Inside, to our delight, we discovered a *chirgai* for cooking that Mirdin said we could use as long as we kept the flame low. Abba, Jandol, and I gathered firewood, Mirdin and Sial tended to the mules, while Moor, assisted by Meena, prepared supper so that soon, a rich heavy smell filled the room, added to by the cinnamon aroma of the chai.

When the meal was ready, we sat in a circle on some torn cots as Abba said a prayer of thanks, after which we dug in. I don't know about the others, but I felt such a sense of accomplishment. Look what we'd done. Who'd have thought we could have made such a journey? It wasn't that we weren't strong enough; I mean, we were country people used to hard work, to traveling long distances by foot. But leaving everything familiar behind as we headed into the unknown with just our courage, some Afghanis, and two balky mules was something entirely different.

After eating, it was wonderful to feel the fire's warmth even when the room became stuffy, at which time Jandol pulled the plastic sheeting open a crack, letting in a sweep of drafty air that also felt refreshing.

In the afternoon it began to drizzle, a soft rain that by dark had turned into a steady downpour. We decided to wait until the rain stopped, and after another hot meal, it was great to rest without having to face another nighttime march, considering that the next part of our journey would be entirely uphill.

Abba told a story:

> Now, some men cast giant shadows while others have no shadows. Instead, they stand in the shadow of the great and claim it as their own. Amir Gulnar was such a man who claimed the shadows of his ancestors to be his own. He was the chief of a horde of marauders who lived on the lower reaches of the Himalayas. When a party of farmers appeared, Gulnar attacked them, and those he didn't kill were enslaved. But some escaped, eventually finding their way to a land of dwarves who, as it turned out, were expert fighters but whose possessions had been stolen, whose lives had been destroyed, whose women had been desecrated by Gulnar and his troops.
>
> The men and the dwarves proceeded to train as soldiers, until, armed to the teeth, they traveled in force to wage war with Amir Gulnar. Infuriated by what he perceived as a parade of fools, Gulnar engaged them in many battles,

> the scars of which can still be seen today on the slopes of those mighty heights. Finally, one of the dwarves, a marksman no older than Sial, hurled his lance at Gulnar and, whether it was luck or fate, severed an artery in the giant's neck. He howled in pain, but none came to his aid, neither his cohorts nor his enemies. He fell to his knees trying to stanch the flow, but it was no use. And so, when King Gulnar died, he died alone, and when it was time to bury him, no one offered to help. Thus, his body lay on the hard ground where he was slain until his bones were bleached white by the sun. And as the sun retreated, at last Gulnar cast a shadow that was his own: a snaggle-beaked wingless crow.
>
> In this way, in death, Gulnar became the man that secretly he always was.

"A cheery tale," Jandol said.

"Indeed it is, son," Abba said. "The moral of the story is a lesson each of you could profit by."

"What moral?" Sial said.

"It's not a riddle?" Jandol said.

"It's not?"

"Well, brother, let's say it's an easy riddle."

"If it's so easy, what's the answer?"

"You must find it in your own heart," Abba said. "No one can tell you."

"I don't think it's a riddle at all," I said. "The moral is, you have to succeed on your own. Fly on your own wings. Not take credit for other's work. You can't rely on the past. You can't rest on the shoulders of those who came before and call them your own."

"Oh, be quiet," Sial said. "I know what it means. After all, I am older than you. And wiser."

"You're a funny guy, Sial. You're the one who's the riddle, not Abba's story. I'll never understand you if I live to be a hundred."

"That makes two of us."

"Hey," Jandol said, "count me in. That makes three." Then he said,

> Once, long ago, during an era of great strife—not unlike our own—there lived a young man named Rokhan who was a poet and a pacifist. One night a voice came to him in a dream and said, "It is up to you to unite the Pashto people as one nation." At first Rokhan resisted. "Why me?" he cried, but night after night, the voice spoke to him until he said, "Enough, I will do as you request." Rokhan organized an army, choosing men who were willing to look death in the eye, who were ready to raise their banners against an enemy fifty, a hundred times stronger, warriors who vowed to put an end to the Mughal tyranny. Ten men became a hundred, a hundred a thousand, a thousand became an army of one hundred thousand men. He became famous among the Pashtoon as Pir Rokhan, the Spirit of the Light, in the war he waged against the Mughal general, Muhsin Khan.
>
> But during the battle of Tarbela, when sheets of fire fell from the sky, when the clash of thunder burst furiously over the burnished hills, Rokhan was taken prisoner. He was executed, and his head was impaled on a stake. Calling him the Spirit of Darkness, the Mughals carried this stake for everyone to see, which so disheartened the fighters that they laid down their arms in defeat. But what the Mughals didn't know was that although they had killed Rokhan's body, his soul remained a vibrant spirit that moved across the earth, rekindling the spirit of the Pashtoon people. Soon they rose up and defeated the powerful enemy, in the process creating their own homeland between the two rivers, the Amo to the north and the Indus to the south.
>
> When this was accomplished, Pir Rokhan's soul was released, and he entered union with the Divine.

Later in bed, I thought about what Abba and Jandol said. I decided that if you wanted to have a proper funeral, you had to perform great deeds like Rokhan. The only snag was that personally,

I didn't care what they did with my body after I was gone. And how many kings had ruled Afghanistan, how many empires had risen to greatness, had promised to last a thousand years, had faded from memory amid drought and mass destruction? The cycle was endless; the wheels never stopped spinning. That being true, why was it that when people saw something beautiful, they had an irresistible urge to destroy it? Greed eclipsed by destruction in the name of glory? Winding up with nothing.

I pictured Amir Gulnar. His eyes were shutters that you couldn't see through. I'd tear the blinds from his eyes and strangle him like a wild dog. No, I couldn't do that. If I did, I'd be just as evil as he was. Besides, what would it matter? One dead Gulnar meant nothing; there'd always be others, an endless procession who'd come with promises, their thin voice tempered like steel, their honeyed words dripping with venom. You must do what we say, believe what we believe, listen when we speak. When they died, their sons took their places and their son's sons, each succeeding generation uttering the same directives, You must listen, you must believe, you must obey. Until yet another Rokhan emerged, another who gave his life in the battle for autonomy. Why did it seem so meaningless to me, this belief that was at the core of most people's minds?

By the following afternoon, the weather cleared, although it was colder than before with a thick mist that rose from the fields off the tops of the stiff grass stalks that weaved in the wind. As we began our climb, our movements somewhat encumbered by the layers of clothing we were wearing, Moor cautioned us to be frugal with the tea for there wasn't much left. We headed southeast on a narrow mountain trail that us upward, in a circuitous route that zigzagged up and around the mountain, going higher and higher. The higher we went, the deeper the carpet of snow that lay on either side.

The climb brought to mind a poem Sandara once read to me, a translation from English that I'd liked, although at the time, the meaning had escaped me. It was only later when I read it in the original that I realized the poet wasn't saying how life was a struggle, but if you persevered, you could find eventual solace. Quite the opposite. She was saying that life was a wearisome trial that inevitably led toward death. Christina Rosetti once wrote,

> Does the road wind up-hill all the way?
> Yes, to the very end.
> Will the day's journey take the whole long day?
> From morn to night, my friend.
> Shall I find comfort, travel-sore and weak?
> Of labor you shall find the sum.
> Will there be beds for me and all who seek?
> Yea, beds for all who come.

With my turtleneck sweater under my woolen *kootsab*, I soon felt too warm, but when I opened it, I became chilled; if I buttoned it up again, it made me drowsy. Once I tripped against Sial, who took me by the shoulder, telling me to watch my step. "If you don't look where you're going, brother, you might wind up as food for the vultures." He was referring to the canyons and gullies that would suddenly appear, precipitous gorges that gaped at your feet while the mountain remained motionless, always leading you upward, always ahead of you, our following steep paths that were nothing more than soupy combinations of melted snow, mud, and rocks.

As we climbed higher, it became colder with an unpredictable wind that caused us to walk with our heads down, the current whipping around us like an angry sea, no one talking, sometimes surrounded by trees, sometimes nakedly exposed, the wind dying down, the path curving sharply one way or the other, giving you a panoramic view of the entire valley overshadowed by the starry sky, then being enclosed by twisted trees that cut off the view until we reached a turning where the path headed toward a lower summit in a more-or-less straight line.

This section of the climb was backbreaking, my only thought being to keep moving, we were almost at the top, don't give in now, not when you've gotten this far, only several more steps, one after another, not much more. It's so close, just think, no, don't think, nothing to think about, close your mind, that's right, one foot then another, look at Moor clutching the bridle of one of the mules and holding on to Meena with her other hand, two ghostly figures shrouded in black. If they could do it, you can too, just don't think about it or about anything.

When we neared the crest, Mirdin turned sharply to the right toward a cleft in the mountain through which you could see a series of farther pinnacles, each more forbidding, each snow-covered peak higher than the one before, summit upon summit, with no sign of anyone, so that if you fell here, if you got lost, that'd be the end of you.

My glance fell on the mules, their gray skin lucent in the moonlight, the steam coming from their nostrils, their pasterns buried in the snow. Mindlessly, I headed toward the opening when I realized that Mirdin was going past it, down a narrow twisted trail that led to a small cave, actually more of a rocky outcropping, set amid a grove of wind-bent pines. We were at the southern topmost edge of the Zazai Forest, a million acres of pristine woods that stretched across the Durand Line, continuing for miles in every direction.

"We are in our mother's arms," Abba said as he looked downward into the forest.

When dusk fell, we began our descent down the Lakarai, which turned out to be comparatively easy with gently sloping trails, nor were there many scary precipices, even though my knees began to ache from the constant tensing. Occasionally, the path did unexpectedly veer one way or another to reveal jagged cliffs, our steps sending small rocks tumbling into the void, but when that happened, I kept my eye on the mules; I trusted those beasts. Suddenly, shrieks of horror burst around us, and we all huddled around each other until Mirdin waved his arms and said to calm down; it was the rhesus monkeys—the forest was full of them—and they were harmless. But their cries sounded as if someone was being torn apart, limb by limb. I remembered Jaat, a Pashto organ grinder with his performing monkey, how he'd come to the Shabak bazaar, turn on a boom box, and the monkey would dance around while we tossed coins for him to catch. I used to think that the monkey was so cute, especially when he ate a banana, how delicate his movements were. But here, where everyone was a potential enemy, every cry a possible life-or-death alarm, nothing was cute; there was no lilting music, and once, when Meena cried out, Moor warned her not to let that happen again.

The Zazai Forest was a darkness in a darkness. We rested for a few hours before resuming our quest. Since Mirdin was avoiding the more straightforward routes, in no time we had no idea in which direction we were going. In places where the leaves were dry, they crunched under our feet, and we had to be extra careful how hard we stepped so as not to make too much noise. My shoes were falling apart—they weren't made for the kind of punishment they were being given—so I tried to avoid the drifts of snow, but sometimes we simply had to plow right through, and soon my socks were soaked.

The hours passed until Mirdin brought us to a halt and said that the Durand Line was less than a mile away. He pulled Abba aside, and the two men conferred for a short time, after which Abba explained that for our own safety, we'd have to travel in pairs, that it was too dangerous to move en masse. He said that he would go with Moor, Jandol would go with Meena, I would go with Sial, and Mirdin would lead with the mules. If we heard any strange voices or noises, we were told not to stop, no matter what. Step lively, no talking, watch where you're going. If we were stopped by anyone and questioned, we were to tell them that we were nomads and knew nothing about the Durand Line, that we'd never heard of it. If you have any problems, don't panic; just keep your wits about you.

When we were ready, Moor kissed each of us. "Don't be afraid," she said. "Keep your heads up high. Remember. We are Pashtoon."

The word rang in my ears. *Pashtoon!*

In Taramangal, the villagers greeted us like family. Malak Kaliwal, the village elder, provided us with lodgings, an abandoned house at the edge of the village. Abba offered to pay, but it would have been unseemly for Kaliwal to accept. How could he ask a spiritual brother for pay? It was against the Pashtoon code of behavior. Even in their poverty, the villagers were generous, and throughout the day, they augmented our meager supplies with bags of rice, salt, sugar, and tea. By late afternoon, we'd settled in, except for candles and some other sundries, which we bought at the village market, really nothing more than a garden shed.

Anxious to return to Tummanai, Mirdin only stayed with us a few days. We'd been through so much together, a bond had been formed that was as strong as a blood tie, even though we hardly knew him and would probably never see him again. Life was funny, I thought as we stood watching his departure. These connections you made, like a flare that briefly illuminated the landscape down to the smallest detail before being swiftly extinguished, leaving you again in darkness. Without Mirdin, we would have never found our way to Taramangal; he was closer to us than a brother, and once he was swallowed by that darkness, we'd never even know if he survived the journey back to Tummanai. A modest man, like Kaliwal, he refused to accept payment except for Abba's insisting he keep the two mules.

Kaliwal came by later, saying he wanted to show us something spectacular. Moor and Meena chose to remain at home, but the rest of us accompanied him. As we stepped around a series of steep rock-strewn hills we came to a shelf that extended out about a quarter mile before dropping sharply down to the valley below. On this shelf there was a massive construction site that sprawled before us, on which, spread out for what seemed like blocks, was a series of half-built, interconnected, one-story brick buildings in all stages of development. Swarming over the various hives, hard hats were operating caterpillar tractors, cranes, and drilling machines. The closer we got, the noisier it became, as if the earth itself were shrieking at the violence being done to what had once been a field of winter wheat. Turns out, wealthy Arab sheikhs and millionaire Punjabis were building a madrassa that would be large enough to house thousands of students.

Kaliwal trembled with excitement. "This is our future!" he shouted above the clamor. "The future of our children and of their children. Is it not magnificent? Does it not thrill the heart and spirit? Being built within walking distance of the Durand Line, a magnificent school that will attract the generations."

When we got home, we asked ourselves how Kaliwal could be that excited over the millions being spent on the madrassa while the people in his village starved, while the children ran around in rags and everyone lived in such poverty, even Srakala appeared wealthy in comparison. As if to punctuate our exclamations, it started to drizzle, just sprinkles at first that suddenly turned into a deluge, which kept on practically the entire week.

After a few days, Jandol and Sial made a mad dash over to the store to buy some candles, but when they came back, they were empty-handed. The shopkeeper said that there'd be no deliveries until the rain let up because the roads were closed. Jandol asked him how long that would take, but the man said it was in God's hands, that the mountains and the skies had their own ways of doing things, their own timetable.

"So now what?" Meena said.

"So now, we have to be patient," Moor said. "Isn't that right, Miwand?"

"What other choice do we have?" Sial said.

"As long as we don't freeze to death," Meena said.

"What I don't understand," Sial said, "is why every time we come to a village, we get stuck. First Tummanai and now Taramangal. What should we expect in Peshawar, fire? A drought?"

"Maybe it will rain chickens," Jandol said. "Then we can have chicken every day."

"Children," Abba said, "enough."

The truth was, in spite of Abba's and Moor's attempts to cheer us up, the news was dismaying, and we went to bed early. On the following morning we almost didn't wake up. The weather had been so abysmal that we decided to keep the heater on. We could always find firewood, so that at least wasn't a problem. That way, when we woke up in the morning, we wouldn't find ourselves in a refrigerator in which the water in our pitchers would be frozen solid. Sial said one of these days we were going to blow ourselves to smithereens, but what happened was worse.

Unbeknownst to us, the ancient heater was leaking carbon monoxide. The only thing I remember about the experience was being forcibly dragged outside by Jandol and hitting my head against the front porch. I heard Moor hollering at Sial to open every window and to pull open the doors. Meena was retching, while Abba, shaky though he was, knelt beside her, holding her by the shoulder. I finally came around, thanks to the discomfort of the rain seeping through my clothes, but it took a while for my head to clear.

Kaliwal replaced our heater with another, but to be on the safe side, we kept it next to the window, which we left cracked open to ventilate the place, and no matter how cold it was, we always turned it off when we went to sleep. It turned out to be Meena who'd saved our lives. Sometime before dawn she'd awakened, violently sick to her stomach, but when she tried to rise, her limbs felt paralyzed. She said she felt as if she were suffocating. Somehow she managed to crawl outside, and immediately the fresh air revived her enough to realize something was happening, and she woke us up.

As the poets say, extreme conditions bring out the best in people—or the worst. I think in retrospect, it was a miracle that we didn't kill each other. Stuck there day after day with nothing to do, nowhere to go, our hope for the future bleeding away. In truth, if it hadn't been for Kaliwal providing us with food, we would have gone hungry.

I would lie on my cot and think about our house in Shabak, of the scent of roses from the garden, of the hibiscus that flourished along the banks of the Auzingianai until I realized that if we had to live like animals, it didn't help to reminisce about irreclaimable past. Meena and Sial were constantly at each other's throats. They'd start before breakfast without wrapping it up until bedtime. Jandol and I began to realize that they amused each other while driving the rest of us crazy, which amused them even more, like two dull knives scraping their blades against each other until they were sharp enough to cut our throats.

On the evening of the heater mishap, Jandol had said he hoped that now with no heating, their lips might freeze. But no such luck. I can still hear Meena's plaintive voice. "My life is draining away, I might as well be dead." Then Sial's. "Shut up, you stupid jerk." They'd snap at each other until Moor raised her hands, a gesture that, more than words, expressed the question "Why did I have children?"

I was no one's darling either. Although I knew it wasn't my destiny to end my days in Taramangal, my belief in my future began to flicker, leaving in its place an irritation I could not rid myself of and which was increased tenfold when I had to listen to Sial and Meena, who inevitably saw the bad side of everything. I finally told them both to go to hell, which made me feel better—well, a little better. A very little, I might add.

One day I slept late, but as I got out of bed, the room started spinning so crazily, I immediately sank back down on my still-warm pillows. Moor said, "What's the matter?" but I had trouble telling her my head hurt because my teeth began to chatter. She told me to get under the blankets while she heated some tea for me. It took me some time to stop shivering. My head was burning hot, and my body ached. When the chai was ready, it had a funny bitter taste that made me sick to my stomach. When I think back about this time, I can hardly remember anything distinctly. It was like being inside a kaleidoscope, my own private slideshow where everything kept shifting into a series of weird shapes, where waking and sleeping fed into each other. I saw Gulapa, only she had razored claws, sharp fangs, and she was fiery, but before I could grasp what she was saying, she changed into Imam Parast, who began chasing me, then Droon and Baz appeared in white.

Whenever I opened my eyes, Abba would be sitting next to me with a concerned look on his face, an expression I found alarming for it said clear as day that I was dying. But I couldn't be dying; I was too young, too healthy. One night I woke up, my heart pounding. The heater was filling the room with carbon monoxide, the place reeked of smoke, and it was freezing. Meena was beside me wrapped in a heavy shawl with only a candle for light. When she noticed that my eyes were open, she wiped my forehead with a damp towel and gave me some heated broth.

What had been a hallucination really marked the fact that I had passed the crisis and was on the mend. Later, Jandol lifted me up to a sitting position while Sial held out a glass of hot milk with honey, much of which I was able to swallow before sinking under the blankets. Then I knew I wasn't dying. Through the plastic-sheeted window, I could just make out the pale sky against which the branches of the trees in their naked splendor struggled to remain aloft, a reminder of the Garda Tsirai tree, especially of the lady in the shawl praying for illumination. Now it was this stranger's face I saw when I thought of Lakhta, whose image was becoming blurred in my memory. It didn't help that I screwed up my eyes as I tried to force myself to remember what she looked like; I couldn't hold on to the picture or of my thoughts. Instead, I watched as the sky darkened until you could no longer see the outlines of the branches. That night I had my first solid food. Brother, was I ravenous; you couldn't hold me back.

So my fever went away; I began to feel more like myself just as the weather became warmer. Now we didn't need a fire except in the evening or sometimes in the early morning when it was pleasant to sit with the door open and the sun streaming in, reading or simply daydreaming over a steaming bowl of cereal. *What a dream come true*, I thought with no irony. *The sun is out.* To be honest, like with the famous egg incident, I loved being the center of attention, but I knew my moment in the spotlight had come to an abrupt end when I asked Sial if he would please fix me a glass of cold lemonade with just a dash of sugar, and he said, "You're not crippled. Make it yourself."

My eye fell on a poster he'd tacked up. You know how you can see something a hundred times without noticing it until, for no discernable reason, it hits you on the head? Upon our arrival in Taramangal, Sial had put up a poster he'd brought from Shabak that showed a vacation resort in Brazil (I think it was Brazil), of a blue ocean rolling onto a beach of white sand. The scene was breathtaking. Along the shore were resort hotels fronted by coconut palms whose fronds were swaying in the breeze. In the foreground, a man and a woman were reclining in chaise lounges, the woman reading a magazine while the man gazed at the ocean with a tall iced drink in his hand. I scrutinized the picture and imagined myself soaking up the sun on that nameless beach, sipping a cold drink as the tide came in. Then, unbidden, came the thought, *Why not?* Why couldn't I? I felt a chill course through me. What made that guy so special that he could be living in the lap of luxury while I couldn't?

The image remained in my consciousness even when, a few weeks later, the weather cleared, enabling us to leave Taramangal and catch the bus for Peshawar. That could—that would be me. Seriously.

CHAPTER SEVEN

The commander's office was at the entrance to the camp behind a wire fence with a couple of armed sentries at the gate as a welcoming committee. Within, the lean, trim Punjabi commander, Sultan Mushtaq Ahmad, as the brass nameplate stated, was at his desk, seated on a black leather executive's chair. On the wall behind him was a bulletin board with photographs of shabby refugees being given bags of grain, their neediness in sharp contrast to this well-dressed officer facing us.

As we stood stiffly before him with inane smiles, he affected a world-weary expression that was mirrored by a clerk who sat across the room from him, typing on an old Royal electric typewriter and glancing up from time to time. The commander's eyes slowly traveled from Abba to Jandol to Sial to me, cold eyes, predatory eyes, their intensity cautioning care should he ask anything. Nodding his head ruefully, he waited for one of us to speak, and in the momentary silence, I noticed the wall clock had stopped working and its hands stood at three o'clock.

After what we'd gone through, to wind up in a refugee camp with its endless jumble of threadbare tents, mud hovels, makeshift enclosures made from dozens of plastic shopping bags sewn together and attached to stilts, to be in this office with our hopes dismantled like the watercolor I'd seen of a sailing ship dashed upon a stone-white reef, was impossible to fathom—it couldn't be happening. In fact, the actual blow hadn't yet fallen, but the fear, the watchfulness, they'd blossomed without so much as a drop of moisture. I say the blow hadn't fallen because unless we could pay the necessary bribes, we wouldn't be allowed to remain in the camp.

Staying with Zakria had turned out to be impossible; his house was inundated by relatives, and with Abba's dwindling money supply, it was imperative that we situate ourselves as soon and as cheaply as possible.

Jarred by the telephone, the commander swooped it up on the second ring, spat out several yeses and nos, replaced the receiver, and snapped his finger toward the clerk, who leaped to his feet. Wordlessly, the commander indicated a pile of folders in his inbox. The clerk picked up the one on top and returned to his typing.

"I wish I could help you, really I do." The commander addressed my father half in Urdu, half in Pashto. "I am not a cruel man, I am not a blind man. I see what the world is like. But my hands are tied. The truth is, I am besieged. Everywhere I go, everyone I meet. Give me this, give me that, just give me, give me, give me. Now you come asking not only for space to set up a temporary home, but the temporary home as well. And to my regret, I have to say that it is impossible. Are you aware that there are over seventy thousand of you people in this camp alone? Seventy thousand! Why don't you stay in your own country? You don't see me coming over and demanding a place to live. It always begins in such a simple way. Only one tent, sir, just one. It doesn't have to be new, my children are young, the sun is hot, the nights are cold. So I give you a tent, and then you want a bed and blankets, and pretty soon, you want a palace."

Now having fired himself up, the commander continued, leaping from point to point, never stopping to take a breath until a riptide of self-satisfaction pulled us under and threatened to drown us in his embrace. When he was finished, he leaned toward us, resting both of his forearms on the edges of his desk blotter.

We waited for him to finish.

"So," the commander concluded as he rose from his chair, "if there's nothing else, I am a busy man." He told the clerk to get the car ready. "Oh, and bring me a Coke. And make sure it's cold. Plenty of chipped ice. Not like the last time."

"I can see you are an honorable man," Abba said to the commander, who was now busy preparing to go.

"I try, I try."

"Why don't you boys wait outside," Abba said, shepherding us out. "I want to talk to the commander alone."

What happened next I could only imagine because twenty minutes later, when Abba and the commander stepped outside, both of them were acting as if they'd known each other since grade school. As they came up to us, I heard the commander say, "Right in the newcomer's section. That's the nicest part of the camp. Lots of open fields. Good for the children to play in. Plenty of fresh air."

As he was pulling on his gloves, a man stepped out of the office, pausing to shield his eyes against the glare. Then he turned in a half circle, placed his index finger below each of his ears, and in a high-pitched reedy voice, called out the afternoon prayer in Arabic. "Allah-Hoo-Akbar, Allah-Hoo-Akbar, Allah-Hoo-Akbar!"

His words were echoed by hundreds of other voices that came from the camp muezzins, their cries melding together, some shrill, some deep, some near, others seeming to rise from the bowels of the earth.

The commander checked his watch with a fleeting expression of annoyance before he assumed a proper mien. "Jala jalala hoo!" he shouted to a crowd of people waiting outside the fence separating the offices from the camp, their cries mingling with that of his.

When the calls for prayer ceased, the clerks came out of their offices, one of them with a pitcher of water that he held for the commander to rinse off his face, arms, and feet. Those who hadn't previously cleansed themselves headed toward the side of the building where there was a collection of ewers on a shelf above a cement water trough. There they followed the same ritual as the commander: first the men followed by the women and children.

Behind the office was a rudely-constructed mosque for the men, basically a large rectangular tent, open on all four sides, with a rug of felt carpeting for the floor. The women and children retreated to a shaded area that had been set up for them while the commander, in his role as mullah, led the men to the mosque where everyone took off his shoes before entering, after which they took their places in rows facing his back.

When I took my place, I felt a foot rubbing against mine, but when I shifted away, the foot moved closer. I dared not look over to see whose foot it was. But even though I remembered that saying "You shouldn't leave spaces because the devil will walk in between," I had the mad longing to smash my foot down on his.

After the commander's air-conditioned office, the heat was unbearable, there was no breeze, and the sweet aroma of jasmine perfume could not cover the smell of sweaty, unwashed bodies pressing against each other. The commander began the ritual by repeating the words, "Allah-Hoo-Akbar." At the same time—and depending upon which Islamic sect you belonged to—you either placed your thumbs below your ears with the palms outward, or you held your hands directly in front of you with your thumbs next to each other and your palms at an angle. Then some of the men in the first group either dropped their arms to their sides, or they clutched their hands together against their abdomens while the men in the second group placed one hand upon another on their chests with their legs apart and their heads down. I was one of the ear-thumb stomach clutchers.

The commander again said, "Allah-Hoo-Akbar." When he did, everyone leaned forward, placing our hands on our knees with our heads down. And again. "Allah-Hoo-Akbar." Each of us stood up straight with our shoulders back, stomach in, and when he repeated, "Allah-Hoo-Akbar," we promptly dropped to the floor with our foreheads touching the carpet and ours arms stretched out straight before us. Again, the words "Allah-Hoo-Akbar," and we rose to our knees and settled in place, except for the few old men who sat on stools. At this point, the entire ritual was repeated three more times until the commander said, "Alsalamo Ull Alikam Wa Rehmatullahi Wa Barakatuh," at which time we turned our heads to the right. He repeated the phrase, and we turned our heads to the left. Now we went through the entire ceremony from the beginning to the end four more times, after which we paused and did everything again two more times. This took about half an hour, until all of us placed our palms toward us with the pinkie fingers touching. The commander said something in Urdu, which I didn't understand, and everyone rubbed his hands against his face as if he were washing it. That was it. Then everyone dispersed.

I held back for a moment—I didn't want to make eye contact with the foot guy—before I ambled out of the mosque with my hands behind my back as if I hadn't a care in the world. No one was supposed to budge during the ceremony. Everything was deadly serious. If any of these men suspected you of being an infidel, they could murder you without fear of rebuttal. But during the ceremony, a dog fly had landed on the commander's back right below his neck. I watched as it inched up, whereby I made a bet with myself. If the commander didn't swat it when it bit him, then he was a truly religious man. But if he did, well, you can draw your own conclusions. I myself had no love for the insect world—indeed, I was allergic to bees, and once when I was about eight, the sting of a hornet caused my whole body to blow up. Luckily, we were visiting my uncle in Jalalabad, and he treated me. From then on I had to always carry medication in case of an emergency. One bite, and I would be among my ancestors. Dead.

So I'm watching this dog fly inching closer to the guy's neck, wondering, *Will he or won't he?* At the same time, I'm also thinking that no one here understands Arabic, including the commander. What a world. Once Khialo asked Kadoo the meaning of something in the evening prayer, which resulted in the mindless mullah slapping him in the face. "You are never to ask questions about God, do you hear me, boy? Never!" We soon realized that Kadoo didn't understand the language either. This image obliterated my obsessing about the dog fly. What was the difference if he swatted it or not? If he was lame enough to follow a religion whose very words were beyond his comprehension, then whether he swatted a fly or not meant less than nothing. Well, except to the fly. To the fly it meant—everything.

Still, I was relieved that no one had noticed me. I didn't want to get into a brouhaha my first day at camp. One of the clerks was taking my family to a warehouse, and I caught up with them.

"How much did you give him?" my mother was saying.

"Who?"

"Don't play coy with me, my dear."

"You mean the commander? Just enough. Not a rupee more. He's given us one week to get our ID papers."

"Well, that's a relief. I was afraid he wouldn't let us stay here without them."

"Money talks."

"Money sings." Sial laughed. "So long as you know the words."

"Well, we have a place to stay, let's thank God for that," Moor said.

"Yes, but what happens when there are no more rupees?"

"When there are no more rupees, you'll have to get a job," Moor said.

"I'm serious."

At the doorway, the clerk fumbled with the keys until Abba stuck twenty rupees in his hand, at which, miraculously, he found the correct one. Inside were piles of blankets, tents, cooking oil, bags of rice, and wheat flour. Everything was stamped UN. In addition to the supplies, we were given one rolled-up tent, our new home.

We boys kept taking turns carrying the cumbersome tent, which was rolled around the stakes; it actually needed two of us on that long walk through the camp to the newcomers' section. When we reached our destination, without much ado, the clerk led us to a space adjacent to the camp cemetery, said good luck, and left. Our belongings were at the compound office, so Jandol, Sial, and I went to retrieve everything while Abba stayed behind to set up the tent.

"One more sardine, and the can will pop open," Sial remarked after we'd set up everything. How like him to say out loud what the rest of us were thinking. "How can we live here? The weather's horrible, there's no air, the tent's much too small. No clean water, no food, no sanitation. This place is a zoo, and we're caged animals."

"Not quite," I said, pointing toward the cemetery. But in that shimmering heat, the headstones themselves seemed to tremble as if the living dead were about to engulf the dead who were still living.

That night, I dreamed I was outside a hospital whose walls were made of twisted wire that resembled writhing limbs. There was a long line of patients waiting to be admitted, their remarks, when I asked what was happening, belied by their healthy appearance. "We're dying," they said. "We need to see the doctor, hurry, hurry."

The scene switched. I was on the opposite side of the hospital watching these same people leave, and they were laughing and joking. "We've been cured!" they shouted happily. "We're free!" I couldn't believe my eyes. They were all in wheelchairs, some with no legs, some had no arms, some were blind. I ran back to the entrance, waving my arms. "Go back, go back, you're in danger!" No one listened, no one heard.

I awoke with a start, my heart racing, and at first I couldn't remember where I was.

The next day, Abba, Jandol, Sial, and I went off to get identification cards (the women didn't need any) at the headquarters of the ruling warlord, Mavlavi Khalis. His compound, located behind high brick walls on acreage half the size of a soccer field, was a fortress. Armed guards at the gate and around the five-story office building, an elaborate pat down, signing in, signing out, countless posters:

> Jihad zamoong Islami fariza da.
> (Jihad is our Islamic duty.)

Inside, the building was crawling with typists, clerks, managers, phones ringing off the hook, typists pecking away, bright fluorescent lights that made everyone look like they were sick. Thank God, it was air-conditioned. At the door where we were directed, there was a line of people, and we took our place at the end, although within minutes, there was now a line behind us until the hallway was filled.

We inched forward. People were standing or sitting, and some were gossiping; the guards would come by and tell us to move, move, move. We'd get up, move another inch, then sit down and wait. Four men in dark business suits wearing sunglasses and carrying leather briefcases came up accompanied by two guards at either end. They looked at us, and one of them said something in another's ear, and they both laughed before continuing upstairs. Voices. Who were they? Did you see those clothes? And those briefcases must have cost an arm and a leg. It may have, but sure as hell it wasn't their arm or their leg.

In this way the morning passed until we finally reached the counter where a bored clerk gave Abba some forms for us all to fill out, saying, "That'll be forty rupees. Next!" We moved to another counter where we completed them; each page bore a letterhead of fancy scripted italics that said "*God is great.*" When we were all finished, Abba gave them back to the clerk, who told us to wait until they called our name. We took our place at the end of another line, which, like the first, quickly grew in length.

The hours seemed to pass over us like droplets of glue that kept us stuck in this interminable position. When Sial, placing his fist on his forehead and closing his eyes, said he was going to faint from hunger, Jandol said that he could use a cold drink, but we didn't want to lose our places in line, so I, being the youngest, offered to go. Anything to get out of there.

I raced downstairs, but when I was out of sight from the front gate, I ground to a halt. What a relief, like entering another world where you could breathe fresh air without inhaling various combinations of fruity men's cologne competing with each other. I wandered around for a while, taking in the sights, before going to one of the countless food stalls where I ordered a Coke, along with a sweet roll laced with buttery honey. This section of Peshawar was churning with activity. Just the cars speeding past me were amazing to someone such as I who'd spent most of his life in a tiny village set down in a vast desert. I'd never seen such a cavalcade, all of those people going somewhere, coming from somewhere, living exciting lives. The sidewalks were also crowded with people of all types, all ages, the place so alive it connected with something alive in me, something I'd always had to suppress lest I drive myself crazy.

Regretfully, I started back at the same time as an old bent man leading a bony donkey stepped into the busy thoroughfare with his head down, paying not the least attention to the traffic That donkey looked like a relic from the Afghan-Anglo war; it was even scragglier than the old man, with both of them moving like two snails. I was sure they were going to get killed, what with cars having to swerve around them, jamming on their brakes, honking their horns. Halfway across, I noticed that the one of his bags, which was stuffed with honeydew melons, became unfastened, and the fruit was about to fall out, but when I called to the guy, he just kept on moving.

Up ahead was a larger stand with more selections than the one I first went to. I ordered four plates of lamb kebab over curried rice, lime sodas, and sweet rolls, carefully wrapping everything up in newspapers, but when I got close to the entrance gate, I couldn't go back inside. I was sure no one had moved since I'd left and that once I returned, I'd be stuck there for the rest of the day.

Across the street from the office building was a block of apartments, their windows reflecting the sun in such a way that the entire building seemed decorated as if for a festival. As my eyes traveled from floor to floor, I saw that the windows on the top floor were covered with black shades, but before I could give this much consideration, something much more charming caught my attention. There was a young woman on the roof hanging clothes on a line, the purple of her dress complementing the blue of the sky. She proceeded in a leisurely, graceful manner, as if she had all day to do it, until, with an impatient gesture, she tore off her head scarf and shook her head so that her hair billowed in the soft breeze. That simple gesture from a girl I'd never seen before, that only I had witnessed, was like a slap in the face of authority, reducing to ashes this grim office building crowded with refugees, this warlord with his myriad rules, his stifling regulations.

Oh, if I could only feel that free. It was youth, pure youth that I saw up on that roof under a sky the color of a cold lake. But it was a kind of youth I only rarely felt. I had to shield my eyes from the glare, which was when she spotted me because she waved and smiled. It was as if no one existed but the two of us. I felt something totally weird coursing through me, something I'd never experienced before, arising from my stomach, a burning sensation that was peculiarly delightful. Her eyes were cameras that were focused on me; she was capturing my image as I was seizing hers. But her gaze frightened me, this fire inside became unendurable. I didn't know what was happening, the sensations turning my excitement into fear strong enough for me to avert my eyes. Then life being what it was, when I did look up again, she was gone. With worlds colliding, I absently tried to reenter the compound, only to be immediately hauled back to reality by a gorilla in a monkey suit holding out a hairy paw while demanding to see my ID. I explained to him that me and my family were applying to get our IDs, but the bastard didn't believe me. Plus, he wanted to know what was wrapped up in the newspaper. Since you could smell the food, I didn't know what to say, my fear that he would take it overriding any kind of logic. I simply glared at him the way Abba used to do when he was pissed off, without saying a word, very effective. It worked here too. The Neanderthal allowed me to pass, albeit quite unwillingly.

When I reappeared, the first thing Sial asked was what took me so long. As you can imagine, I was in no mood for him or his reality. All I could think was, *Where was my youth?* That girl was an image of what I wanted, of something that existed somewhere inside me, a state of being that I longed to express. It was then I realized I'd lost my appetite. The very smell of the food made me queasy.

"So what did they say?" Moor asked when we got back.

"They were impossible," Jandol said. "They said we needed proof of who we are. Can you believe that?"

"Proof?"

"The boy's right," Abba said. "In order to get the papers, we have to prove our identity. No proof, no papers."

"But you were gone all day. What took so long?"

Abba shrugged and held out his hands, palms up.

"Well, you'll just have to give them proof," Moor said. "Take Zakria with you next time. He knows who you are."

"They won't accept Zakria," Jandol said, "They want either a mullah or a warlord from Hisarak."

"The office was a disaster," Sial added. "A real madhouse. It seems that everyone's leaving Afghanistan."

"What are we going to do?" Moor asked.

"There are more doors to knock on," Abba said. "Other warlords. I will pull some strings."

"I hope those strings don't snap off in our hands," Sial said.

"Abba will grease them," Jandol said.

"With what?"

"With shekels," he said, rubbing his index finger against his thumb in the time-old gesture.

"It's not money they want," Abba said. "Not really."

"What do they want?" Meena asked.

"Our souls," Jandol said. "That's what they want. Our souls."

"Don't talk foolishness, all of you," Abba said. "We will go to see Zakria in the morning. He'll tell us what to do."

"You're right," Jandol said. "Don't listen to me. I'm just tired."

Later in my makeshift bed, with the sounds of the camp percolating around me, thin voices that carried in the night, an occasional cry, the fragrance of cooking, footsteps hurrying by like whispers along dusty paths, I thought again about the girl that I saw on the roof of the apartment house. I wondered how old she was, what her name was; I wondered if she was married. I wondered if we would ever meet each other. But what would I say if we did meet? I'd be tongue-tied. Again, I experienced those same stirrings running through my body. The next time we went, I'd wait outside at the exact same spot for as long as it took. Who cared about ID cards, who cared about bribes and warlords with their iron fists? I was still thrilled by the picture of her tearing off her head scarf and how her hair had blown in the wind.

As for our identification cards, even with Zakria's help, it took some doing. We had to return to that same office building over and over to be questioned by various officials, with Abba forced to hand out many well-placed bribes, before we were able to get the proper papers. But in the end, we did get them, so at least one obstacle was out of the way. Also, and most importantly, we had temporary papers allowing us to stay together in the camp without having to send a family member to fight in Afghanistan. These had to be renewed every six months. What with so much happening, the girl in the purple dress faded from my thoughts, replaced by angry warlords and their equally obnoxious minions. The Gods of War, a proper honorific, since their longing, their fierce hunger, was to destroy everything around them. Improvident to the extreme, for what did they wind up with, especially as they aged, as whatever youth these monsters once had became brittle, dried out, without substance. A world, a process rather, that I hadn't made, that Abba had fought to survive in, that each of us had to confront. These were the thoughts that occupied my mind, as well as the consequent feelings that they created.

It didn't take long before I wasn't sure if I'd made the whole thing up about the girl. But in some deep place within me, I knew I hadn't, that she represented a promise that I would fulfill.

So now our life in Kacha Garhi began. We could come and go as we pleased now that we had our papers, which meant that if the city police stopped us, we only had to pay a bribe rather than being escorted to prison. But we still had to watch our step, given that the camp was infiltrated by ISI-controlled warlords and *mavlavi* spies. Our main goals evolved around conserving what money we still possessed, getting enough food to eat, keeping our mouths shut—especially Mr. Movie Star—and staying out of trouble.

Every day Abba and Jandol went looking for work while Sial and I would go hunting for fuel to cook with—wood, cactus, old newspapers, roots, leaves. In addition, we were the family water bearers. Jandol had taken two large oil cans, rigging them up with straps, which he attached to a yoke. Five to six times per day, we'd walk the mile to the pump to fetch water, each of us taking turns carrying it home. I hated it, but at least I was developing broad shoulders.

The camp was split up into various numbered divisions. Once a month, from the first to the seventh, our section of about six thousand families would go to an assigned warehouse to pick up our rations. The guards would open the doors promptly at eight in the morning and close it by three. The first time we went, we didn't get there until 8:30 a.m., which was a major mistake given that because of the crowds, we wound up spending the entire day waiting, only to be turned away and told to come back tomorrow. We had, however, learned our lesson since from then on, we were there at five in the morning, and even then we had to wait for hours, sometimes because the food hadn't yet been delivered. The monthly rations per family consisted of a two-liter can of cooking oil, four kilograms of sugar, a bag of powdered milk, a small amount of black tea, and a hundred-kilogram sack of unmilled wheat, which we then carried to an adjacent store where we exchanged it for flour at a 20 percent loss.

"What a *dosaq*," Sial said. "When I get out of here, you know what I'm going to do? I'm going to go live in Nuristan where it's always cold. That's what I'll do. Live in a house made of ice, and whenever I'm thirsty, I'll lick the walls."

We were sitting in the shade of our tent. The heat was crashing down in waves that were almost visible. Wave upon wave shimmering before my eyes. It was too hot to talk; it was too hot to think. Even the shade was like an anvil. Sial languidly took a sip of lemonade and spit it out. "This stuff tastes like crap."

"Go get some ice."

"You go."

"It's your lemonade, not mine."

Sial didn't move. "Doesn't it ever rain here?"

"Sure it does. It rains sand."

"Remember that fish I caught, that giant fish? Me and Meena. We woke up when it was still dark. No one was up but us. Everything was so quiet. You couldn't even hear the birds. Sitting by the river. This tug on my line. Meena and me grabbing the fishing pole with her shouting, 'Reel him in, Sial! Reel him in!' Only the fish was too strong, and we both went flying into the river. Those were the days, you know? I didn't realize it then how precious those moments were."

My eyes fell on the water trough that was near the tent; they were used in the winter to collect rain so that mud walls could be built. There were probably thousands in the camp. But in the summer, all of them were open cesspools, nothing but ordure, human and animal. It smelled from here to high heaven, with flies buzzing and lizards and spiders scrambling around; nothing to catch in that trough, nothing except disease. It was pointless to think about the past; the past was dead. It was the future we needed to focus on, each day, what we have, not what we had. What we will have once we get our lives together, once we—I suddenly heard something.

"Sial, wake up."

"Shut up and leave me alone."

"Wake up, I hear something."

"What? Voices in your head?"

"Whirlybirds. Two of them."

We both squinted up at the sky, watching as they buzzed overhead with the dust rising up and the tent flapping.

Our curiosity was aroused, and we followed them to a nearby field where one was landing while the other circled above. The entire area was surrounded by Pakistani special force security guards with AK-47s. They were standing at attention, like predators waiting to pounce, observing every move, every step, ready at the slightest provocation to fire. A couple of the guards, with their heads ducked down, opened the cabin door, and two sheikhs emerged, followed by a Pakistani general, in turn followed by two blond men in pinstriped business suits. Each man was carrying a camera with a zoom lens. Accompanied by yet more guards, the camp commander stepped forward; everyone shook hands, after which he made a little prepared speech.

"They've come to photograph the animals," a woman next to me said. "Just like we were monkeys in a zoo."

"The children think it's some kind of game," said another.

"What's going on?" Jandol said, coming up to us.

The same woman who'd spoken before said, "It's showtime."

As if on cue, the photographers began clicking away. This went on for about half an hour, and for the entire time, the security helicopter circled noisily around. Then without warning, everyone packed up and left, including the guards in their trucks. Within moments, everything was quiet, a certain solemnity in the air from what had just occurred. Then even that slipped away, making it seem as if none of this had happened, as if it had all been a weird dream.

On the way home, Jandol said that now our smiling faces will be on the covers of newspapers all over the world, the happy, contented refugees.

"Sial, you will finally be famous."

"Screw you."

"You don't want to be famous? After all your moaning and groaning?"

"I want to eat. I'm hungry and I'm hot. I'm burning up. I want a cold drink. Look, there's a guy with ice. Let's get some."

"Do you have any money?" I said to Sial.

"Sial and money," Jandol said. "I never thought I'd hear those two words in one sentence." He dug into his pocket and handed a couple of rupees to Sial, who walked up and gave the iceman his order. The guy was like a pneumatic drill the way he chipped off the ice with his pick. He weighed the ice on a scale and placed it in a plastic bag, and we hurried home.

When we got back, Sial said, "Hey, I'm going to make the cover of *Time Magazine*. Some guys just took a picture of me, and he said I should be a model."

"Yeah, a model airplane," I said.

"What are you two talking about?"

"It's true," Jandol said. "Some guys dropped down from the sky and went around taking everyone's picture. Pro photographers. One of them asked Sial to pose."

"Dropped down from the sky?" she asked.

"You know," Sial said, spreading his arms and making helicopter noises. "With cameras. God's cameras."

We ate outside, sitting on small carpets. Meena prepared tea, and when it got dark, we lit the kerosene lamp. There were fires everywhere, and you could hear the wood crackling and the various smells of cooking.

"Someone just walked over my grave," Meena said.

"What's that?" Sial said.

"I felt a chill."

"It's that light from the cemetery," Moor said. "Someone's digging there. They do it at night to prepare for the burials the next day. It's too hot when the sun is out. Haven't you seen them? Or heard them? It doesn't mean anything. People die."

"This whole camp gives me the creeps," Meena said. "How long will we have to stay here?"

"We will stay here until we're ready to leave."

"Look out there," Meena said. "We're surrounded by dead people. Everywhere you go, everyone you see. Skeletons."

Moor said for her to hush.

"I'm not going to—"

Sial suddenly stiffened. "Oh my god, Moor's right. There's a dead man coming here. He's got a long white beard, and he's carrying a bloody scythe. Oh my god, he's coming right at us. Let's get out of here."

With a dramatic cry that segued into a giggle, Meena threw herself into Moor's arms, hugging her around the neck.

"Both of you, hush up," Moor said, disentangling herself.

"He started it," Meena said.

"I did? You did."

"Well, I'm going to finish it," Moor said.

"No one wants to hear the truth," Meena said.

"You're right, daughter," Abba said. "Because the truth right now is obvious to each of us, and we don't need to be reminded."

It was funny, I thought, watching them. Meena really believed in what she said, but Sial was a pukka troublemaker; he fed on drama and on conflict. Then when everybody was at each other's throats, he'd shrug in his superior way. And who knew what he really believed? I doubted if even he did.

"You know what I like about you?" Sial said to Meena. "You're never happy. I like that. It makes me feel there's someone more miserable that I am."

Meena leaped to her feet. "I hate this place, and I hate you." She rushed inside the tent. Everyone stared at Sial.

He smiled ingratiatingly. "What did I say?"

"What did you say?" Moor said.

"Now you're picking on me. As usual. Always pick on Sial. Well, I'm sick of it."

"When I was a young girl," Moor said, "we never had arguments. We were happy, delightfully happy. We had a beautiful house and beautiful friends. None of this fighting."

"Oh, Mother," Sial said. "Don't tell us stories that never existed."

"I'm telling you, our lives were beautiful," she said. Before Sial could reply, the kerosene lamp began to flicker before abruptly going out. Moor said that we needed to get fuel tomorrow, not to forget.

With the kerosene lamp extinguished, the moon seemed to fill the sky with its pale tender glow.

It was March already; six months had passed. August to September being the worst, but unlike our village, the winter months were mild, although the rain was incessant. What a deluge. I can still hear its drumming on our tent, a sound I enjoyed at first. But when the rain continued, when it looked like our tent might fall apart any minute, when our nights became chaotic with damp bedding accompanied by the splatter of rain on our faces, Abba said it was time to do something. So he and Jandol went to a lumber yard where they bought pinewood planks, which they used to buttress the slanting roof of the tent. This was so successful, they did the same with the flooring, in addition to which, they built a low cement wall made to keep out the drafts and to seal the corners. In this way, our living quarters became quite hospitable. I couldn't understand why others around us didn't do the same since everyone had the same problem keeping dry.

"We've got to keep our focus," Moor said as she poured rice into the cooking pot while I removed the dhal from the *nagharai*, placing it on the ground. She lifted the pot of rice, put it on the fire, and covered it. "Our determination, our aims, our objectives. We didn't leave our home to come live in a refugee camp or sleep in a tent." The fire had dwindled, and she knelt down and pushed some more wood, piece by piece, until it rose higher. "We came here to better our lives, and that takes ingenuity. It takes thought and knowledge. But where to find them? They say if you close a door, a window will open." My mother was still a beautiful woman, and she worked hard taking care of all of us. Lila. A musical name. She was not much more than five feet tall.

Around this time, guards in jeeps with PA systems began driving around the camp for weeks, announcing that the famous founder of the Jamiat-e-Islami, Qazi Saib, was coming to Kacha Garhi to bless us, to inspire us with his words, to enlighten our souls. What an honor. This man, this humble Pakistani scholar whose entire life has been dedicated to Islamic causes, will give a speech on the necessity of jihad, for Afghan refugees to join the Mujahideen in order to fight the oppressor, the Communists.

Sial and I were late when we reached the tent, which stretched across an entire field near the commander's compound. Outside was a banner:

> KEY TO THE HEAVENS—JIHAD! JIHAD! JIHAD!
> QAZI SAIB
> Friday, July 16, 9:00 a.m. to 8:00 p.m.
> Refreshments will be served.

By the time the guards searched us, handed us eating utensils, and found two empty seats, Qazi was already speaking. "I still remember that day. August 14, 1947. The day Pakistan, our great mother, gained her independence. No longer were we chattels of British India, no longer were we controlled by infidels. It was a day of great joy for everyone, a day of great happiness, of hope for the future of our children, our beloved sons and daughters who would no longer have to suffer. But for some of us, it was also a day of great sorrow. Of blood and sacrifice.

"I see all of you looking at me in astonishment. How could this be? How could such a significant event cause such personal sorrow? At the time I was a young man, and I had just gotten married, and my wife and I were living in Delhi. My wife's name was Aisha, and we had a little boy named Abdul Jalal. He was a happy child, and he loved to play outside in the grass, trying to catch the sun. And when I came home from work, he would wave his arms and laugh. We were a happy family, we were a joyful family, we were an honorable family. The only thing we didn't have, the only flaw in our lives, the only lack, was our freedom.

"But great changes had been in the air, enormous changes whirling around us. Talk and rumors and gossip. Emotions began to run riot, neighbor plotting against neighbor. A thousand years of hostility between Muslim and Hindu brought to a head. The Hindu Gandhi wanted to keep us prisoners of India, but our beloved Mohammad Ali Jinnah, who was a greater man, a far-seeing man, a visionary, an intellectual, a freedom fighter, he wanted to create the Islamic state of Pakistan. A state for all Muslims the world over. And it was he who succeeded, he who fought and died for us, he who created Pakistan. For now we have our own land, finally, our own borders. But bought at a price, as you all know."

Our seats were close enough to see Qazi's face. We were also underneath one of the speakers, and the volume was almost earsplitting. I stared in disbelief as he took out a handkerchief and dabbed at his eyes. *The guy is a little theatrical, but boy, is he was good*, I thought. *Very, very good.* Even I was excited by the way he reached out to the audience, and when he said that all of us were Muslim brothers, were one, had gone through the same experiences, had faced the same hardships, had lost family members, had lost possessions, home, state, country, even I felt something come over me. A voice shouted from the crowd, "Nara-e-Takbir!" followed by many responses. "Allah-Hoo-Akbar" was repeated and repeated.

Qazi bowed first to the left, then to the middle, and then to the right. He smiled at the audience, and it was so quiet you could hear a pin drop. He took a sip of water and continued his speech, placing the microphone close to his lips and speaking softly.

"August 14, 1947. There had been rioting all that month, but that night, they were going to make the official announcement for the independent state of Pakistan. I had been working with the Muslim League night and day, seven days a week, twelve hours a day, sleeping in my office. I couldn't remember that last time I had seen my wife and my child. When the rioting began, I sent them to stay with my parents. That night I left work early so that I could be with them when they made the announcement over the radio. It was dark out by the time I was able to leave, and you could hear gunshots, and fires were burning, and people were running and shouting. It was chaos. Absolute chaos. No trams were running, and it took a long time. My parents lived in an outlying suburb, but once I passed through the heart of the city, things quieted down, and I felt safe. Everything was quiet and peaceful. There were no streetlights anywhere, and when I reached our house, it was pitch-black. The first thing I noticed was that the door was ajar. I pushed, but something was holding it in place, and I had to elbow my way inside. 'Where is everybody?' I said. No one answered. Outside, a dog started barking. I took out a match and struck it. From that moment on, nothing was the same."

Again Qazi paused, once more dabbing at his eyes. He stared out at the audience, his glance going from person to person. "My youth was gone, my childhood was gone, my love was gone. My wife, my children, my parents, taken from me on a dark night as if the price for the birth of a new world was death. I knew then there was no security, no final resting place. That our beloved Pakistan, born that night, would always need to be defended, to be protected and loved, to be cherished and needed. For that was all any of us would ever, could ever, depend upon. Our mountain ranges, our rivers, our deserts, our beautiful cities that have grown and prospered. And now, my Muslim brothers from Afghanistan, it is time for you to rise up and take hold of your country the way that we rose up and took ours. It is time for you to defeat the infidels who have invaded your land and taken over your schools and your hospitals, your factories and your farms, taken over your government. You must be strong, you must be ruthless. You must rid yourself of these predators. Destroy those schools. Destroy those hospitals. Blow up those dams. Burn those factories. That is the great service that you can render to our God and for your country. Give up your petty cares for something greater, for angels who are waiting for you in the wings."

With these details, his whole demeanor changed, and in an instant, he raised his fist like a wrathful god, his voice ringing out. "*Jihad is the way! Jihad is the path, jihad is the answer! Death to the Communist infidels!*"

In answer to these phrases that he continued repeating, the audience began to shout with him, "Jihad, jihad, jihad! Death to the infidels! Long live Islam!" Their voices, mounting in volume that sent shivers up my spine for they sounded like a holy chorus through whose expression the very soul of the earth was speaking, vibrated through these men, a wall of sound, of intent, the fire of their voices burning the soul, burning my soul while leaving it whole. I too shouted along with them.

Everyone rose to his feet. The chanting grew louder; our collective voices filled with joy, with fervor. Sial had raised his fist along with the others as his feeling cut a swath through his usual sarcasm to a reality that he himself always kept locked up. I was inspired by all of it, particularly by Sial, such that when our eyes met, they were unabashedly filled with tears.

At the height of the uproar, servers came down the aisles loaded with trays and handed out cups of tea and sweet biscuits. Stands had been set up where people could fill out forms in order join the Mujahideen. Sial said to me, "Let's get out of here," and we made our way to the entrance where a guard asked us if we'd signed up. Sial said we definitely had, that we couldn't wait to fight. The guard patted him on the back, saying, "Mashallah," Arabic for thank you.

On the way back, we passed the rear of the tent where there was a black BMW waiting with two men standing with their heads tucked into their chins. A flap was lifted, revealing Qazi, who stepped out, surrounded by more guards. He sat down at a table where he was served a sumptuous meal of chicken kebabs with various hors d'oeuvres and treats that looked like they'd been especially prepared for him. He fastidiously picked at his food as if he were an English monarch at a formal state dinner, this old man with his gray beard, on a hot day, in a camp overcrowded with penniless, half-starved refugees.

A young boy crept close to him, staring speechlessly while the old man ate his lunch, the hunger in the boy's eyes apparent for anyone to recognize, even great leaders. Qazi didn't deign to glance at him, but after he left, the guards who came out to bus the dishes told the boy to get lost. He moved a little but continued to stare as they collected the leftovers. As he walked away, I saw him straighten his shoulders.

I was growing older. I wanted to know about everything. I was always asking why until everyone in my family wanted to wring my neck. But I had this impulse to understand how the universe operated: religion, politics, love, fate. That's how my mind ran. In circles. I always saw comparisons between things that people didn't see. I guess you could say I had a kind of metaphorical take on the world. Big things reminded me of small things and vice versa. Societal events reminded me domestic crises. If my mother burned the soup, I felt the world was going to starve. I saw these connections everywhere; it was as if the whole universe was like a web of interrelated strings, as if I was running my fingers across them, but what it meant was beyond me.

I knew, of course, that there was a right way and a wrong way, but often I couldn't tell which was which. I knew, for example, you couldn't put chicken eggs under a duck because when they hatched and the duck began to swim, the chicks would drown. Imam Parast had taught me that lesson when we were in Hisarak. But other things weren't so obvious. I needed to learn, I was hungry to learn, and not just about chickens and ducks or how to tote water on a yoke and sleep in a drafty tent and spend hours hunting for fuel. So many questions, so many feelings, feelings I had no name for, and thoughts that sprang up from nowhere and led me nowhere. One day I was joyful, and the next miserable, sometimes hour by hour. Confidence one minute, confusion the next. I observed people, how they walked and talked, what made one person able to roll with the punches while another couldn't.

CHAPTER EIGHT

"NOW, ABBA, HEAR ME out," Jandol said. "For the past few weeks, I've been spending a lot of time at the Kochi Bazaar, and I noticed that the fabric stands are always very busy, but the sellers continue to run out of material. So I started thinking. Lahore is the fabric center of the world, right? Only it's three hundred miles away, and the vendors have to close up shop to go there to buy material. It's much too time-consuming. Another problem is fashions change here so quickly that sometimes they come back with fabrics that nobody wants. It's like they're gone so much, they can't keep a finger on the pulse. So here's my idea. A delivery service, we start a delivery service. We go to Lahore and buy fabrics on the cheap, bring them back here, and sell them. I'm not saying we'll make a fortune, but I think a couple of trips a week should make a big difference. I figure we can clear a few hundred rupees every trip. Then we can save our money and find us a place to live outside of the camp."

Our eyes turned toward Abba.

"So what do you think, Father?" Jandol said.

Before he spoke, Sial said, "Boy, Jandol, you're always thinking. I envy you."

Abba shook his head and said, "I am not thrilled by your plan."

"I see," Jandol said.

"Son, I know you have good intentions, and your plan is essentially a good plan. But it's like trying to build a fire with a block of ice."

"Well, I for one like it," Sial piped up. "I think it's a fantastic idea. Then we can get out of this hell."

"Is that so?" Abba said stonily. "And what is any plan worth if you don't have cash to carry it out with? Fabrics, even on the cheap, cost money, transportation costs money, taxis, hotels, food. The list goes on and on. Who's going to pay for it? You?"

"I would if I could, you know that."

"Sial, be quiet," Jandol said.

"But I'm agreeing with you."

"I'd rather have you on the other side."

"Don't be so hard on your brother," Moor said. "He's only trying to help. You'll think of something."

"Something," Jandol said. "But what? One thing's for sure, we can't go on living like this too much longer."

"I agree," Meena said. "This isn't living. It's not even existing. I'm not sure what it is."

"Meena, you hush," Moor said. "Let the men talk."

"Father," Jandol said, "is there no way to raise the money? What about Zakria?"

"I doubt that he has anything. As it is, the refugees living with him are unable to pay rent, and he's been feeding them day and night."

"So he's out. Is there anyone else?"

"You know the answer to that, son, so why ask?"

"Why indeed?" he said softly, as if to himself.

As time passed, the darkening sky brought with it a chill in the air. We went inside our tent where Jandol lit a lantern and hung it on a hook that was attached to the center pole, its wavering light making us look like fading ghosts.

"What a tinderbox," Sial said as we crowded together in a tight circle.

The truth was, all of our relatives, beginning with Abba's brother in Jalalabad, were in Pakistan; there was no mail; and traveling was dangerous, if not forbidden. Other than Zakria, we knew no one in Peshawar. Borrowing money was hopeless. Why even ask? Jandol's plan, our futile replies, Abba's decision—they were merely copies of other plans and talks and decisions by means of which we had attempted to come up with an escape route, especially now, with yet another terrible summer soon upon us. Instead of reaching any sort of agreement, we had only wound up going in circles and getting on each other's nerves until even the most innocuous remark had the power to cause a conflagration.

To add to our discomfort, as usual we were hungry, given that there was never enough food, and what we did have (lentils and rice) filled the stomach but not the soul. No more apricot pastries, which Meena loved, or rice pudding with cream that I could never get enough of, no more skewered lamb kebabs or beef stews or yoghurt made from goat's milk, the very thought of which was enough to bring tears to the eyes. The lack of variety, of never having enough even of these, of time hanging on our hands with nothing to do, and surrounded by a mass of starving, luckless people—this was our life. Along with these physical privations, the sense of hope was something else that we were forced to relinquish, lest it eats us up inside and turn bitterness into a homicidal rampage, such as what sometimes happened in camp.

My thoughts were spinning with all of these quandaries, none of which appeared to be capable of resolution, when I saw Moor dig into the drawstring satchel where she kept her valuables and pull out her sandalwood jewelry box, which she placed on the carpet in front of Abba.

"What is this for?" he asked edgily.

"It's for you," she said, kneeling down and offering to him. "It's for all of us."

My father would not meet her eyes. When he spoke, his voice was sepulchral. "I am not taking your jewelry. Period."

"Mine, yours, what's the difference? It's ours. Our protection."

Sial lifted up one of the bracelets, holding it in the light. "You think you'll get money with this stuff? You've got to be kidding."

"Do not interfere," Moor said. "And give me that bracelet." She took off her antique sapphire earrings then slowly twisted off her diamond wedding ring and held them momentarily in her fist before placing them on top of her jewelry box.

Abba stiffened. He picked up the ring to return it to her, but she reached out, enfolded both of her hands over his, and nodded yes. "Miwand, do you remember what you said to us? Jewelry, clothes, automobiles—you can always replace them. But you can't replace our lives. Do you remember saying that? Well, ever since we came to this camp, I have watched my family fall into despair, give up goals, live uneducated, useless lives. I cannot stand by any longer and let that happen. We have to do something. We can't end our lives in a refugee camp, begging for food. I will not let that happen. If you won't take my jewelry, I will go into the city myself and sell them for whatever I can get."

A week later, Abba and Jandol left for Lahore.

Opening the door, Sial and I greeted the director of the Abu Jafar Madrassa, Qari Ejaz-Ull-Haq, in the Arabic manner, to which he gave the traditional reply. Without bothering to glance at us, he asked what we wanted to see him about. Sial said we would like to be admitted to the madrassa. He asked our names, but before either of us could answer, he closed his eyes and began moving his lips at the same time that he began fiddling with his prayer beads.

We stopped speaking, at which time he stopped praying and again asked us what we wanted. But the moment Sial began to speak, again he began to pray, which forced Sial to speak over his murmuring. Somehow he must have communicated our reason for seeing him because he handed us the admission forms, telling us to go into the next room and come back when they were completed.

We filled out the forms and returned to his office, but when we handed them to him, he seized upon our names, slashing them both out with a red Magic Marker. He told us that we could not use our names, that they were not Islamic, although what he meant was that they were not Arabic—and this, even though he was a Punjabi. He then paused before saying that from then on, I was to be called Abu Bakar, who had been a great caliph, and Sial was to be called Abu Azam, after the fearless warrior who sacrificed his life in the name of Allah. "From now on, those are the names you will go by. These men shall stand before you and before God as heroic figures from the mists of the ancient past. It is up to you, in your devotion to Islam, to keep them always before you as role models. Be grateful. You boys have just been reborn."

Abu and Abu, I thought, forcing myself not to smile as he went on to tell us the daily schedule. School began before sunrise with morning devotions. After prayers, breakfast was served. Classes were held from eight until twelve thirty. Afternoon devotions were at one, after which lunch was served. When the meal was over, the day students, such as Sial and I, were sent home. On our first day he told us to report to his assistant's office so that he could show us where our classes were held as well as give us our school supplies and eating utensils.

"Do you have any questions?" he asked.

We said no.

"I have something for you," he said. He called out to one of the guards, and he gave us each a blanket along with a bag of dates. We thanked the director.

"Allah is with you," he said, coming from behind his desk and putting his arms around our shoulders. "Remember that God is with you. For you boys are the future warriors of our noble cause. The crown of the Mujahideen."

"So, Abu Bakar, what do you think?" Sial asked when we were far enough away to talk privately.

"Ah, Abu Azam, it is not I who thinks. It is Allah."

"I hope this idea of yours doesn't get us into trouble."

"It won't if you keep your mouth shut. Don't start complaining from here to heaven, and we'll be safe."

"I understand, little brother, but what'll happen when Abba and Jandol come back?

"Let's worry about that when the time comes."

"They're going to kills us."

"So what'd you think of the director?" I asked, but when I stepped forward, a stone had gotten stuck in my sandal that necessitated my having to hop in order to dislodge it. The stone later turned out to be a lifesaver, but more of that later.

"You know what I think of those guys. They're all crackpots."

"Wait a minute," I said, bending over to unstrap my sandal and shake it out.

"When I'm a famous movie star, I will remember these days and laugh."

"Well, that makes one of us."

Our first morning, we stood lost amid the stares of a thousand students, each of us pushed together, shoulder to shoulder, in the open space in between the outspread wings of the madrassa, boys of various ages and backgrounds, each with his little white cap or black turban. I felt sad because they were bound together while Sial and I were not only interlopers but heretics.

After prayers, it was time to eat. The boarding students returned to their dormitories where they were served while the rest of us broke up into different lines. There were quite a few food stations at which breakfast was ladled out: paratha, halvah, and tea. Well, we had come to fill our stomachs, so at least that part of the regimen was acceptable.

Sial and I had barely finished when we heard voices coming from loudspeakers. "Inshallah, classes begin in five minutes!" The words seemed to reverberate everywhere, a startling sound among the murmuring of boys' voices. We wolfed down the rest of our breakfast while the whole madrassa became a beehive of activity. Sial and I made our way to the assistant's office, and he pulled out our folders from a filing cabinet.

"Which one of you is Abu Bakar?"

I said I was, and he told me to report to Jeem-23 on the third floor. Then he told Sial—Abu Azam, I should say—that he was in Alef-11 on the first floor.

Reaching my classroom, I found it was already overcrowded with students sitting on the floor in front of rows of long low tables. I squeezed myself in between two boys near the back of the room, trying not to disturb them, which was nigh impossible. The thin carpet did nothing to cushion you from the hard cement floor, making it hard to find a comfortable position.

Presently, the teacher, an ascetic-appearing man dressed in white except for a pink scarf, handed out copies of the Holy Quran and then returned to the front, where he sat cross-legged facing us. He closed his eyes and began moving his head up and down and mumbling words of prayer, words spoken so softly I couldn't make them out. After a while, he opened his eyes, and they were red with tears. He told everyone to turn to a certain chapter. When he said that, all of the students changed their positions so that no one had his back to the holy book, which was forbidden. Raising his voice, the teacher began to recite the verses, swaying from side to side, swept away by the words. Not one boy in the class, all of whom were Pashtoon, spoke Arabic, and consequently, no one understood what he was saying, but the feeling from the teacher seemed to affect many of them, and they began swaying and reading aloud with him, words they didn't understand and mispronounced but tried to catch.

A shadow fell. I glanced up. The teacher was hovering over me. He asked me in Pashto to read aloud from the Quran, but before I had hardly begun, he interrupted me and corrected my pronunciation. Every second word. The more he corrected me, of course, the more flummoxed I became. Until he moved to the next student and the next and the next. They also stumbled over the words. Well, why not? It wasn't our language. Anyway, this went on until the end of the class. Four hours. One of the boys raised his hand, sticking his pinkie finger up to indicate that he needed to be excused to use the bathroom. Later I did the same, staying out as long as I could.

I found the fervor at the madrassa relentless, belief ran rampant, opinion unquestionable, from students and teachers alike. After school, to clear my head, I'd go hiking in the neighboring countryside until the feeling of something heavy began to dissipate, and I could breathe again. On the one hand, the camp, which was our life. Unspeakable conditions, worse than prison, and no way out, unless you had money. Without money, you were dead. Without money. On the other, the madrassa promising eternal bliss—well, in heaven, that is. In this way, since you would be rewarded after death, you could live in a tent with nothing and wait peacefully to die. All you needed to do was to give up your soul. Once you'd done that, the golden gates would swing open.

So the choice was give up your soul or your body; you couldn't have it both ways. In my case, I realized that nothing had reality for me unless I could touch it, could see it, and could feel it. That's why I wrote poetry, really, to embody sensation, to give an image to thoughts and feelings, to make real what was insubstantial.

It goes without saying that I kept my opinions to myself since, strangely for a school, you were enjoined not to question anything. None of the teachers liked to be challenged, even those who gave you special treats or who recommended a doctor friend when Moor was sick, which went against their doctrine that doctors were infidels. What a world was the madrassa, filled with voices having as much meaning as sand scattered on the desert floor.

Sial said that one day he was going to laugh about this, which he probably mentioned just to annoy me in that the only time he laughed was when somebody else tripped on the banana peel, never him. Anyway, in some strange way, I was beginning to agree with him. The absurdity was hilarious—would be hilarious, that is—if it weren't so heartbreaking. To see such young eyes turn all cold and dead, the end of innocence but not the beginning of knowledge or guilt, the beginning of entrapment. I could continue for pages, but you get the idea.

Forced to remain quiet while some jerk in a white robe waved a riding crop in my face, I wondered what had made me choose to attend in the first place. What had piqued my curiosity to such a degree? I'd told Sial it was a way to get two good meals, but that hadn't been the true reason. The fact was, I'd heard so much about the madrassa, both good and bad, that I wanted to see for myself. Now I had seen, and what I saw revolted me.

Across from me were fields that led to mountains, mountains that were crisscrossed by passes, the most famous being the Khyber Pass where past, present, and future were forged in an eternal triumvirate, but others as well that had witnessed the rise and fall of empires, of entire civilizations that had lasted hundreds of years and that were now nothing more than relics half-buried under the earth. I took off my sandals, digging my toes into the soil. I wanted to climb those mountains, and the touch of the cold earth brought me back to reality, even as I spent hours every day with those who would drag me away from what was real, as if they were rogue waves. I knew the direction my life was destined to take—or rather, I should say, I was certain which direction it would not take. Still, we remained in school.

Initially, I avoided the other boys, but at the same time, I didn't want to isolate myself in any kind of way that would bring too much attention to me. So I did make some friends, although

I remained cautious as to what I said since there was a grapevine that was invisible but omnipresent.

A month passed. At home we asked ourselves where Abba and Jandol were. At school, Sial and I were careful not to say anything that could be misinterpreted. Each day made me more positive that I was part of the living, part of my family and my surroundings, while they were part of the dead. I wanted to conquer the world; they wanted to escape it. It was all they ever talked about: death, heaven, hell, fire, and gardens bursting with fruit and beautiful sinuous virgins. Images only they could imagine. No wonder they went around giggling half the time; the other half was spent weeping and beating their breasts.

Saturdays were the worst since that meant six days of this unending tedium. Reading and studying in a language I barely understood, teachers repeating everything they said, stuck like a zombie in a classroom of the lobotomized.

The review was held in a cramped corner room on the second floor behind the stairs. The windows at the rear were opened to the Khyber Road, which, even at this early hour, was busy with traffic. Inside were three mullahs who I didn't know; they were from another madrassa who used to go around testing students, as well as one of our own substitute teachers. They all stared at me.

"Salamalikoom," I said.

In front of me was a heavyset middle-aged man with a thick grizzled beard and wearing aviator reflection sunglasses that completely hid his eyes. When you looked at him, you saw your own face in each of the lenses, but the image was distorted by the curvature of the glass. From the way the others deferred to him, I figured he must be the chief honcho. He raised a tin cup to his mouth and spat out some tobacco juice and motioned for me to come closer.

"What did you say?" he said, dabbing at his lips with a handkerchief.

"Salamalikoom."

"Repeat this with me. You do not say 'Salamalikoom.' You say, 'Alsalam-ali-kom Wal Rehmatullah-Walbarakathuh."

I stumbled over the words, and he made me repeat them until I got them right.

"Good," he said, "Wallikom-Ul-Salam Wal Rehmatullah-Walbarakathuh. I am Mavlavi Fazlulrahman. And this is Mullah Fazlulah. You probably have met Mullah Saydulhaq, and this is Mullah Qutbudin." Then he had me repeat the greeting to each of them, and they replied with the customary phrase and nodded.

Mullah Qutbudin was hunched in his chair with his mouth slightly open, wiggling his fingers and his eyes twitching, his whole body trembling. A real cockroach. I felt a shiver just being near him. "What's that book?" he shrieked and pointed. "That book!"

"Book? What book?"

"The book you're carrying. What is it?"

Oh, man.

"Well?"

"It's just a book."

"Just a book! What book!" He talked a mile a minute.

"Well…" I hesitated, trying to stall for time, but I couldn't think; meanwhile, the *mavlavi* held out a beringed hand. "Give me the book."

"It's poetry," I said as I handed it to him. I felt suspended. Here I was standing like a criminal on a thin carpet whose edges were torn and frayed. And all because I'd forgotten about that stupid book.

Meanwhile, the *mavlavi* took his own sweet time, leafing through the pages. "You know what the Prophet said about poetry!" the cockroach hissed, but the *mavlavi* asked him to be quiet. Finally, he closed the cover and placed it on the floor. He told me to come closer, and when I did, he reached for my right hand and covered it with both of his. I felt awkward, but I did as he asked. Outside, the blaring of horns grew noisier, and the sun shone directly through the curtainless windows, and you could feel the room getting stuffier. There was a scroll on the wall I hadn't noticed before, and it was crooked, and I had the urge to run over and straighten it. The *mavlavi's* hand felt damp and comfortless.

"I want you to listen carefully to what I say," he said. "Poets are evil. That is what the Prophet said. Evil. They are the enemies of God. They are rebellious and will not follow the dictates of Allah. Do you know what happens to men who refuse to listen to God? They're drawn and quartered and fed to the hyenas, and their souls are sent to hell where they burn forever. Do you know what hell is like? Fire and ash, smoke. Pain and suffering. Suffering for eternity. The fire that burns and does not consume itself." He spoke softly, as if he and I were alone. Then he released my hand, picked up the book, and held it in front of me "Do you know this man?"

"Who, Ghani Khan? No, I don't know him. Not personally. Is that what you mean?"

"I'm asking you, do you like his poetry? Do you want to drink wine in this world? To have women in this world and not when you are in the bliss of heaven? Here's what I think of his poetry." He gave the book to the Mullah Qutbudin and told him to get rid of it.

The cockroach held the book between his thumb and index finger, as if it were toxic, and he scurried over to the window and threw it out and scurried back to his seat, and the *mavlavi* said to me, "It is now time to take the test. I am going to ask you some questions. Are you ready to begin? All right then, if there are eighty infidels and you kill sixty of them, how many are left?"

I didn't know what to say; was he joking, was this a trick question? Again, I could feel their eyes on me. "Twenty," I said.

"Yes, good. In a battle, ten Mujahideen are fighting against fifteen Communists. Five of the Mujahideen are martyred, but with the help of God, the other five kill all of the infidels and capture twenty virgins. How many of the virgins can each man have as a slave?"

I knew the answer immediately, but I waited for a few seconds. "Four."

"How did you come to that conclusion?"

"Well, ten Mujahideen minus five equal five. I divided twenty women by five and concluded that each man would get four."

"Ah, a math genius. Okay. Now let me ask you a question about physics," he said. "Can a man go to the moon?"

"Yes, he already has."

Without warning, the cockroach leaped up with such force, I almost jumped myself. "Who told you such nonsense? No one can go to moon! The moon is in the seventh sky, you idiot." He picked up his chair and again took his seat, muttering the entire time about how boneheaded I was.

All I could answer was, "The seventh sky?"

This time the *mavlavi* spoke, but now, having asked me questions fit for a five-year-old, he went into a long rambling explanation about the seven skies and how we can't even reach the first, even though the earth might either exist in the first, or it might be separated from all seven, but that no matter whether we could reach the first sky or not, the moon was nevertheless in the seventh sky, and that was absolutely impossible to reach; it was too far away. One minute he called them skies and the next spheres and then heavens. When he was finished, he leaned back in his chair and waited for me to say something. But what?

After a moment, he said, "When I was your age, boy, I wanted to know everything. I asked many questions, but no one could answer me. My family lived in the mountains, and at night, the sky was on fire. Where did that fire come from? Life was difficult on the mountains, work was hard, and money, who had any? We suffered, we aged and died, and for what? I left those mountains, boy, and I came down to the valley. I wanted to understand, I had to—my hunger was a burning fire in my soul, and I would not rest until I had the answer. I could not."

He gazed at me and through me, and then his eyes swept up to the ceiling. "Never mind. You are no physicist. Well, neither am I. What does science know? How can they help us? Can they tell us what electricity is made of? Can they turn night into day or day into night? I have one final question. Now take your time and think before you answer. This is the most important question of all. This is the question that will carry you to the heavens. How do you know there is a God?"

I mumbled some inane reply, half swallowing my words, and they glared at me.

"The boy's a fool," Mullah Fazlulah said. "He thinks the earth revolves around the sun."

"The boy's an ignoramus," Mullah Qutbudin said.

"These Pashtoon. But one must make allowances," the *mavlavi* said. "Listen to me, child. The earth doesn't move around the sun. That's a fable, a fairy tale. It means nothing. The earth rests on the horn of a bull of immense size and proportion. When there is an earthquake on earth, that means that the bull became tired and shifted the earth from one horn to the other. I know you might find this difficult to believe, but you are here to learn. Indeed, this is why we were sent to help you. You may go now."

That night, Sial didn't return from school.

CHAPTER NINE

When Sial didn't appear the next morning, Moor and I went to the police station, which was next to the Peshawar airport. As we were stepping inside, we were unceremoniously elbowed out of the way by a couple of thickset policemen bringing in a young crazy-eyed prisoner who was flailing his arms in a useless struggle to free himself. They handcuffed him to the armrest of a bench, but he started pulling at the chain and hollering at the top of his voice. They told him to shut up, but he ignored their command until one of the guards smashed him on the shoulder with his nightstick. This quieted him down.

The place was a busy hive, and we didn't know what to do, who to speak to. Against the far wall were a series of adjoining cells, each meant to house no more than about five to seven prisoners, judging by their size, but I counted fourteen in one cell and nineteen in another. My eyes were drawn to a boy who was holding the bars, half-asleep, a scarecrow; he looked like he hadn't had a decent meal in weeks. His hair was matted, his mouth half-open, eyes closed, not much older than me, maybe younger. Above his cell was a portrait of Mohammad Ali Jinnah, the founder of Pakistan, a formal state photograph, blown up, colored, airbrushed, the eyes like two hot coals that followed you, that burnt into your soul, into your thoughts. *I am watching you.*

Moor asked one of the cops if he could tell her who was in charge of missing persons, and he wrote our names on a pad, told us to take a seat somewhere, that he'd get him.

The acrid smell of chewing tobacco, the sound of phlegm hitting a metal spittoon, causing it to rattle, cops that could have used a good shower, arrogant, implacable, busy, busy, busy with their hands out for bribes, given that the government only paid them three hundred rupees a month, not nearly enough to feed a family.

Two of them crossed over to the prisoner handcuffed to the bench where they began hassling him, rattling off questions like machine guns. When he didn't answer quickly enough, one of them yanked him to his feet, or at least he tried to, but the handcuffs weren't long enough. Instead of standing, the prisoner wound up leaning far back against the lobby wall with his back pressed against the bench, at which point the cop reached into the guy's pocket and extracted a small amount of hash. Well, supposedly he found some hash, since the usual scenario was for cops to surreptitiously slip drugs into a prisoner's pocket. I knew about this because one time, Sial and I were at the Peshawar bazaar shopping when we were stopped by a policeman who asked to see our papers. This was before Abba had gotten them, but although Sial tried to explain our situation, the policeman said he would need to search us. Luckily, Sial was too smart; he jumped back and asked the policeman to show him his hands first. I guess the policeman had a sense of humor because, when he held them up, we saw a plug of marijuana in between his index and his third finger. "Where did this come from?" he said before telling us to get moving.

My thoughts came to an abrupt halt when the guard held up his hand and said, "Kabuli chars" before punching the prisoner, a real punch. He dropped his shoulder, swinging his body. There was a lot of force in that punch, which meant he knew what he was doing; you could see that, a guy who enjoyed his work. The prisoner, with a sharp intake of breath, seemed to fade right in front of us. When another punch landed, he didn't try to evade it, but he took it, shaking himself like a dog. The cop yanked him forward by the waistband, tearing the prisoner's pants, which slid down his legs. He pressed his open palm against the prisoner's face, slamming his head against the wall. The prisoner staggered and then slipped down, half on the bench and half on the floor with his pants around his ankles. His legs twitched, and then he was still. The two cops pulled him to his feet, pulled his pants up, and dropped him down on the bench before they sauntered away.

The man next to me—he looked like a scholar with a wide temple, gray goatee, and eyeglasses—leaned over and said, "In the United States of America, you're innocent until you're proven guilty. According to the Napoleonic Code, you're guilty until you're proven innocent. But here you're guilty until you're proven guilty."

We wound up spending the day in the police station, but when we got back to camp, we didn't know any more about Sial than we had the day before. The following day, we asked around the camp, but as we expected, no one knew anything, or if they did, they weren't talking. I then went to the camp commander only to hear the same story—he didn't know anything. He had enough trouble trying to maintain order in the camp to get involved in the problems of its inhabitants. He suggested we try the police. The most logical place to ask for information was also the last place we could go, namely the madrassa, which when I even mentioned it, both Moor and Meena made me promise I'd never do such a thing. They were afraid that the same thing might happen to me. For although none of us said it out loud, we were almost certain that we'd never find out what happened to Sial, not know if he were dead or alive; such fates were not uncommon, even here in Peshawar.

We counted the days until Abba and Jandol returned from Lahore. They'd been gone for weeks. What could they be doing? What was taking them so long? But with no way to contact them or they us, we were left to wait. Time hung on our hands like weights pressing against our spirit.

Sial. It was funny, most of the time, my brother drove everybody crazy, so temperamental, you never knew what to expect. One minute "How can I help you?" The next "Get the hell away from me." Not to mention those stupid movie star posters of his that covered our bedroom walls.

I remembered back in Srakala the time I'd colored eggs to celebrate the end of Ramadan; I couldn't have been more than seven or so. I carefully wrapped each egg in newspaper, placed the eggs in a bath towel with the ends tied, and we set off for the bazaar, he and I. Well, in our village was a pack of feral dogs who hung around looking for scraps; they were quite ferocious, worse than wolves. On the way to the festivities, they began trailing after us. Sial went bananas, picking up a handful of rocks, taking aim, screaming at them until they lunged after him, at which he clambered up a tree to safety while continuing to taunt them. It happened so fast. One minute they were running toward us, then suddenly, I was in the middle of a maelstrom of snarling dogs while Sial was laughing as if it was the funniest thing he'd ever seen. I tried to run, but I tripped, and the towel with the eggs went flying out of my hand, which turned out to be lucky.

True, the eggs were ruined, which meant going to the festival empty-handed like a fool. True, I'd worked for hours diligently mixing the watercolors and making elaborate designs. But the good thing was, the dogs were more interested in the eggs than in me. So did he apologize? Did he say he'd never do such a thing again? No, he said I was stupid for not running along with him. That was the thanks I got. What Sial needed was a good swift kick in the butt. Something to remind him that other people existed. But the truth was, he was still my brother. I loved him.

Besides, I couldn't kick him if he weren't here. So I decided to act on my own.

Impervious to the wet May heat, the madrassa stood before me, austere, inaccessible, but not regal, more a factory or a hospital like the one in my dream, transforming healthy people into limbless zombies. No matter. I was determined to find out what happened to my brother; he couldn't have just vanished into thin air, not him, not Sial. My plan was to rifle through the school's files to see if I could find any information.

Having waited until afternoon prayers, I circled the madrassa until I came to the section of the rear wall where there was a telephone pole just outside. I squatted down to give myself leverage then sprang up, taking hold of the first rung with one hand while wrapping my arms and legs around the pole and pulling myself inch by inch until my knee was on the first rung. Then I took hold of the second rung and did the same maneuver until I had one foot on the second rung while I held onto the third, which left me slightly higher than the top of the wall. By leaning over with my right arm extended, I gripped the outer edge of the wall, balanced myself on the rung, and flew forward, swinging my other arm over my head so I wouldn't slam into the concrete. Then as I was about to slither down, with a burst of manic energy, I hurled my body upward, pulling as hard as I could. I wound up straddling the wall where I lay for a moment before letting myself drop down to the ground. I was in. They only checked you when you came in, so when I was done, I'd just mosey out without a care in the world.

It was still a few minutes before the call for prayer, and as the field began to fill up with students, I made my way to the verandah. I reached it just as the mullahs and teachers came pouring out from their classrooms. I hid behind a ceramic flower pot in the shape of a gigantic ewer, which was filled to overflowing with climbing ferns on wooden stakes. When everyone was settled and the service began, I sprinted inside. The building was deserted, not a sound from any of the classrooms, the only voice coming from the mullah leading the prayer. Amplified by the loudspeakers, his words rose in pitch until they resembled the anguished shriek of a cuckoo devouring its young. I only had a short time, half an hour at the most.

I came to the office where they kept the student records. My plan was to rifle through the files to see if I could find out any information about Sial, but the door was locked. Great, every other door unlocked except the one I wanted. The door to the adjacent office was half-open, and I went in, climbed out the back window, made my way to the records room—this time luck was with me in the form of an open window—and climbed in.

The records room was dingy, with rows of ancient metal filing cabinets, concrete walls, floor tiles either broken or missing in places. Scarred by boots, stained with chewing tobacco, it was like being in a war zone. In the corner beside a walk-in closet (I checked, couldn't be too safe), there was a water cooler from whose broken plastic spigot droplets were spilling out. Indeed, there was a puddle on the floor. Hanging from the ceiling were several naked lightbulbs, along the electric cords of which were hundreds of dead midges.

As I began to hunt for Sial's file, I soon discovered that everything was in great disorder. None of the filing cabinets were organized in any way so that the *A-B*s were next to the *W-Z*s. Then when I thought I'd found the right cabinet, none of the folders was in alphabetical order. Each cabinet had four separate drawers, each drawer stuffed with thick files, most of which were tied together, although some were scattered around. This was going to take forever. I heard footsteps. I'd been so engrossed in my search, I hadn't realized that prayers were over, meaning it was time for lunch. Well, I'd have to come back tomorrow.

I closed the file as quietly as I could, but as I was about to leave, I heard voices on the other side of the door accompanied by the click of the lock. I was almost at the window, but it was too late. I ran into the closet where I hid behind a pile of boxes at the same time as the door opened.

After my heart stopped beating like a kettledrum, I relaxed—sort of. I mean, what else could I do, have a heart attack? But apparently, they weren't going anywhere; they just sat making conversation that I couldn't make out but could only hear soft voices droning on like bees buzzing around the petals of a rose—and I was the rose. This was one of those situations that you joke about later but which, at the time, could have been disastrous. If I'd been discovered, they'd have thrown me in prison, probably for years. Recently, they'd accused a twelve-year-old student in one of my classes of spying, and he'd been executed. So this wasn't some kind of schoolboy prank where I'd get ten demerits. Now though, I find it comical to think of my hiding in that dusty coffin, in that dingy office, waiting for those men to leave. At the time, I was terrified I'd be caught. I don't know how much time passed.

Finally, I heard them close the door and lock it, but still I waited just to make sure that they weren't coming back. After waiting a short time, which seemed to take forever, I cracked the door open a smidgen and ascertained that the office was empty. This time I systematically examined the files until I finally found Sial's school records. I flipped through it, but it was written in Urdu and Arabic, which I couldn't read, so I stuck it in the small of my back inside my pants.

Then, so that they wouldn't discover my theft, I began to mix up a lot of the files, placing one person's file in another's folder, mixing up the loose papers. That done, I tried the door, but it was locked, so I climbed out the window and headed toward the main entrance.

"Stop!"

I continued walking.

"Stop!"

I turned around.

A guard came up to where I was, spitting out a wad of chewing tobacco. "Where do you think you're going?"

"Who, me? Outside."

"Where outside?"

"To the bazaar."

"Like that?"

"Like what?"

"You know what I'm talking about."

"What?"

"You really don't know?" The guard folded his arms against his chest and stared at me with an expression of arrogant disdain. "Where's your turban?"

My hands flew to my head. "Oh, I'm sorry. I forgot to put it on."

"How could you forget your turban? Did you forget your pants?"

"No. I'm sorry, I'll go back and get it."

"Not so fast," he said, taking out a notebook and pen from his shirt pocket. "What's your name?"

I smiled at him and said, "Why don't you let me go, and I'll get my turban, and everyone'll be happy?"

He didn't look too happy when I said that. Again he asked me to tell him my name, and I made up one, which he dutifully noted. Before he returned the notebook to his pocket, he examined the name carefully. I couldn't tell what he was thinking; he was wearing those mirrored aviator sunglasses they all wore. I took a step backward as if I was going to get my missing turban, but he took hold of me by the collar and said to come with him.

We headed straight toward the entrance. Most of the students were either inside the dorms or out on the shady lawn in front, although sometimes boys would pass by arm in arm, or they'd be lying on the grass under the wall holding hands and talking quietly. Along the western wing of the madrassa, there were banks of sunflowers drying in the sun, great grasping flowers with their bright yellow leaves.

I started limping. "Wait, wait," I said. "There's a stone in my sandal."

He tightened his grip and slowed his pace, but he continued walking. His heavy onyx ring dug into my neck. I leaned down, unstrapped my sandal, lifted it, and shook it, all the while hopping up and down. But as I replaced the sandal, I raked my fingers along the gravel until I had a fistful of the stuff. When we reached a fairly empty section of the walkway, I raised my left foot, and just as he stepped forward, I stamped down with all my might on his toes sticking out from his sandals. Immediately, I yanked off his sunglasses with such force they snapped in half, threw the sandy mixture in his eyes, and sped off.

When I turned the corner of the building and reached the front gate, I slowed down, nonchalantly exiting. The minute I walked out, as you can imagine, I sped away. The streets were mobbed with people. It was market day, but I kept running, not daring to look back until I lost myself among the crowd and then made my way to camp.

That night after our usual supper of rice and lentils, I took out the file for Moor and Meena to see, telling them the whole story. Moor was alarmed by my behavior, but I brushed away her fears. "I'm like the wind," I said. "Where I come from and where I go, no one knows."

"No matter what, we need to stick together," she said, giving me a hug. "We haven't lost Sial, I can feel it in my bones. He'll walk in here like nothing's happened, and if we get excited, he'll say we're so dramatic."

"I'm frightened," Meena said.

"You'll see I'm right, my girl. You'll see."

"I agree with you," I said. "But the first thing we need to do is find someone to translate these notes without knowing exactly what it is."

The next morning, I copied everything on different pages, which I then cut into smaller sections so that no one I spoke to would know what it was about, after which I went around asking different people if anyone could read Urdu or Arabic. It took some doing, but in the final analysis, it wound up being less than useless. Simply some scattered notes that didn't amount to much.

Meena said that she kept imagining the prison in Warsak. This was a notorious jail built by the Mujahideen to house infidels, with its reputation for brutality and murder. It was said that there was only one way out—being tossed in the Warsak River to feed the fish. One thing was for sure: the only way we were going to find Sial was having enough money to bribe the right officials. But who had money? With Abba and Jandol gone, the only person we could turn to was Pamir, who was in Kabul.

This was an extremely risky journey, especially for men over twenty-one who could be forcibly drafted into the Communist-controlled Afghan Army, even teenagers, sometimes even boys with valid student IDs. Those cards were worth their weight in gold, and a thriving black market had sprung up, but nevertheless, I had one, and it wasn't ersatz either.

After years of combat, Kabul itself was still held by the Russians, and Pakhtunistan was under the aegis of the insurgents, resulting in a trip that led from danger to danger. If Pamir didn't have any money, well, at least he had access to the jewelry, which could be bartered. Moor didn't like the idea but could think of no other. The question was who should go? Initially, Moor and Meena were planning on making the journey until one day, while my mother was talking to us, she said she felt dizzy, that the heat was making her feel faint. She lay down for an hour, but the same thing happened a few days later. Meena said it was the food—or the lack thereof—that was affecting her health, that none of us getting enough, those small bowls of rice or lentils, those thin servings of moldy cheese, but never enough of these to feed one person, much less the five of us. Normally, we'd added to the meals by buying meat and eggs, but with Abba and Jandol gone, with our money dwindling, even that became impossible.

It became clear to the three of us that, like it or not, Moor was too fragile to undertake such an arduous journey, that Meena could not possibly go by herself, and that I would have to go with her. We would have to trust luck as well as the fact that at sixteen, I looked years younger and that we wouldn't be caught.

To travel from Peshawar to Kabul, you needed to take three buses—one to the border, then another to Jalalabad, and then a third from there to Kabul. Once we reached Jalalabad, we were going to go to our uncle Shamshad's house and spend the night. Shamla's place was too small, what with her, her husband, their children, and Bibi.

On the way to the first bus, I told Meena that if the KHAD stopped us at a checkpoint, she was not to even glance in my direction but to keep moving. "Make up a phony name," I told her. "You don't need papers, so you'll be safe." If on the return journey we were questioned or searched and they were to discover the money, she was to say she didn't know me, but that I had asked her to carry it because I was afraid of being robbed. "But let's keep our fingers crossed," I said, "that God will protect us."

Meena told me not to worry, that she thought it was going to be exciting. Anything was better than being in camp.

The first bus was crowded as usual, but we got two seats and sped onward until we reached the border, which was located at the edge of Tourkham, more a town than a village due to the bus lines that converged there. There was a flurry of nervous excitement among the passengers as we disembarked and stood in line at the checkpoint. There were two of them, one manned by Pakistanis on the Peshawar side and Communists on the Afghan side. When it was our turn, they just waved us through both of the checkpoints without even asking to see my papers or asking us any questions. As we crossed over the Tourkham Bridge, we stopped midspan to gaze at the valley as it undulated for miles until it was lost to view. It filled the imagination. Places, people, the future.

The end of the bridge was located in the opposite edge of Tourkham, which apparently stretched between the two countries. We went to a food stand by the bus stop, where Meena ordered a large plate of *pakora* while I got samosas, and we sat down on a bench, luxuriating in such a wonderful meal, particularly in light of what we had been dining on for the past few months. It was fresh, hot, spicy with chutney, the taste and smell bringing back my childhood in a sharp nostalgic way that even memory itself could not accomplish, along with a sense of being home again.

The second bus ride was a lesson in futility, the difference between the Afghan bus and the one in Pakistan being like night and day, a distinct indication of the modern world as compared to the world of the past. Whereas our ride to the border had been smooth sailing on a modern highway, the road to Jalalabad was a different story with the driver having to really keep his eyes peeled. Not only did you have to be careful because the Communist tanks had broken up the road, leaving huge ruts and pitfalls, but also because of land mines planted by the insurgents. Many bridges had been blown up, which meant endless detours, the worst being the time we had to get off the bus while the driver rode up a narrow lane, crossed a river where the water wasn't too deep, then come back to pick us up. It took over an hour.

We finally reached Jalalabad, a distance that should have been covered in forty-five minutes from the border but lasted almost four hours. There were no phones in the station, so we couldn't call my uncle Shamshad even though he, being a doctor, was one of the few Afghans who actually had one. But outside was a line of *gadai*, horse and buggies, and we took one to his house.

When our uncle opened the door, he was surprised to see us, considering he hadn't heard from us in such a long time, but when we told him the reason for our journey, tears came to his eyes. "What can I give you?" he asked. "Money, food?" On the morning of our departure, he filled our pockets with Afghanis while his wife made us enough food to last a week. "Just in case," she said.

Family, what else meant anything? Always family. Always our hands linked when there was a crisis.

Uncle Shamshad went to fetch Shamla and Bibi, which resulted in more hugging and weeping on Bibi's part. Shamla had just borne her second child. It felt so good to sleep in a real bed, to have traditional Afghan dishes; we let ourselves be talked into staying for a few days. Any longer would have caused me plagues of guilt given that during those several days, I had to remind myself of the importance of reaching Kabul. But I made a promise I'd come back someday so that I could lose myself among his many books and daydream in his garden. Such a kind couple, my uncle, Abba's older brother, with many sons and daughters at home or living abroad, those nearby joining us at meals. The sound of laughter, a sound we hadn't heard for ages—it felt good, it felt wonderful. Sial was the adventurer; he was the man of action. I was the poet; I was the one meant to study in crowded libraries filled with heavy volumes. Instead, we'd changed places, he and I. I was living his dream while he was stuck somewhere in a room with bars on the windows.

No matter how down in the dumps we felt, Kabul was like a shot of adrenaline. Much greater than Peshawar. We'd gotten Pamir's address, which was in a section of town called Kala Zaman Khan, but when we got off the tram and managed to locate the house, we found that it had been commandeered by a group of Communist officers as some kind of headquarters. The same was also true of the little storefront in downtown Kabul that Pamir was using as an office. Nevertheless, our spirits remained lifted. After living under the strictures of the camp, which was governed by the Mujahideen with their Sharia laws, it was quite an adventure to be in a city again among so many different people, even the government officials who streamed out of the Makrooyan complex and the Communist soldiers in their khaki uniforms.

I was affected by the number of beggars, some of them without eyes, others without arms or legs, the glories of war. They pulled at your clothes, and they shook metal cups at you. It was heartbreaking; it was impossible. Why would people do such things to each other? Greed, that's all it was. But pretty soon, you become inured to such catastrophes. Nobody paid them any attention; they didn't even bother to look away but stared at these poor fools with contempt.

My eye was caught by two boys snaking their way through the crowd with their eyes intently watching everybody. They edged up to a lady who was holding a large bag of groceries, and while one of them said something to her, the other snatched the bag from her arms, and they both raced off.

"Did you see that?" I said to Meena, but they'd already disappeared.

"Now what do we do?" she asked.

Once we got our bearings, we went around to every shop and house within walking distance, up one street and down another, but no luck. No one knew him. By the time we were through, it was getting late and we were both tired and hungry. More than once I wished that I were living somewhere else, someplace normal. Whoever heard of a city with no street addresses and no phones and no directories and no bureaus where you could find out where someone was living? Here, the most important thing was to remain invisible, to *not* stand out in any way. Going to the Communist authorities for anything was out of the question, you were just buying yourself in trouble. Typically, there wasn't a Russian in sight except for those in charge. Afghan against Afghan. It was pathetic. I decided that the best plan was grab a bite and then to go to our old house in Koti Sangi. Abba had rented the place to a widow with two young daughters, and my thought was that maybe she could tell us where Pamir was living. At the least, she'd let us spend the night there, and in the morning, we could ask around. A week later we found him in a little attic room near the University of Kabul.

Actually we didn't find him, we ran into him one morning when he was on his way to school. He was living in student housing, keeping pretty much to himself, pretty much under the radar, since he knew that if the Communists discovered his family was living in Peshawar, they'd suspect him of being an insurgent. Since every bank was in the hands of the Communists, Pamir had stashed his savings in a crawl space in the ceiling. It turned out that he was making good wages selling jewelry, although not from Afghan customers but from the Communists, who were having rings and pendants made that they sent home to their sweethearts.

CHAPTER TEN

When we told Pamir the reason for our journey, he gathered up his cash—years of savings that he'd hidden beneath the floorboards under his bed—and took it to local moneylenders. Arrangements were made to transfer the funds to Peshawar, an extremely risky enterprise since your only proof was a *hawala* that you'd show to the *saraf* in Peshawar, all we could do is pray that he'd honor it; since if he didn't, you had no recourse, given that the entire transaction was illegal and you had nothing but a piece of paper as proof. Pamir wound up using two moneylenders, just in case, since he was sending a large sum of money. But no matter how careful he was being, since there was no mail or telephone from Kabul to Peshawar, there'd be no way for him to know if we received the money, unless Meena and I traveled back to Kabul to tell him, which we weren't about to do. If we were ripped off, that would've been the end of us—so much in our lives depended on luck and street smarts, but they only went so far. Anyway, when the terms with the two sarafs had been agreed upon and Pamir handed over the money, he made sure to keep enough to pay his bills as well as to take us out to lunch and then to a movie. What a treat. When we returned home, Moor said she hadn't had a good-night's sleep since we left. The next day she and I went to each of the sarafs in Peshawar, and accept a commission from the second guy—which Pamir had already paid in Kabul, by the way, but what the hell?—we received our money. I counted it, of course, and nothing had been stolen. Now, it was our turn to take Moor out for supper. Eat, eat, we kept saying.

Life is funny; weeks and months pass, and nothing happens, and then, within a short time, your world is turned upside-down. Only a few days later, Sial came crashing into our tent, mumbling to himself, quite filthy, his head bloodied, and hardly making any sense. He was ravenous, and after washing up and eating, he fell into a deep sleep and didn't wake up until the following afternoon. We tried to discover where he'd been, but every time we asked, he told us to leave him alone. This was the situation when, several days later, Abba and Jandol came home, somewhat the worse for wear.

"I'm so happy you two are here," Moor said. "You'll never know what we've been through while you were gone." She then proceeded to tell them about Sial's disappearance for a month and then his unexpected return. "We still don't know what happened, and every time we ask him, he bites our heads off."

"Don't worry, Lila, I'll find out what happened," Abba said.

"Wait till he wakes up."

"He's in terrible shape," I said.

"Yes, he's really in bad shape," Moor said. "That boy. And where have you two been? What took you so long? We thought you'd been kidnapped. You go away for three days and come back six weeks later."

They told us there were hundreds of traders in Lahore looking to buy fabrics, but since they themselves knew nothing about the business, they didn't stand a chance of competing, not that they didn't go around talking to various manufacturers, which accounted for their being away so long. They were actually at the station waiting for the bus home when they picked up a newspaper, in which there was an article about the Shama Corporation—which manufactured cooking oil—and how they were expanding so rapidly, they needed more wholesale subcontractors. Abba applied for a contract and was told that their operation was not based on trust, that they needed to be paid upfront and not, as was usual, on a monthly basis or after some time when the business flourished.

"So, here we are, back where we started," Abba said.

"Not exactly," Moor said.

"How's that?"

"Show them, son," she said to me, and I handed Abba the money from Pamir.

"What's this?"

"This is our future," Moor said.

"Did you guys rob a bank?" Jandol said.

"Better," Meena said. "Much, much better."

"You can thank your brother Pamir and my two little ones here," Moor said and told them about our trip and Pamir's generosity. "He's a good son, my Pamir, my firstborn. I knew he wouldn't let us starve."

"This is unbelievable," Jandol said.

"Isn't it? Now that we have enough money to leave this camp, we don't need to suffer anymore."

While she was speaking, Sial stumbled stiffly out from the alcove where he'd been sleeping, half hidden by some bags of wheat. "My head is pounding," he said. "Is there any aspirin around?"

"I'll get it," Meena said, and jumped up.

"Okay, okay, okay, stop staring at me like that, all of you," Sial said, his eyes on Abba. "So it was like this. A mullah came around to the madrassa with this bright orange turban and asked if anyone was interested in learning how to become a fighter. After he was done going on and on about how great it would be to battle against tyranny, to struggle for freedom, a bunch of guys raised their hands, and without thinking, I did too. I mean,

I thought it'd be some kind of adventure, you know, shooting guns, climbing mountains, I thought I could become one of those important honchos, the guys who do the kicking and not the ones who get kicked like us. Maybe I could earn enough rupees to get us out of this hovel. I don't know. But right from the get-go, I knew I'd made a mistake. Like they wouldn't let us go home and tell our families what was going on. You don't think I'd just up and leave without telling you? I'm telling you, they wouldn't let us. Instead, they packed us into two buses, about eighty of us, drove to Nowkhaar, fed us, and, before we resumed our journey, blindfolded everyone. Man, they weren't kidding about taking precautions about where they were taking us.

"The bus was like an oven at first, but later it was like an icebox. I fell asleep, and when I woke up, we were in a training camp in the mountains somewhere, a huge place, hundreds of tents, soldiers running around, target practice, people hollering at each other. They assigned us to various tents, and from then on, it was train and pray, train and pray, train and pray from morning until night. Our commander was a real pig. All he ever talked about was blowing up cities, killing people, destroying hospitals, schools. Oh, yeah, he was a real dreamer. Bullets that glowed in the dark, forced marches when it was twenty below, and then bivouacs in the snow, I thought I'd freeze to death. And then those hateful lectures about the infidels, about holy wars. Like this kid I knew, he got into trouble over some religious thing or something and just disappeared, like one minute he was there and the next—poof! You couldn't ask where he was or you'd disappear too.

"Believe, it didn't take me long to realize that I'd messed up. Really messed up, this time. Worse than the donkey. So what could I do, I asked myself? I couldn't stay, and it seemed impossible to leave. Well, the truth is, if it hadn't been for summer, I'd have been stuck there for the entire year, there's no way I could have climbed down the mountain during the winter. Even so, the nights were freezing, like I said, but the crazy thing was, getting away was actually kind of easy, they didn't think anyone would have enough nerve to even try. As it turned out, all I did was say I had to go to the bathroom, and then I sneaked into the tent used for cooking and stole some food and took off. I hid during the day and hiked all night long, just like we did when we left Tummanai, I stole food from orchards and farms, I was never sure of my direction, I'd hear footsteps or voices and drop to the ground hardly daring to breathe until they were gone. Anyway, I reached a road, and a truck came by, and I jumped in the back, and the guy drove to Mansehra, and from there, I found my way back home."

Abba returned to Lahore, paid for a contract, and when he came back to Peshawar, he rented a storage space on University Road, where he began selling cooking oil to shopkeepers, restaurants, and housewives. For such an odd business, a business we knew nothing about, it turned out that there was quite a demand for cooking oil. He and Jandol were busy right from the get-go. It really gave my father a zest he hadn't felt for a long time. The next thing we did after the business began was to find a rental house in an upscale neighborhood, one where you stood the least chance of being hassled by the ISI. The house was on the Arbab Road, just a few blocks from University Road where the buses ran, so it was easy for us to get around. Sial and I shared a bedroom, a situation that didn't feel homey until he began putting up his movie posters, those garish displays of slender, seductive temptresses who smiled at you, who beckoned you, their kohl-black eyes shooting arrows into your heart. O, their eyes burned through my body, their long thick hair blowing in the wind, these women in their purple dresses who called me when I awoke, who waved good-bye when I went to sleep. Sometimes my body would burn; I was afraid I had fever.

Several months I was walking with Sial down the Arbab Road in Peshawar on our way to catch a bus to the Sadar Bazaar. The weather was mild for January; it was Friday, so no school, which was a relief, given that I was still having a lot of difficulty understanding Urdu. We passed by Dr. Sheraz's dental office where Abba had gone to have an infected molar extracted and wound up losing two teeth. In the window was a sign that said TEETH ARE WEALTH, KEEP YOUR HEALTH, TWENTY-FIVE YEARS EXPERIENCE. What rubbish, Sial said, indicating the sign, he could've have done a better job with a pair of household pliers.

"You wouldn't laugh if it were your teeth," I said.

"You're still pissed off at me."

"I'm not pissed off at you. I'm pissed off at myself for risking my life to try and rescue you."

"Well, what can I say? You're quite a guy."

"Yeah, I'm quite a guy." I shrugged. Sial was wrong about so many things, but this time, he pinned the tail on the donkey. "You put yourself in danger, you made your family suffer, me and Moor and Meena for nothing. You were stupid and you know it. And don't try to make any excuses. You're lucky you're alive."

The Sadar Bazaar was busier than before. It was so busy you could hardly move. Horse-drawn vegetable wagons with vendors hawking their wares, bicyclists clanging bells, motorcyclists with women in burkas holding onto them, revving their engines, practically running you down; men in BMWs, blasting their horns, slamming their brakes, ordering you to get out of the way. The smell of barbecue, the acrid smoke rising from the skewers, the crackling of meat, restaurants packed with customers, with sonorous Pashtu music emanating from the speakers, romantic Afghan tappas from the ancient past. We headed for the Abaseen, it was jammed, and Sial got in line for a table while I stayed outside, hungrily looking at the meat hanging on hooks that were protected by mosquito netting, freshly killed chickens, lambs, goats, entire beef carcasses—the animals slaughtered according to the rules of halal, meaning that they were healthy. When you gave your order, the waiter would tell one of the cooks, usually there were three or four sitting in a row in front of the meat, and the cook would take the order, cut up your selection, weigh it on a scale, dice it, and sauté it with vegetables in pans that were placed on mud ovens directly outside. If you were smart, you'd go with the waiter to tell the cook exactly which cut of meat or chicken you wanted. I watched the *samawarchi* making tea; his arms never stopped moving. He sat cross-legged at the entrance, stirring an enormous bowl of steaming milk, which was constantly being replenished by the busboys. Next to the milk bowl was a huge boiler for heating water, which was also continually being refilled, on the other side of which were containers of black and green tea. Waiters would rush up with teapots into which he'd spoon out the proper amount of tea, then came the water, and then the milk.

One pot! Five pots! A hundred pots! And the food after all those months in Taramangal and in the camp, I was always hungry.

"Now, this is the life," Sial said, sitting back in his chair. "You know something, little brother. I feel so good today. It's the Sadar, no one knows my name. Just imagine, we can walk anywhere, go anywhere, without anybody noticing us. It gives me a whole new outlook on life."

When the waiter came, I ordered spicy chicken *karahi*, Sial asked for *sikh* kebab, and we shared a pot of milk tea. When the order came, we savored the food. We didn't wolf it down, and with the tea that we sipped, we didn't bolt it down, with hardly any conversation. When he was finished, Sial wiped the corners of his mouth with his napkin, put the napkin on the table, took a sip of tea, placing the empty cup on the little saucer and signaling the waiter for the bill. "It's too noisy in here, let's go someplace where it's quiet and get dessert." After we paid, we went to a little teahouse at the far end of the bazaar, which specialized in cinnamon rice pudding.

Dessert rice pudding was delicate with a subtle mixture of cinnamon, milk, and rice whose little globules melted in your mouth.

He leaned across the table and took hold of my hand. "It's such a relief to have all that behind me and be back home."

"Oh, Sial, quit sounding like an actor in a B movie."

"An actor? Really? Like who?"

"King Kong."

"Very funny. You should be a stand-up comedian."

"Well, at least I can stand up."

On the way out, as Sial was collecting our change, a woman passed by, close enough for me to catch the scent of her perfume. I kept staring at her, she was so exotic, so sweet, so warm, so unavailable—all women were unavailable to me. And then she was gone, swallowed by the crowd. Sial came out, and we went to a stall and bought some dates and headed home.

"Let's walk a little before we take the bus," Sial said. "I want another cigarette."

"Give me one."

"You're too young."

"Come on."

"Well, don't tell Abba," he said, and we lit up. The dates were delicious, but the smoke tasted awful, and I started coughing.

"You're wasting that," Sial said and took it from me and put it out and placed it back in the pack. "These things aren't cheap." He wrapped his fingers around his cigarette and held it to his mouth and squinted one eye like hoodlums did in Hollywood movies, and when he exhaled, the smoke drifted away in lopsided rings. "You know what?" he said looking around, "I'm going to soak up all this stuff, all this local color. And you want to know why? Because when the camera"—and here he framed his face with his hands as if a camera were actually coming toward him—"dollies in for my close-up, the audience will see a thousand years of history in my eyes. They will see a proud people reflected there. They will see war and death, but also the triumph of life."

We passed by the Sadar Stadium. A soccer game had just ended, and streams of people were exiting from all directions, and Park Avenue was turning into a major traffic jam. Just ahead, two guards came rushing out of the Iranian Consulate and pulled open the heavy iron gates, and out came a black Cadillac limousine with tinted windows and Iranian and Pakistanian flags flying, accompanied by three officers on motorcycles, one of whom sped ahead until he was in front. We watched as it merged with the traffic and then continued up Park Avenue, where it was quieter; and soon there were no pedestrians around and little traffic, except for the buses that came trundling along every five minutes. Great decorated behemoths with spires and chains and tiny minarets were attached to the roof, like circus elephants on wheels.

"Save some for me," Sial said and reached into the bag. He popped a date into his mouth and spit out the pit, and I did the same.

"Hey."

"I bet I can spit farther than you can," I said.

"No way, brother."

"*Hey!*"

We both stood side by side, stamping the ground. "At the count of three, we will spit the pits. One...two...three."

We both took a deep breath and spat as far as we could.

"Hey, I'm talking to you."

We turned around. Three bearded men in ivory Arab garbs came toward us. Ghosts from the deserts of the East. Mantis religioso. Brainwashed, fervent, so sure of themselves. One of them was a small, wiry man with a parrot beak, a thin face and narrow, hard eyes blackened with mascara. The other two followed close behind, one of them lumbering like a gorilla with heavy shoulders, no forehead, thick lips, his arms dangling by their sides. The other guy had a distinct limp, but he was as fast as a snake.

"We've been watching you for the past half hour," the man with the parrot beak said. He was not quite half as tall as Sial, and he had to look up when he talked to him.

Sial raised his eyebrow questioningly and pointed to himself. But he said nothing.

"Maybe he can't speak," the man with the limp sniffed, taking a handkerchief out of his pocket and blowing his nose.

"Do you know where dates come from?" the man with the parrot beak asked. His voice was soft and gentle.

Sial held up the bag and shook it. "These dates?"

"They come from the Holy Land."

"The Holy Land? Which Holy Land?"

"Which Holy Land?" He gave Sial a look in which pity and incomprehension fought for ascendancy. "The Land of the Prophet." He placed his hand on his heart and said, "Peace be upon Him." The other two repeated the phrase.

Sial shrugged indifferently. "Which Prophet?"

The man with the parrot beak stiffened, and when he again spoke, his voice was cold. "All dates are holy and the pits are holy. They must be treated with respect. Keep them always wrapped up in silk, and every time you touch one, pray to Allah."

"These boys are more Arabic than the Arabs," Sial said to me, "There's one fruit in the whole Arabic world. Dates. Hey"—he turned to the three men—"why don't you pray to our fruit, we've got plenty. Aren't they holy?"

Sial handed me a date and popped another in his mouth. They were the last two, and he crumpled up the bag, and we both spit out the pits. When we did this, the man with the parrot beak rapped Sial under the chin, and Sial popped him on the head with the bag. The parrot man pulled his arm back and was about to give him a right hook, but before he made contact, Sial shoved him in the face with the flat of his palm, and blood spurted out of his nose. He fell backward and tripped over the folds of his clothes and landed on the ground.

The gorilla made a lunge for Sial, but I jumped over and wrapped my arms around him and stuck my leg in between his. He was too strong for me, and he flung me away, but I held onto his *thoub*, and the fabric ripped apart all the way up to his shoulder. He was about to lay one on me when Sial came from behind and grabbed him by the neck and held him in a chin lock. The man with the limp slithered around Sial from the side and tried to pull him down with a double-leg takedown. I quickly grabbed hold of his beard and pulled it so hard that some of the hair ended up in my hand. He held on to Sial, but I made an enormous effort until I wrenched his arms away and got him lying facedown with me on his back. I pulled up the ends of his thoub and tied it around his legs. Then I whipped his *shumagg* off; it was like riding a bucking horse, but I managed to get his hands tied together. I turned to help Sial, but the gorilla was falling from his arms, gasping for air. Sial let go, and he dropped to his knees, holding his throat and moaning.

Sial picked up a few of our date pits and walked over to the man with the parrot beak who backed up as we came closer and held his arms in front of him. "From now on," Sial said, "we've learned our lesson, you've taught us well. We will wrap each date pit in silk."

"What are we going to tell Abba and Moor?" I said when we got on the bus.

"Let me handle it."

Of course, letting Sial handle something meant that he'd shine and I'd be shoved into the background, which is exactly what happened. He said that three men tried to attack me and that he saved my life. I didn't say anything, who cared? I was a rock and the waves were sculpting my sense of livingness. They never stopped.

Winter was the rainy season in Peshawar, but when it was clear, I used to go around on my Chinese commuting bicycle, it must have weighed forty pounds. Two gears, hills were murder. But I had a basket in front, and I'd bring something to nibble on. The farthest I ever went was to Palosai, a farming village about ten miles to the north. If the bike was cheaply made, the tires were even worse though, and I hardly ever went anywhere without getting a flat. I became pretty adept at fixing them. Two or three times a week I rode to the Afghan Information Center, which was owned and run by a friend of my father's who published a weekly journal devoted to political issues. Before the Russian invasion, he'd been head of the Political Science Department at Kabul University, and now every year, he wrote a statement condemning the occupation that was read to the United Nations General Assembly. He had a well-stocked private library where he would let me sit and read, and I'd spend hours poring over Pashto poetry books and philosophy and watching Hollywood cowboy movies on his VCR. America, I thought, land of earthquakes and dangers, the Wild Wild West.

But this time when I drew near to the front gate, there was a man's body spread out on the gravel, half covered with a blanket and surrounded by onlookers. One of them lifted the edge, and there was my father's friend lying in a pool of blood with the entire back of his head shot off. The last time I saw him was when Abba and I had tea with him in his office. He had been warned time and again by the ISI not to write incendiary articles about them, but he had ignored their threats, and I remember Abba telling him to be careful and to stay out of trouble. "Those guys don't kid around," he said, "They're serious lunatics." But his friend told him he could take care of himself.

So here he was, a dead body riddled with bullets, lying on a dirt road. I didn't stay long; I bicycled over to my father's office and told him what had happened. Later when I got home, he was sitting alone in his bedroom, and I sat down next to him. But where was he? This man with his stoicism and his silences, silences that separated him from everyone. If he would only talk to you, tell you how he felt. I used to wonder what would happen if he ever let himself go, would it be like a volcano erupting? The only one close to him was Moor. Not even Moor. So I didn't try to intrude upon him, I simply sat next to him.

In front of our house, there was an apple tree, and in the early morning, the branches were bearded with dew, but when the sun rose, the dew melted, forming tiny drops that cascaded downward. In the spring, flowers sprouted on the branches of the tree that were white, tinged with pink, until the tree was teeming with blossoms. There was a lilt in the air when you sat under it reading, with white peals drifting onto the pages. It was sad too, because in a few weeks, they disappeared; summer arrived, at which time the tree was covered with green leaves and apples began to form, hanging from the boughs, but you no longer sat beneath the tree because it was too muggy.

"I can't remember it ever being this hot," Meena said, languidly fanning herself with a palmetto fan.

"Not in Shabak," Sial said. "It was protected. Here we're prey to the elements."

We were outside on the verandah.

"When are they going to fix the electricity?" Moor asked Abba.

"When they get their bribes," Sial said, uncrossing his ankles and yawning. "It's so hot."

"Just think," Meena said. "Although it's not much, we do have fans, but no electricity." As if to emphasize her words, the lights flickered, and for the next five minutes, they went on and off until they stopped and didn't go back on.

"Now what?"

"Now we sit in the dark," Abba said.

"I'm always in the dark," I said. "Even when the lights are on."

"You know, son," Abba said. "You have a philosophical mind." He reached into his pocket and took out some almonds and dropped them in my hand.

"We might as well enjoy the heat," Jandol said. "Who knows where we'll be next summer."

"We'll survive," Moor said. "Bibi's been a refugee twice. Not once. Twice she had to give up everything and leave everyone. Twice she had to start again with nothing but her own wits. One time when the British forced her family their land, and now with the Russians and her having to give up our house in Srakala and move to Jalalabad with Shamla. That is the stock you come from on your father's side of the family: strength, the ability to bend when the storm blows and to spring up when it's over, to spring up stronger and smarter."

"Don't worry," I said, "I know how to take care of myself."

"We all do," Sial agreed. "Each of us in his or her own way. Look how far we've traveled."

"It's because we have pure hearts," Abba said, "and clear minds that we can see our way through anything."

My mother laughed. "Oh, honey. Your mother was born here, and now you've come back."

After everyone went to bed, I turned the lamp down, its flickering glow swallowed by the immensity of the night sky that shimmered with the stars of summer. I stretched out against the pillows. Voices: If you don't learn from your experiences, your path will always be rocky. Without winter, there can be no spring. I hear the strains of triumph that burst agonized and clear. You either accept the impossible or risk being thrown to the wolves. In other words, you turned the impossible into the improbable, turned that into the probable, then turned the probable into the possible. Yes, I was a creature of words, lots of words.

The next day I was coming home from school on the Tango Adda Road. Our teacher had assigned us to write a paper, I forget on what, but it had to be written in Urdu. I had struggled for a week, but my comprehension was too rudimentary. That morning when we got our papers from the teacher, he'd drawn red slashes across each page. I was disappointed, especially at the prospect of another lecture from Abba about how they'd hired a tutor, so why was I still unable to comprehend the language? I was embarrassed but what could I say, it was like trying to hold water in my hands. But when I stepped into the living room, a familiar voice greeted me, our raspy, grizzled neighbor Ali, Anisa's husband. I dropped my rucksack down upon which I sank to the kot hugging my knees.

"Tell me something, Ali Hussain-Zada, how long did it take you to learn Urdu? Six months? Five years? Maybe you don't speak it even now, but why should you? Why should we?"

"Ah, my young scholar, it's the price of war. Wars are like aging oxen, the older and weaker they get, the more they cost you. Anyway, I have my own problems. I have a barren wife, my beautiful Anisa with her green eyes and pale skin, so elegant, so fashionable. But this is not for your innocent ears."

"My ears are no longer so innocent, Ali."

"Ah, Miwand, you're back and with tea and desserts. But how can I drink tea, how can I eat pastries when I'm so unhappy? I married Anisa because she was so appetizing, so succulent, like a ripe pear ready to be picked. But now look at me. The pear is rotting in my hands. I ask you, I ask God, why am I being punished? What sins have I committed? I pray five times a day. And each time I pray, I ask God for help and forgiveness. But does He hear? Look at me," he said, pulling up his shirt. His back was covered with welts. "Every Muharam, I beat myself with chains until my skin bleeds. I walk in the procession, I go round in circles, my body torn, tears spring from my eyes, I rub salt in my wounds. And all for nothing. Nothing. I'm telling you, Miwand, it's killing me. I can't hold my head up among my friends. When I die, who'll take over my fruit business? Who'll carry on the family name?"

"Ali, you have many years ahead of you. It will happen when the time is right."

He sighed deeply and tragically. "I took her to the doctors. Those ignoramuses. They're like vampires, they suck your blood with their needles and their medicines, their x-rays, checking you up and down. No privacy, robbing you of your last rupee."

"What did they say?"

"They said there was nothing wrong with her, gave her some vitamins to take, sent her home, and gave me the bill. Nothing wrong with her? If there was nothing wrong with her, why did I take her there in the first place?" His voice rising, he took a swift sip of tea with a trembling hand.

"What about you? Did you go to the doctor?"

"I'm a man, there's nothing wrong with me. You know as well as I do, it's always the woman's fault. But I have another ace up my sleeve.

"You are a resourceful man."

"You bet I am. Have you ever heard of Pir Sayeed-Hazrat-Agha?"

"Of course. But remind me, who is he again?" Abba said.

"It's not who he is, it's where he is."

"Where he is." Abba said, drawing out his words.

"Yes," Ali answered solemnly, "he's so close to God that all he has to do is sneeze and God wipes his nose."

"What if he doesn't sneeze?" I said, "What if he coughs?"

"Don't makes jokes. I am a man at the end of his rope. If he can't help, I'll have to take a second wife, and with Anisa eating me out of house and home, I'll go to ruin."

"Why don't you tell Anisa to call you Papa?" I said.

"It's not the same thing," he said, taking out a pinch of snuff, holding it to his nose, and inhaling. He tearily sneezed into his handkerchief. "Wait until you grow up and get married, then you'll see."

Pained as he was, he managed to eat quite a few of the little custard pies Moor had made accompanied by copious cups of milk tea. But when I reached for a second helping, Abba told me to forget it, that I'd ruin my dinner. Ah, life, is it ever fair?

Jandol said that Ali had nothing between his ears but emptiness. "I'm surprised he doesn't fly off into outer space. You know, rejoin his people."

"Now, son, don't be too hard on poor Ali, he has many problems," Abba said.

For the next few weeks, I didn't hear anything about Pir Sayeed-Hazrat-Agha until one Friday afternoon. I was out in the front yard doing my homework when Anisa came rushing up to me, telling me to put my paperwork down, that she had something urgent to tell me, something that couldn't wait. "Guess what? I am to be honored. I am to be presented to the great Pir Sayeed-Hazrat-Agha, a direct descendant of the prophet whose hands will heal me so that I can give him lots of babies."

"Are you serious?"

"I'm as serious as pneumonia."

"That sounds pretty serious."

"Don't laugh, I'm supposed to be thrilled. My face hurts from smiling so much."

"Anisa, tell him how you feel."

"I can't, he'll kill me."

"He won't kill you. Besides, you're not thrilled."

"I can hardly wait. Do you believe me? Well, forget it, I'm lying. I don't care if I never have any children."

"If that's the case, you owe it to him to tell him."

"I did try, but he refuses to listen. After all, what am I? Nothing but a sacrifice. Sold by my uncle Pidram in Kabul. And for what? So I could live in poverty with a man old enough to be my grandfather? How would you like that?"

"I wouldn't like it. Neither would Meena. But Ali, well, he may not be the sharpest knife in the drawer, but he does have a kind heart."

"What are you talking about? Who cares about knives or drawers? Or kind hearts? It's my life I'm talking about. At least he doesn't beat me."

"Why don't you leave him? Why do you stay with him?"

"Where would I go? Back with that uncle of mine, so he can sell me to somebody else to pay for his drug habit? Or maybe have a bunch of holy bastards marry me by the hour. Become a *segha*."

"A temple prostitute? You?"

She placed both of her hands on my arm. "I want you to talk to him. Please say that you will. He trusts you. Even more than your father. He trusts your opinion, he always says so. With grown-ups, he always thinks they're after something, but with children, they bear their hearts."

"I don't know what I'd say. Besides, I'm not a child."

"You'll think of something."

"Why don't you ask Abba?"

"I can't. I'm too ashamed."

"Well, if you think it'll help, but he's pretty set on taking you."

As she got up to leave, she said she had one more favor to ask. "In the likely event that you won't get thim to change his mind, will you come with us?"

"Hopefully, that day will never come."

But the day came. We were going to walk, but Ali—insisting it was too hot, that he didn't want to arrive stained with sweat—hailed a motorcycle rickshaw. When we dismounted, I could feel the hot pavement right through my sandals. Outside the Pir's compound, there was a line of devotees, many dressed in rags. I wondered if the hopes they'd brought with them would be assuaged in any way. Everyone had come with offerings, mostly livestock. Ali had brought a basket of artfully arranged bananas balanced on ripe, glistening mangoes. We took our place in front of a couple with a little girl holding a baby goat in her arms. The woman was wearing a burka, the man was moving his lips in a silent prayer.

After not moving for a while, the line began to inch forward until the little girl came to the front gate. But when the attendant reached out for the goat, she held on with all her might before her father ordered her to let go. The attendant handed the goat to his assistant who noted the gift in an account book. I felt sorry for the little girl, apparently no one had told her that she was going to have to give away the goat. When it was our turn, Ali smiled obsequiously as he handed over the basket. "It's only a small gift, I am a poor man, I wish I had more to give, I—" The attendant took his offering, wrote the information down, and motioned for Ali and I to join the men and sent Anisa to the women's section.

Within the compound, there was a path that led away from the Pir's house to two large tents; they resembled gazebos, set up adjacent to each other, one in which the Pir saw the men and the other for the women. The tent for the women was enshrouded with heavy curtains while the men's tent was open on all four sides. There was a royal Indian sofa piled high with multicolored silk pillows, with candles burning, and the ground covered by Oriental rugs, the smell of sandalwood incense pervading the air. Around the perimeter of the men's tent were hundreds of devotees sitting on rugs with their eyes closed, bobbing their necks back and forth, and clucking like chickens, "Allah-hoo, Allah-hoo, Allah-hoo."

The Pir hadn't yet emerged, and in the shimmering heat, the devotees seemed to be a mirage of chattering insects in the heavy air. In a way they weren't much more than spirit, living skeletons whose only aim was to see the holy man, to offer him what little they had managed to eke out in order to be blessed by him. That's all they hungered for, his blessing that would transform their lives as if God Himself had touched them. Ali and I found ourselves a place by the entrance to the men's tent, but there was no shade and my clothes were sticking to my body.

Suddenly a man's voice erupted in a shrill cry, "Nara-e-takbir!" A bodyguard came bursting out of the Pir's house, brandishing an AK-47. The crowd of devotees, like some great beast awakened from a thousand years of sleep, leaped to their feet as one, responding joyfully, "Allah-hoo Akbar!"

The guard's voice rose even higher, "Nara-e-takbir!"

"Allah-hoo Akbar!"

As he came rushing past me, he raised his AK-47 and fired a round into the sky. "Nara-e-takbir!"

"Allah-hoo Akbar!"

More guards with assault weapons positioned themselves around the inner side of the compound.

All eyes were fastened upon the house. Pir Sayeed-Hazrat-Agha appeared, framed in the doorway. The moment they saw him, everyone dropped down to their knees, bowed their heads, then rose up on their haunches with their eyes fastened upon him. He was quite a sight, dressed all in black and standing without moving, his eyebrows slightly raised, his hands behind his back, and his chest pushed out. He stepped out onto the porch, gazing slowly, regally from left to right, back and forth. No one dared to breathe lest they miss something. When he held up his hand in greeting, there was a long, drawn-out murmur along with the sounds of many hands slapping their hearts as everyone dropped to their knees. Except for me. I felt as if I were witnessing an armada of human beings being buffeted by the wake of a great life-giving force over which they had no control but whose movement would hoist them on their way. I felt like an idiot, but I refused to kneel down in front of him or in front of any of those muckety-mucks. No way, especially not for Ali and not even for Anisa. Instead, I put this silly smirk on my face as if to say, Hey, don't worry about me, I'm harmless, a little slow on the uptake. But surrounded by his bodyguards, the Pir passed by me with all of the mien of royalty, sweeping grandly into the men's tent where he took his place among the pillows on which he leaned with his arms outspread.

Presently, he raised his index finger at one of the guards who stepped outside the tent and said that the Pir was ready to see the devotees. In this way, the show began. As I said, everyone but me was kneeling, and when the guard made his announcement, they remained on their knees and crawled single file toward the tent. As each man entered, he crawled over to the Pir, kissing his hand where it was resting on the pillows upon which he was granted a brief audience. The Pir listened to their problems, their wishes, their transgressions, hopes, desires, difficulties. A young man hopelessly in love, an old man close to death, a transgressor wanting forgiveness from God, a husband without children, a father who couldn't feed his brood, a poor man wanting wealth, a *chaudri* wanting peace. They came to him to mediate between themselves and God. He would say a few precious words, hold out his fingers; he had four rings, jeweled with precious stones, and the man would kiss one hand while with the other the Pir waved toward the next in line.

The man and the little girl in front of us finally got their chance to speak to him. I waited by the entrance and listened as the man told the Pir that his daughter had fever blisters in her mouth. The Pir nodded sagely, motioning for her to come closer. Instead, she hid behind her kneeling father who was forced to push her forward. The Pir placed a hand on her head, another below her mouth, told her to open wide, and lowered his face until his lips were directly above hers. Everyone in the tent craned forward. Tears were streaming from the little girl's eyes, but she held her mouth closed. The Pir took his thumb and index finger and placed them on her lips until her mouth was wide open. Then, the Pir leaned down as if he were going to kiss her and spat a large globule of saliva directly into her open mouth. "Now, God will bless you, inshalah," he said to the startled girl. The father prostrated himself, and when he rose, he was crying. He thanked the Pir, took the little girl by the hand, and backed out, bowing the entire time.

Finally, it was Ali's turn. He wormed his way over to the Pir, kissed his hand, and the Pir asked him what he wanted. Ali went into an anguished diatribe about Anisa. When he was finished talking, he held his hands together in a gesture of entreaty, looking with tearful eyes into the dry eyes of the Pir.

"My future is in your hands," Ali said. The Pir closed his eyes and prayed, finishing by blowing some air from his lips into Ali's face.

"On the wings of prayer soars the eagle of love," he said. Then without turning, he snapped his fingers at a guard. "Bring me my book of wishes," he said. A moment later the guard returned holding a leather-bound book in his hands, palms upward, as if he were giving the Pir a blessed offering. At first the Pir ignored him. He examined his own fingernails, he adjusted his turban, he moved a pillow closer, while the guard waited without moving. Finally the Pir acknowledged his presence, and the man whispered, "Holiness." Ali was entranced, especially when the Pir held the book for him to see. I noticed then something I hadn't seen before. The Pir had a large ugly purple birthmark behind his right ear. It was shaped like an eggplant.

"What is your wife's name?" he asked Ali.

"Anisa."

He stood up, and when he did, everyone in the room got to their feet with their eyes closed, their heads bowed, and their lips moving. Without a word, the guard brought him a large bowl of water and a towel for him to clean his hands, after which the Pir made his way to the women's tent. At the same time, the guard with the bowl went from devotee to devotee, spooning out some of the liquid for them to drink. When they came to me, I shook my head. I realized I was thirsty. The sun was brutal, high in the cloudless sky, burning down on you.

I stepped over to the water tank, and when I went back to the men's tent, I almost tripped over a devotee lying on the ground, his entire body vibrating as he spewed out yet more incomprehensible clucking noises, duck noises. People were watching him fixedly, but it was obvious that no one knew what to do or what to make of him. Someone said he was being tortured by the spirits of the devil, and another said that it wasn't the devil, it was his past deeds, that the devil couldn't come in here. The Pir would save him, that he'd know what to do.

"Someone has to get him."

"No, we can't disturb him. He's with the women."

"How long will he be there?"

"Don't ask so many questions."

"What a lucky woman to have the Pir all to herself."

"When is he coming out? I've been waiting for five hours to see him, to touch his sandals."

All eyes were on the women's tent. The Pir eventually materialized, and immediately he was surrounded by a crush of devotees who began chattering like canaries and pointing at the prostrate man. The Pir allowed them to lead him toward the man, over whose body he said a brief prayer that he repeated three times. Then he bent down gently patting the man's shoulder, telling him to get up. When he spoke, the man's trembling ceased; he opened his eyes and smiled. He pulled himself to his knees so that he could kiss the Pir's beringed hand. "You have saved me from the perils of hell," he said before addressing the devotees in a voice of deep thankfulness. "The Holy Pir has saved me, the Great One has saved me!"

I had had enough, more than enough. I walked back out the gate and sat against the wall where there was some shade. After a while, Ali and Anisa came out.

"The Pir has decided," Ali said. "He's going to *chila* my beautiful Anisa. Now all of our problems will be solved."

"Isn't it wonderful?" Anisa said. "Our dreams will come true. I will bear many sons and daughters." A *chila*. I pictured the whole drama in my mind. Anisa would be dressed in her most elegant clothes; she would be brought back to the women's compound. Once there, she would be cleansed, showered, and then given a small room where she would meet the Pir. Him and no one else. Ali would bring her saffron mixed with hashish, which would be burned while the Pir performed various religious rituals so that the souls of the little children, which were being held in abeyance by evil forces, could be freed. The process could take months, and all that time, Anisa would only have contact with the Pir. Ali would empty his savings to pay for everything. And the great Pir Sayeed-Hazrat-Agha, who was a direct descendant of the Prophet and who could change one's destiny, especially when he was surrounded by bearded goons with AK-47s, would bring forth new life in Anisa's barren body.

What a world, I thought. When I told Sial, he said he wanted to become a Pir.

CHAPTER ELEVEN

Jandol and I were on our way to Afghanistan. The bus went from Peshawar to Parachinar, which was the last stop on the line. From there we would catch a lift to the border and then proceed the rest of the way on foot. It'd been Abba's suggestion; he wanted us to check up on our properties in both villages so as to see if we could collect any money that was owed to us. Atal, Gulapa, and Khialo were living in our home in Srakala, in exchange for which they were put in charge of the farming. In Shabak, for a portion of the crops, Lakhta and Samsoor had agreed to look after our house, the water mill, and our livestock. In addition, he wanted us to see if the car was still there with the hope that one day we could get it.

We had waited until school was over before taking off. The Mujahideen were winning the war, which left the Communists, who had vacated the countryside, barely able to hold onto the larger cities. Relatively speaking, as far as the Mujahideen went, it was safe to travel, although you still you had to be careful. They had an extremely efficient justice system. Accuser, judge, and executioner were the same person, your sentence hastily carried out at the end of a gun barrel.

As we were crossing the mountainous Kohat District with its magnificent views that carried your imagination to the end of the horizon, the bus driver kept having to pull over to allow the timber-laden semis coming from Afghanistan to the Punjab to pass on the narrow twisting road. After they clattered by, he would shoot forward, causing a spray of gravel to shower into the valley a thousand feet below. In Parachinar, some Mujahideen who were driving a rented Datsun as far as Taramangal needed paying passengers, and we were happy to oblige.

When we arrived that afternoon, we were shocked at the changes that had occurred in the past two years. Expecting a tiny village where we'd be greeted by the same elder as before, we instead found ourselves in a burgeoning city whose unpaved sidewalks were crowded with people, hotels, shops, construction sites, and lumber yards by the dozen. Jandol said the entire countryside must have been decimated. Donkeys laden with guns, trucks carrying troops and artillery, SUVs with warlords—it was like being in a nerve center.

There was a stream of insurgents, with their machine guns and handheld rocket launchers, fierce hostile men, their eyes glaring mistrustfully as they marched in one direction toward Afghanistan. From Afghanistan came the refugees whose lines stretched as far as the eye could see, mostly women, children, and old men. On the same road the refugees were taking, loaded semis with their gears shrieking descended toward Taramangal at breakneck speed, forcing people to jump out of the way or be run over.

"God is great! God is great! God is great!" You could hear their voices reverberating everywhere, almost as loud as the Russian fighter jets that you could hear but couldn't see. It was a lot to take in. When it got dark, we ate at a teahouse, after which we ambled around until we found an inexpensive hotel.

The next day we stocked up on almonds, walnuts, raisins, bags of trail mix, samosas, dried meat, rice, as well as some basic camping equipment, including a couple of thermoses that we filled with hot chai. We had a lengthy trek ahead of us through the Zazi Forest, up Mt. Lakarai, then however long it took us to reach Tummanai where we hoped to borrow some mules for the trip down to Shabak. At least this time we could travel during the day now that the Mujahideen had American stingers to chase off the Russian jets. We tried to find a shop that sold fabrics to bring as gifts, but other than the few grocery stores, the only things you could buy anywhere were guns and ammunition, even small cannons. And drugs, fifty-pound potato sacks overflowing with heroin, cocaine, and marijuana.

In the last store we went to, some Pakistani officers stomped in with their heavy steel-toed boots, one of them going over and sticking his finger into a sack, which he brought to his tongue. "Masha-Allah, Masha-Allah," he said to the shopkeeper, who rubbed his hands together and grinned obsequiously. "You look like an honest man. Now show us the real stuff.

"Colonel Sa'ab," he said. "*Chai pilo*, come with me." He lifted a curtain, and all of them went into the back. Jandol put his arm around my shoulder, and we headed out.

No one bothered us. It was the same when we reached the area around the Durand Line. The only reminders of the past were the rotting skeletons of the outposts that stood bent over like tired ghosts. I remembered the last time we'd been here, how terrified we were, how dangerous it had been. I couldn't help but feel a sense of dislocation that increased as we descended the rise that led into the Zazi Forest to face crisscrossing gravel logging roads winding through what looked like a million tree stumps. The various roads coalesced at the base of the Lakarai, turning what had once been a single-track mountain trail into a wide busy dirt road, the only danger being that you could get run over since the drivers were so reckless. Our hike up the mountain was punctuated continually by groups of dispirited prisoners with their hands shackled, being guarded by Mujahideen fighters.

We took our time. Sometimes there were shortcuts up steep gnarled trails that twisted away from the road, which they rejoined at much higher levels. Midway to the summit, a convoy of empty trucks came driving up, and when the last one came close, we climbed into the bed. Jandol held onto the railings while I hoisted myself up to the *jangla*, which was a decorative balcony directly above the driver. The road was so jarring, it was like being on a circus ride.

High in the sky, a red-tailed hawk was wheeling around in wide circles, and I watched until it disappeared behind a series of distant snowy peaks. *It wouldn't find much to eat here*, I thought. *Nothing but carrion.*

When the truck reached the crest, the driver slowed down, enabling us to jump off. We decided to spend the night, placed our sleeping bags behind some boulders away from the road, and went about gathering scrub to build a fire. For supper we whittled twigs, stuck them into our samosas, and held them over the flame, careful not to singe them. They were spicy and delicious, and the tea from our thermos had retained their heat, the salty nuts with the raisins for dessert a perfect complement to our meal.

We could see all the way from Mingul to Zadran to Azra, beyond which, though they were hidden from view, were the Tummanai Mountains that led to home. Everything—and I mean everything—was denuded, forests once alive with vegetation nothing but naked scars, parched valleys strangled by thorny brush that writhed seemingly in the moment of an agonized death. Jandol pointed out a field bright with color that at first confused us until we realized they were coming from thousands of flags that had been put up to honor the those who'd been killed. So neither edelweiss nor flowering pomegranate trees nor delicate blossoms that grew along the rocky heights and along the edges of the valleys. Nothing but these flags of death, with tree stumps for tombstones, fluttering in the wind, waving at us, whispering to us, "Death took me, it can also take you." It was impossible to comprehend how, within two years, not even that, our country had been so completely devastated. Perhaps no one would want it now; perhaps the invaders would leave, and the land would heal. *How sentimental*, I thought, because I knew how long would it take before things returned to normal. Minimum ten years, maybe fifty. Maybe never.

As we looked out, the sun turned the land misty orange before sinking behind a snow-covered peak, the scene immediately darkening into a blur through which nothing moved except for a soft breeze that carried the odor of rotting flowers.

The next day when we reached the Azra River, we found that it had overflowed its banks, spreading a viscous film of oily water over the entire area, including the trail we'd planned on using. Forced to make our way as best we could, we found that the worst part was the first few miles, after which the ground became dry again, although in places, we had no other choice than to slog through murky water. The farther we got from the Lakarai, the quieter everything became, no semis, very few refugees. It was peaceful but still depressing, the stagnant river water emitting a funky wooden smell.

I slipped down from the bank and stepped into the gunky mess, and when I pulled my foot out, it made a sucking sound. "Hold on," I said, and I took out a towel from my backpack and wiped myself off. "Why are you smiling?"

"I am smiling because I'm unhappy, and when I'm unhappy I smile. That way everyone thinks I'm happy."

"What a philosophy."

"I am smiling because the sun is out, and it feels good. It was freezing last night."

"I know, my feet were like ice."

"Those poor uneducated fools."

"What's that?"

"Our own people allowing this to happen. Causing it to happen."

There were blackberry thickets whose berries were ready to be picked. We emptied our trail mix into one bag and filled the other with the ripest we would find. I was so intent on eating them, I slid down a steep incline, unable to stop my legs from moving like a toy soldier that had been wound up, certain that if I fell over my legs would keep going back and forth. Luckily, perhaps symbolically, I landed on my feet.

Farther on we rested, had some of the dried meat, then stood on the banks of the river skidding rocks across its surface. According to Jandol, success depended on how you curved your wrist for the throw. I never was able to master that flick that he said was necessary, although as it turned out, my rocks skidded much farther than his. He'd hunt for the perfect stone, balance it in his hand, take a position with his legs slightly apart, pull his arm across his chest whereupon he'd flick his wrist and fling the rock, only to see most of them sink below the surface. Now Sial would have been furious, but not Jandol, who always knew how much thought, how much feeling, to give to a situation, either good or bad.

"I want you to remember this," Jandol said as we moved on. "That stone throwing is a symbol of life. You never know what to expect."

I thought about what he said, so glad to have him for my brother. "Jandol, can I tell you something?"

"What?"

"Oh, nothing. Forget it!" I shouted, running ahead up another incline.

In the first hours after dawn, as we headed through the Tangai Pass, hiking up the winding road to Srakala. We were buffeted by the fluctuating funnel of wind that always whipped through the gap in the mountains. The Azra River, now called the Nawar, began to break up into smaller streams that bisected each other like spider veins on the legs of an old man. And as became readily evident, the old man was the Nawar Valley, now nothing but a wasteland. Other than packs of feral dogs sniffing around, which made me nervous as hell, the entire valley was empty, nothing was growing, no crops to harvest. Still, we were unprepared for what we saw when we ascended the trail to Srakala. I remember that Jandol had been ahead of me, but when he reached the crest of the hill, he simply stood there without moving. I was about to ask what was going on until I saw what he saw, realizing no words would suffice.

The village had been leveled. Strictly speaking, there was no village—no enclosing mud walls with their heavy wooden gates, no villagers, no houses, no livestock grazing on the tender summer grasses. Everything was gone, even the venerable *chinar* trees that had been here for five hundred years on which we used to attach ropes for swings during festivals. A few crumbled walls, two or three foundations, the south tower of the fort that was cracked in places and riddled with bullets—that's all that was left. The silence was oppressive except for the wind from the Tangai that you could hear moaning and whispering. A blackbird sprang out of the brush with a screeching cry, flapped its wings, and circled around overhead before landing on the tower.

As my eyes followed, I saw a plume of smoke, which I pointed out to Jandol. Someone must be living here, but when we headed toward it, the stillness seemed to wrap its fingers around my throat, tighter and tighter. I hurried forward, but before I made much headway, Jandol took hold of me, warning me to slow down. "We don't know who's there. It could be dangerous."

I didn't care. I hurried forward, the dust whirling around me until I heard a familiar voice. Instantly the years fell away to reveal a gullible five-year-old entranced by a woman who I thought the wisest in the world, telling a story about alien monsters who lived in the Auzingianai River and who ate little children. There she was. Gulapa. Squatting in front of a hovel made from tree branches, mud, and rocks with an awning held in place by sticks, she was stirring something in a pot over a fire. Before she could respond, Atal and Khialo appeared, carrying bundles of sticks along with a bucket of fish. Gulapa was ageless, Khialo stood a head taller than me even if he was skinny as a rail, but Atal had was gaunt, withered, his grayish hair almost totally white. Our greetings were warm but subdued.

"The fort was completely destroyed, except for my vegetable garden," Atal said.

"Our poor garden," Khialo added. "All the cucumbers were shriveled up like the johnson on a dead monkey. But you, my friend," he said to me, "you've changed. You're growing up."

"Only on the outside. On the inside, I'm the same. But our new house, our car, what happened to them? Our swimming pool? Can they be completely destroyed? At least we still own the land."

"What a luxury," Gulapa said. It was the first time she looked directly at me, as usual, the smoke from the hookah slowly curling from her lips as if she were on fire internally. "You own the land where nothing will ever grow, the poisonous soil where you dare not step or risk being blown up by a land mine."

"I guess we've all changed," I said.

"Yes, but I am not the same on the inside. On the inside there is no—ah, might as well forget it."

"Forget what?"

"It's not important. Life goes on. So what brings you two our way? Sightseeing?" She handed Jandol the pipe. "This is very special tobacco."

"What's special about it?" I asked.

"We have it."

"Gulapa, no matter what you say, you'll always be the same," I said, instantly realizing that this wasn't so, that she had changed, as had the rest of us, and in deep essential ways, internally and externally.

Jandol handed the pipe to Atal, but Gulapa took hold of it before passing it to her husband. As the afternoon waned, we sat there taking turns with the hookah.

"This is just like old times," Jandol said.

"Sure, as long as we don't look around, isn't that right?" Gulapa said.

"What made you stay here?"

"That is a long story," Khialo said. "But one that can be reduced to one word—stubbornness."

"Is that true, Gulapa?" I said.

"Don't make fun of me. Do you remember when you came back from Kabul? Same thing happened, only this time they had better bombs. Isn't that right, Atal? Tell them, Khialo. They probably think we've lost our minds."

"We have," Khialo said. "Completely. But not our courage. That we haven't lost."

"Not yet."

"Tell us what went on," Jandol said.

"Not yet, not now," Atal said. "First we eat. Isn't that right, Gulapa?"

"Do you hear me contradicting you?"

"Where's our house?" I said. "There's nothing there. And where is everybody?"

"Are you deaf? First we will eat. I presume you've got some goodies in those rucksacks of yours."

We'd completely forgotten. Indeed, we had some samosas left, along with trail mix and tea. Gulapa had made rice the night before and set about cleaning the fish. All in all, a pretty good meal to be had in the middle of nowhere, in a deserted world, a peopleless world, a country decimated by war, ruled by death. We even had dessert.

"I was frying *parata*," Gulapa said. "It was early morning. These bums were dead to the world. Suddenly, I heard planes. Jets. Then all hell broke loose. The whole house shook, everything was moving. I called out, 'Atal and Khialo,' and they came running into the kitchen. They thought I was dead. I'd spilled boiling oil over myself, I fried myself, look, you can still see the scar." She pulled her sleeve back to reveal an angry white splotch that looked like a map of India. "All day it went on, hour after hour and all through the night and the next morning. It was enough to drive you out of your mind. The Communists had sent an entire brigade to retake the region, but by then the Mujahideen were fully armed. It was a blood bath with us in the middle. But the Mujahideen were no match for the Russians, and they were forced to flee to their mountain retreats.

"Srakala and Shabak were disaster zones, the entire Hisarak District, although we didn't know that at the time. But here, so many casualties, the dead, the wounded. The worst were the children, and there were no surgeons, no hospital, no medicine. We used your hujra as a temporary hospital, and some of the young men went in search of medical help. We'd been swept up in the tide. We'd swept anyway. After all of our prayers. Russian helicopters came dropping flyers printed in red, the ground was littered with them. It looked like a million rose petals were dropping from the sky. Followed by tanks with loudspeakers. Military band music. Marching music. Drumrolls. Then came the soldiers, they were everywhere, eyeless robots. You could only see their boots, their black shiny boots. They went from village to village, accompanied by that dreadful music whose clamor came from ten different directions, one minute blasting your ear, the next a faint tremor that was equally crushing. If the bastards hadn't brought doctors with them, I don't know what would've happened. They bomb us, and then they heal us.

"How many counterattacks from the insurgents. How many nights when the gunfire went on until dawn. They also had their own loudspeakers. 'Allah hoo akbar, Allah hoo akbar.' Too bad their aim wasn't as good as their words. More like a blind man throwing a donkey, it could land anywhere. There were a group of nomads who'd set up camp nearby when one of the Mujahideen set off a rocket. Not one living soul survived that attack from those stupid fools. So tell me who was worse, the Communist bastards or the Mujahideen. But, like I said, they were no match for the Russian artillery. When the shooting was finally over, announcements were made that everyone was to meet outside Fort Jafar the following morning. When the sun rose, those of us who could gathered together like they told us to. Hurry up and wait, isn't that what they say?

"It was almost noon before they drove up in lorries and began unloading bags of food, clothing, and medicine, boxes and boxes. That's when the doctor arrived, along with some nurses. Khialo and I took them to the hujra so that they could help the wounded, and when we returned, they were setting up a stage. They had their own generators, their own PA system. Nobody knew what to expect, but we found out soon enough when a colonel, I think he was a colonel, he had enough medals to sink a battleship, came on stage, introducing himself and saying that the commander was going to speak to us. Another hour passed. But when he appeared, I couldn't believe my eyes. I was expecting a fat oily limp-lidded son of gun. So who comes out? The handsomest man I have ever seen. He couldn't have been more than twenty-five, but I was ready follow him barefoot into the desert.

"'We are here to help you,' he announces. 'We have come to free you. Free you from suffering, free you from starvation, from fear. Where are your hospitals? Where are your schools? Where are your universities? We have doctors and nurses, we have engineers and teachers. We will rebuild everything from the ground up. We are not your enemies. The Mujahideen are your enemies. They are robbing you day and night. They are haters of civilization, of progress, of equality, of growth. They are bees in your mouth. They are tumors in your soul. We are your allies, your friends.'

"That was all. No long boring speech, not from this man. Of course, did it matter what he said? If we said for them to go home, they'd kill us, and if we welcomed them, the Mujahideen would do the same thing. You could hear whispering among the villagers, but no one dared say a word, no one was that stupid. Well, no one except that fool Shakar, who was sitting practically under the stage. He raised his hand as if he were in the third grade, and when granted to speak, shouted loud enough for everyone to hear, 'You're good and they're good. We're the ones who are bad. If we weren't here, you wouldn't be here, and they wouldn't be here. It would be better if we didn't exist!' From the mouths of fools.

"A few days later the same colonel, accompanied by several fellow officers, came to our home and told us through an interpreter that we had to leave by the end of the week. 'What about all of the commander's promises, food and education, how we're going to be free?' I said to the interpreter. Well, as you imagine, it wasn't easy talking this way. For instance, who knows what the interpreter told him, but one of the officers who was Afghan said, 'Don't bug us, lady. We're here to help you, and we don't have much time. This has nothing to do with you personally.' I said to the guy, 'Thank God it's not personal.' After they left, I discovered he was right, it wasn't personal. They were kicking everyone out, they were going to use our village for their headquarters. 'I'm not moving,' I told Atal. 'Let them shoot me, I don't care.' I meant it too, I would have stayed if it hadn't been for these two pussycats. But where to go, where would it be safe? It was Khialo's idea to go to Jookan. It was off the beaten path, pretty small change, no one went there, maybe they didn't know it existed. So that's what we did. Like you, we traveled at night. The less anyone knew of our movements, the better."

Gulapa held the hookah in a death grip and inhaled with such force the tobacco caught on fire and turned amber.

"We were the last to leave Srakala," Atal said. "The last to leave and the first to come back. But we came back to nothing."

"We stayed in Jookan for two years," Gulapa said. "We could hear fighting, continuous fighting like corn popping in a vat of frying oil. The Mujahideen were night owls. They always waited until it was dark before they attacked. It was like a thunderstorm. Sometimes the sky like lightning, like fire. But during the day the Russians returned their fire, gunning down anything that moved. Jookan was small potatoes, like I said, nobody there but us chickens. And life goes on. It's funny, the whole world is coming to an end, the battles are ferocious, two giants trying to kill each other, but what do you worry about? Did your fool of a son remember to buy sugar for our tea? Ah, God, why? I want an answer. But whenever I ask, whenever I throw myself on His mercy, all I ever hear are my husband snores."

"Don't be so poetic," Atal said. "Talk facts."

"What do think I'm doing? Fact, the tide began to turn. Fact, the Russians were spread out over thousands of miles of rough country of which they knew nothing, districts where the Mujahideen had spent their entire lives. Fact, the Mujahideen could focus their attacks, much more effective. The Russians were thousands of miles from their homes, fighting a war they knew nothing about, while the Mujahideen were fighting for their land, for their families, for their God. In addition to which half of them were crazy, the Communists never knew what to expect. They were dealing with men who weren't afraid to die for their beliefs. They'd just as soon die as live. They thought that if they got killed, they'd soon be in bed with seventy virgins. For a year the Russians hung on, but the noose kept being squeezed tighter until finally they strangled on their misguided dreams of glory, of conquering the world.

"When we came back, it was the same story as the first time we had to vacate the premises, only worse. Much worse. There were no premises. What the Communists hadn't destroyed, the Mujahideen did. Until there was nothing left. As you can see. Now the Mujahideen are running the show."

"She means the Major," Atal said. "He's the one in charge."

"The Major?" I said. "Wouldn't you know that he'd come through in one piece."

"Now he rules over life and death."

"With an emphasis on the latter," Khialo added. "Definitely."

"We came back to nothing," Atal said. "To blackness, to emptiness."

"Worse," said Gulapa. "Much worse. The Major put Mohammad Din in charge, although if you ask me, it's that shrew of a wife, Shatoo Khala, who runs the show. Tell them, Atal, tell them."

"I can't believe that," I said. "I thought I'd never see those two ever again."

"So did we all, boy, so did we all. Instead, they come back here in a bright red Land Cruiser."

"What do they want?" Jandol said.

"What do you think they want? Money," Gulapa said. "They keep pestering us to pay taxes, and I keep telling them, 'Taxes? Taxes? On what?' God forbid, you make one Afghani, and they want two. It looks like we're going to have to move on. Maybe go back to the land of rocks and salt."

"She means Jookan," Khialo said, "where you can't make a living and can't grow anything."

"Do you have any better suggestions?"

"Yes. How about someplace that's farther away than three miles from here? Someplace far away."

"We can't hide every time someone drives past," Atal said. "There aren't enough caves or bushes."

"You should hear them. All they talk about are their souls," Gulapa said. "Their souls and our souls and the souls of our souls."

"Meanwhile, our sandals have no soles," Khialo said.

"Meanwhile, you have to ask permission to take a breath."

"No matter what, you'll always wind up on your feet."

"At least you have faith in me."

"I couldn't get over it," Atal said. "My garden flowers, my *chambili*, were still alive."

I couldn't help but look around in dismay. The whole area was a wasteland—debris, ruts that would turn into quagmires when the rains came, the air filled with dusty motes.

Noticing my expression, Gulapa said, "I forgot to give you your grain money."

"Don't worry about it," Jandol said.

"Fair is fair," she said. "Khialo, go inside and bring back our bag of treasures."

He did as she asked, returning with a small sack in his hand.

"What, are you frozen?" Gulapa said. "Open it up."

Khialo pulled out a dried ear of corn, but Jandol, ignoring the gesture, pulled out some bills from his wallet and handed them to Atal, who looked embarrassed but took the money all the same.

"I wish I had more. Perhaps when I return I can figure a way to get you some."

"Return to where, might I ask?" Gulapa said.

"Peshawar."

"You two roosters. Well, there's nothing for it. I'd be there too if I weren't strapped with these two good-for-nothings."

"Aw, Adi," Khialo said. "What would you do without us?"

"What about Sandara and the others?" Jandol said. "Azmoon, Lakhta, Samsoor?"

"We don't know," Atal said. "Shabak, there's still some buildings standing. For some reason it didn't get hit as hard as we did. But I don't know."

"You haven't you checked it out?"

"We cook," Gulapa said. "We have smoke. Let them come here."

"Don't listen to her," Khialo said. "We only came here a few weeks ago. We've hardly settled down."

"And now we have to leave again." Atal said.

"I would think you'd feel better if you could see some of your old friends," Jandol said. "Surely not everyone is gone."

"There's no point," Khialo said. "Nothing but ghosts. Frail, lonely, frightened ghosts."

Gulapa sat motionlessly, her skin pale, her lips twin gashes over a chin that was beginning to lose its firmness, haloed by tendrils of thick black hair that cascaded down her dress.

"Hey, I'm antsy," I said to Khialo. "Is it safe to take a walk?"

"Just lead the way, brother."

"Whatever happened to the great imam?" I said when we were beyond the hearing of the others.

"Imam Parast? Hey, he's an important man now. Mohammad Din is the right testicle of the Major, and Shatoo is the left. And Parast is a pubic hair."

"Be serious," I said. "What does he do?"

"Who knows what any of those fungi do. Except suck out our life's blood."

"Why don't you come to Peshawar, then you won't have to worry about them?"

"Oh, sure. Try to make Adi move from her beloved Hisarak that only exists in her imagination. My father does whatever she tells him to, you know that. He lacks inner fiber. And me? Well, someone has to look after things. Adi's in her dream world, Jandol has his garden. You ask me, this goes back to Droon. When he got killed, it did something to her, although she'd die before she admitted it. But he was the apple of her eye. Nevertheless, we may have to move, even if Adi doesn't want to. Mr. Right Testicle warned us if we don't start paying our taxes, he's going to take me away with him. Can you imagine, joining one group of hooligans to fight the other? It makes you think, huh? I mean, it's so black-and-white, no moral ambiguities, no subtleties, you know? Ever since I can remember. If you ask me, no one'll be satisfied until we're all dead. Maybe not even then.

"We hated the king, and then the Communists took over, and we hated them, and now the Mujahideen are taking over, and we say, 'Bring back the king.' It's like that old story, the gravedigger who stole the coffins. You remember that story, after people were buried, he'd go back and steal the coffins and leave the bodies to rot. All the villagers hated him, they cursed him, they couldn't wait for him to die and go to hell. And when he finally did die, everyone was jubilant. They couldn't believe their good luck. The only problem was, the son turned out to be worse than the father. Not only would he steal the coffins, but he'd take the bodies and shove a bayonet up their ass. 'Oi,' the people begged, 'Bring back the father!'"

We walked along a smooth path that skirted the near side of the Auzingianai River, but the warm air remained thick, dry. Even the evening light had a sickly greenish tinge, as if you were treading underwater. Floating on the black scum of dissolution, the mountain's crags were like old men in wheelchairs with thin claws for hands. I unbuttoned my shirt and took out a handkerchief and wiped my forehead.

All of the spidery little streams snaked off in different directions until they joined the river to create an area where the current was slow and the water deep. I was hot, tired, my whole body aching from the walking my brother and I had done, so I suggested we take a swim. The water was an ice-cold shock at first, until you splashed around enough to get used to it. Then you could have floated for days. Where the river narrowed and the current was stronger, you had to kick hard to get back upstream. I dived below the surface, the water pressing me from every side as I paddled my legs, forcing myself to go farther down until I couldn't hold my breath any longer and sprang up to the surface. When we climbed out, I felt refreshed. After we wiped ourselves off with our shirts, we lay on the bank until we were dried by the sun.

As soon as Jandol and I finished breakfast, we headed to Shabak. There were no bridges, which necessitated our having to search the bank until we found a place where the water was shallow enough for us to wade across. As we climbed out the opposite shore, I wondered what had happened to the pomegranate trees that we'd planted, but they were gone, swept away by the river or by bombs, who knew?

As Gulapa'd said, Shabak was luckier than Srakala. In Srakala, no one was around except for Gulapa's family, but in Shabak, with some houses still standing, a sense of menace could be felt, particularly when we heard our footsteps on the dirty gray roads heretofore unnoticed. Our house was nothing more than a bombed ruin—the roof had caved in, every window and every door was smashed, the glass, the wood, the furniture, books, everything gone, nothing left but spiders, scorpions, the fruit trees in our garden charred beyond recognition, the swimming pool with its cracked cement, its clogged drainage, awash with brackish water, every vestige that told of family life obliterated. No, there was nothing here. As for the car, there was nothing left except for a dented bumper.

A group of young boys was playing soccer up ahead, but when their mother or caretaker saw us, she frantically called them to come inside. Once we turned into the passageway that led to Lakhta's home, we saw up ahead that her front gate was hanging at an angle from one hinge. No one was inside. The flat tires were piled on the verandah, Samsoor's rusty tools were in the same greasy box, and there were strips of cowhide hanging from the wall, but no one was there. Indeed, no one was there, and there was no sign of recent habitation; no vibration is perhaps more accurate for the sense we had of the place.

We asked around but could get no information. It was like walking through a dead land populated by ghosts. Familiar faces, the voices of friends, were no longer there; everyone evaded our questions in this eerie village in which no one knew anything. We tried to locate Tofan's mother, but she was also gone.

Later when we questioned Gulapa and her family, the only thing they knew was after the first series of bombings, which had been extremely violent as well as nonending, most villagers had taken off, and no one knew where they were. "You might as well ask the wind where it blows," Gulapa said. Hearing her remark, trying to talk to Khialo, seeing Atal's taut expression, I felt I'd been thrust into the past, that we'd grown so distant, they were like figures from my childhood.

I was flipping through a photograph album that brought back memories but did not instill these memories with life. The only emotion I felt besides nostalgia, which I hated, was an uncontrollable desire to shut the book and move on.

Jandol and I left the next morning. Gulapa and Khialo urged us to stay longer, but Atal said to go in peace, that we would meet again, but he was mistaken. This was the last time we saw any of them.

At the time of this story, Badshah Khan, known throughout the country as the pride of Afghanistan, was a very old man, having reached the age of ninety-six. He was tall, stately in his traditional Pashtoon clothes, his head covered by a white veil that flowed across both of his shoulders and down his back. Standing beside his friend Gandhi, with whom he joined in a battle for Indian autonomy, he towered over him. His home in the ancient town of Charsadda, about twenty-five miles northeast of Peshawar, was the destination for Afghans worldwide who sought spiritual and political enlightenment. This compound, consisting of home and hujra, was situated on a promontory that overlooked the place where three rivers converged—the Jindi, the Kabul, and the Swat—to form the mighty Indus River, which Afghans called the Abasin, the River of our Fathers, that separates Pakhtunistan from Punjab, flowing for over a thousand miles until it merges with the Arabian Sea.

CHAPTER TWELVE

It was Abba's idea for both Jandol and me to have a consultation with Badshah Khan, to which we halfheartedly agreed, neither of us actually believing that he could help us, this man who was the progenitor of vast movements and alliances held in such esteem by the Pashtoon people. What attention, we asked, could he pay to what would be a trifling affair for him? What worth a death, a disappearance? But the truth was, after our trip to Afghanistan, Jandol went around in a moody silence while my own despair hadn't gone away but exhibited itself in a malaise of epic proportions, something I'd never experienced previously. Maybe despair is too grandiose a description, but I felt as if my life were over, the intensity of which was like a physical punch in the gut against which I no longer had the spirit to fight.

Jandol, just as much at loose ends, was unable to help me but shut himself up in his own world. Ironically, though we'd seen Gulapa, Khialo, Atal, it was as if they'd disappeared into the mists of the past whereas Lakhta, Sandara, Azmoon, Samsoor, who we hadn't seen, never left our consciousness. Instead, at least with me, they remained as a vibrant presence. Adding to the grayness, when Jandol said that our possessions were gone, including the precious car, a gloomy spell fell on everyone, particularly Sial, who'd really looked forward to gadding about in it. In the face of what seemed insurmountable problems, how could anyone help us, even Badshah Khan, and the sole reason we agreed to meet him was to please Abba.

Anyway, Jandol and I hoped that perhaps some good would come of it. Our only other option was to numb out, not feel anything, be like the man with the proverbial elephant in the room. If only I could stop remembering Lakhta's little house, the gate smashed against the wall, the few paltry possessions lying helter-skelter, everything about to crumble into nothingness. I couldn't get that picture out of my mind.

When the three of us arrived at his compound, a tall thin beardless young man standing by the gate introduced himself as Sangeen Wali, Badshah Khan's grandson, and led us inside. The large grassy open space around the hujra was crowded with followers on cots, which were arranged in a semicircle around the old man who was in the process of giving a lecture. I thought he'd be a peacock in a golden pavilion surrounded by bodyguards with other-worldly music piped in when he spoke. But the setting was nothing extraordinary: a cot, a samovar for tea, platters of cakes and fruit, the man himself, perhaps because of his age, not at all commanding or forbidding. When he spoke, everyone and I strained to listen before his words sank into the heavily incensed air like whispers from a distant time.

"You see, son, he is a being of light," Abba said, but Jandol and I doubted our father's description. We were in darkness. There was no light.

How can I explain the impact of meeting Badshah Khan? Physically, simply an old man with the visage of an ascetic, tall, rangy, not an ounce of fat on his frame, his carefully chosen words separated by lengthy pauses, during which he appeared to be meditating. But these are mere physical attributes. What was spellbinding was his charisma, his gaze that seemed to reach inside you and ferret out your secret hopes and plans. You knew right away that you were in the presence of a great man. You could feel the vitality that stirred within him, even as the human shell seemed to be fading before your very eyes, even as you yourself seemed to deepen, become stronger, more able to face adversity—an experience so unlike that of meeting most people who tried to make you smaller. He referred to us as his sons and daughters, observing that we were not refugees but citizens of in a country that, though it was now in the hands of the Punjabi, had once been part of Afghanistan. That is, until the British created the Durand Line and later when the entire area was ladled into the stew that became Pakistan.

How could one be a refugee in his own land? He described a way of life that had been spent in peace and harmony, a way of being unchanged since the beginning of civilization. He told us how a young woman once came to him and said, 'I have no country, no home. I own nothing but what I carry on my back.' He asked her, 'What did you carry on your back?' 'Not enough to get by,' she answered. But she was wrong, he told her. She carried her destiny on her back, for nothing was written. Nothing. Her destiny, our destiny, was in her hands, was in our hands.

"That's what I say to you who sit before me. I have witnessed much that is terrible and much that is wonderful. I have been exiled more times than I can remember. I was in prison for twice the length of some of your lives. Thirty years. And I still say to you that experience is the fire, that we are the metal being shaped by the fire. Iron has no value unless it can be transformed. And this transformation is our destiny…for we are the blacksmiths… of our soul. I have witnessed much that is terrible. And much that is wonderful. I have been called an infidel, a troublemaker, a traitor. I have been an exile, I have been a prisoner, still I am none of these things. Those who call me their enemy are wrong, misguided. I am no one's enemy, and no one is my enemy. I am a simple man. I am not simply one of you. I am you. No better and no worse. And when I die, bury me in Jalalabad."

Around noon, the old man held up his hand to indicate that he was finished for now, resting his head on some pillows and appearing to deflate into himself so that only the outlines of his being were visible, as if he were no longer made of flesh but was an expression of spirit.

Sangeen Wali, aided by a cadre of volunteers, began distributing fresh lemonade and biscuits while everyone was milling around, talking quietly in little groups. I needed to be alone. All I could think was that next to him, I was nobody. Even if he claimed to be an ordinary man, how many ordinary men had lived such extraordinary lives that they were thought of as the heart and soul of Afghanistan? I was only a screwed-up kid.

I stepped briskly outside the walls of the hujra and headed to the open fields, where it felt good to breathe the air that smelled of fresh heather, the sounds of the earth expressed by the insects chirping, the feeling of the breeze, the distant rustling of the rivers. The world was joyful, but I was despairing. How could this be? How was I different from the trees or the fields around me? Weren't we tied together in endless loops and spirals, all alive, all conscious?

When I returned to our seats, Abba and Jandol weren't there, which was when I noticed that Badshah Khan was gazing directly at me. At least I thought he was, but though I had the urge to look around, I forced myself not to. He patted the pillow next to him, motioning for me to come sit beside him. That was quite an honor, and I stepped over to him hesitantly, but he immediately made me feel as if we were friends. He offered me chai that was aromatic with cardamom and asked me about myself. I told him a little about my life, but I refrained from saying how things actually were since we'd gotten back from Afghanistan, how I couldn't understand anything, how everything was upside down, how I tried not to think, not to remember. My thoughts flew around my mind like crows, hyenas of the air, swooping down, tearing out the eyes of the dead. Would I ever shake those pictures from my memory, pictures that shook the very foundations of my world? Now, I no longer believed in anything. If someone smiled, I asked myself what they wanted. Every stranger was an enemy, every friend a potential traitor whose sweet words hid sharp thoughts.

I knew that Badshah Khan said there were no enemies, but accepting something like that, something that ran counter to all recent experiences, I found impossible. My temper was hair trigger. The slightest remark anyone said, I'd jump down their throats. Then I'd apologize, and the next time it'd be the same. How could I tell this sordid story to the greatest twentieth-century leader that Afghanistan had produced, a man tireless in his fight for Pashtoon reunification? Why would he be interested in me? No wonder I couldn't find my tongue, no wonder my cheeks burned.

A peaceful silence descended over both of us as we drank our tea, broken finally by his telling me there was a man he wanted me to meet and asking Sangeen to show me the way to his studio, which was on the grounds. The door was open, but no one was home, and Sangeen told me to wait inside while he went to find him, that he was around somewhere. The studio, bright with sliding glass doors that opened onto a walled garden, was filled with books and sculptures. On the walls were oil paintings, charcoal sketches, and delicate watercolors of nature scenes, all of them unsigned but obviously by the same artist. One painting struck me by its size, covering almost an entire wall. A winged creature, half-man, half-woman, with one breast exposed, the rest of the body veiled by tendrils of strategically-placed rusty locks, was standing on a temple dome with arms outstretched. Directly above, the sun, a spattering of yellow blotches, bore into the figure with shards of gold thick enough to have been applied with a kitchen knife. Below the temple was an ocean of what appeared to be spectators with their arms raised in supplication while in the background, honed by black angry clouds, rose the serrated heights of a great mountain range.

I heard footsteps. A man entered. "Ah, I see you're studying my painting," he said.

"It's incredible."

"I've been working on it for the past three years. It incorporates everything I've learned so far. Color, tone, density, clarity. As you can see, I like to play around with perspective. See how enormous the figure is compared to the crowd below? And the sun?"

"I see what you mean."

"People always ask why is it a he and a she and I always say, 'You tell me.' But truthfully, it's neither. Well, it's both. It's the portrait of an idea, of an ideal. I wanted to show the viewer that both men and women are equal, and that if we work together, we can rid our lives of poverty, early death, and hunger. You must be asking yourself why only one breast is uncovered, why not both?"

"Yes, I was wondering."

"Well, of course, there's the initial shock of seeing a naked breast, which exposes our own narrow-mindedness and hypocrisy, of how we sexualize women and turn them into serpents."

"I wasn't sure."

"No matter. My true intent was to show the viewers the danger, actually the stupidity, of only seeing one side of a situation without delving into the depths, of never keeping abreast, if you'll pardon the pun. Did you notice the clouds in the background? They represent the influx of ignorance that obscures every thought. See how they seem to be moving toward the viewer while the mountains seem to be moving backward? That's where I was playing with the perspective. Step back a little so you can see the full effect."

I did as he asked.

"The most important part of the picture is the mob. Their arms are raised, but none of them has a face. It's one continuous coat of paint, making them simultaneously thick and thin. By blending into each other, by lacking individuality, they're just a crowd of frightened helpless…blobs. They look up with awe, veneration, hope, but the reality, ah, that is different. This icon, this savior, is nothing more than a projection, a figment of their collective consciousness, an externalization of their inner fantasies, both of the crowd as well as of the viewer. In this way, the viewer is actually part of the painting. You see, we are all culpable. I am Mushtaba Khan. And you?"

I told him my name and said, "I recognized you when you came in. I want you to know I've read all of your poetry."

"My poetry?"

"I've read every word, even memorized verses."

"I accept the implied compliment. But please have a seat. So, my young friend, since you've read my work, there's something I'd like to ask you."

"Shoot."

"What is poetry?"

"I'm sorry?"

"What is poetry?"

"Don't you know?"

"I want to know what you think."

"Well, sir, for me, poetry is an expression of feelings. Deep feelings. And thoughts."

"But feelings are feelings, thoughts are thoughts. What makes them poetry? In fact, given that everybody has feelings and thoughts, why isn't everyone a poet?"

"They don't have the imagination to put it together. The words."

"What about the words? What makes a word poetic?"

"Fitting the word to the picture you want to describe."

"You mean you choose words through your imagination? But what makes you choose a particular word?"

"I don't know. I just…I know it when I see it."

"You mean, you use your feelings to decide, right?"

"Yes, I use my feelings to create a universal language that readers can identify with."

"So your feelings are what you use to find the right words to create a universal language that readers can relate to."

"Yes, that's exactly right."

"So poetry is not feeling."

"Come again?"

"Poetry is a language of feeling created by feeling, but it's not feeling, per se. Is that right?"

"I think so."

"So again I ask, what is poetry? We know what it's not. It's not an expression of feeling."

"Well, feeling is what you feel, and language is the expression of what you feel, something you can put down on paper and work on and…something that actually exists. You know, like you see a bird fly across the sky and then it's gone? But if you write it down, it'll always be there."

"Is that why you write? To capture the bird, to put it in a cage of words?"

"Yes, that's right. I mean, not a cage." There was a string hanging from the waistband of my pants, and I started nervously rolling it between my thumb and index finger until the seam began to unravel. "Definitely not a cage. No way. That's why it's universal."

"Where do they come from, these words of yours?"

"They come from me."

"In that case, how can they be universal?"

"Well, they don't literally come from me. I try to tune into—everyone has common feelings. And the words I look for, well, I just try to find the right words to express these common feelings in a universal way."

"You still have told me how you find these words."

"Well, it's like I said, I use my feelings—no, not my feelings, my mind, I use my mind, my thinking, to find words that will express the feeling."

He paused for a moment while I continued tugging at the thread and hoping they wouldn't fall off when I stood up.

"Tell me something," he said. "Do you exist?"

"Do I—of course, I exist."

"Can you prove it to me?"

"I live, I eat, I sleep, I breathe, I have hopes and ambitions."

"And therefore you exist? Suppose I said that doesn't prove anything. Suppose I told you, you don't exist, that no one does."

"I would think you'd lost your mind."

"Ah, perhaps I have. Perhaps that is what makes one a poet. To lose your mind as well as your immortal soul, to give up everything you believe to be true, give it all up. What do you think?"

"Then it means we're nothing."

"I asked if you existed. Remember, when we're born, we're nameless, and when we die, we're forgotten. It's all temporary. Ashes to ashes, dust to dust, as they say in the West. While we live, we're like musical instruments that the elements of nature play on. Do the storms, the earthquakes, the fires have names? What do you call the rain?

"Let me tell you a story. One time Badshah Khan was leading a protest against the British in the bazaar in Mardan, he and a gathering of his Red Shirts. When the British officer in charge asked him who he was, Badshah Khan looked directly into the man's eyes and said, 'I am no one, and I have no name.' The officer ordered his troops to present arms, and they raised their rifles. 'You can kill us all, but you cannot kill our spirit,' Badshah Khan said. 'For we Pashtoon are as anonymous and plentiful as rain-soaked wheat. When the rain ceases, we will spring up again, stronger than before.' The soldiers put down their rifles in defeat.

"I'll tell you something else. In 1947, when the Indian National Congress voted for the creation of Pakistan, Badshah spoke out publicly against it. 'You have thrown us to the wolves,' he told the Congress. 'You have broken your promises to the Pashtoon and given us over to those who hate us.' Thrown to the wolves. For Badshah Khan, as well as for millions of other Afghans, this meant arrests, interrogations, imprisonment, the firing squad. But he never gave up his mission, not even when his brother was murdered. Not even when he himself was sentenced to be executed. He said that he wasn't afraid to die but that he would not compromise his beliefs. 'On the day that I give up my ideals, that will be the day of my death.' If the government hadn't changed hands, they'd have hung him. But through all of this, no matter how revered he became, he remained a simple man. Even today if you ask him, he will say that his name is not important.

"It is the same with poetry as it is with him. The words are nothing. People think if they know the rules, they can win the game. What they don't realize is that the minute they think this way, they've lost. For there is no game, and there are no rules. It's all made up, it's all a projection. And whether they have any reality in their lives or not, who can say? Can you?"

"I can honestly say I have no idea," I answered softly. "None whatsoever."

That night lying in the dark, I thought about what had happened to me that day. There was Badshah Khan the wise old man and Sangeen the charismatic young man linked together, arm in arm, on the same path, the never-ending journey toward…toward… And the creature on the temple dome, the famous poet who didn't know what poetry was—the blobs of color with their hands grasping at an illusion—all of them were circling around my head in restless quivers of probability, the possible, the nonenviable, orbiting around the son. I could hear Sial snoring, oblivious to the world, my brother with his dreams of fame and glory. A door in my psyche, one previously bolted, was opening, turning what I'd thought real into nothing more than smoke and mirrors. But who was turning the key? Not I, not consciously. At the same time, I knew that this door had to open, that it symbolized the difference between being a puppet like Pinocchio or springing to life as a three-dimensional living being. That's when I realized you could learn as much from an idiot as you could from a genius. What was poetry indeed? Poetry was consciousness clothed in images, a volcano of words that erupted from the deepest recesses of the self. Lakhta's face and Sandara's eyes flashed before me, and I wondered where they were, were they alive? I'd find them, no matter how difficult. I'd find them, and I would save them.

It was a mild afternoon in early September, and my whole outlook was buoyed by the changes that had come about by the fruit trees shedding their leaves to reveal succulent pears and apples turned gold, the nip in the air that shook the pomegranates, ugly, shriveled on the outside, ambrosia when you broke them open, the myriad vendors selling grilled corn on the cob that they heated in burnt sand. The thousand-year-old Kissa-Khwani Bazaar, which was the storytelling center for the entire region, was in full swing; and as I passed different groups, as I heard the sounds of many competing voices, I wondered if, in a thousand years, someone like me might walk down these same streets and ask himself what it'd been like when I was alive. There was a famous section where booksellers had set up stalls and shops, which is where I was headed.

It was funny how great I felt considering that that morning I'd awakened with a foul taste in my mouth, tired, restless, already bored by the prospect of spending the day at Abba's office, although it couldn't be too much worse than school. Abba was doing some trading in Lahore and left Jandol and me in charge. He didn't ask Sial, who had to spend all of his time with his tutor since he was having problems with his studies, although how any of us learned anything was a mystery to me, not because we lacked ability but because the lessons were in Urdu, and we were still struggling to learn the language.

Sharply at eight, Jandol and I opened shop only to find ourselves sitting for three hours with no customers, Sunday being the slowest day of the week. Jandol was not in an expansive mood, but when I said how antsy I was, he suggested I mop up the floor. The place was really in crisis mode; every time you took a step, you'd leave footprints in the dust given that the floor hadn't been swept for months, the warehouse was a minefield of dented cans of cooking oil beaded with sweat, and Abba's desk was covered by papers scattered helter-skelter, on which ledgers were stacked precariously, making it impossible to find anything. What a way to conduct a business. It was obvious that Abba didn't like what he was doing. He was no fool; he just wasn't a small man. He wasn't concerned with petty details. His was the type of mind that needed an occupation that would challenge him, not a constant battle with petty men in a life of debt, of worry, his only protection the selling of cooking oil. No wonder he lost interest and let things fall into disorder. I'd have done the same thing.

Just then the door swung open, and a fast-talking customer came hurtling in, arms akimbo. "Hey, boss man, whaddaya, whaddaya?" he said, and without giving either of us a chance to respond, he asked about the price of a dozen kilos of oil. Upon hearing the figure, which came to 250 rupees, the guy immediately began haggling with Jandol, saying he was only willing to pay 150.

"You've got to be out of your mind," I said.

"Let me handle this," Jandol said. "Okay, 225."

"No way."

"No way?"

"Hey, the guy down the street sells it for 175."

"Well, go down the street."

"I can't, he's out of oil."

"Well, when we're out of oil, we only charge 125."

They finally settled on two hundred, and Jandol and I helped the customer haul the cans onto his buffalo-drawn wagon. I looked at the buffalo with his sad eyes, his beard, his equanimity, and I thought about the three of us grunting and straining, the customer's finicky gestures, Jandol's worried frown, my own desperation, while this beast looking like something from prehistoric times and weighing two thousand pounds simply stood and waited as if he had all the time in the world. It's like I said, everything was upside down, topsy-turvy. He was a beast of burden, lower on the evolutionary scale, born to serve man, and yet he knew more about life than the three of us did.

"Boy," the customer said, climbing up on the wagon, "you guys are tough cookies to do business with."

Silently, we watched him as he slapped the reins to hurry the beast along, which had absolutely no effect other than to make him more frenzied while the animal moved at his own slow, deliberate pace. What a strange guy with his weird lingo, trying to make a buffalo jump through hoops.

I hung around the office for another hour until Jandol, exasperated by my restlessness, gave me fifty rupees and told me to beat it. "Go play soccer with your buddies. Go to the movies. The world will keep on spinning."

"What about you?"

"Don't worry about me. I have some studying to do for school."

I didn't need much convincing. So here I was. When I reached the bookseller section—some enterprising souls even spread their wares on carpets—I went from stall to stall as well as from store to store. Of course, I well knew, there were thousands of titles in Arabic and Urdu, but in Pashto, there were but few, mostly religious diatribes or poetry, bad poetry. I didn't care. I could read some Urdu, and I could examine the pictures, no matter what the language. This love of mine for books was relatively new, but I realized that I loved the written word more than movies, much more. Books allowed me to immerse myself in other destinies, other worlds. In addition, the more I read, the greater my vocabulary, so that I found myself able to describe things more accurately, with more finesse.

The last bookstore I went into was rightfully called the Ocean of Books since it filled a huge warehouse with shelves from floor to ceiling. On a display table as you entered were oversized photography books, and I began browsing through *The Pride of Pakistan* that contained photographs of Kashmir (paradise on earth) and Lahore (the future of industry) in full, living, breathing color. Life appeared so peaceful, the mosques in their bejeweled splendor, the factories filled with smiling workers, palaces burned umber in the burning sun. I became so absorbed that I lost all sense of reality, borne as I was by this splendid work. Just imagine, somewhere there were people who had expensive cars, who lived in fancy apartments, who dined at four-star restaurants and went on vacations to the Indian sea. Hardest to bear were the smiling youths attending college in order to build a better future for their country, themselves, and their descendents.

My reverie came to an abrupt climax in the form of two men, one a square-jawed stocky gentleman with thick scraggly eyebrows—I should say eyebrow since it stretched from one corner of his face to the other with no break—and an older, shorter, stouter individual with liver spots who was unable to stop smiling.

"Pardon me for interrupting," the stocky man said. "My name is Chowdri, and this is Nawaz. And you?"

"Call me Amir."

"Well, Amir, we wanted to ask if you'd seen any books about India. Specifically the Taj Mahal."

Nawaz shrugged. "My oldest son wants to see it."

"And I keep saying, who can afford such luxuries?"

"Can I help it if my son's adventurous?"

"And whose fault is that?"

"What? You see, sir, he blames me."

"Well, who would you blame?" Chowdri said.

"Don't listen to him," Nawaz said. "He's a good one with the words. But that's about all he's good at."

"Do you hear that? He's calling me useless."

"Yes, but I say it with great affection."

"And I say this about the Taj Mahal." Chowdri lowered his voice. "The British should have bombed it years ago. It's an abomination to humanity."

"An abomination?" Nawaz said. "You're only saying that because my son wants to go to Agra so that he can enrich his mind. Whereas your brats—"

"Leave my children out of this."

"All they ever care about is how to avoid doing anything."

"If your son wants to enrich his mind, we have a perfectly good Taj Mahal in Lahore."

"But he wants to see the original."

"Ours is the original."

Boy, what chowderheads, I thought.

"So what do you think, sir?" Chowdri asked me, his eyebrows seeming to swallow the entire upper portion of his face.

"Oh, definitely the temple in Lahore," I said. "It's much older than the one in Agra. And it's more beautiful by far. Why, there's no comparison, no indeed. Not that I've ever been to India. Just looked at photographs. Has either of you ever been there?"

"I have," Nawaz said with a toothy smile. He was about to pat my shoulder when I feinted to the side, quickly picked up a book, and pounded the cover with my fist.

"You see this book? This book tells the real story about India, about how Gandhi was a liar and a thief. Take a look at it. Go on, read it, I dare you." I pushed the book at Nawaz so hard he had to take it or risk getting pounded in the stomach.

"Hey, this is a cookbook," Chowdri said, reading over Nawaz's shoulder.

I stretched around so I could see the title. "Would you believe that? Who takes care of the stock in this store? This is supposed to be the Indian history section."

"Well, it is a book on Indian cuisine," Nawaz said.

"There's no such thing," I said, picking up one book after another and dropping them disdainfully. "I'm looking for…no, not this one either. Let me see, I know it's here somewhere. I'll find it. This book proves how two-faced India is and how they would like to crush our beautiful Islamic state. All I can say is, I wish we had some bombs so we could blow the Taj Mahal to kingdom come."

"A volatile young man," said Nawaz, laughing uncertainly.

"I'll wager your son feels the same way as I do."

"My son is a student."

"You're sure about that?" I said.

"Of course I'm sure."

"Because I wouldn't blame him. Not one bit. But what can one man do? What can any of us do?"

"My son is a man of peace."

"Then why does he want to blow up the Taj Mahal?"

"You're the one who said he wants to blow up the Taj Mahal."

"That's all right," I said softly. "I don't blame you for being careful. The ears have walls. But you can trust me, my lips are sealed." I emphasized this by placing my index finger in front of my lips and screwing my eyes until they were half-closed.

"You've never met my son."

"Please, no more," I said. "I can't be involved in your personal dilemma. I have enough problems of my own."

"Ah," Chowdri began, but I interrupted.

"Excuse me, but I don't have much time. I have to meet my… my brother, yes, my brother. But it was an honor to speak with such intelligent men. A genuine honor. And don't worry, they won't get a thing out of me. Not one single thing. Good-bye."

With that I turned on my heel and exited, but I had only taken a few steps when in the distance, I saw Lakhta and Sandara strolling arm in arm among the throngs of people. I tried to catch up with them, but the bazaar was so jammed, I had to continually push my way through, and I lost sight of them. By the time I got over to where I'd seen them, they were gone. I must have spent hours looking, but to no avail; they'd disappeared as completely as if they'd been mirages. It was shattering. I thought I'd even recognized Sandara's shawl. I couldn't have been mistaken. I'm not that delusional; my feet are pretty much on the ground.

By the time I was home, I'd decided that I must have been seeing things. It was impossible, projecting my own images on two total strangers who might not even have resembled either one. Nevertheless, for the next few weeks, as soon as school was over, I'd hurry over to the bazaar and hang out. But finally, I gave up. My disappointment was so profound that from then on, I avoided going to the bazaar. I didn't want to go through such a turmoil again. I'd thought I was beginning to accept the fact that they were gone from my life, but seeing them or whoever I'd seen brought the pain back, and it hurt just as much as when Jandol and I had come back to Peshawar after our visit home. It was like a physical ache.

I had to leave Peshawar. That's what I needed to do because I was driving myself crazy. I saw the future like a pelican diving in the sea of the past where it caught its meals. My future only existed in the past; it fed off it. Soon there'd be no me at all, I'd simply be pulled under. But how and where, how and where? Abba had no money, no influence. But I guess I knew right from the get-go where I wanted to go. America.

When I imagined my being in the United States, I never looked back. I would immigrate to America, go to school, find a job, make something out of my life. I wouldn't take that long. Then I'd come back. I was determined to locate Lakhta, Sandara, and their family. But a youth without money in a war-torn country? Impossible. A determination was born in me then that impelled me forward on the long journey ahead of me.

I continued going to see Badshah Khan, eager to learn, never getting enough to read. This went on for months, every Friday, our one day of no school, often with Jandol, but mostly by myself. There were times when the old man spoke, but most of the time he was content to drink his tea and stretch out on his cot while Sangeen Wali welcomed visitors. If the weather was inclement, we would remain crowded inside the hujra.

I got to know Sangeen pretty well. He was studying political science at Khyber University in Peshawar and was planning to run for office after he received his degree. The two of us would engage in great conversations, swapping ideas, usually about the future and what we wanted from life, with each of us challenging the other, but just as often fooling around, cracking jokes. He wasn't much older than me, not even twenty yet, only three years. We'd both be wreathed in the smoke from his ever-present Red & White, which he invariably lit as soon as we were away from the compound and left hanging from a corner of his mouth even when he was talking. It was a wonder he didn't poke his eye out.

I also spent time with Mushtaba Khan, although he was never what you'd call an idle conversationalist. Whenever we spoke, it was like going through the wringer. I could never simply ask him how he was without his asking me what I meant so that by the time I explained, I'd forget what I'd originally said. The fact was that even though he certainly had an oversized personality, what he said was usually so convoluted, I couldn't follow him, although it didn't take me long to realize that half the time he didn't make any sense. I asked Sangeen what his story was, but he simply waved me away. "Don't take things so seriously," he said. Anyway, it was his poetry that mattered, not his personality.

Often Badshah Khan wasn't feeling well, and when he came outside, he had to be supported by Sangeen. On many occasions, the famous balladeer Sardar Ali Takar would perform Pashto folk songs, accompanying himself on the harmonium. Once while he was singing, I went over to a table on which there was a stack of Pashto newspapers, magazines, and manila folders. I picked up an armful, which I carried to the corner of the verandah where there was an ancient sofa. Careful to avoid the broken springs, I made myself comfortable and began leafing though the folders, which were filled with photographs from World War II, specifically of the freeing of concentration camp survivors in Poland and Germany. One of the captions said, "British soldier drives a bulldozer to push bodies into mass grave at Belsen." Auschwitz, Treblinka, Dachau. A portrait of Hitler. A Russian soldier raising the victory flag over the Reichstag, with the photograph in black-and-white, except for the flag that was bright red. Hermann Göring at the Nuremberg Trials, his face a study in fear and fury. A young soldier who didn't look much older than twelve or thirteen carrying a bronze cast of Hitler's head under his arm. Jewish children in striped prisoner clothes behind barbed wire. A selection at Chelmno with the main camp in the background. Jews being deported from the Warsaw Ghetto after the uprising. A pyramid of corpses beside a ditch. There was more. The battle of Normandy. Grim faces. A dead solder lying on the beach holding a wooden cross. Eisenhower speaking to a group of young soldiers: "The eyes of the world are upon you." The atom bomb. Hiroshima. One hundred thousand dead. Only a few buildings left standing. The Nagasaki cloud. Korea. Vietnam. A shell-shocked soldier, a girl who'd been napalmed, the execution of a Vietcong spy, blowing the guy's brains out. I read the articles; there were too many to go through in one day or ten days, so many stories, reports, diaries, most in languages I couldn't understand, with neatly typed Pashto translations stapled to each of them.

The more I read, the more I realized how little I knew. I knew nothing about World War II, the Korean War, Vietnam. How was that possible? I felt so ridiculous, I was afraid to mention it to Sangeen, even though it wasn't my fault. It was the fault of my education, first at the hands of the Communists and then by the Mujahideen. When the Communists were in charge, they taught you who Lenin and Marx were, and of course, Mr. Death himself, the great Joseph Stalin. But that was all we learned. And here in Peshawar, all we'd ever been taught was that on August 14, 1947, Pakistan was created. A constipated, overpopulated third-world country of a billion people squatted down, and from its bowels out came something new, clean, and wonderful, an Islamic state. With only the slightest of nasty smells.

Speaking of insides, mine were boiling up even as I tried to keep in control. How could we live in such ignorance and fear? No wonder the Mujahideen were able to take over with hardly a struggle. Oh, it was pitiful, but I had no time for pity.

In that year, I learned more about the condition of the world, about history, politics, about the West, about Europe, about Russia than I had my entire life. My resolve only hardened. I would go away from Afghanistan, and I would go to school. I would find work and save my money. I would come back, and when I did, I would find Lakhta and Sandara. Their disappearance continued to cast a blight on my family, especially me and Jandol. Lakhta was too vital a presence to simply vanish into nowhere, and Sandara had survived so much, surely she must have survived this war.

"I want to go to America," I said one night. "I want to go, and I'm going to go. I've made up my mind."

Sial at once began to chide me from behind some weird comic book he was reading, on the cover of which were ghouls being shot out of spaceships. "Who is going to pay for it?" he wondered. "You don't have any money, brother."

"Well, I'll earn it."

"Oh yeah? How?"

"I'll figure out a way. Maybe I'll become a pharmacist."

"I doubt that."

"Well, I won't become a pharmacist. There must be something I can do."

But I knew Sial was right. If I worked until I was fifty, I'd never be able to save enough to fly to the United States, not to mention the various bribes to get out of the country. But even if I managed that, how would I find a job in the United States? I wasn't a citizen, I didn't speak English, there would be no guarantee that I could stay there beyond a tourist's visa. How would I manage?

The only thing I remember about the plane trip was the noise and chaos, and then it was quiet and you couldn't see anything outside and the food was okay. The stewardess was beautiful, and she smiled and asked me if I needed anything. But I was lost in my own world. All I could do was think about Sial, that fool, that goddamn fool with his jokes and his whining and complaining, his dreams of being Mr. Big of the Silver Screen, his famous disappearance and equally famous reappearance. I loved him, he was my brother, but I didn't trust him, his entire universe was built on such flimsy stilts even the gentlest rain could bowl it over, leaving it in total disarray so that the rest of us had to sandbag the structure before it collapsed, for which we got no thanks but instead a litany of bitter reproaches—now his foolishness exceeded anything that had come before, had screwed up to the nth degree and left me feeling sad and guilty and helpless.

It began almost a year ago with his sudden change of plans. After having convinced me that leaving Peshawar was impossible, and after I'd begun to resign myself to spending the rest of my life in a country governed by people I hated, who we all hated, he jumped ship, began apostrophizing about the intoxication of escape, of making it in a new world—Europe, the US, South America, it didn't matter where, anywhere but here. The problem was, how to get enough money. More than once we spoke to Abba, and he always said that we needed to be patient and let him think about it, that maybe there was a way but that he wasn't sure. Then, out of the blue, last month, Abba again asked us if we were serious. We said that we were, and then he told us he had the money for us to travel out of the country, not a lot but enough. Then came the bribes and the false passports that the smuggler wouldn't even allow us to see until we were on the way to the airport because he was afraid we'd go away without paying him.

Then, going to the airport in Lahore, where the smuggler had bribed one of the customs officials and then standing in his line with our new passports and trying to remember our names, reminding me of when we both enrolled in the madrassa and the headmaster had changed our names. My heart was hammering, I was afraid to look anyone in the eye as the interminable line crept slowly forward. At last, when I was about to hand over the passport to the customs official, another official opened his window and motioned for Sial to come over. Sial didn't move, but the official rapped on the counter for him, and others in line began mumbling and staring at Sial who went over to the guy and gave him his passport.

I stood in front of the customs official, but he was distracted and hardly glanced at my passport, he just stamped it and waved me through. But after Sial handed his papers to the other official, the guy called over a few of his buddies, and all of them began examining both Sial and his passport, finally pulling him physically out of the line and parading him into a room behind the desk. If he'd only kept his head, I still think he'd have managed to fool them. But he blew up and began flailing his fists, and things turned in a wild mêlée before they could subdue him. I watched helplessly. What could I do? If I so much as said a word, they'd arrest me too. I was powerless. The world, the future, they were opening before me, and at the same time, the past and present were closing down like a rattrap.

No, I don't remember much about the journey. It wasn't until months later that I found out what happened. Sial was back at home, but getting him free cost more than if he'd taken ten trips.

I was no longer a young fiery rebel ready to take on the world, but what, or rather, who was I? A scholar? Well, I was in San Francisco State University, an escapee, yes, that too; an immigrant whose face would be recognizable but whose soul would be foreign. I had left my youth behind when I flew off first to Germany and then to the United States of America, but had I attained adulthood, or was I stuck in some kind of limbo, neither here nor there? I wasn't married, I hardly thought about women, I had a lot of acquaintances and few friends. To make up for all this, I concentrated on school studies and on work—I was the shift manager of a small coffee shop in Walnut Creek. Four years I'd been there. I dreamed to become a US citizen, which, when it finally happened, left me amazed and confused in equal measure. And all those years when I hadn't been ready to return home, when I didn't have the money, although that wasn't the main reason. It was something else, something deeper, some fear that only became actualized in dreams that I could barely remember when I awoke.

When Gorbachev realized that winning the war was hopeless, he began to withdraw his forces from Afghanistan, leaving Mohammad Najibullah in power. It took from January 1987 to February 1989, at which time ten years of Soviet occupation came to an end. At this juncture, the Mujahideen came from every direction and made their way to Kabul. There was constant fighting between them and Najibullah's army, but city after city, village after village, fell into the hands of the Mujahideen. They took over Kabul in 1992 and eventually the rest of the country. Once they'd achieved their goals, the West ceased to be involved, a decision that allowed the Saudis, Iranians, and Pakistanis to expand their influence.

In 1992, Sibghatullah-al-Mojaddidi was chosen to be the new president, forcing Najibullah and his family to take refuge at the UN compound. Mojaddidi's reign lasted only two months, at which time the extremist Sunni, Burhanuddin Rabbani, the head of the Nation of Islam, was put in power. Shortly afterward, war broke out within Rabbani's government, notorious warlords such as Ahmad Shah Masood, Gulbadin Hikmatyar, General Dostam, Mohammad Mohaqiq, Abulrab Rasul Sayaf, Ismail Khan, and their subcommanders fought each other, resulting in the deaths in one month of sixty thousand Kabulis. The ISI, led by General Hamid Gul, realizing that Rabbani was a failure and that they might lose control of Afghanistan, brought in the Taliban.

Originally, the term Taliban *translated loosely as religious students. In Afghanistan, the term is still used in its original meaning, though in the world it refers to violent religious extremists who have been indoctrinated from an early age. In the words of Lenin, "Give me the first five years of a child's life, and he will be mine forever." This is how the Taliban keeps in power as it is made up of young people, mostly Afghan refugees, who are taught in ISI-controlled madrassas in Pakhtunistan. The difference between them and the Jihadists is that the latter, though they are as radical, are grown men with their own agendas and don't follow the dictates of the ISI as do the members of the Taliban.*

In 1994, the first major gathering of the Taliban occurred in Quata, Pakhtunistan, after which they were sent en masse into Afghanistan. Their first major military activity occurred on their march from Maiwand and ended in the capture of Kandahar and the surrounding provinces. This was an initial step toward taking over the entire country. Afghans were tired of the Jihadists, the struggle was halfhearted, and the Taliban spread out in increasing numbers throughout the land. Scattered groups were reorganized by the ISI as a way to overthrow the Mujahideen government and take control. To achieve this, the ISI placed the Taliban under the leadership of Mullah Omar, known as One Eye. Propaganda was so ubiquitous, espousing the Taliban's ruse of helping the people, that Afghans threw down their guns and welcomed them as brothers.

Rabbani was ousted from office, and the country was placed under the control of Mullah Omar. When the Taliban took control of Kabul in 1996, Najibullah was castrated, dragged by truck through the streets, and publicly hanged. The warlords who had been involved in internecine warfare fled to the Panjshir Valley in northern Afghanistan. They formed the Northern Alliance, and formerly battling warlords from all over Afghanistan made a truce and joined them.

From 1996 until 2001, the ISI-controlled Taliban ruled the country with Hurricane Omar in charge. But after 9/11, the Taliban was ousted from Afghanistan, and the warlords who had formed the Northern Alliance were put back in power, under the leadership of Hamid Karzai, who was appointed as president. The return of the warlords who had been responsible for mass murders and whose former rule had devastated the country angered the Afghan people. The ISI and the Iranian government took advantage of the situation and infiltrated the country in such a way as to create more divisiveness and more conflict. The Northern Alliance began to work hand in hand with Iran, whose objective was to overtake the country. This is a scenario that continues through the present day.

The wind is cold and the trees are dead, and on the dead branches of the dead trees, flocks of mutant birds flap black wings, squat and featureless creatures forged in the hellish turmoil of war. Yet there is a grandeur in the land that cannot be diminished, though many have tried, a sense of destiny bordered by mountain range and desert waste and by a people whose courage never ceases to amaze.

PART III

CHAPTER THIRTEEN

As the plane taxied down the runway at Peshawar International Airport, I could feel my heart racing with excitement. After more than a decade in the United States, I was coming home. It was raining when we landed, and along with the other passengers, I dashed over to the grimy brick terminal—needles to say, it was considerably smaller and dirtier than the one at SFO—where you picked up your suitcases and had your passport stamped. Off in the distance was the police station, which, in my mind's eye, conjured up memories of hoodlum cops beating up a demonstrator or whatever he was. The present ceased to have any reality as once more I breathed the sordid air and witnessed the passing show, the parade of prisoners and police officers, the confusion, the violence, how insignificant Moor and I felt.

I was brought sharply back to reality when it was my turn to face the immigration officer, who spoke rapidly to me in Pashto. "So did you have a nice trip?" he asked.

"It was fine," I replied, handing him my passport.

He examined it as if it contained hidden codes that only he could decipher. He held it close to his eye and then at arm's length, looking at me and comparing the photograph, with an expression louder than words that said, "Aha, another rat from the sewers of the West come to bleed our country dry."

"I see you've come all the way from America."

"Yes."

"What are you doing here?"

"I came to see my family."

"Oh boy, oh boy," he said, still holding my passport. "America, lots of money."

I shrugged, and when he grinned somewhat conspiratorially, his gold-filled incisors caught the light. "Maybe you have enough to buy me tea?"

"Chowdri, Saib, I've come all the way here from California, twenty hours on a plane, and do you want to know why I came here?"

"To see your beloved family?"

"I came here just to pay for your chai."

"I see we understand each other. After all, what's a few shekels between Muslim brothers, eh?"

I slipped him a nice new crisp twenty, and he pocketed the bill, stamped my passport, handed it to me, and shouted, "Next!"

The minute I stepped outside, I left the twentieth century for a setting made up of crowds of men in loose-fitting shirts that hung below the knees, women in bright scarves and veils, crumbling edifices, ancient automobiles, horse- and oxen-driven wagons, camels laden with supplies led by men in desert nomad garb, taxi drivers hustling fares, and boys playing soccer in the park that was adjacent to the airport. I'd barely placed my suitcases down when I was surrounded by cabbies, two of whom lunged for my suitcases simultaneously and proceeded to shove each other out of the way. At that moment, Jandol and Sial came rushing over, got hold of my luggage, and motioned for me to follow them.

"Come on, those bastards'll eat you alive," Sial said.

"When did you get here?" I asked as we hurried away from the throng.

"A couple of weeks ago."

"I was afraid you wouldn't make it."

"I promised, didn't I?"

"Yes, you promised. How good it is to see you."

They had a taxi waiting. We piled my bags on the front seat, and the three of us squeezed into the back. Jandol told the driver the address, and the vehicle sped off with a squeal of rubber. I'd forgotten how crazy Afghan cabdrivers were, worse than New York.

"So here you are again," Jandol said. "My successful younger brother from America."

"Hey," Sial said. "What of your successful brother in London?"

"I thought you're working as a busboy."

"I'm on my way up."

"Call me when you get there," Jandol said with such high spirits that his words were like an embrace. "I'm glad both of you are here. It's been too long. Too many years."

"What was going on with you and that officer?" Sial asked. "We saw you inside talking to him. What'd he want?"

"That weasel. I'm lucky he let me through."

"He give you a hard time?" Jandol said.

"He tried, but luckily, I have magic fingers. All I had to do was conjure up twenty bucks, and he was my friend for life."

"Twenty dollars here's like a thousand rupees."

"I hope he enjoys it," I said.

"So tell us what you've been up to."

"Where shall I start? There's school, work, studying."

"And love?"

"Hey, not so fast," Sial said. "I want to know what America's like."

"America's like a dream. To live in California, to be free to do what you want and think what you want. Where shall I begin? Believe me, before I go back, you'll hear plenty. What about you two?"

"Well, like Jandol said, I'm starting at the bottom, but I want to open my own café. Serve authentic Pashto dishes. I'll make a fortune."

"And you, Jandol, are you still teaching Pashto to refugees?"

"You wouldn't believe the conditions these people live in. It's terrible. Much worse than when we were there. Starvation, disease, overcrowding. The corruption is mind-boggling. But the children, how anxious they are to make something of their lives. It's the children who matter, they are the future—if we have one here. Some of those children were born in camp, and they've spent their entire lives there, it's all they know, that and war. But their determination to make a future for themselves and their families, it makes me feel that any despair I might experience on their behalf is an indulgence.

"There's one boy in my class right now, he lives in a tent with his grandmother. Eleven years old, and already he's seen his parents blown to bits right in front of him. That boy has such a spirit that I know he'll succeed. He himself says that nothing will stop him."

"He sounds like you when you were young," I said.

"Perhaps," Jandol said. "Anyway, it's children like him who give me hope."

"Tell him about Meena," Sial said.

"She came to live with us a few months ago."

"That jerk of a husband kicked her out."

"Moor wrote something about that," I said. "But she didn't divulge any of the details."

"Well, brother, look at it like this," Sial said. "When I say he kicked her out, I'm speaking literally. She was really a mess when she came here."

"Shad," Jandol said. "The human fish. Lots of bones. If you're not careful, you'll choke to death."

"Well, he'd better keep away from me," Sial said. "That is, if he knows what's good for him."

"I'd advise you to stay out of it," Jandol said. "It'll only make things worse for Meena."

"That so?"

"You don't live here. You'll leave, and she'll be left with the consequences. He'll never let her see her kids again."

"The son of gun."

"Calm down, boy," Jandol said and turned to me. "Abba's back in the jewelry business. He sold one of our houses in Kabul, and with the money, he set up another wholesale company, though on a much smaller scale."

"Yeah, there's only two or three people working for him."

"I still can't believe Pamir's gone," I said.

"I feel sorry for Abba," Jandol said, "He feels responsible because of the way it happened. Pamir was coming back from the mines, always an iffy proposition thanks to the fighting between the warlords and the Taliban. Moor hated it when he went. 'It's too dangerous,' she used to say, but there was no one else around who could be trusted. So what happened was, as much as we could make out, he got a flat, but when he pulled over to the shoulder, he accidentally tripped the wires of an IED that was half-buried there, and the car blew up. Abba carries on as best he can, and now whenever someone has to drive to the mine, he goes himself in a rented car. But every time he goes, Moor gets tied in knots. I don't know how long this will last, this business I mean. Can't say."

"Pamir always felt responsible when it came to family," Sial said. "He'd have gone no matter what."

"I always feel that we could've been closer if it hadn't been for circumstances," I said, "Now, it's too late. Maybe it always was too late."

"Did you know he got married?" Sial said.

"Just," Jandol said. "They'd only been together for a few months when it happened."

"She's moved back to Jalalabad to live with her family."

Our conversation tapered off, and we rode through the familiar countryside in the shadow of my brother's death, his and countless others, each diminishing the other, each adding significance to those who'd gone before and would come after, the kaleidoscope that never stopped turning, the sound of the wheels a warning refrain: don't get caught, don't get caught, don't get caught.

"Would you believe it," Sial said, "that there are still clients who owe Abba money from when you were here?"

"No one has any money," Jandol said. "Even the wealthy are land rich and money poor. Actually, we were lucky to unload our house, and even then Abba took a loss."

"So, Sial," I said, "how are you getting along? And how come you haven't married?"

"His English isn't good enough," Jandol said.

"First money and then honey," Sial said.

"One of these days I'm going to come visit you. I've always wanted to see London."

"I wish you would. Just don't forget to bring a raincoat."

"Rains a lot?"

"More than a lot. But at least you can leave your apartment and not worry about being arrested and shot. I worked my ass off to get asylum there. Now, I'm a permanent resident, and I'm on a list to become a citizen."

"Has either of you heard anything about Lakhta or Sandara?" I said.

"Not a word," Jandol said. "It's as if they'd dropped off the face of the earth."

"We should have brought them with us when we left Shabak. It was criminal leaving them behind."

"They wouldn't have come," Sial said. "You know Lakhta wouldn't have left without knowing where Azmoon was, and Sandara wouldn't have gone off without Lakhta."

"I know, I'm just saying. What about Khialo and Gulapa and Atal?"

"I pity the man who tries to arrest Gulapa," Sial said.

Takal, a suburb of Peshawar, was about a half-hour ride from the airport on what had once been a bone-jarring mud road but was now a modern two-lane highway jammed with traffic, which caused our taxi driver to continually stick his head out the window to holler at the other cars and to veer perilously from lane to lane. The villages we passed hummed with activity while in between hugging the highway were hundreds of mud huts.

My parents' house turned out to be nothing special, but there was a garden, and it did afford privacy behind its high walls. Upon my arrival, Moor came running out and threw her arms around me while Abba stood in the doorway. When I walked over to him, we clasped each other like two grown men of the world, after which I kissed Meena. It was a shock to see her grown up. I remembered her as a willowy teenager, not a married woman with children.

"Shamla wrote and said she was going to come," Abba said. "But I forbad her traveling. It's too risky. Even for a woman, especially for a woman. But she wrote and sends you two her love."

"Let me take a look at you," Moor said to me. "If only Pamir were here to meet you. And Bibi."

"Now, Lila, let's be joyful."

"Yes, you're right. Sial, show your brother where he's to sleep and help him unpack. You probably want to bathe and rest, my son, and then I have planned a real Pashto meal to welcome you home. I hope you're hungry."

"Are you kidding? That airplane food was awful. I'm starved."

For the next couple of weeks, we had a wonderful time going around, eating out, taking in movies, going to teahouses, the bazaar, renting a taxi to take us to the Bagh-e-Naran Park in Hayatabad. Moor said she hadn't had as much fun in years, although Meena, for the most part, remained subdued and didn't say much, which wasn't like her.

One day after lunch, Jandol and I were in the garden. The weather was perfect, with a soft wind that rifled the leaves of the trees, causing tiny ripples to flicker.

"It's good to see you relax," I said. "You're always so keyed up."

"Moor says the same thing."

"Tell me what's going on."

"It's my thoughts, they weigh on me. On my soul, brother. On my mind and soul."

"I'll tell you something, Jandol, even if we don't see each other for years, and even if we're worlds apart geographically, our spirits dance together and will always dance together."

"I know what you mean. That's the way I feel about you. And it's the way I feel about Lakhta and Sandara."

"You've never heard anything?"

"It's like I said. They seem to have vanished."

"Well, somebody must know something."

"Who?"

"I don't know. Somebody."

"Afghanistan is full of somebodies who turn out to be nobodies."

"Jandol, I have an idea. Let's rent a car and drive to Hisarak. We can travel at night, stay out of trouble. Besides, what can the Taliban do to us? I do have an American passport."

"What world are you living in? You think they'd care that you have an American passport? They'll kill you just to lay their hands on it."

"I'm not afraid."

"You should be."

"Will you think about it?"

"Yes, I'll think about it. But I'll tell you right off, Moor and Abba will hit the roof."

"Brother, I've been on my own for a long time. To be honest, I follow my own star."

"Is that the real reason for your visit, to locate them?"

"You know that's not true. It's just that—"

"What?"

"Oh, nothing."

"It's just that not a day goes by that you don't think about them?"

"How did you know?"

"I suffer the same affliction," Jandol said. "Did you think my heart was closed?"

This didn't surprise me. I knew he longed to be with Sandara. "Well, in that case, you can see what I mean. Anyway, there's nothing worse than not knowing. Even if they're dead, it's better to find out."

"Let's not bury them yet, brother. Let's hope that they're alive. Azmoon might have returned for all we know, and Lakhta's nobody's fool."

"I wonder what Gulapa and Khialo and Atal are up to?" I said.

"I heard they're still in Hisarak but that they moved away from Srakala, but I don't know where. Not that there is a Srakala anymore. Nothing but ruins, I hear."

"This whole country is a vale of tears," I said. "A shadow of its former greatness."

"Well, I for one don't sit around feeling sorry for myself. Actually, I'm too busy most of the time. Especially with my work in the camps."

"Maybe I shouldn't have come back," I said. "Or maybe I shouldn't have left in the first place."

"Call me an optimist, but I believe that peace will come in our lifetime, and I want to be here when it happens. The Russians left, we never thought that would happen, and the warlords, and as of now, the Taliban are besieged on every side. You'll see. Maybe then I can do something productive. Maybe open a school that's not in a refugee camp."

"I know you'll do it, Jandol. I can feel it."

"Brother, I've really missed you."

"Me too," I said.

Moor came over and said that Ali from next door heard I was home, and he was asking about me. "He sent his oldest son

Khalid to invite you for supper. He said to bring your brothers, but Sial doesn't want to go."

"His oldest son? I thought they were childless?"

"God has worked miracles."

"This should be interesting," I said to Jandol.

An hour or so later, we'd just taken our seats when Anisa brought in a tray of hors d'oeuvres, placed the tray down on the cot, and scurried back into the kitchen, quite a different picture from the feisty girl I remembered who'd faced an impossible future with tightly balled fists. Ali asked me about my life in California, but even before I could elaborate, he said that in America, there was no one as great as Pir Sayeed-Hazrat-Agha.

"This is a man who converses with the angels," Ali said, floating on an intake of breath and speaking during its release. "Every night, all night long. They tell him that he must help people, that he must intercede for them with God. You have no idea how many people he has saved. I'm not only talking about his beloved patrons and followers but regular people, ordinary people, the rich, the poor, the sick, the lonely. A great mass of suffering individuals caught in the maelstrom of war and devastation. He knows everything, he hears everything. Even now, especially now. You think we're here alone, but he's listening to every word we say."

"Every single word?" Jandol said, but his irony was lost on Ali.

"And if the *chila* is difficult for women," Ali continued, "well, of course it is, spending twenty-four hours a day in one cubicle made from the bones of dead wolves, never going out, bathing five times a day, anointing yourself with perfumes. I don't have to tell you. But you remember that my darling Anisa was barren. No doctors could help her. You remember how distraught I was, how confused. I loved Anisa, but if she couldn't have children, I would have had to take a second wife. But two wives in one kitchen? And what if the second wife was also a tree with no fruit, what then?"

Jandol uncrossed his long legs and stretched out on the cot with his hands behind his head, looking bemused, in contrast to Ali, who was as fidgety as a moth on a lightbulb. He was continually tapping his feet, playing with his hat, scratching his head, smiling, frowning, pulling at his scanty beard. His reverence for the pir, who talked to winged figures bathed in a white light, filled his soul, whose shallowness made it easy to fill, but equally easy to overfill. You had to be extremely careful, which, apparently, the pir was.

"Well, you know Anisa," he went on. "Stubborn as a goat. What I had to go through that first time to get her to see the pir. Remember? She only agreed when you said you'd come with her. Women. Well, anyway, after that first *chila*, nothing happened. I mean nothing. Months passed. Finally, I went back to see the pir to explain my problem, and he said Anisa obviously hadn't followed his instructions. 'I'm a busy man,' he said to me. 'I don't have time for such foolishness. You can bring your wife one more time, but that's all. And make it soon.' When I got home I said to her, 'Look what you've done. I wouldn't blame the pir if he never wanted to see you again.' She wept, she beseeched, she begged me to give her another chance, that she'd do whatever the pir wanted her to."

"She did what?" I said.

"Once again I took her for an audience. The pir's generosity is as deep as the deepest well. Of course Anisa could do another *chila*, he said. He'd be honored to help her. This time she stayed for a month. When she came back, her entire demeanor had changed. In the past, even when I begged her not to insult God, she used to go around singing while she did her chores, but now, no more disrespect and no more songs. She began to write poetry in praise of God. I'd chide her about them, they were always so dark and depressing. 'Anisa,' I'd say, 'life is not as terrible as you make it.' Well, she put her notebooks away. For good. Yet another improvement. Again and again, I'd remind her that when a woman disobeyed a pir, she could be stoned to death. But I would smile when I said this and gently kiss her on the cheek. 'Don't worry, my divine rose petal, you're safe with me.'" Then in a breathless voice trembling with emotion, he said, "Oh, blessed God, at last He heard the voice of our great pir. When Anisa told me that she was with child, I fell to the floor and wrapped my arms around her and wept. It was a miracle. The first of five, I might add."

Ali clapped his hands, and a parade marched in, four boys and a girl who kept giggling every time she looked at Jandol. "These are the fruit of my loins. Children, say hello. This tall one you see, Khalid, is my pride and joy."

They stood around awkwardly while Anisa brought in a pitcher of water so that we could clean our hands before eating. The food was delicious and plentiful. Sitting cross-legged on the cot with the food spread out on a *dustarkhan*, eating with my fingers as I always had, my life in Concord faded, and it felt as if I'd never left Afghanistan. The chai was steaming hot, the dessert plentiful, creamy cardamom rice pudding, and each of us took seconds.

On the way home, Jandol said, "We should eat out more often."

"We definitely should."

"I'm serious."

"Anisa didn't say a single word during the whole meal. But Khalid, he's as bad as his father. Yak yak yak."

"I loved it when you asked him what he was studying at the madrassa," Jandol said. "And he said the meaning of heaven. And you asked him if he'd ever seen heaven, and he said he will."

"What's with Anisa? It's like she's not the same person I knew."

"She weighed her freedom against her survival."

"Everyone makes compromises."

"But in Anisa's case, they were sacrifices rather than compromises."

"Those children really run roughshod over her. Why doesn't Ali do something?"

"I don't think he knows what do to. God knows what they're taught at the madrassa. Nothing helpful, I can tell you that."

"What about you? Are you looking forward to getting married and being a father?"

"I don't look that far ahead. The truth is, you can't make plans in Peshawar. Life is too uncertain."

"I feel the same way," I said. "Even in California."

"In California it's only a feeling. Here it's an obsession."

"Not for Anisa," I said.

No, her life is mapped out. She's more than ten years younger than me."

"Not from the front."

Their graves, placed next to each other, were at the farther end of the cemetery on the opposite side of a dry narrow gully. The grounds themselves were enormous, so many dead, fulfilled, not fulfilled, row upon row, ornate monuments and mausoleums abutting simple headstones and granite markers. But in spite of the thousands buried here, I experienced a sense of vacancy whose emptiness spoke volumes about the reality of life after death, or most likely the nonreality. Already I was beginning to forget how Pamir looked so that when I conjured him up in my imagination, he was like a photograph that is slightly out of focus. But Bibi, who'd been such an integral part of my life, always loving, always ready to listen, to help, reading to me so I'd fall asleep, when I was sick taking care of me, making soups and sumptuous treats, with her it was as if she hadn't died. So it was that in this dusty necropolis with its nonexistent secrets, without even a spasm of spiritual energy to illuminate the darkness within or without, merely this void, this nothingness, I felt as if Bibi were among us, just out of eyesight.

"There lies our grandmother and our brother," Jandol said. It was hot and windy, and dust whirled across the two graves, and the air smelled like smoke, and it too was dry.

Moor placed a candle on each one, but when she tried to light the wick, the dry wind kept blowing it out, and she gave up. "This way the candles will last longer," she said, and Abba helped her up.

"She was extraordinary," Abba said. "Nothing could get her down. The worse the circumstances, the straighter her backbone. But in the end she was human, like the rest of us, and after the years of struggle and deprivation, she didn't have the stamina to fight anymore."

"It happened quickly," Moor said. "I was sitting by her bed, and one moment she was here, and then she was gone. No pain, no suffering, her heart gave out. So different from Pamir, our oldest son, our firstborn. The struggle to live, the hours that lasted a lifetime."

"I don't want to talks about death or dying," Meena said. "Once you start, you can never stop. Let's talk about…about something else."

"You're right," Moor said. "We can't keep mourning forever. We can't look back always. But, Meena, just for a few moments here now, let me embrace the past, let me remember things as they used to be. Let me say good-bye."

"Lila, you speak with great wisdom," Abba said. "You speak from the heart. We live and die. It is our destiny, so it is good to face dying with equanimity. Bibi lived a long meaningful life, a remarkable life. If it was difficult, if many sacrifices were called for, whose life isn't one of suffering as well as of joy? But she was always surrounded by people who loved her, reflecting them and highlighting their lives as well as her own."

"But Pamir?"

"Ah, Pamir, he was too young, much too young," Abba said.

"I have no more tears," Meena said. "Neither for Bibi or Pamir. I've used them all up."

"Don't worry, Meena," Moor said. "Things will change, you'll see."

"What will I see?"

"You'll see that there are wonderful surprises just waiting for you."

"The only surprise I want is to see the man I married with a bullet in his head."

"Meena, you mustn't say such things," Moor said. "Not now and especially not here."

"Why not?"

"You must show some respect for the dead. And the living."

"Who's to tell me what I can and can't say? But you're right, what's the use of talking of things that you cannot repair. The dead must be left behind so that the living can continue forward on this dark path where good and evil are so entangled, you can hardly tell one from the other. So I go on. I go on. I don't look back. Really, I don't." Meena's words burst from her like a series of popping balloons. She lifted her shawl and began to twirl around the grave.

Watching her, I remembered another hot day and another woman stamping her feet in the approximation of a dance—Gulapa, when we'd returned from Kabul. How similar and yet how different from Meena. Hers a dance of rage, Meena's an awkward demonstration of grief.

"Meena, compose yourself," Sial said. He took her by the arm and gently pulled her aside.

"Leave me alone."

"You're making a spectacle of yourself. And of us."

"Who cares?" she said and tried to break free, but Sial's grip was too strong. "You're hurting me."

"Then stop struggling."

"Bibi won't know, I'll prove it. Bibi, get up. Dance with me. Please. See, she doesn't move."

"Let her dance if she wants to," Abba said. "It's her way of memorializing the dead."

"You heard Abba. Let me go," she said, yanking herself from his grip and skipping around.

"Brother, that husband of hers, how I'd love to run into him on a dark night," Sial said, and he placed his fists together and twisted them with a jerk.

On the way back to the bus stop, we walked past fields that were flat, and beyond the fields, the wasteland glittered gunmetal gray in the dense afternoon air. Meena and I had been at loggerheads ever since we were children. I remember once when we were still living in Srakala, Abba brought me a shiny red truck and a doll for Meena. But she wanted my truck and said she'd trade me. I told her to forget it, and we got into a tug-of-war with the truck and pulled the two front wheels off. "Now look what you've done," she said, stamping her foot.

I took hold of her doll and pulled the head off and threw it at her. Moor was furious with both of us. But then when we'd moved to Shabak and I was depressed because my coloring books and crayons had been inadvertently thrown away, Meena kissed me on the cheek and said that I could have hers. That was so long ago.

"Shad proposed to Meena right after you left for the US," Jandol said when we were alone later that night. "We wrote to you. He seemed to be a genuinely caring man, someone who'd be a shoulder for Meena to lean on. After all, he's Kamkai's cousin."

"Not the best reference."

"No, not the best. But we didn't know how bad at first. Well, we soon found out. You see, lies are like playing cards. You have to place one upon another, but the slightest movement, and the cards come tumbling down. Within six months of the wedding, things began to go haywire. Turns out, he's one of those religious hypocrites who loves telling everybody what to do. Poor Meena, I felt sorry for her. She'd come to our house for a visit but say she couldn't stay too long. When we asked her why, at first Meena made up a whole bunch of excuses until finally she told us that Shad became physically violent when she was late. Sial was ready to kick the guy's ass, you know how excitable our brother is, but it wasn't long before he forbade her to come, even for a short visit.

"We tried to talk to Shad, Abba and I, not Sial, he'd have only made things worse, but whenever we went over there, he was too busy. Meena told us that he punished her for what he called our interfering. Sial said Meena should leave him, but she couldn't because of the children. She was afraid he'd take them away, and she'd never see them again. It was really frustrating for all of us. Then when the Communist regime crumbled in 1992 and the Mujahideen entered Kabul, turning the city into a slaughterhouse, Shad was right in there with them along with Arab pedophiles, crazed Pakistanis, and the Taliban, who turned madrassas into glorified terrorist labs. He rose in the company of others on the bottom who were elevated to the top. Each neighborhood was controlled by a different warlord, and Shad, formerly a minor clerk with the insurgents, joined up with one of the most powerful. He was always willing to help someone one rung above him, doing what needed to be done and saying what needed to be said. He wound up with his own office, his own staff. What he actually did never made clear to us. What was clear was that he had his own guards, a government house in Jalalabad, and a chauffeur to drive him around. As his world expanded, Meena's shrank.

"Anyway, when they went to Kabul, that's the last we heard of them until about a year ago. We were already in bed when Moor woke us and said someone's at the gate. Abba and I went out to see who it was, and we found Meena lying half-conscious against the wall. She had bruises all over her, and it turned out she had three fractured ribs. Eventually, she told Moor that Shad had been abusing her for years. During their marriage, she was pregnant most of the time. She has four children. It was when she was in an advanced stage of pregnancy with the fifth that Shad told her he had arranged to marry another woman and that from then on she would be their servant. But when the child was stillborn, he threw her out."

"I wish you'd written. I'd have come back."

"I'm glad you said that," Jandol said. "But that's exactly what we didn't want you to do. At least you were safe."

"So what's going on with her?"

"Her mind is gone, her moods come and go. Sometimes she's fine, but at other times, it's like what happened at the cemetery. She just does these incomprehensible things. Then she doesn't remember what she did. There's nothing we can do. We've taken her to doctors, such as they are, and they've all shaken their collective heads. When she's too out of it, we have medication, if we can convince her to take it.

"I want to hear her and Sial snapping at each other. I want... what does it matter what I want?"

"I hope I'm not bothering you," she said stiffly.

"Anisa, my dear, we were just going to have tea," Moor said. "Please join us."

"I'd be honored.

"So how are you?" I asked.

"Good. I'm good. And you?"

"I'm good."

"That's good," she said. Her voice was a whisper, and she wouldn't look anyone in the eye. I told her how much I enjoyed eating with them, but she barely acknowledged my remark.

"It seems like I'm always coming here when I have a problem."

"That's why we're here," Abba said.

"It's Khalid. I'm at my wit's end."

Moor said, "What's wrong?"

"Ali's brother and his wife came over for supper."

"And?" Sial said.

"And Khalid said that I burned the rice."

"So you burned the rice," I said. "So what?"

"You don't understand," Anisa said, nervously twisting her hands.

"Tell us, Anisa," Jandol said. "What's going on?"

"I know what you're going to say. That it's my fault. That's what Ali says. I'm a bad mother. My children have no respect for me. But it's Ali who has no respect for me, and the children follow his lead."

"Ah, my dear," Moor said.

"What happened?" Sial said. "Khalid said you ruined his dinner, and then what?"

"He dumped it on the floor and stomped out. I was horrified. But Ali said the boy had spirit, that he'd grow up to be a fine warrior. How could Ali have said that to me in front of his family?"

"If you want, I'll speak to the boy," Abba said.

"Oh, don't do that. Please. If Ali even suspected I was talking about him behind his back, oh, you can't imagine the beating I would get. No, you can't breathe a word of this."

"Anisa, relax," Abba said. "You know that you can trust us."

"Besides, it's not Khalid's fault. It's that teacher of his, Imam Hayatullah Khumari, he's the one who's behind all of this. He encourages Khalid to misbehave, and he's blinded Ali with his crazy ideas. He tells him that women are subhuman, that men are kings. It's horrible."

"Some of those imams are subhuman," Sial said.

"I keep asking myself, 'Why is he spending so much time with a twelve-year-old boy?' Once I mentioned this to Ali, and he looked at me as if a piece of dung was speaking."

"Anisa, this is terrible," Moor said. "You mustn't let him treat you like this. You must do something. But what?"

"Yes, Lila, I know, I know. But what?"

"I don't listen to women."

"Who do you listen to?" Jandol said.

"I listen to God."

"And God tells you to disrespect your mother?" I added.

"It's the other way around," Khalid said.

"What? Your mother tells you to disrespect God?"

"Of course not," Khalid said. "God tells me that women are weak creatures, born to serve man."

"Is that so?" Jandol said.

"Yes. Father says she's an infidel."

"He should know," Jandol said. "How many infidels have you met lately?"

"Other than you two?"

"We're not infidels," I said. "We're your friends."

"I don't need friends, I have—"

"You're quite the holy boy, eh?" I said. "I guess you know all about right and wrong."

"Why are you bothering me? You're not part of this family."

"We're trying to help you."

"The only way you can help me is to go away and let me be. I am the favorite pupil of Imam Saib Khumari. I go to the biggest and best madrassa in Peshawar, Madrassa Haqania. I'm one of the top students. The imam gives me lots of presents, beautiful kites that look like butterflies, special desserts, and money to buy clothes with. He promised me that when I'm older, I can go to a special camp where they let you use real guns with real bullets. Once he took me to one in Mansara, but they wouldn't let me shoot anything. I can't wait to go. Father is behind me 100 percent. But her"—he indicated his mother, who was in the living room sweeping up—"she keeps telling me it's all nonsense and foolishness and that I'll only wind up hurting myself."

"Hey," I said, "maybe they can strap a vest around you and blow you up, and that way you can go to heaven and cavort with the angels."

"I would be honored to be a martyr."

"You wouldn't know if you were or weren't," Jandol said.

"What do you mean?"

"He means, you'd be dead."

"Just because you came from America, you think you know everything."

"I know this: if I talked to Moor the way you talk to Anisa, Abba would have killed me."

"And what a loss that would've been," Khalid said.

"Kid, you've got a big mouth," Jandol said. "One of these days someone's going to flatten it for you."

"Look, you've made your pitch, so bug off."

When we returned home, we found Moor in the kitchen chopping potatoes and dropping them into the stew she was cooking, and I told her what had happened.

"Portrait of a young terrorist," Jandol said.

"If he was in the US, he'd either be behind bars or on a therapist's couch. He's nuts."

"You're wrong, brother. If he'd had a decent education, he'd be a different boy."

"I don't know. Maybe. Who's that imam he was talking about? Is it the same one that there was so much talk about?"

"The one and only," Jandol said. "And it's not just talk from what I've heard."

"Poor Anisa," Moor said. "She's had her share of trouble. But of course, we all have."

"It's the world we live in," Jandol said.

"Now you're the one who sounds cynical," I said.

"Not cynical, brother. Realistic. You can't live in a fantasy world, not here, not now. You always have to watch your back."

"So what about Khalid?" I said.

"What can we do? The wolves are in charge, and they dress up like sheep, and everyone goes 'Baa-baa.' Right up to the slaughterhouse."

"What did you hear about the imam anyway?" I asked.

"Plenty."

"Maybe it's all just talk."

Jandol and Moor glanced briefly at each other, and Jandol said, "It's a rumor with a heavy tread. You can feel the vibrations from miles away."

"What Jandol means is the way the imam—and not just that particular imam but others too—the way they look at boys," Moor said. "They look at boys the way a man looks at a woman. You can feel it."

"We have the same problem in America," I said. "Only there it's the priests. It's funny, I just realized something. Imams and the priests are always dressed in black. These great big black things. Just like giant bats."

At that moment, I remembered something I'd noticed the moment we met. Khalid, this gift of the gods, this paragon of virtue with his warped ideas and his skewed view of reality, this future holy warrior who couldn't wait to wrap his fingers around the bore of an AK-47, had a birthmark behind his ear shaped like an eggplant.

CHAPTER FOURTEEN

Across the road from my parents' house was a Pashto bakery where they made the traditional flat bread that we loved, and for breakfast, one of us would walk over and buy it hot from the oven. We'd spread goat cheese on the bread, and the cheese would melt, and we'd have strong milk tea spiced with cardamom and honey. One Sunday while I was waiting in line at the outdoor counter, two men in front of me began talking together, and one of them—he looked to be about fifty, thin, clean-shaven, heavy mustache—was counting his rupees. They noticed that I was looking at them and introduced themselves. The thin man had been a colonel and the other man a professor.

"Day-old bread, that's what we've sunk to," the professor said cheerfully.

"Who needs fresh bread when stale bread is sweeter?" his companion answered. He was wearing gold-rimmed glasses, and one of the temple arms was bandaged at the frame, and they hung crookedly on his nose.

"Hear, hear, brother!"

"He used to teach economics, and now he doesn't have two rupees to rub together."

"Who does?" I said.

"You can say that again," the colonel said.

The line inched forward. As customers got closer and shouted their orders, the baker would attach a hook to one of the loaves, flip it over like a pizza pie, and hand it to the man at the counter, who gave it to the customer. Everyone was in a hurry and there was a lot of complaining, people saying they were late, that they couldn't wait.

"Can I tell you gentlemen something?" the professor said.

"This line's so long, you can tell us the story of your life, professor, starting with the birth of your grandfather," the other man said.

"I used to think this was all my fault. Me and my generation, that there was something wrong with us, something sick, that we had brought everything upon ourselves. Even when they fired me from the university. Here I was supposed to educate the young, to teach them so that they would have a better life, but what did I teach them? Nothing. So getting canned was no big deal."

"I wouldn't say nothing."

The professor straightened his glasses, put his arm around the colonel's shoulder, and let out a great roar of laughter. "Listen to him. The cold war victim. Blaming himself so he can feel that he has some control over his life."

"And what's wrong with that?"

"You're right. Nothing's wrong with it. I found out when we moved here from Kabul. I went back home to get some of my stuff, and they wouldn't let me inside. When I started to argue. two soldiers came running over with AK-47s. Now I'm practically a beggar with three growing children at home, but I'm happy."

"He says he's happy. Who knows? Maybe he is. I was a colonel in the Afghan Army. I had a command of twelve hundred men. So they give us orders, the Russians, they send us to the mountains around Kunar and tell us to get rid of the Mujahideen. Tanks, heavy artillery, rockets, it was quite a show. So what happened is, when we got there, I ordered all of my men to throw down their arms, and I told the officer in charge, 'We're here to join you, we're your brothers, we want to fight *with* you, not *against* you.' What do you think they did, those stupid murderers. We were rounded up, handcuffed, and blindfolded. When my lieutenant colonel asked them what was going on, they shot him in the head." He pointed his index finger at the professor's forehead, lifted his thumb, and brought it down. "Bang. They stole everything we had, even our underwear, and marched us off to their prison compounds. For the next year, they kept moving me from one cell after another, who knows why? There were endless hours of interrogation, and when I didn't answer to their satisfaction, I was beaten, tortured. It was my rank. They thought they'd caught a real live one."

"It was the ISI," the professor said. "The great masterminds of the Middle East."

"I was one of the few lucky ones. I escaped."

"Maybe not so lucky, eh?" the professor said.

"Oh, I was lucky. I'm alive. Even if I'm down to my last rupee and work like a dog."

"Ah, but you're moving up in the world. You have a shoeshine stand."

"Yes, I'm moving up."

"At least you have a job. It's more than I have."

"Hey, I'm grateful for every pair of dirty shoes. Who knows, maybe I'll be the shoeshine king of Peshawar one of these days."

When they reached the counter, they bought their bread and then I got mine, and we said our good-byes and headed in opposite directions.

In the afternoon, Sial and I went to grab a hamburger at Chief Burger, which was located in an area of the city called the Jahangarabad. On the way I had some vague idea of getting a shoeshine from the colonel, but I couldn't find him anywhere. The closer we came to the Jahangarabad, the more we could see how it had changed. Where there had been empty fields, now there were buildings, some five stories high, others of mud, concrete, candy shops, restaurants, butchers, yoghurt makers. It was exciting; it really showed how resilient people were. Wars, endless wars, and still we went on with our lives. It was exciting, and I felt part of it.

Chief Burger, which had once been a small mud hut with wooden benches and a temperamental gas generator, was now a Pashto version of McDonald's where hamburgers cost so much only the rich could afford them. Even so, the place was jam-packed. Directly in front, as if to thumb his nose at progress, a spindly hollow-cheeked man was loading hundred-kilo bags of grain onto an equally gaunt donkey. But when he lifted the last bag onto his shoulder and heaved it across the tops of the other bags, the weight was so heavy, the donkey fell back on its haunches with its front legs pawing at the air. The poor animal was panting and snorting, and I felt sorry for him. The man ran in front and pulled on each of the wooden shafts, but he couldn't move the donkey. A couple of bystanders came over and grabbed the shafts, and they managed to get the animal back on all four feet. The man thanked them and led the donkey off.

After we finished, we went out to the square to a quiet place to have tea. I couldn't get over the extremes that seemed to be everywhere. Truly, Peshawar wasn't where the east met the west; it was where the centuries collided.

A well-dressed man sitting beside us finished drinking a bottle of soda and threw the glass in the street without a thought. How infuriating. I took it personally. Who cares about anything, who takes care of anyone? But was I any better? After all, I had left, I went away, and I didn't stay here. But if I had stayed, what could I have done? I couldn't even help that poor donkey when you came right down it. That beast of burden was a metaphor for an entire way of life. Here it was the twenty-first century, and a man was using an overburdened donkey to transport goods.

"Today's hot topic, today's hot topic!" the newsboys were shouting. "Get your paper!" They came rushing over, and we bought a paper. The headline was like a gash of blood across our faces for it announced in large letters that the Taliban had destroyed the Buddha of Bamyan. There was a giant photograph, and the headlines said, "Mahmood-E-Buddh Shikan." Underneath the destruction was a photograph of Omar, a sneer plastered on his cruel face with his thick gray beard and cold eyes and bent nose. They were crowing about it, thrilled to have destroyed what they called idols.

My head began to spin, and I had to lean over for a moment as a streak of dizziness came flying through my gut. Inside my mind, the past and the present were colliding into each other at the speed of memory. For the Taliban it meant a wild victory, but to me, to the Pashtoon people, it was an evisceration of our identity as once again those bastards were taking something away from us that we loved and nurtured and held sacred. To then read such a glowing article, perfect in the way it so completely skewed facts in the wrong direction, was shameful, mortifying. I'd been in the United States for ten years, I'd become a new person, a new citizen of an exciting country with school and work and friends. But deep in my soul, I was Pashtoon! Just as Moor had said when we were crossing the Duran Line. That was a mantle I would never willingly remove. Could never.

Sial could see I wasn't feeling well and said for us to go home. For the next few days, I was incommunicado, just as the rest of us was, except for Meena, who had her own autonomous moods. For the next few days that's all I thought about. I realized that they bombed us from the outside, but when they robbed us from within, it was dismaying in a way that no bomb could ever be. The destruction of the Buddha was like a reenactment from ancient times, as if Mahmood had risen from his grave. I thought about the king Mahmood, who invaded Delhi and leveled every holy site and stole all the gold he could find, though it was much less than what the Hindus offered him if he would leave their temples intact. And now in 2001? A stupid Urdu newspaper calls Mullah

Omar, who was the caliph of the Taliban, the new Mahmood-E-Buddth-Shikan, as if he'd done something wonderful. It was too deep for tears, too painful for absurdity, which it was.

Everyone said it was the ISI, that's who it was. Muslim against Hindu. People against people. Religion against religion. If you do this, I'll do that. But what was behind it all? And then I realized, if you destroy the Buddha in Afghanistan, then you alienate the Hindus in India. They then destroy the mosques in India, and a civil war starts. And Pakistan sits in its web like a spider while India collapses internally, and then it lashes out and cuts everything into pieces, drops their nuclear bombs.

No, that wasn't it; it seemed too big. What about this? How best to strike at us? Destroy our treasures. And what was most distressing was that it had been carried out by Afghans. That was what I couldn't understand. That's what got to me. Self-destruction. I thought of Badshah Khan. What would he have thought of the Pashtoon destroying their own Buddhas? It wasn't the Communists; it was our own people destroying their own ancestral roots. Brainwashed by the ISI. But maybe that was wrong, maybe they weren't brainwashed, maybe there was something evil and terrible in all of us, who knew? A longing for death. No, they were brainwashed. How? The madrassas, those foul pits. And poverty. It's harder to brainwash someone with a full stomach.

I thought about Khalid. I'd seen him the other day and asked him what he was learning in school, and he told me that they were teaching them that statues and pictures were against Islam, against religion, against God. They must be banished. Destroyed. I remember asking him what would happen then, and he told me that there would be a new heaven, only it would be on earth. That's what they taught. A pure Islamic state for the first in a thousand years. "Think of it," he said. He looked like a kid in a candy store. He held his fingers wide in front of him, and he smiled, and I felt like I wanted to kick him. What could I say to this kid? No, he was brainwashed, no doubt about it. But it wasn't just the madrassa—it was his parents, Ali, not the brightest spark in the fire, and his mother, who was too weak-willed to stand up to him.

I thought about living in California and how different everything was. Really, destroying this Buddha, why, it would be like the mayor of San Francisco blowing up the Golden Gate Bridge and having the *Chronicle* say what a great deed it was and that now everything in life would be wonderful. The destruction of such an ancient temple shook the foundations of who I was and what I wanted to do with my life. I asked myself, *Was nothing sacred?* It was as if Afghanistan was a dead body, and these *heroes* were robbing the dead at the same that they called themselves the messengers of the light. Breaking the bones and eating the meat. Soon there'd be nothing left.

I imagined a beautiful mansion surrounded by a lush garden being razed to the ground until nothing is left except a gate, a gate to nowhere, and when the wind blows, you can hear it creaking back and forth.

"Abba, what's going on?" I said. "Has everybody gone completely crazy?"

Sial was flipping through a magazine, and he said, "The Taliban."

"Watch your language," Abba said. He looked tired. I hadn't noticed until now because he never spoke much and he was always calm, but he had aged considerably since I had last seen him. There were dark circles under his eyes and two deep lines that ran from his nose to the corners of his mouth. But still his voice resonated with authority. "Anyway, son, you're wrong if you think it's the Taliban. They're just tools. Dummies. It's who pulls the strings. They're the ones who are responsible."

"You mean the ISI," I said.

"Yes, the ISI. They tell the Taliban what to do, and those fools listen to them."

"Doesn't the Taliban know that they're making fools of us in the eyes of the world? That the ISI wants us to look like barbarians? And who are they, after all, just a pack of Pakistani terrorists with their hands stuck in the cookie jar."

"The cookie jar?" Sial said.

I pulled his ear, and he jerked his head away. "Money from oil, little boy. Oil."

"People are gullible everywhere," Abba said. "Even in America." He picked up a pencil and began rolling it between his thumb and index finger.

"Yeah, great. Only everyone thinks we're violent, uneducated, and irresponsible."

"Everyone wants Afghanistan," Abba said. "But without the people."

"We need to stop the ISI once and for all."

"And how do you propose to stop the ISI?"

"We could poison their *dal makhani.*"

"It's talk like that, that made us send you away. Just remember, a loose tongue can be cut out of your mouth. And don't shake your head at me like that, I know you, I know how you can be. Remember, you'll be home in a few months, but we have to live here."

"You call this living? You live like prisoners of war. You have no voice, no words. People who have no voice are dead to me."

"Is that what they teach you in America?"

"That's what they teach you everywhere."

"Well, they don't teach that here. Not when we have a guillotine hanging over our head."

"That's my whole point," I said. "You're the ones who made the guillotine in the first place."

"And how did we do that?"

"By letting outsiders take over. Don't you see, Abba, you have no life, you have no future. When we visited Bibi's grave and I saw my friends buried there, people who were young and who had their whole lives ahead of them, and what did they get? A bullet in the head."

"I ask you again, what is your answer?"

"My answer is simple. You can think of yourselves as victims, or you can stand up and fight. There is no other choice."

"Talk is cheap. You talk loud, and you want to change the world. But what have you done? They were many like you who shouted and talked, and you can meet them. Just follow the vultures."

"There wouldn't have been any vultures if these shouters and talkers had a great army behind them. If they were united. If everyone stood up for them. How many Afghans are there? Twenty millions?"

"Things will get better, I promise you. Things will change. It just takes time."

"You're just sitting with your head in the stocks. Waiting for the blade to fall. They will destroy you—in a way, they already have."

"Young men rant and rave, and old men sit and wait. We are waiting. We have been here since the beginning of time. We know what's going on. We're patient. When the time comes, we'll act."

"The time will never come unless you act. Right now. In this moment."

"We'll build a bigger and greater Buddha," Abba said. "How about that?"

"Greater, bigger," I said. "And who's going to stop them blowing that one up too?"

"Don't be so sure, son. Anything can happen." Abba stood up and stretched. It must have been ninety degrees inside, and our fans just seemed to blow the hot air from one corner of the room to the other. He opened the front door and said, "Looks like rain. The sky is dry, and it looks like rain."

"Do you really think it'll rain?" I said. I was getting drowsy from the heat.

"It looks like rain. The clouds are coming. So is your brother, Jandol."

"I hope it rains," Sial said.

"It looks like it will."

"It's so hot today. My clothes are sticking to me."

"You're not used to our weather anymore. I'm going for a walk. Sial, come with me, you need to get out, you're looking too pale. Sial, put the magazine down and come on."

He was sprawled on the cot reading a movie magazine, and he looked up at my father and said, "Can I have an ice cream?"

My father didn't answer, which was answer enough, and they went out together. The street on which our house was located had no name, and I watched as they disappeared into the hazy distance.

We still had the newspaper lying around, and I picked it up, went outside, and threw it in the trash. Soon nothing was left except the sensation in my hands of having touched something that impressed its dark spirit on my skin. And yet, hope burning in my heart, I wondered if one day these animals might also be torn to shreds and be carried away by the arms of the wind. I thought of the horrors of the Inquisition and of Stalin and Hitler; I thought of all the carnage they had brought about, the death, the destruction. Each had turned the world upside, but though they left their stamp on future events and though their regimes had been mighty and great and their victims numberless, they too had vanished and now only existed in history books.

Then one morning, I was wandering around downtown Peshawar, and I saw Samsoor, and nothing was the same afterward. He was sitting at an outdoor teahouse reading a newspaper. I recognized him immediately—the same scraggly befuddlement at the exigencies that life threw his way writ large. I couldn't believe my luck after all these years of wondering and hoping and waiting to see Samsoor, who'd surely have news about Lakhta and Azmoon, maybe Sandara. I touched his shoulder, and he looked up and at first he didn't recognize me, not until I told him my name, and then he rose to his feet and gripped me by the shoulders. Then he asked me to join him, and I took a seat and gave the waiter my order. At first, we spoke desultorily, but I wasn't going to leave until I found out about Lakhta and Azmoon, no matter how befuddled he might appear, no matter how painful it might be for him to open old wounds. I could barely contain myself. I had to know.

"Tell me," I said, interrupting him, "where is Lakhta and Azmoon?"

Samsoor paused and sipped his tea and wiped his mouth with a little napkin. This is the gist of what he said.

Azmoon was heading to the market outside of Shabak and listening to music on his boom box, the lilting voice of Bakht ZaMina thrilling his soul: "Oh, my beloved Afghan hero, defend your borders, and when you return after the defeat of our enemies, then I will weave my long hair like a carpet, and I will let you sleep on it as long you wish." At some point he was stopped by a band of heavily armed Jihadists. The leader was none other than the long-vanished Tofan. When Azmoon saw him, he placed his boom box on the ground and threw his arms around him.

"My brother," he said, "tell me what you've been doing. So many years have passed, and look at you. You've grown into a fine man."

"I've always been a man," Tofan said, disentangling himself.

"Even when there was thunder and lightning," Azmoon said, "and you were afraid, and Khialo and I had to comfort you?"

"You have a good memory, Azmoon. Perhaps it will serve you."

The others crowded around the two men.

"Tell me, Tofan, what are you up to? Everyone said you ran away to join the insurgents. Was there much hard fighting? Danger?"

"I am a man on a mission," Tofan said. "For such as we, there is no fear."

"What mission is that?"

"To rid the land of infidels."

"A noble mission," Azmoon said. "I'm proud of you, proud for all of us, for our souls will never be our own until we reclaim the land."

"The land? Whose land?"

"Yours and mine."

"How is it yours?"

"Well, of course, it's not mine. Or yours. It's theirs."

"Those are inflammatory words, Azmoon. The truth is, this is not your land or my land. Or theirs, whoever your refer to. This land is God's land."

"Ah, God. Sometimes I wonder if there is a God. How could we be any the worse off if there were none?"

"Do you consider yourself an enemy of God then, is that what you're implying?"

"Don't even say that, brother," Azmoon said. "You know how sincere I am, how thoughtful and respectful. It's just that…I don't know…why doesn't God help us? Why does He ignore our cries for help? We don't ask for much, we only ask for our freedom, is that so much to ask?"

During their exchange, two things happened. First, Azmoon hadn't actually digested Tofan's tone of voice, or if he did, he figured he was tired or angry or in a bad mood. The second was that Azmoon had left his tape player on, but when the tape ended and he reached down to turn it to the other side, Tofan pushed his hand away, knocking the tape to the ground.

"Quit horsing around," Azmoon said, picking it up.

"Those who listen to music are the enemies of God," Tofan said. "Surely you don't want to be such an enemy. Now give me the tape."

"You want the tape? Here, take it. I have others."

Tofan wiggled his finger between the tape and the cassette, and he spooled it out and tore it off and threw the tape into a ditch by the side of the road.

"Hey, what's that all about?" Azmoon said. "I thought you want to take it with you."

"It is taught that a Muslim who kills the enemies of Allah and Islam shall enter heaven after his own death. In heaven he will be rewarded with golden palaces and gardens lush with bright flowers as well as other more tasty delights. Now, take you and me, for instance."

"What about you and me?"

"If I killed you, I would then become the beloved of Allah. I would be fulfilling my religious duty in the same way that our butchers follow halal when they slaughter cows, sheep, and goats."

"Kill me? What are you talking such nonsense?"

"You're the fool. You're the infidel who listens to forbidden music."

"I happen to like forbidden music. And if I remember right, there was a time when you did as well."

"Are you making fun of me?"

"Of course I am. Because you're being ridiculous."

"You need a lesson."

"Well, maybe some other time, I've got to be off." Azmoon picked up his boom box, but before he'd even taken a step, he was surrounded. Hands were placed on his shoulder, and he was spun around in a dizzying, mocking whirl.

"You Godless infidel," Tofan said softly, musically. "You son of a dog."

"What are you doing, showing off for these others? You know you don't have to. They already know you're a madman."

"Strong words from a monkey's son."

"And who's son are you?" Azmoon said. "Do you even know your father?"

"Who's son am I? I will tell you." Tofan grabbed the boom box out of Azmoon's hand, raised it above his head, and before Azmoon could stop him, smashed it on the ground. Then Tofan's followers grabbed him and bound his hands and feet with their scarves. Tofan then lifted his boot and kicked him to the ground. Azmoon struggled to free his hands while Tofan grabbed him by the collar and dragged him behind some bushes. He pulled a bayonet off his AK-47 and held it against Azmoon's throat.

"Allah-Hoo-Akbar, Allah-Hoo-Akbar, Allah-Hoo-Akbar," Tofan chanted. "God is great, God is great, God is great." He pulled Azmoon's head back by his hair and cut his throat with such force that the knife got caught in the bone, almost decapitating him, his blood spurting out of the gaping hole while his body shivered and danced and his fingers grabbed at the earth.

"Allah-Hoo-Akbar, Allah-Hoo-Akbar, Allah-Hoo-Akbar!" the others shouted. "God is great, God is great, God is great!"

And Tofan, rising to his feet, replied in a soft voice, "Allah-Jala-Jalala-Hoo, Allah the most merciful and kind. What is done is done. Leave him for the crows."

When they brought Azmoon home, Lakhta stitched the head to the torso so that Azmoon's soul would find peace on his journey toward the ineffable. Maybe it was that that unhinged her mind. Because from then on, Lakhta wasn't the same. Her mind was always off in some distant land where no one could follow. She'd sit outside for hours, even in the rain, even when it was snowy or hot, waiting for a son who would never return. Samsoor thought she'd recover from the shock, but a year had passed, and she was no better than before. Except for the rare lucid moments when she snapped to and realized that Azmoon was dead. Then she'd start sobbing uncontrollably. Samsoor didn't know which was worse, her waiting for Azmoon to return or knowing he was gone.

"When they murdered my son," Samsoor said, "they killed my wife as well."

I asked him what he meant, and he said that Lakhta was gone, that she'd disappeared shortly after Azmoon's murder, and he hadn't seen or heard from her since. He'd been asleep, and when he woke up she was gone, taking nothing with her but the clothes she was wearing. Hoping to be reunited, he'd remained in Shabak, but the village was a ghost of itself, almost peopleless, like a graveyard. When he could take no more, Samsoor came to Peshawar, and he's been here ever since.

So Lakhta was gone, I thought. Well, I'd find her. I'd get Samsoor's address and go over and see him. He must know something, even if he didn't know that he did. When I asked him about Sandara, he knew even less. One day she'd been there, and the next she wasn't, and he had no idea where she was. She'd left during a bombing raid. Then there came weeks of heavy fighting, he said, and you had to find someplace that was safe, and he'd hidden in the caves that fronted the mountains leading to Tummani. Maybe she'd been killed, probably she was.

But no, I thought. Not the beautiful Sandara with her gypsy eyes and arched eyebrows, her high cheekbones framed by thick black wavy hair, the soft sinuous way she moved, every gesture that of a dancer. It was inconceivable to imagine her obliterated, blown to smithereens, unrecognizable.

Dusk burned out the light from the sky and it was dark, and we were engulfed in the fiery decline. Bereft, futureless, easily distracted, Samsoor was a frail figure among the hordes of frantic pedestrians trapped in their own universes, like city dwellers everywhere.

We parted company, and as I watched him being swallowed by the crowd, I realized that I would never see him again, that I wouldn't visit him, I wouldn't talk to him, that he'd told me everything he knew, that it was no use, I would only upset him. The man was a shell. Perhaps, if I listened closely, I could hear Lakhta calling, her voice rising with the wind in an unceasing current. And then it seemed as if Lakhta and Azmoon, as if Sandara and Gulapa, Khialo and Shakar, Bibi and Pamir, everyone I knew, all the people of my village who I'd never see again, were addressing me, as if they were everywhere, part of me and part of the evening sky. I realized that I might never see any of them again, but that, at the same time, neither would I ever be free of their touch for they were as much me as was my own heritage, my own genes, the color of my hair, the tone of my skin. I comprised each one. But how I would miss Lakhta.

"Oh, the wind, the wind is blowing, through the graves the wind is blowing. Freedom soon will come, then we'll come from the shadows." The Northern Alliance, some of whom were against the Pashtoon people, upon the eclipse of the Taliban, were brought to power. Instead of attacking the terrorists in Afghanistan, they sought to eliminate the Pashtoon who comprised 65 percent of the population. The Northern Alliance split up into factions, little and big wars were fought, wars that were caused by ethnic hostility, revenge, and tribal disputes, until at the current time, the fate of the country is still uncertain. Such internecine conflicts continue to make it difficult, if not impossible, for international and coalition forces to have a clear grasp of the situation, without which they can do very little. Additionally, such confusion only serves to increase the feeling of mistrust felt by the Pashtoon toward them. Such mistrust enables extremists to harness their own forces while exploiting the anger and ignorance of others. Oh, the wind, the wind is blowing…

(i) Shahi Sadat with his friends

(ii) From left to right: Lt. Col. Donold, Col. Danaho, Lt. Col. Munster, and Shahi Sadat

(i) Shahi Sadat with Afghan soldiers

(ii) From right to left: Maj. Gen. John W. Nicholson Jr, governor of Urzgan, governor of Paktika, governor of Ghazni, Shahi Sadat, two Afghan generals and their staff

(1) Left to right: Shahi Sadat, Lt. Col. Shull, Maj. Gen. John Nicholson, Liam Wasley, and Tim Standaert both State Department's rep in a grand opening of girls school in Assadabad, Kunar

(ii) Group photo during women's day

(i) From left to right: Fox news reporter, Shahi Sadat, Governor Wafa, Lt. Col. Pete Munster

(ii) Shahi Sadat is distributing aid from USA to Afghan refugees who returned to Afghanistan.

(i) Shahi Sadat and Lt. Col. Munster in a local Jarga

(ii) Shahi Sadat and Col. Schwizer in Camp Selerno

(i) From left to right: Pakistani Gen. Nasser, Shahi Sadat, and Afghan Gen. Akram

(ii) Governor of Wardak Province and Shahi Sadat

(i) Shahi Sadat in Afghan gathering

(ii) Shahi Sadat with Provincial Reconstruction Team in Assadabad

MAR 23 2007

(i) Portrait of an Afghan woman by Zartashtai Babai

(ii) Portraits of Ghandi and Badshah Khan by Zartshtai Babai

(i) Lt. Gen. Benjamin Freakley and Shahi Sadat

(i) Governor of Nangarhar and Shahi Sadat

(ii) From Left to right: Maj. Gen. John Nicholson Jr, Shahi Sadat, Lt. Gen. Karl W. Eikenberry

(i) Shahi Sadat with USA soldier

(ii) Shahi Sadat with other Afghan refugees' children

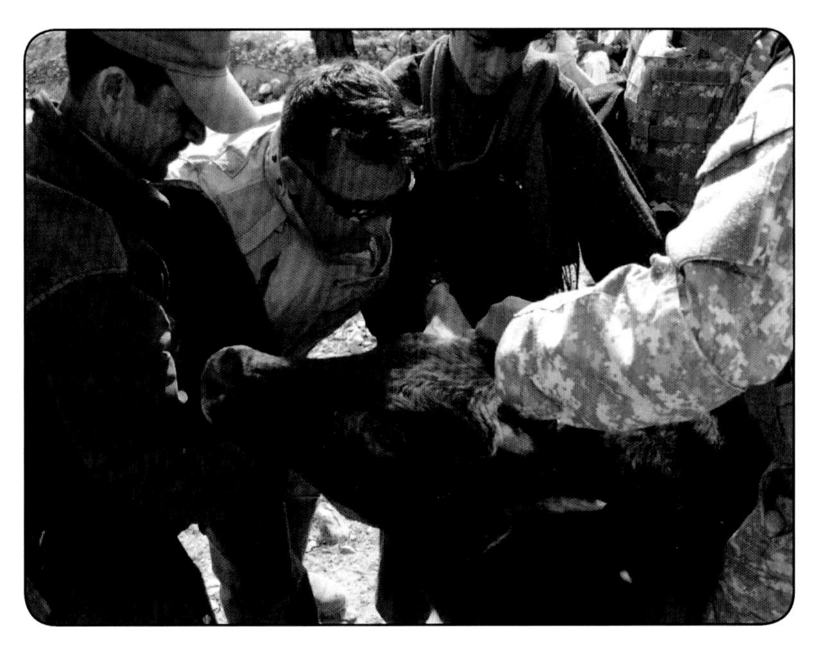

(i) Shahi Sadat with his team helping farmers and their livestock

(ii) From Left to right: Afghan generals, governor of Paktia, Maj. Gen. John Nicholson and Shahi Sadat

(i) Lt. Gen. James L. Terry and Shahi Sadat